A Collision of Two Worlds

Geraldine Ann Ford

Thank you to Carolyn Jones who gave me a couple of excellent ideas to add to the plot and Teri-Jayne Bigger who did a proofread for me.

I dedicate this book to my beautiful family and all my wonderful friends who support me.

By the same author
When the Spirit Moves You
On the Dickens' Trail
On the Writer's Trail

Chapter One

Katie Morgan had no idea that a catastrophic life-changing event would happen on this ill-fated day; the day her parents had decided to drive to Cornwall for the 1985 Whitsun bank holiday weekend. They owned a successful antique shop and led extremely busy lives. Business was thriving and they didn't have much time for vacations. However, right now a change of scenery and some relaxation was much needed, and they were really looking forward to it.

The charm and magic of the Cornish County with its tiny coves, beautiful beaches, and rugged landscape had lured them once again. They had stayed in most of the seaside towns and many of the picturesque villages over the years.

Katie had fond memories of Cornwall as she grew up. Her dad taught her to swim, and she loved swimming in the sea; her mum called her a water baby. Her best friend Sue often went with them, and they spent hours of fun together.

She felt a bit uneasy as she waved goodbye to her parents from the doorstep. But she thought it was probably because she had just broken up with her boyfriend. He had popped round that morning and being a caring and sensitive person, she hadn't found it easy to finish their relationship. She decided to end it after a year because although Mark was kind and dependable, he was boring.

Katie had already had holidays in the Canaries, Italy and the Maltese Islands before she met Mark and she wanted to travel more but he was happier at home; she enjoyed the arts especially music, literature and poetry but he preferred football. She was beginning to wonder why they had got together in the first place. She was only twenty-three, but she wanted more out of life than Mark ever would.

Shirley and Alan Morgan preferred to drive the scenic route to Cornwall. They found a charming country pub where they stopped for a snack and a loo break. It had low wooden beams and an amazing old fireplace which had once been used for cooking. In the 1700's it was an inn where the coach and horses stopped on their way to Truro. Travellers would have relaxed and enjoyed a good repast and the horses would have cooled down and been given something to eat; needing a rest before they resumed their arduous journey pulling a coach full of passengers and hefty trunks.

Interesting prints on the walls showing the history of the building could have kept them chatting to the landlord for a long time. Instead, they decided to be on their way having planned to arrive early evening so they could relax and have a leisurely dinner in the hotel.

Plans have a habit of going haywire and they soon found themselves being diverted onto the M5 because of a massive water leak. With copious amounts of the valuable liquid gushing out of a broken water main the police had to take control.

Ten minutes later Alan joined the inside lane and merged into the slow-moving cars. Shirley had a strange feeling in the pit of her stomach but tried to push it to the back of her mind. She dozed as the cars started moving at a faster pace.

Thirty minutes had past, and Alan would heave a sigh of relief when he was able to leave the motorway and join the A.30 to Bodmin. He had been driving in the outside lane to avoid the bottleneck, but he wanted to get off the motorway as soon as possible and so did Shirley. Putting his left indicator on so he could move into the central lane did not seem to be working; the cars were not letting him in.

An old Cortina came into sight on the other side of the motorway; it was swerving violently. Fortunately, there wasn't much traffic on that side, but Alan couldn't believe what he was seeing. The driver lost control and went through the only opening in the central safety barrier for miles. It was a head on collision, and they died instantly.

In a matter of a few, chaotic and surreal minutes Shirley and Alan were gone. They worked hard, had a great future ahead of them, a steady and happy marriage, a wonderful talented twenty-three-year-old daughter, and a beautiful house. But they had departed this world because of a drunk, out of control young man.

What had been a classic and well looked after Jaguar, Alan's pride, and joy, was now a mass of mangled metal and broken glass with two crushed bodies inside the wreckage. The Cortina had buckled on impact and the eighteen year old, who hadn't been wearing a seatbelt, was thrown through the windscreen. Now his broken body lay on what was left of the bonnet covered in blood and glass. Two families were going to receive heart-breaking news before the end of this inauspicious day.

It felt cold in the hospital mortuary, very cold. Katie Morgan stood desperately trying to compose herself while waiting for the sheets to be pulled back. The sparkle that had been in her bright blue eyes just two days ago had gone. Instead, they were swollen and red with so much crying and dark circles were forming. Her long black and lustrous hair was dishevelled, and her beautiful heart shaped face was tear-stained and taut with anguish. She had a pounding headache through lack of sleep and the feeling of nausea swept over her.

Aunt Ellen, her mother's sister, was by her side. She had mousey blonde hair shaped into a pixie cut that never looked out of place, but the strain of the last two days was beginning to show on her usually cheery face. She had offered to identify the bodies of her beloved sister and brother-in-law to save her niece yet more torment, but Katie had insisted on doing it herself.

A police liaison officer was close by waiting discreetly for the bodies to be formally identified. He could never get used to seeing relatives agonising over their loved ones.

Katie nodded to the attendant to let him know she was ready for the terrible ordeal. He lifted the sheets but left their bodies covered up to the neck, so she wouldn't see the appalling injuries. Cuts and bruises had been disguised as much as possible, but their faces were still black and blue after such a horrific crash. They gasped, finding it hard to believe what they were seeing. Placed outside each sheet, in case they wanted to hold them, was a hand; they looked alien to her. Standing in between her beloved parents she took hold of each of their hands but was shocked at how cold they were. They looked waxy and she knew their spirits had long departed.

She couldn't stop thinking about how cruelly they had been taken away from her and the tears rolled down her cheeks into the creases of her neck. She didn't have the energy to wipe them away while saying her goodbyes. Ellen's tears came unchecked too when she said goodbye to her dearest sister and brother-in-law.

6

It was all too much for Katie and her aunt steadied her as she staggered back gently steering her towards the door. They had identified the bodies and now she wanted to get her niece as far away as possible, wondering how she would ever get over her loss.

Chapter Two

It had been eight-thirty in the evening before Katie was told the tragic news. It was by chance that her best friend, Sue, had telephoned earlier to ask if she could come round. They had been friends all through their primary and grammar schools and enjoyed each other's company. Sue had trained as a nurse and worked in Farnborough Hospital in Kent and Katie was a dental hygienist at Guys Dental Hospital, London; they had both ended up working for the National Health Service.

Sue could be outrageous at times and Katie loved that about her, although her parents raised an eyebrow when Sue encouraged her to dress as a punk. Knowing that teenagers often struggle with their identity they decided not to make a fuss as it would probably be a passing faze; this proved to be right. Sue's parents, however, weren't so accommodating and the more they admonished her the more outrageous she became.

Armed with a bottle of wine and some snacks she arrived just after eight. Katie gave her a warm welcome. "Here, give me those and I'll put them in some bowls. The corkscrew is on the coffee table, and you know where the glasses are so you can do the honours she called as she walked towards the kitchen."

By the time Katie carried the snacks into the lounge Sue had opened and poured the wine.

"Cheers!" They both chorused as they clinked their glasses together.

"Let's hope 1985 gets better. I'm glad the miner's strikes are over but I'm sick of Margaret Thatcher."

"Oh, don't let's talk politics, Sue."

"Okay," she sighed. "Show me your new CD player instead."

Katie opened the left-hand door of the television unit. "Voila!"

"Wow, it looks great. They certainly are compact discs and a lot smaller than our records." Sue was impressed.

"I only bought a few to start with but they'll be easier to store. What do you want on? The Smiths? Sting? Dire Straits? Talking Heads? Thompson Twins? Whitney?"

"I don't mind. You choose."

Katie didn't put anything on as there was a knock. She looked puzzled. "Who on earth can that be?"

"Well, you won't find out if you don't go and open the door. You never know it might be a couple of hunks," Sue joked as she leant over to top up their glasses.

"Oh, very funny," called Katie as she entered the hall, but stopped in her tracks. Through the bevelled glass panels of the front door, she saw two dark figures who looked suspiciously like police officers.

There was another knock which was louder and more urgent than the first and she felt sick to the pit of her stomach. Slowly and deliberately, she reached out to open the door with trembling hands. It was as if she already knew a tragedy had befallen her parents.

"Miss Katie Morgan?" asked the older constable.

"Yes."

"Can we come in please?"

At first, she was paralysed with fear until he repeated his question. She showed them into the lounge where Sue was looking through the CDs. She was surprised to see two policemen following Katie who looked like she was about to pass out.

"I'm afraid we have some bad news so you may need to sit down." He was trying to be as delicate as possible, but it was never easy. Sue, realizing something awful had happened sat down next to her and held her hand as if to soften the blow.

The following fifteen minutes were a blur to Katie as she was told of the fatal accident on the motorway. It was a head on collision and had taken the emergency services two hours to cut them free. The other driver had also died instantly.

Katie couldn't take it all in. It was as though he was talking to somebody else. She couldn't comprehend the fact that she wasn't going to see her parents walk through the front door telling her all about their long weekend away. Never again would she see her dear mum bustling about in her new dream kitchen preparing the evening meal; or her lovely dad pottering around in his garden wearing his green wellington boots all caked with mud and bits of grass. No more would she hear them discussing the state of the antique market or talking lovingly about a new piece her dad managed to secure at the auctions, and she would never again hear her mum play the piano.

Sue let the policemen out and she stayed with Katie until Ellen arrived from Edenbridge. The only family she had left was her dear aunt who came as soon as she was told the devastating news. Ellen had to keep her eyes on the road while she was driving which wasn't easy as she sobbed all the way. Shirley was her only sibling, and she was gone. "My beautiful, kind, compassionate, talented big sister dead at forty-six," she cried. "How can that be? And Alan … he's like a brother to me. I can't bear it … but I must be strong for my poor niece."

Neither of them slept much in the next few days and Katie was in a kind of a trance which was understandable after the shock of having to identify her parent's bodies. Ellen had also found it a terrible ordeal, but her main concern was Katie. Guy's Dental Hospital gave her compassionate leave without hesitation when Ellen phoned to tell her boss the terrible news. She was also given compassionate leave from the grammar school where she taught English. She hated letting her pupils down, but she had enough to worry about and there was the funeral to arrange. She was hoping it would give her niece something to focus on.

"Darling, are you getting up? It's eleven o'clock and we need to discuss the funeral arrangements. I know how difficult it is for you, but we don't have much time."

"I know auntie," Katie replied, as she pulled herself up in bed and straightened the duvet so Ellen could sit next to her.

Ellen scowled. "Can you please stop calling me auntie it makes me feel ancient and I'm only forty-one."

"You'll always be auntie to me."

She looked at her niece over the top of her reading glasses she hadn't bothered to take off.

"Okay ... Ellen."

"Do you want to go to the chapel again?"

"No, definitely not. I've seen enough death and they aren't there are they? She cried angrily. "I still can't believe I won't see them again. I never thought I'd be an orphan at my age," she began to sob.

Ellen reached out and took hold of her hand. "I wish I could bring them back," she said, sounding miserable.

Kate wiped her eyes with a sodden tissue. She still had a bad headache and all she wanted to do was sleep. "I'm sorry."

"What for?"

"For being so wrapped up in my grief and forgetting you've lost your sister."

"My sister and my best friend. She was always trying to protect me especially when we were young."

"From your dad?"

"Mostly yes. At least Shirley had some good memories of him before he started drinking. Your grandad Reg would change from a mild-mannered man to an aggressive one after a drinking binge, but when he wasn't drinking Shirley said he was lovable. He would insist on putting us to bed and would carry us up the stairs one by one on his shoulders dropping us onto our beds. Shirley said mum would tell him off for getting us excited before our bedtime. I was only a toddler and can't remember that far back but it was always nice to imagine him sober."

"You had a hard childhood, and I had an amazing one."

"It wasn't all bad. Mum was marvellous and we had some good times together when she wasn't working."

"Did she ever think of leaving your dad?"

"Well, if she did, she didn't tell us, but she did say many times that he couldn't help it. Alcoholism is an illness she told us. He only started drinking to forget the terrible things he'd witnessed in France during the war; especially after his best friend got his head blown off a few yards from where he stood."

"What a terrible thing to happen. It's difficult to imagine something like that. No wonder he started drinking and who could blame him."

"Mum said dad didn't have an ounce of aggression in him. She said he was a people person and loved his job restoring furniture. The last thing he wanted to do was fight for King and country, but he had no choice. Eventually he went into a clinic to be dried out and when he came home it was lovely because he seemed more normal if a bit subdued. Mind you we didn't really know what normal was regarding our dad and we still tip-toed

12

around him. It wasn't long before he started drinking again even though he had promised mum he would stay off the booze.

"It must have been dreadful for you all. Poor gran!"

"It was and after he fell and died from a brain haemorrhage mum said she had always felt he wouldn't make old bones."

"How awful! I was so lucky I couldn't have asked for better parents … but … now they're gone, and I don't know what to do," she sobbed uncontrollably.

Ellen curved her arm around her niece's neck and drew her dark-haired head to her shoulder. She felt helpless but at least Katie was crying again and not walking around in a daze caused by the shock; that was much more worrying. "We will get through this darling I promise," Ellen said as she stroked her hair and kissed the top of her head while praying for guidance.

Katie did not know how she had coped at the funeral. Somehow, she managed to listen to her parent's favourite music tracks as they entered and left the chapel and the eulogy that she and Ellen had written between them. It encapsulated the lives of her dear mum and dad beautifully and the celebrant read it with such feeling; it was truly a celebration of life.

"We got through it, Katie!" Ellen said as the last of the mourners left followed by Sue. The caterers were clearing up and packing their things away. "We did your mum and dad proud."

"Yes, we did auntie … we did."

"I thought we'd agreed that you would never call me auntie again." Ellen was trying to keep the conversation light as her niece looked exhausted.

Katie smiled weakly.

13

"Would you like a glass of wine now that everyone has gone? We don't need to stay stone cold sober any longer and have you eaten anything since breakfast?"

"Yes, to a glass of wine and no I haven't eaten anything since this morning."

"I'll pay the caterers then I'll bring in some snacks as there was quite a bit of food left over and I know how you love Vol-au-vents."

"Thanks Ellen." Katie didn't have much energy left as she sat on the soft brown leather sofa, but she was hungry, and she needed to eat something. Even if she took herself to bed, she knew she wouldn't be able to sleep. Already the funeral played out in her mind like a video, and she saw the curtains closing in front of the coffins once more.

Tears started to fall but something made her look over at her mum's piano in the alcove. Their wedding photo was on top with two pieces of Lladro either side. Katie smiled because they were her mum's favourite figurines, and she couldn't stop staring at them. The one to the left of the photo was of a woman holding a baby and it was called, 'A Mother's Embrace.' Her dad bought it for her mum when Katie was born. On the right of their wedding photo was a figurine called, 'Together Forever.' He had bought that one for their 10th wedding anniversary. It portrayed a man and woman, obviously in love, and he is taking her hand in his. This was the figurine that she saw move slightly; she couldn't believe her eyes but as she started to doubt herself it moved again.

Ellen had found the caterers packing up all their stuff ready to load in the van. She helped them with the last few bits and pieces, paid them and saw them off. They'd even left a casserole, new potatoes, and broccoli for their dinner; all they had to do was heat it up. Ellen put a plate of Vol-au-vents and some crisps onto a tray with two glasses and a chilled bottle of wine. It was only four-fifteen so a few snacks wouldn't spoil their evening meal that's if either of them could eat it after so much spent emotion.

The lounge door opposite Shirley's piano was wide open so walking into the room on the cream soft pile carpet with slippers on meant Katie hadn't heard her come in. Ellen saw her staring at the figurine just as it moved for the second time. Standing rooted to the spot Ellen gasped.

"It moved Ellen … it moved!" she cried. "I'm not going mad … I saw it move!"

"I saw it too darling." Ellen replied as she put the tray on the coffee table. "I saw it for myself."

"Together Forever, that's the name of the figurine. "Together Forever! Mum and dad are sending us a message.

"It seems they are indeed," replied Ellen, as she moved closer to her niece and put her arms around her. "Come on darling let's go into the dining room and eat our snacks. You can't stand here all afternoon willing the figurine to move again. Let's just be grateful we both saw such a wonderful thing happen at all."

"I didn't think you believed in an after-life."

"I've never disbelieved it just wasn't something that I thought much about unlike your mum and gran."

"That's true mum's insight was passed down from Gran. But what I don't understand is why she didn't have any bad feelings about going away? Mum often had strong feelings, as you know, and she was always right."

"We will never know whether she had one of her hunches or not."

"Why didn't I say anything to mum and dad about my own uneasiness concerning their trip to Cornwall?"

"Now darling, please don't start blaming yourself. You know how excited they were. Even if you had told them of your feelings, they probably still would have gone. Their hotel was booked, and their bags were packed."

Katie and Ellen sat up talking for hours after the incident in the lounge. They did manage to eat some of the meal the caterers had left them because they both felt a little happier since observing the figurine move. It might have only moved an inch, but they had both witnessed the phenomena which was amazing.

Chapter Three

Katie found herself walking round the house. She had never been far from home, apart from holidays abroad. Now she was on her own the house seemed silent and empty as she walked from room to room feeling utterly desolate. It was crying out to be filled with happiness once more the happiness she had taken for granted.

The garden had been her dad's pride and joy and his green wellingtons still stood by the back door of the kitchen. She kicked off her slippers slid her feet inside the boots and walked outside. It didn't matter that it had started to rain she just wanted to walk round the garden and remember. Tears were never far away and seeing her dad's well-kept herbaceous borders made her well-up. Both her parents loved the flowering cherry trees and the miniature weeping willow next to the rockery was her dad's particular favourite. She was oblivious to the dark grey clouds overhead, the rain falling on her head and running down the back of her neck. She stood in the middle of the well-manicured lawn her tears mingling with the raindrops.

Ellen had gone back to school and Katie was able to return to Guys Hospital. The staff were kind but a bit wary because they didn't want to upset her. She threw herself into her work and it was good to see some of her regular patients. Gaining some semblance of normality was imperative after such a drastic change in circumstances. Katie loved hospital life but when alone in her surgery she often welled-up and it was difficult not to break down in between appointments.

Another thing that worried her was the letter she'd received recently from Darren Butler's mother asking if she could visit. Receiving such a heartfelt letter from the mother whose son had killed her parents left her dumbfounded; she had placed it on the telephone table in the hall and there it had stayed for the last three days. How on earth could she face this woman? And yet her heart went out to her because however appalling the circumstances she had lost her son.

John Simpkins, the family solicitor, helped and supported Katie with everything to do with the business and the house. On hearing the news, he had been as shocked as everyone else because he'd known the family for several years and he was a tremendous help. John advised her to sell the business because although she was interested in antiques, she had no intention of giving up her job as a dental hygienist which she enjoyed immensely; she would invest the money wisely with John's help. She didn't want to keep the house either as she was not happy living in it anymore. It brought back too many memories which were excruciatingly painful, so she decided she wanted sell that too. John and Ellen tried to persuade her to rent it out rather than sell but she had already made up her mind. Katie could be tenacious when she wanted to be, and tenacity was something she was going to need in large measures if she wanted to move on with her life. One thing was certain though to enable her to sell the house she would have to go through her mum and dad's things; this would take all the strength she could muster.

Ellen offered to stay so she could give her help and support through yet another ordeal. Moreover, she wanted to be there with her niece when they sorted through photos and memorabilia. She missed her sister so much it hurt. Shirley and Alan had been her rocks when her marriage of nine years broke down. Divorce had not been something she'd ever considered even though her and Pete had not been content for some time. But when she found out he was having an affair with a close friend, Anna, and it had been going on for more than a year she was devastated.

Feeling betrayed and let down it took a long time after he moved out for Ellen to regain her confidence. Having an affair was bad enough but the fact that it had been with one of her closest friends was a dreadful blow. Not only had Anna sat in her home sharing her confidences eating her food and drinking her wine but she had been sharing her man too.

Fortunately, she was able to buy her husband out so she could remain living in the three-bedroom cottage she adored. He didn't want any of their furniture either because he said he'd never liked any of it anyway which was news to Ellen.

Pete moved in with his lover, but she insisted he had to take all his personal belongings with him or the whole lot would go to the nearest charity shop. Anything that was too painful to keep such as presents from him also went to the charity shop; she had the cottage completely re-decorated as if to banish all traces of him.

He had always liked her hair shoulder length, but she had been threatening to have it cut short for as long as she could remember. Now that he was no longer in her life, she felt empowered, so she told her hairdresser to cut her hair short, extremely short in fact. She loved her new pixie hair style. It felt daring and liberating.

"But Ellen what about school?" Katie asked, when she spoke to her aunt on the phone.

"It's okay darling all the exams are finished, and we'll be breaking up for the summer holidays next week."

"Already? I think I must have lost track of time. I have been so depressed in the last couple of months."

"Understandable. I haven't been too good myself, but work helps. Besides, West Wickham is nearer to Bromley than Edenbridge so it will be a shorter journey until the end of term."

"Thank you so much. I wasn't looking forward to doing it on my own especially now that Sue has moved up to Manchester to live with her boyfriend." Katie had been crestfallen when her best friend had moved away.

"I can imagine what her parents are saying about her 'living in sin'."

"Well, there isn't much love lost between Sue and her parents is there, especially her mum. She takes every opportunity to upset her own daughter with disparaging remarks. You would think she'd have been proud when Sue qualified as a nurse, but it doesn't seem to have made any difference."

"Yes, I remember you saying that at the time, poor love! But it's just a shame she moved away when you needed her most."

"I have a few good friends Ellen but Sue's the only one I would want to help me. I do worry she's moving in with Rob too quickly though just to get away from her mother. Anyway, when shall I expect you?"

"I'll pack a case before I leave for work tomorrow and take it with me. Then I can come straight to you after I've finished for the day. I have my key so I can let myself in. Why don't we have a takeaway when you get home from work?"

"Yes, let's do that! See you tomorrow … bye."

"Bye Katie." Ellen put the phone down wondering why life was so terribly unfair at times.

In her lunch break the next day Katie saw an advertisement in The British Dental Journal for a dental hygienist in Dubai, in the Middle East. The United Arab Emirates to be precise but she had never heard of the UAE before. Tearing the advert out of the journal and bringing it home so she could read it again was a good idea. She didn't want anyone at work asking questions.

Pulling the world atlas from the bookshelves in the upstairs study and blowing a light layer of dust from it she looked for the relevant page; she discovered it was on the Gulf extremely hot in the summer months and comfortably so in the winter. Katie sat staring at the advert lying on her mum's desk for a long time. What if she applied? And more importantly what if she was offered the position? It would be a new start away from the painful memories and doing the job she loved. I'm sure there'll be many applications she thought to herself though it does state you must be single and have experience of working in a busy dental department in a hospital setting; that will narrow it down and Guys Hospital certainly has a good reputation. Getting away from the house and starting afresh was her main priority and she would gain valuable experience too.

A beautiful smell wafted under her nose bringing her back from her reverie and she recognised it straightway, Chanel No. 5 ... Shirley's one weakness.

"Mum, I know you're here. I love you so much. Please guide me in making the right decision," Katie said aloud feeling excited knowing her mum was close, but the beautiful scent had already disappeared.

Ellen had been unpacking her small case in the spare bedroom next to the study when she heard Katie talking. She knocked on the door which stood ajar.

"Are you okay darling? I heard you talking, and I thought I heard you say mum?"

21

"I did say mum. She was here Ellen I know she was. I could smell her favourite perfume."

"Chanel No. 5."

"Yes, and for a few minutes it was overpowering."

"I'm not surprised as she did most of the business admin in here and she loved this sunny room overlooking the garden."

There was a knock at the front door.

"That'll be our dinner I'm ravenous! I'd better go down and pay him."

Katie was reluctant to leave the study, but she was hungry too, so she followed Ellen down the stairs. She took the advert with her and the letter from Darren's mother she had been pouring over again.

"I'll get the cutlery and plates," Katie said as Ellen shut the front door.

"Okay," she replied as she took it through to the dining room."

Forty minutes later they sat back savouring the splendid food they had just consumed.

"That was delicious thanks Ellen. That's the first decent meal I've eaten for a long time, but I'll be paying from now on."

"Don't let's worry about who is going to pay next time."

"But you'll be busy at work then coming home to help me sort things out, so I insist on feeding you."

Ellen patted her niece's hand, "We'll see about that darling you know I like to pay my way."

"Mum and dad certainly left everything in order. John sold the business in no time and I'm thankful for that. I couldn't bear to go into the shop ever again. He says if I'm serious about not wanting to keep the house that there shouldn't be a problem selling that either. So, I'll be well-off," she remarked bitterly, and tears started to flow. Katie laid her head on Ellen's shoulder. "I feel guilty," she said between sobs.

"Why?"

"Because they should be here to enjoy the money after all their hard work."

"Like you said, everything was in order as you would expect it to be. Your mum and dad would have made sure there was a written will despite their young age."

Katie sat up and dried her eyes.

"If I'm honest I also feel bad about the amount of money they left me. It was more than enough to pay off my entire mortgage."

"I'm so pleased for you Ellen even though I know you'd rather have your sister back. I'd like to give you some more money when the house is sold."

"Oh no! I'm not going to let that happen."

"But …

"No Katie. I have a beautiful cottage in a gorgeous part of Kent, a good career and money in the bank. No darling, you have your whole life ahead of you and your parents worked hard so you could have what they didn't have when they were young."

"I guess … but …

"No buts. Now you said you had two things to show me when we'd finished eating."

Ellen was surprised when she read the advert Katie handed her and it must have shown on her face.

"You think it's a bad idea. I might not even get an interview let alone the job."

"Not at all I just want what's best for you darling. And, as for not being called for an interview that's not likely, is it? But don't you think you should take a bit more time to think about what it is you want?"

"I know I was in a dreadful state for a few weeks and I'm glad I went back to work eventually but I've done nothing else but think about my future. I love my home but as mum used to say … 'A house is just bricks and mortar it's the people living in it that make it into a home.' It's no longer a happy house not for me anyway but it can be for somebody else."

"I do believe you've inherited some of your mum's wisdom and at such a young age."

"I've changed since the accident and I'm sure mum is guiding me."

"Yes, I'm sure she is and if she was here now, she would tell you to follow your heart."

Katie sat deep in thought for a few minutes then remembered the letter. "Oh, I nearly forgot to show you this. It's from Darren Butler's mum," Katie said as she picked it up from the sideboard and handed it to her aunt. "Let's go through to the lounge. I'll make some coffee while you read it."

Ellen read the short letter from Diane Butler asking if she could visit Katie because she felt responsible for the actions of her son; the young man who had crashed his Cortina into Shirley and Alan's car while drunk. She looked pensive as Katie walked into the lounge with a pot of fresh coffee and a jug of cream.

"When did this arrive?" she asked as she put the letter back in the envelope.

"Four days ago. I read it and left it on the telephone table for three days wondering how she had the audacity to write to me; it made me so angry. Yesterday I took it up to the study as I was going to leave it in the desk drawer, but something made me read it again."

"Will you let her visit?

"I wanted to talk to you about it first Ellen."

"She's coming all the way from Bristol so she must be desperate to see you."

"I know and now that I've calmed down, I think I'll phone her and tell her to come while you're staying here. I can't help feeling sorry for her she's lost her son in such a senseless and tragic way."

"And she must live with that knowledge for the rest of her life. Yes, I think you're right to allow her to visit, though it's not going to be easy for either of us."

"I'll phone her now before I change my mind," Katie replied, as she walked into the hall with the letter in her hands.

Ellen hoped her niece would be able to cope when face to face with Darren Butler's mum. More importantly, would she be able to keep it together for her niece?

"She's coming tomorrow morning Ellen," Katie announced as she walked back into the lounge.

"That was a quick phone call. How can she make it all the way from Bristol by tomorrow morning?"

"She's staying with her sister in southeast London, so she doesn't have far to come, and I just want to get it over and done with. Sorry Ellen, I should have asked you first ... I didn't think. Do you have plans for tomorrow, especially as it's Saturday?"

"It's okay you don't have to apologise I understand. And no, I don't. A couple of friends from work want to meet up with me at some point but they know I'm here helping you pack and sort through your mum and dad's things, plus it's 'Live Aid' tomorrow. You said you wanted to watch it while we go through some more bits and pieces. But we'll wait and see how you feel ... after she's been."

Katie suddenly looked exhausted. Her head was full, and she needed to try and switch off. "Let's not think about it anymore tonight. Did you bring the film?"

"Yes, it's in my bag," Ellen said as she bent down to retrieve the video. "This may help to take our minds off things. 'Return to Oz' especially for you, my darling."

"Wonderful!" Katie replied, as she made herself comfortable on the sofa. 'The Wizard of Oz' had been one of her childhood favourites. "It will be interesting to see if it's as good as the first," she quipped as Ellen put it in the video player. But Katie didn't pay as much attention to the film as she would have liked; plus, she'd had a sleepless night as well.

The following morning, she found herself opening the front door to Mrs Butler at exactly ten-thirty. She showed her through to the lounge and introduced Ellen. An awkward silence followed.

The mother of the young man who had killed her parents was sitting in her dad's favourite armchair. Darren's mum broke the silence. "There are no words to describe how sorry I am for the loss of your parents Miss Morgan. I can't tell you how mortified I am that my son was driving his car under the influence. It should never have happened."

"Well, we're all agreed on that!" Katie hadn't been expecting a neat, well-spoken, and obviously intelligent woman. "Why? That's what I want to know ... why?"

"Yes," said Ellen. "Why was your son driving when he was drunk?"

"He had a huge row with his father because he wanted Darren to go to university. Darren had other ideas. His dad is domineering, and his demands are often unreasonable ... he has a temper and can get physical. I tried to intervene because it was upsetting my fourteen-year-old daughter, but it just made matters worse and when my husband raised his arm to hit me, the argument escalated into a brawl. Now my son is eighteen he tries to defend me, and things have been so bad recently. I was planning to leave my husband and my sister had offered us refuge. She's a widow and has a large house in Forest Hill; that's where I'm staying with my daughter."

"But why was your son drunk? repeated Ellen.

"I'm not making excuses for Darren, but the row had been so violent, and his dad threw him out of the house. I can only imagine he went to the pub but what he was doing on the motorway I have no idea. I have never known him to drink and drive … he is usually a responsible young man … was." Tears flowed down her cheeks, and she reached in her handbag for a hanky.

Now they were all crying. Diane for the loss of her only son and the terrible guilt she felt. Katie and Ellen for the tragic loss of Shirley and Alan and for the wasted life of a young man who had obviously had a bright future ahead of him. It seems he was a decent young person with a bully for a father.

Diane Butler looked broken, "I haven't come for sympathy or to beg forgiveness. I just wanted to explain what happened prior to the crash. I feel it's my fault," she said between sobs. "If only I had left my husband sooner this would never have happened."

"You can't blame yourself for your husband's behaviour or your son's actions," remarked Katie.

"Oh, but I do, and I will for the rest of my life." She looked over to the piano. "Is that a photograph of your parents?

"Yes, it is." Katie replied and went over to the alcove where she picked up their wedding photo and took it to show her.

"What a fine couple … they look so radiant."

"They were the best parents anyone could have."

"And Shirley was a wonderful sister," remarked Ellen.

"Our lives will never be the same without them," Katie said looking miserable.

"I must go. I've taken up enough of your time," Diane said, as she got up and started walking into the hall. Katie and Ellen followed.

"We probably won't see each other again Miss Morgan."

"No, probably not but good luck," she said as she opened the front door.

"Thank you for agreeing to see me." And with that she walked down the driveway to her car parked on the road. Diane Butler didn't look back, but they could see her shoulders shaking as she climbed into her car; she stopped to compose herself before she drove away.

"The poor woman. I just hope she and her daughter have a better life away from her husband," said Katie as she shut the door.

Ellen put her arms around her niece. "You did well darling. I'm so proud of you."

They both felt completely drained, but before they went back into the lounge, Ellen fetched the brandy from the dining room.

"I think we both need a stiff drink."

"I don't feel anger towards her son anymore," Katie remarked, after drinking some of the brandy. "I did feel vengeful for a few weeks but that has passed. I feel so sorry for his mum. Not only has she lost her son, but it will be like a life sentence knowing he was responsible for the crash."

"You are a beautiful person inside and outside darling and you have a lot of your gran in you. 'Best revenge is a life lived well!' That's what she used to say. The war ruined her marriage, but she never blamed anyone, not even the Germans. So, you must live the rest of your life as best you can."

Katie nodded with all the energy she could muster.

"Drink some more brandy, you look pale and exhausted. Do you still want to watch 'Live Aid'?"

"I'd love to Ellen, the line-up looks amazing, but I think I'll go and lie down. I can hardly keep my eyes open especially after drinking brandy."

"It seems to have calmed you down though and if it makes you sleepy all the better."

Katie slept for three hours but as soon as she woke, she was immediately haunted by Diane Butler's face. Not surprising after the traumatic situation, they had found themselves in earlier. So much was going round in her head; the advert for the job in Dubai; the thought of going through more of her parent's belongings and of course just thinking about her mum and dad brought fresh tears to her eyes. She lay wide awake staring at the ceiling then she turned to look at the photo albums on the top of her dressing table. She had been looking at family photos a lot in the last few days.

She thought of her mum who had always been a warm kind-hearted person and would help anyone in need if she could; despising injustice she would invariably stick up for the underdog.

Her gran, Lillian, had come from a modest background in Lambeth but this didn't impede her love for the arts, and she managed to buy a second-hand piano for her and the girls. Lillian could play from memory because when she was young, she refused to learn to read music preferring to do her own thing.

Ellen never really showed an interest; she was a tomboy and loved sports. Shirley liked to draw, listen to music, and play the piano so when she married Alan the old piano came with them. But as the years went past it was invariably in need of tuning, so he bought her a new one for their 25th wedding anniversary.

Katie and her dad got so much pleasure from seeing the look of surprise on Shirley's face when it was uncovered. It had been a mammoth task making sure she was out of the house and having the piano delivered at the right time.

Lillian, Katie's gran, had worked hard so her daughters could have a good education trying to compensate for their father's excessive drinking. Moving into a small rented terraced house in Catford, southeast London was a blessing; it was owned by friends of theirs and the rent was low. Shirley and Ellen loved having a garden to play in when they were young, and Mansfield Park was just down the road.

They adored their mum but feared their dad, Reg, and the three of them dreaded him coming home from the local pub. Lillian would send the girls off to their rooms, but they would hear their dad shouting downstairs trying to provoke their mother into an argument. He wasn't violent but mental abuse can be just as damaging. Some evenings Reg was so inebriated her small frame would struggle upstairs with him so she could put him to bed. No way would she let him sleep it off downstairs because the last thing she wanted was the girls seeing him in the morning when they came down for breakfast.

Trying to keep their lives as normal as possible was becoming increasingly difficult and Lillian wondered if she could take much more. It wasn't long after she had this thought that Reg died suddenly after getting drunk and banging his head on the front doorstep, so Katie never knew her granddad.

Having been blessed with loving and supportive parents and a secure childhood Katie knew how lucky she was. Shirley and Alan had been happy in their small house, but they wanted to live in a more affluent area. Choosing West Wickham was a great idea because it was on the edge of the country, and they loved to go on picnics and walks.

Both her parents had been children in the war. Shirley's family had survived those six terrible years but Alan, who had been evacuated when he had barely turned five, lost his mother, baby sister and both sets of grandparents during the Blitz. His dad got killed on the Front, like so many others, and the only thing Alan had of any value was a small photo of them all looking happy and relaxed on a day out at Sheerness. It was found in the breast pocket of his dad's muddy blood-spattered uniform when it was sent back from France.

Doug and Alice Fordham looked after Alan from 1939. They took him in when he arrived at the village hall. He was among a few other frightened and confused evacuees carrying their belongings with gas masks round their necks.

They made him very welcome in their three-bedroom cottage in the beautiful village of Dereham in Norfolk. Their only child, Albert, was serving in the RAF as a pilot. Sadly, Alan had to go and live with a distant elderly aunt after his family was killed in London. She wasn't exactly enamoured with the idea but felt it was her duty to take him in. To a small boy who had lost the only family he knew she looked austere with grey hair that was pulled back into a bun, dark eyes, an unsmiling mouth, and a back that was always ramrod straight.

She lived in Camberwell in southeast London. They were in constant danger from German bombs, so after a few months he was sent back to Dereham for the remainder of the war much to Doug and Alice's delight.

Albert's Spitfire had been shot down five months before while Alan was living in London, and they were devastated. Transferring all their love onto him helped him to forget he was an orphan. After the war, his aunt

31

let him go and stay in Dereham in the school holidays and he treasured his friends there. Back then there weren't many cars on the roads and the country lanes, especially the hilly ones, were perfect for bike riding. On one steep lane they'd have to wheel their bicycles up to the top then they would zoom down with their legs outstretched, laughing, and shouting to one another

It wasn't long after he left school and started working in an auction house in Lewisham that his aunt died. Alan arranged her funeral and paid his respects but hardly anybody came and there hadn't been much love lost between them.

It was a different story with Doug and Alice as they were like parents to him. He always stayed in touch and visited when he was able to get time off work. Doug died of a heart attack in 1955 and Alice seemed to age after that. She fell asleep in her armchair one night and never woke up; her cleaner found her in the morning looking peaceful with a slight smile on her face.

She left the cottage to Alan to keep or sell as he wished, and he was overwhelmed. It enabled him to buy a small house in Catford near to where he worked. He invested the rest of the money because he wanted his own business one day when he'd learned as much as he could about antiques and auction houses. Alan's family had lost everything in the war and after all the love Doug and Alice had shown him, he wasn't about to waste his inheritance from these two wonderful people.

Katie reached for the advert which was on her bedside table. Reading it at least three more times she decided she would phone the contact number on Monday morning. She loved her job at Guys and her parents had been so proud when she qualified three years ago, but it just wasn't the same anymore. Understandably, her colleagues and some of her regular patients were afraid of upsetting her since her parent's deaths. This caused some of them to feel awkward around her, creating an atmosphere that had never been there before. A fresh start in another country would mean nobody need know about her tragic change of circumstances unless she wanted to tell them.

To her delight, she was asked to attend an interview the following week, which resulted in a second interview the week after that. This was a tremendous boost to her confidence which had plummeted in recent weeks. It proved to be extremely successful, and she was offered the job in Dubai.

"I'm so happy for you darling," Ellen said as she opened a bottle of champagne. The cork came out with such force it bounced off the wall causing them both to laugh. "Here's to a wonderful experience in Dubai," she said, as they clinked their champagne flutes together.

"Thank you. I'm elated and petrified at the same time."

"Of course, you are it's only natural, but it's going to be a new adventure. You'll have the same career but in another country." Ellen had concerns, but she told herself she was being irrational. Such feelings were bound to surface when your nearest and dearest was going to live so far away. "I'm going to miss you Katie," Ellen said with tears in her eyes.

"Don't get upset. I'm going to miss you more than you can imagine, but I'm not leaving until the first week in November. It's nearly four months away."

"At least by then you will have sold the house if the buyers John was telling us about still want to pay cash. Imagine having that much money to play with."

"John is certain the couple will get back to him tomorrow. He is such a good friend besides being an

33

excellent solicitor. Did you know that he and dad got to know each other when Alice left dad the cottage in Dereham? John helped him invest some of the money from the sale?"

"Yes, I remember your mum telling me a long time ago."

"I feel safe leaving it all in John's hands."

"Just imagine if your dad had decided to leave London and live in the cottage all those years ago, he might never have met your mum."

"He did say once that he was tempted but he loved his job in Lewisham and felt that was where he was meant to be. I'm so glad Tom came to the funeral. Him and dad have been best buddies ever since they met at school in Dereham, and it was great to hear stories of their childhood."

"Yes, it was."

"What strange times they grew up in and what wonderful people Alice and Doug must have been. They told dad that as soon as they saw him looking lost and alone in the village hall amongst the other evacuees that they were drawn to him straightaway. The church committee wanted them to have another lad, but they asked for Alan, or so the story goes. It's hard to imagine being wrenched away from the family you love at five years old and finding yourself in a place alien to you."

"It doesn't bear thinking about."

"It would have been lovely to have known dad's side of the family. If only they had survived the war."

"There were so many like your dad who lost everything. But this isn't getting the packing done. November will be here in no time at all, and you will need to be ready."

Looking round the spacious dining room, when Ellen had taken the glasses through to the kitchen, she recalled her mum's love of entertaining. The antique dresser was Shirley's pride and joy and was home to a beautiful Spode bone china dinner service. On top of the sideboard were the crystal decanters; one with her mum's favourite Harvey's Bristol Cream; one with her dad's Glenfiddich Whiskey and the other filled with Courvoisier Brandy for after dinner.

Her mum used to like six to eight guests even though the table seated ten. She thought, if you had too many, some would end up having conversations between themselves which defeated the object. On the odd occasion when Katie appeared, she'd had the confidence to join in the discussions round the table as she'd always had a mind of her own. Sometimes they would play backgammon after the meal, and she would play too if there was an odd number.

Katie didn't want to part with certain things and after Ellen had chosen what she wanted to keep she was going to put some of it in storage. Thankfully, her mum and dad had not been hoarders. She smiled to herself as she remembered her mum saying, 'A cluttered home is a cluttered mind!' All their spare stock for the business had been in the storeroom above the shop and was now sold. A week before the crash, Katie was in the stock room with her dad as he showed her some of the new pieces he had purchased at the auctions, plus a few bits from a house clearance. It made her feel utterly miserable to think they had only just extended their business and silent tears flowed down her cheeks.

Chapter Four

It was nearing the end of October and Katie's friends and colleagues at Guy's were wishing her luck with her new job. A farewell party was organised in one of the lecture rooms in the hospital and they gave her such lovely gifts. Carol, her boss, made a moving speech and hoped her new life in Dubai was going to be everything she wished for. There had been tears and hugs all round as she'd always been popular.

She left her job two weeks before she was due to fly to the Emirates so she could catch up with friends and spend time with Ellen, also, the new owners wanted to move into the house. It had been a harrowing day when Ellen came to collect Katie with her belongings in two suitcases. They had already taken some of Katie's clothes to the cottage in case she needed them when she came to stay, especially the winter ones. John Simpkins was going to organise the removal of the last of the furniture and they were grateful for that. They walked from room to room, but Katie became overwhelmed with grief, so they locked the front door for the last time and drove to Ellen's cottage in silence.

Suddenly it felt like she had a mountain to climb, and she wondered why she had applied for the job in the first place. Had it been bravado? Was she doing the right thing? Would she like it? So many thoughts were buzzing around in her head, and she felt apprehensive to say the least. It was too late to back down now. Her life had changed beyond all recognition, and she needed to make the most of this new opportunity, to build a new life for herself, to 'spread her wings' as her mum would have said.

Standing in front of her parent's memorial stone was distressing but she wanted to visit the cemetery before she flew to the Middle East. Ellen promised to look after it and said she would come here as often as she could. Katie missed her mum and dad dreadfully, but she didn't need to visit this garden of remembrance to talk to them.

Rose trees were in abundance and a beautiful weeping willow was close by, its thick green wands rustling violently in the intensity of the November wind. It was the perfect setting because Shirley and Alan both loved roses and her dad had planted a miniature weeping willow tree in their garden.

Ellen had to go to the cemetery office, so she left her niece sitting in the middle of the bench close to her parent's stone. She was going to meet her in the car park. Katie wrapped her coat tight around her to keep out the chill and wished the wind would die down. It was extremely cold even though it was only the first week in November, and she was looking forward to some sun. Sensing her parents around wasn't unusual and today was no exception but she had never actually seen them. However, the feeling that they were sitting on either side of her on the bench was so strong that she fully expected to see them looking solid. What she did see were two diaphanous figures and she was stunned into silence. For a few seconds she could smell the scent of her mum's perfume and then her dad's aftershave, just long enough to know it was them. But the power of their love left her in no doubt at all. The warmth from their arms enveloping her whole being was the most beautiful thing that had ever happened to her.

A few days later, Sue and Ellen went with Katie to Heathrow Airport. Her aunt had cooked a fabulous meal the night before, as Sue had arrived from Manchester three days earlier to spend some time with her best friend. Before Katie went through to the departure lounge, they sat and had a coffee together. It was too early for breakfast and none of them were hungry anyway.

"Well, this is it!" Katie remarked nervously when they had finished their drinks.

Ellen leant across and squeezed her hand.

Sue got up from the table. "You are so brave."

They hugged each other. "I don't feel brave, Katie replied."

"You can always change your mind, darling."

"I know Ellen but it's going to be an experience if nothing else and I can always come back if it doesn't work out."

"You certainly can," her aunt said with tears in her eyes. "I will miss you, Katie." They held each other close swaying gently.

"I'll miss you too … love you both," she said as they finally let go of each other.

"Love you too!" Sue and Ellen called after her as she walked off towards the departure lounge without looking back. She couldn't look back because she was quietly weeping.

Katie couldn't quite believe she was at Dubai Airport in The United Arab Emirates, though she had always promised herself she would travel to more exotic countries. She wandered along pushing her luggage, taking everything in. It was certainly different to any other Airport she'd been to. It was a large ultra-modern building with the distinctive Arabic style and the Arabic language sounded quaint as she weaved in and out of the colourful crowds. She had never seen such a cross-section of people under one roof before.

Fascinated by the Arab dress she found herself unintentionally looking at a group of local women. It was strange to see their faces covered all but their eyes; there was hardly any flesh to be seen underneath their attire. She averted her eyes when she saw the women pointing at her obviously agitated by her gaze. Pushing her trolley once more she hadn't noticed two suave looking men walking in front of it. Bumping into one of them caused a small bag to fall to the floor with a thud.

"Oh, I'm so sorry," she cried as she bent down to retrieve it.

"Please, don't apologise. It was my fault I wasn't looking where I was going."

For a few seconds, their eyes met, and Katie couldn't help noticing his were deep brown and sparkling; she felt her cheeks starting to glow. It was difficult to tear her eyes away from this handsome, Arab gentleman and she realised he was asking her a question in perfect English.

"Would you like me to get you some help with these?" he asked, pointing to her luggage.

"No ... it's all right, thank you, somebody is coming to meet me."

"I will say good-bye then," his smile lit up his whole face and showed the most beautiful white teeth.

"Good-bye," she half whispered, and smiling to herself, she walked on. But something made her turn round and she was surprised to see him standing there, staring after her. It seemed they didn't want to put out the spark that had been ignited between them. The older man, who looked extremely annoyed, tugged at his sleeve and they both walked off in the opposite direction. Katie felt embarrassed and flattered at the same time and she was puzzled by this sudden, deep attraction for a total stranger.

It was a few minutes before she could get him out of her mind, and she began to feel lost and alone in this noisy airport. Knowing somebody was meeting her didn't help suppress her concern. Once more she started to question herself. Had she done the right thing leaving England? Would she settle into her new life? Well, whatever she felt she certainly needed a new beginning, but at this precise moment she wanted to run. Trying to calm herself, she began to take a few deep breaths. "It's too late now," she mused. "I am here, and I must make the best of my new adventure." She vowed to herself she would think positive.

"Katie Morgan?"

She jumped when she heard this friendly English voice calling her name. It stood out amidst the many foreign voices around her and brought her back from her reverie.

"Yes."

"Sorry, I didn't mean to make you jump," she said, as she picked up one of Katie's bags.

"I'm Beverley, but you can call me Bev, everyone else does. I have a car waiting. I expect everything feels strange, but you'll soon get used to it. How was the flight? Did you enjoy the wonderful view of Dubai Creek as you flew in? It seems ages ago since I arrived for the first time. Oh, I'm sorry I do go on don't I," she said, as they reached the car. Looking at each other they both laughed. Katie felt sure she was going to be good friends with Beverley. She liked this friendly chatty young woman already and began to feel less apprehensive as she climbed into the back seat.

"Thanks for meeting me, Beverley … er … Bev. I was feeling conspicuous standing there." She told her what had happened when she found herself staring at a group of local women and how they had started pointing at her. How she had turned away quickly and pushed her trolley into the most gorgeous man.

"I'm not in the habit of gazing into the eyes of every man I bump into, not that I bump into many, but there was something about him. I can't explain it. Still, I don't suppose I'll see him again."

"It was probably his charm that attracted you. Arab men, or should I say Emirati men can be very charming, especially when they're dressed in western clothes. Just don't ever marry one." They both giggled at the sudden seriousness in Bev's voice.

"It's lovely and cool in here."

"Yes, the air conditioning is such a relief in the summer when it's 120 degrees. Thankfully, you've missed the fierce heat. November is hot, but certainly not as bad as July or August."

"I wonder if I'll ever get used to the heat. I've never been one for sunbathing."

"You will if you don't stay out in it too long for the first two or three weeks. Mind you, there's so much to do here you won't want to be lying in the sun all day. Wind surfing, scuba diving, sailing.

"I'm not very sporty though I do love to swim."

"Wait till you see some of the hunky instructors," she grinned. "And on Chicago Beach there are catamarans for anyone to use. Sometimes we go out in them for a sundowner, with beers and a picnic. It's a good life here, Katie."

"What about work?"

"There's plenty of time to tell you about that. You haven't got to start for another couple of days, so you can settle into your apartment and get used to things. Oh, by the way our boss sends his apologies. He would have met you himself, but he got called to a meeting. Anyway, I'm

41

sure you'd rather have me for company. He's a good man but you looked worried enough without having Mr Baker looming up behind you."

They both chuckled.

Katie felt relaxed in Bev's company. She hadn't laughed much in the last five months; she'd been too worried about her ensuing trip to the Emirates, plus, in the early days of her grieving, she'd felt guilty when she found something even remotely funny.

"Look, there's the hospital you're going to be working in." Beverley pointed to a large and extremely modern building. It looked luxurious compared to the hospitals in England; the grounds were beautiful with emerald green lawns, and an abundance of colour in the vast flowerbeds. There were many exotic plants she had never seen before and palm trees lining the driveway to the main entrance. It looked more like a hotel than a hospital.

"Wow, my colleagues at Guy's would be amazed if they could see this."

"You'll have to send them a photograph."

A few minutes later the car stopped outside the compound which to Katie sounded more like a prison rather than a block of luxury apartments overlooking a large communal swimming pool.

Climbing out of the car the heat was more noticeable. The driver took her luggage out of the boot, and she paid him.

"Phew, it's hot!"

"Yes, and it's too hot to do anything. Anyway, I'm sure you're feeling tired after your long journey," she said as she helped Katie carry her luggage up the back stairs. I'll show you round your apartment then leave you to have a rest. I'm only next door, so just knock if you need me." Bev gave her a reassuring look. She knew what it was like on your first day in a strange country and not knowing anybody.

"Thanks Bev, you're so kind."

Half an hour later Katie was alone in her apartment feeling much happier than she had been earlier. Bev was so friendly and helpful, and she could not help liking her. She was pleased to know they were going to be working together, as she was to be her dental nurse. Tired though she was she wanted to have another look round before a much-needed rest.

Finding a bottle of white wine in an ice bucket sitting on the kitchen table, with a note from Mr. Baker made her feel welcome. He said he was looking forward to seeing her in his office the day after tomorrow. And he would personally show her round the dental department and introduce her to the rest of the staff. Well, he certainly sounded down to earth, and she was looking forward to meeting them all.

Katie liked her apartment. It was furnished with American Colonial style furniture which was both beautiful and comfortable. Lounging on the sofa she sunk into the large soft cushions, which were a pretty floral print in pastel colours with curtains to match. A wall unit opposite the sofa looked a little bare, apart from a couple of plants and a small television. It wouldn't take her long to fill the shelves with a few of her personal belongings and she would feel more at home when she unpacked her books. The kitchen, bathroom and bedroom were all a decent size and she marvelled at the pink and grey marble floors throughout the apartment; it was so cool under her feet. Yes, she was going to like it here.

Unable to keep her eyes open any longer she walked into the bedroom and flopped onto the double bed, the plain burgundy cotton quilt cover and the cotton sheets felt so cool. She decided a shower would have to wait until she'd had a rest. Not having been able to sleep on the plane meant that right now, sheer exhaustion was about to overcome any feelings of excitement or apprehension that she might still have. She slept soundly for the next three hours.

A feeling of panic swept over her when she woke suddenly, rubbing her eyes and wondering where she was. It took her a few moments to realise she was lying on her bed in her new apartment in Dubai. Focusing her eyes, she looked at her watch. Oh damn, she had forgotten to alter it, then she remembered the alarm clock on her bedside cabinet. Bev had made sure this was showing the correct time. She was going to knock later to take her to meet some of the others in the complex. They were going to have a swim before dinner. It was six o'clock, so she would have plenty of time to unpack and have a shower before Bev came back. What would she have done without her on her first day in such unfamiliar surroundings?

The feeling of loneliness swept over her again like a tidal wave and she was tempted to jump on the next plane back to England. How she missed the house already but there was no going back. It had been sold and she didn't want to live there after her parents had passed away.

Katie was going to miss her friends, she thought, as she looked round for somewhere to put her empty suitcase and holdall. She had unpacked all her things and put them away without being conscious of doing it. She hadn't been aware of the silent tears rolling down her cheeks either, which now broke into sobs. It was unusual these days for her to become so distraught with grief, but she was in a strange country and feeling homesick.

Deciding a shower would do her the world of good, she wandered into the bathroom as the tears subsided. She wiped her eyes with the sodden tissue she had rolled up into a ball while thinking how glad she would be when she saw the back of 1985.

Chapter Five

Lying on a sun lounger at the side of the pool, Katie was taking in her now familiar environment. It was a large complex with accommodation for a considerable number of hospital staff. The ground floor apartments had patio doors opening onto a small, paved area which was screened on both sides by a wooden lattice fence about six feet high and five feet wide. There were blue, pink, and white climbing plants with the prettiest little trumpet flowers she had ever seen weaving in and out of them. Two steps down to the coloured paving stones surrounding the pool, there was patio furniture and sun loungers at intervals put there entirely for the comfort of the residents. On the first floor where Katie and Bev lived, they had balconies overlooking the swimming pool. They loved to sit here late at night when the complex was lit up with little white lights. It was enchanting!

Three months had passed since she had arrived in Dubai, and she was thoroughly enjoying her new life. Thoughts of the house and the memory of that awful day of the accident had been relentless but now they receded a bit further to the back of her mind. It was strange but comforting when sadness threatened to engulf her, and the feeling of calm came over her instead. It was at these moments she felt a presence in the otherwise empty room. She knew it was her mum and she wasn't frightened, but she didn't tell anyone for fear of being ridiculed. Apart from, Ellen, of course who listened with interest when they spoke on the phone.

Life in the Emirates was great. It made her realise she had been a little over protected, mainly by her dad, when she was a teenager. Working abroad was something she had never contemplated but then she never thought her life was going to be turned upside down, as it had been.

"You look deep in thought Katie." It was Reece the Dental Technician. She hadn't heard him approaching.

"Hello Reece."

"I'm not disturbing you, am I?"

"No. And yes, I was deep in thought. I never considered for one minute I'd end up living and working in the Middle East."

"Why not?"

"Because I was happy with my life until ..." she hesitated. "Well ... let's just say I needed to get away."

"I'm glad you did. It's improved the quality of my life having you around."

"Oh, go away!"

She took the cushion from behind her head and threw it at him playfully.

"Why did you come out here, Reece?"

"I wasn't enamoured with the National Health Service salary. I want to earn enough money out here so I can go home and start my own business, but I'm not in a hurry."

"So, you want to settle down in England then?"

"Yes, eventually, but at the moment I can't think of anything better than sitting here with you."

An awkward silence followed and lasted for a few minutes. Katie felt uncomfortable whenever Reece became too intense. Most of the time he had a relaxed demeanour, but he obviously had feelings for her and couldn't seem to hide them. She liked him as a friend, and she wanted to keep it that way. He was the same age

47

as her but was rather immature and he had a peculiar sense of humour, which made him seem younger still. He was pleasant looking with a cheeky smile, but his thick black hair always looked untidy because he had a habit of pushing his fingers through it.

Kind and congenial though he was, he was not her type. She found herself attracted to older men. Men with a bit more class and style, who treated her like a lady, but also respected her views. A man who opened car doors for her and pulled her seat out at the restaurant table before she sat down to a meal. Some women would say she was old fashioned, but she knew what she liked.

Deep down she wanted to find a man who did not think she was foolish because she liked staring at a full moon, especially when it was sending silver threads of light across the ocean. Someone who would walk along an empty beach with her holding hands would be her kind of man enjoying together the feel of the waves lapping over their bare feet. A tall order she thought to herself, but she couldn't help being an incurable romantic. She noticed Bev making her way towards them and she was relieved to see her.

"Hi, you two. I hope you haven't forgotten about the meal tonight."

"No, Bev of course I haven't. I'm looking forward to it. Are you Reece?" Katie asked, trying to bring him back into the conversation.

"Yes, it sounds great!"

"It's a lovely idea, Mr Baker taking us all out for a meal. I'm feeling hungry already and I've only just had my lunch."

Katie laughed. "All you ever think about is food."

Reece got up to leave. "I've got an urgent job on, so I'm going back to work for a while. See you both later."

"Oh dear," said Bev when Reece was out of earshot.

"Did I interrupt something?"

"No, you did not!"

"You know Reece thinks the world of you."

"I know, but he's not my type."

"I don't think he's anyone's type, is he?"

"Don't be so unkind."

"Well, you know what I mean, he can be childish sometimes."

"Maybe, but he has lots of other qualities."

"You never have a bad word to say about him. I'm sure you two are going to end up together."

"For goodness' sake, I've only been here for three months and you're trying to marry me off already. Can we change the subject or better still let me go to sleep and dream about a handsome rich Sheik coming to take me away to his dazzling white palace?"

Bev smiled. "If you like Arab men that much there's always Mr Moborak the consultant who fancies you. Every time you walk past him his eyes nearly pop out of his head and he's not short of a bob or two either."

"Here you go again."

"At least you can pick and choose Katie?" Bev remarked, suddenly sounding utterly miserable.

"What's wrong with you?"

"Oh, nothing much," Bev muttered stretching herself out on the sun lounger. "I think I'll have a sleep as well and dream about the delicious Chinese meal we're going to have tonight."

"Is your diet getting you down again, Bev?"

"What diet? I haven't stuck to it all week and I'm certainly not going to spoil my visit to the high-class Dynasty Chinese Restaurant tonight worrying about it," she retorted.

Katie was taken aback.

"Sorry, I didn't mean to snap at you like that."

"It's alright."

They both lay in silence each with their own thoughts. It was hot, but not too uncomfortable and soon Bev dozed off. Katie stayed awake and gloried in the thought that she could have been stuck in England with the cold, wind, and rain.

Relaxed, but not sleepy, she was feeling hurt because Bev had barked at her a few minutes ago. It was upsetting to hear her sounding so miserable. She had been such a help when Katie first arrived in the Emirates. Many times, she had gone next door for a cosy chat because she was homesick and missed her friends in England. She couldn't understand why she was always putting herself down as she wasn't that much over-weight. Bev was attractive with a round face and fair hair shaped into a bob which framed her good looks and twinkly blue eyes, which were full of mischief. She was always smiling and had a lively personality which made her popular with the hospital staff.

Katie suddenly remembered Greg who was a radiographer. Somehow, he had got himself an invitation to the meal tonight. She was always going on about how handsome he was.

"Bev, are you awake?"

"Well … I am now," she answered sleepily.

"You really are touchy today," Katie commented, wondering if she should broach to subject.

"Sorry. What is it?"

"It's so unlike you to be irritable. Is it because Greg is going to be there tonight?"

"What does it matter if he's there or not I'm sure he won't be interested in me."

"Here you go again, putting yourself down. How do you know he's not interested in you? Is he taking anyone else?"

"No."

"Well then!"

"Well then, what? I'm a size sixteen, what is commonly known as fat. It's all right for you, you've got a gorgeous figure."

"But it's not me he stops and talks to in the hospital canteen, is it?"

Bev looked thoughtful.

"And it's not me he's hoping to see tonight."

"What do you mean?"

"Oh, come on Bev, he made sure he got an invitation and you and I are the only unattached females going. Besides, he's never said more than half a dozen words to me."

"He's shy." She was quick to defend Greg.

"I know he's shy, but he always manages to talk to you."

"Yes, he does, doesn't he?" Bev looked thoughtful. "I do like him."

"Right then, your make up must be perfect and I'll do your hair for you. You can wear your new blue dress which you look terrific in and ..."

"Hold on ... there is one slight problem if I wear my new dress."

"What is it?"

Bev had a grin on her face. "I will have to wear my 'I can't believe it's a girdle' and big knickers to hold my stomach in."

They burst into fits of giggles.

"You are funny and it's good to see you laughing again. Come on, let's have a swim before the others get back from the souk."

51

"No, let me stay here in peace and daydream about Greg."

"Well, it's certainly an improvement on dreaming about the meal you're going to devour tonight. Come on!"

"Do I have to?"

"Yes. You're always moaning about having to diet. If you exercised more, you wouldn't have to suffer so much, would you?"

"Alright, alright." Bev got up with reluctance but feeling much more cheerful than she had done earlier.

They both dived into the pool, which was like plunging into a warm bath. After a good swim, Katie could not think of anything more luxurious as she lay floating on her back with the sun's rays warming her whole body. She was looking forward to their meal in the Ramada Hotel. Up until now she had only seen it from a taxi, and it looked splendid with its marble steps leading up to the massive glass doors of the entrance. The young chap on the door resplendent in his outfit, which was that of an Indian Rajah, bright and colourful compared to the doorman at the Hilton in London. Not that she had ever visited the Hilton Hotel, but she had walked past it a few times and seen the ladies going in with their terribly expensive furs and jewellery.

"Katie, I'm getting out," called Bev.

"I won't be long."

"It's getting late, and we've got to get ready," she remarked.

"Ok, I'm coming."

They climbed out of the pool, grabbed their towels, and made their way back to their apartments. Katie had a nervous stomach and couldn't make out why. It was not her who was hoping to ensnare her man in the Ramada Hotel, but she could not be rid of this fluttering feeling.

Maybe she was nervous for her friend, she thought, as she threw her swimsuit into the laundry basket and stepped into the shower.

Katie had been in a few hotels in Dubai but this one was the most luxurious and she wondered how her boss could afford to pay for them all even if he did earn good money; he was a generous man.

Reece took her up in the glass lift to see the largest stained-glass window in the world. It was the same height as the building and was magnificent. There were black and white marble floors all the way through and some of the tallest plants she had ever seen. Palms, ferns, rubber plants and others she did not recognise, with a kaleidoscope of colour. In the foyer there was a charming fountain made of white marble; the water changed colour every few seconds and it had a hypnotic effect on her.

"Are you coming?" cried Reece. "We're about to go into the restaurant."

"You bet. I wouldn't miss this for the world."

It was high class. She wondered if she would ever settle down in England again as she was becoming too used to the way of life in the Emirates. They had a large round table. Mr Moborak, the consultant, was sitting opposite her which was to prove embarrassing as nearly every time she looked up, he was smiling at her; the others did not seem to notice. Reece was sitting to Katie's right and was trying to make them all laugh. Bev hadn't been able to hide her pleasure when Greg asked if he could sit next to her, and already they were deep in conversation. Well, Bev was doing most of the talking but Greg did not seem to mind at all. Mr Baker was sitting next to his wife Maureen, and he was making her laugh. He was a very funny man and could make most people around him feel at ease. Don and June, the two

53

dentists, were sitting either side of Mr Moborak. They kept trying to bring him into their conversation without much success. Katie thought he was a strange man, and she certainly didn't give him any encouragement.

During the meal, which Katie thought was exceptional and nothing like the Chinese food she had tasted in England, she got a peculiar feeling in her solar plexus. There was a tremendous heat on the back of her neck and a warm feeling which ran through her body. Naturally, she thought it was the red wine and was putting the glass gently back onto the tablecloth when a waiter came over. He held out a silver salver with a small piece of paper placed on it.

"Madame, the note is for you."

"Me?" She hesitated before taking the piece of folded paper. She could still feel the heat on the back of her neck as she read the words. *Please turn round so I can look into those beautiful sky-blue eyes once more, Nabil Khalifa.* She did turn round and saw him sitting a few yards from their table. Katie hadn't noticed him when they had entered the restaurant, but she certainly recognised him now.

Nabil smiled at her and raised his glass and she reached for her glass without taking her eyes from his and raised it also. His smile was warm and genuine, and he looked even more handsome than he had done at the airport when she bumped into him with her luggage trolley. She had been embarrassed, but he had been courteous and charming.

By this time, everyone sitting at the table had noticed but Katie was oblivious until she realised her heart was thumping so loud, she wondered if they could all hear it too.

"Who's that?" asked Bev, as Katie turned back to face them all.

"That's the man I bumped into at the airport. Do you remember me telling you about him in the taxi when you met me?" Katie spoke quietly so the others couldn't hear but Reece had heard.

"You're not getting involved with a local man, are you?"

"I'm not getting involved with anyone, Reece."

"Well, it certainly looks as if he'd like to get involved with you."

"What?"

"Sorry, but you've got to be careful. You know what Arab men are like."

"No, I don't know what Arab men are like. Only what everyone keeps telling me."

"You've got to admit he is rather gorgeous!" Bev quipped.

This remark brought Greg into the conversation. "Yes, and very charming no doubt."

"The whole table will be discussing my love life in a minute," Katie cried, beginning to lose her patience.

The same waiter came back with three bottles of expensive champagne. "From the gentleman who sent the note, madame. The champagne is for you and your friends." He then proceeded to place the three ice buckets on the table while another waiter brought crystal champagne flutes.

Suddenly everyone was smiling. Mr Baker lent across to her and said, "I didn't know you mingled with the rich?"

"How do you know he is rich Mr Baker?"

"You can call me Ted when we're out for the night, Katie, the others do."

"How do you know he's rich Mr Bake ... er, Ted?"

"You can tell by the clothes for one thing. I expect he's having a business meeting."

55

"Oh," she said thoughtfully.

"Well, the champagne's excellent," commented Bev raising her glass.

"Let's toast eh … what's his name again?"

"Nabil Khalifa," Katie replied, feeling conspicuous. Luckily, the next course had just arrived, and everyone was too busy anticipating such culinary delights to notice.

"This is delicious," exclaimed Bev as she tucked in.

"It certainly beats Mr Chang's takeaway," remarked Katie who was glad to change the subject. "I wouldn't mind doing it again."

"I'll bring you if you like."

"I didn't mean it like that, Reece. You can't afford a place like this."

"Well, we would have to do without the champagne."

Bev gently prodded Katie in the arm. "I'm dying to go to the loo will you come with me?" She said in a quieter voice.

"Yes. Excuse me Reece," she said rising from the table and pushing her chair back.

They found the ladies room but were not expecting anything quite so elegant. A pink marble floor and more gigantic plants, enormous floor to ceiling mirrors with gold frames and even beautifully designed sofas to sit on, if one so wished.

"Wow, I wouldn't mind staying in here for the rest of the night. Anyway, I thought you needed to get away from Reece."

"Oh, I can handle him. I think he was jealous of my admirer especially when the champagne started flowing."

"Think he was jealous he was green with envy. Katie what are you going to do about your new friend?"

"What do you mean 'my new friend'? I don't even know him. And who was the one who told me never to get involved with the local men?"

"Yes, I know, but there's no harm in a couple of dates, especially if he can take you to expensive places."

"I'm not that shallow Bev and I do have money of my own you know, so I don't need a man to take me to posh restaurants."

"Yes of course, sorry, but … I wonder when you'll see him again?"

Her question was soon answered when five minutes later they walked back into the foyer. They nearly collided with Nabil and his two companions who had just walked out of the restaurant.

"We have a habit of meeting like this."

"Oh, hello. Thank you for the champagne … it was extremely kind of you."

"Think no more of it. Can I talk to you for a few moments?"

He turned to his companions said something in Emirati and they walked off before she had the chance to answer him. He then turned to Beverley and asked her if she minded.

"No, of course not, I'll get back to the others," she replied a little put out.

"I don't even know your name?"

"It's Katie."

"A beautiful name for a beautiful lady."

She was a little embarrassed and didn't answer him.

"I suppose you think me presumptuous sending notes and champagne to a strange young woman, but I don't feel we are strangers."

"I know what you mean," she said feeling the fluttering in her stomach again.

"I have often thought about you."

"You have?"

"Yes, I wondered where you were in the Emirates and what you were doing. I couldn't forget your beautiful blue, but sad, eyes."

How perceptive, Katie thought to herself. "I'd better get back to the restaurant, they'll be wondering what's happened to me."

"Yes, of course. I must not keep you from your friends."

"Can I ask you something?"

"You can ask me anything," he replied, spreading his arms wide. He was pleased to be in her company for a few more minutes.

"When you sent the note and the champagne, how did you know whether I was with anyone or not?"

"I'm sorry if I've made the wrong impression. I wouldn't have done it if I thought you were attached to the young man next to you, but you had the look of boredom on your face most of the time he was talking. It's not good when a man's company bores a lady. Please, if I am wrong then I apologise profusely."

"No, you're not wrong."

"You don't know how happy it makes me feel to hear you say that."

His smile lit up his whole face and his eyes sparkled.

"Well, I should go back."

"I look forward to our next meeting. Goodbye Katie."

"Goodbye Nabil." She started to make her way back to the restaurant. She knew he was still looking at her, but she couldn't turn round not in a busy place like this.

"You came back then?" Bev remarked, as she slid into her seat.

"Yes," she replied, somewhat distractedly. Her thoughts were already elsewhere, and she couldn't eat another thing. The night was nearly over, and they'd all be leaving soon. She wanted to be back in her apartment so she could be alone with her thoughts.

Reece, who was feeling dejected, didn't look up but gave his whole attention to the contents of his desert. Fifteen minutes later when they had all finished the last dregs of the champagne Ted Baker got up from the table.

"I'll go and order the taxis. I hope everyone enjoyed the meal?"

They all agreed it had been excellent and thanked him.

"There's nothing like a bit of luxury now and again." He went into the foyer to order the cars. He came back a few minutes later with a grin on his face.

"It seems I don't have to order taxis. Your friend," he looked at Katie, "has sent two chauffeur driven limousines for us and apparently they are waiting outside and will do so until we are ready to leave."

They all gasped and looked at Katie, who was just as surprised.

"Well folks, I suggest we leave now, as we've got work in the morning."

"We're certainly going home in style," said Bev excitedly.

On their way out of the hotel Mr Baker caught Katie gently by the arm so he could talk to her.

"I made a few enquiries when I was finding out about the cars. Nabil Khalifa is from a local and well-respected family. He is extremely rich and has never married. I hope you don't think I'm interfering."

"No, of course I don't, but I don't suppose I'll see him again."

"Oh, you will Katie, you will, just be careful."

Forty minutes later she was alone in her apartment. It had been difficult trying to get Bev to leave because all she wanted to do was discuss the unusual events of the

59

evening. Katie, however, had insisted she was too tired even to think about Nabil Khalifa, so Bev had eventually retired to her own apartment. She smiled to herself. Bev was a good friend, but she could sometimes be a tad overpowering and she was relieved when she had finally gone next door.

Katie made herself a cup of coffee, took it into the living room and sat down on the sofa, putting the coffee on the floor where it eventually went cold. The events of the evening kept going over and over in her mind and she continued to sit there thinking of Nabil Khalifa.

"I look forward to our next meeting," he had said. Maybe he was rather too sure of himself, she thought. But she did have the overwhelming feeling that she was going to see him again. What was she thinking? I hardly know him. I've come out here to work not get involved with anyone, least of all a rich Emirati who probably has a string of women. Mr Baker said he wasn't married but that doesn't mean much. He must be about thirty, so why hasn't he married? Yet the way he looked straight into her eyes and the warmth that emanated from him, the way she was drawn to his dark brown eyes, which appeared to smile when he looked at her, nothing else seemed to matter.

He was handsome but how many times had she heard Bev say, 'Don't get involved with an Arab!' On both the occasions she had seen Nabil he'd been dressed in western style clothes which made her forget all about customs and religion. Younger Arab men seemed to be more relaxed about such things, or so she thought. Eventually Katie dozed off, too tired to drag herself into the bedroom.

Chapter Six

"Katie, I don't believe it, there's another bunch of roses arrived for you."

"Oh no, what am I going to do? The whole place is beginning to look like a rose garden," Katie moaned, as she looked up from her patient who was trying hard not to laugh.

Bev was now standing at the sink cleaning instruments ready for the autoclave when Mr Baker put his head round the door.

"Katie, could I have a word with you when you've finished?"

"Yes, Mr. Baker I'll be about five minutes," she replied apprehensively throwing a questioning glance at Bev who was pretending not to hear.

"How embarrassing what is he going to say?" Katie questioned when they were on their own again.

"He'll probably laugh knowing him," Bev smiled, she could see the funny side of everything.

Five minutes later she was sitting in her boss's office, her cheeks turning pink.

"Mr Khalifa is certainly trying to tell you something, Katie."

"Yes, Mr Baker."

"Don't look so worried. It's just that if anymore roses arrive, I don't know where we're going to put them."

"We'll be finished soon, and Beverley is going to help me take them home."

"You'll be hiring a truck then," he said smiling.

Katie laughed. "Could we send some round to the wards?"

"Yes, good idea. I was going to suggest that, but they're your roses. I'm sure they'll be appreciated, and it will stop Mr Moborak from complaining."

"I am sorry I didn't realise he was. I'll see to it straight away."

"Don't let Mr Moborak worry you, but let's hope no more arrive before the end of the morning."

"Thanks for being so understanding Mr Baker."

"That's alright Katie, but have a word in Mr Khalifa's ear, will you please?"

"Yes of course," she answered, getting up from the chair and making for the door as quickly as she could.

"Katie," Bev called out from the reception area.

"Oh, don't tell me more roses?"

"No. I was just going to say your last patient has cancelled, so if you want me to help you with this lot, we can do it now."

"Bev, I can't possibly take them all home."

"Well, we'd have to make two journeys."

"No, I've decided to send some of them round to the wards. Can you please ring one of the porters for me? But don't tell him who they were for or who sent them, otherwise it'll be all round the hospital in no time; I'll be too embarrassed to go into the staff restaurant. I'll tidy up the surgery then we can get out of here with the rest."

Katie sat doing some paperwork and writing up the patient's notes, but she couldn't concentrate. Mr Baker had asked her to have a word in Mr Khalifa's ear but how could when she had no idea how to contact him. How had he found out where she was working? They'd only spoken for about five minutes in the hotel last night. She smiled to herself. How romantic he is. She'd never seen

62

so many beautiful red roses in one place before, apart from the shops in England on Valentine's Day.

The telephone rang and made her jump. It was the receptionist.

"Katie, there's a phone call for you, it's a Mr Khalifa. Shall I put him through?"

"Er ... yes please."

"Hello Katie. Will you dine with me tonight?" he asked taking her by surprise.

She hesitated.

"If you're otherwise engaged, we could make it another night."

"No, it's alright, I'm not doing anything and thank you for the roses."

"You're welcome. I'm glad you like them."

"Well, who wouldn't like them but there are rather a lot."

"Sorry about that I got carried away. Can I have your address so I can pick you up ... say about nine o'clock?

She gave it to him and they said their goodbyes, but she was still holding the telephone in her hand when Bev came back into the surgery.

"Are you alright?"

Katie looked up. "He rang."

"Who rang?" She asked as she tidied the patient's records ready to take them back to reception.

"Who do you think? Nabil of course!"

"Oh."

"He's asked me out to dinner tonight."

"Wow, he doesn't waste any time. I suppose you said yes?"

"I did. You said yourself he's gorgeous," Katie was puzzled by Bev's sudden change of attitude.

"Yes, I know, but you could have said you were busy tonight, couldn't you? I mean just because he's handsome and rich doesn't mean you have to jump as soon as he asks you out. You could have kept him waiting for a few days."

"I know, but to be honest I can't wait to see him again. I wonder where he's going to take me?"

"First things first, we've got to get your roses home."

"Oh yes, sorry Bev. It's a shame we didn't bring both our cars to work today," she said as she helped Bev switch everything off and put the white covers over the equipment in the surgery. "Still, I suppose we'll manage."

"Yes, if you sit in the boot."

"Oh dear."

"It's all right, I'm only joking. Most of them will have been taken to the wards by now."

They walked out into the reception area to see how many were left as Mr Moborak was coming out of his room.

"I do not know what this place is coming to Miss Morgan. We cannot have this sort of thing going on you know. This is a dental department," he stated sarcastically.

"Mr Moborak I was just about to take them home."

"What must the patients think?"

By this time, they had armfuls of red roses and could hardly see where they were going. Katie peered over the top of the beautiful blooms. "I'm sure the patients were delighted for me, at least my patients were."

Mr Moborak looked as if he was going to choke and he spluttered ... "Good-bye Miss Morgan," and strode back to his room.

They were struggling towards the lift and neither of them could control their giggles. They received peculiar looks from some of the staff and patients and smiles from others.

"What must the patients think?" Bev mimicked. "What a load of … he's so jealous. He's always fancied you, Katie. In fact, I think he's in love with you. Poor old sod!"

"Don't be wicked. Anyway, he's not old."

"Well, he's too old for you," Bev replied as the lift arrived.

On the way home she was rather subdued after all the laughter. The two of them had lots of fun together, but now she was thinking about Nabil; she had that fluttering feeling once more. Was she always going to feel like this at the mere thought of him? There had been a few boyfriends in the past and some she really liked but this was different. Although she hardly knew anything about him, she felt as if she had known him all her life and she knew he felt it too. Maybe they were kindred spirits? This was the sort of thing you read about in novels, and she could not believe it was happening to her. At least it had taken her mind off the first anniversary of her parent's deaths; the day that had changed her life forever.

Bev's chatter brought her back to the present. "What are you going to wear tonight? It had better not be anything too seductive or else he'll have you in his harem as soon as he looks at you."

"Very funny Bev, but all the same I don't want him to get any ideas on our first date. I've made that mistake in the past."

"So, what are you going to wear?"

"Oh, I don't know. It's too hot to be thinking about clothes."

They arrived at the complex and went up the back stairs to their apartments.

"Thanks for your help. You really are a good friend," said Katie, as they laid the roses in the bath.

"Do you want help arranging them?"

"No, it's okay. I'll enjoy doing that, but you could lend me a couple of vases. I only have two and I'm certainly going to need more than that."

"Yes of course. You put the coffee on, and I'll run next door and fetch them."

Ten minutes later they were sitting in the living room.

"Bev, in all the excitement I forgot to ask about Greg. Are you seeing him again?"

"As a matter of fact, I'm seeing him tonight," she said grinning like a Cheshire cat.

"That's great! I'm so pleased things are working out for you."

"I know he's shy and nothing like your Nabil, but he's lovely. I'm cooking him a meal and it's going to be something special."

"I'm sure it will be special. No one can cook like you."

Bev looked thoughtful. "My diet will go out of the window though."

"It won't hurt you for one night, will it?"

"No, I suppose not. Anyway, I'd better get going. I want everything prepared so I don't have to charge around later. Have a lovely time tonight."

"And you, Bev."

"I'll see you in the morning. I'm glad there's no work tomorrow, so we can have a long catch up," she said as she walked out into the hallway.

"Can't wait! See you tomorrow."

What a glorious smell, she thought, as she sat on the side of the bath looking at the flowers and breathing in the scent. Suddenly she felt lightheaded, she thought it was the smell of the roses in such a confined space, but then she sensed somebody was in the room with her. Not a physical presence, but a presence all the same. This feeling did not frighten her but made her feel calm and tranquil.

Katie got all the vases together and began to arrange the flowers, all the time thinking of Nabil and how romantic he was. She put most of the roses in the lounge but saved some for her bedroom. A few minutes later she lay on her bed suddenly feeling tired; sensing a presence in the room again as she dozed off. There was someone leaning over her and the voice she heard in her head sounded like her mother's. Opening her eyes in amazement, she thought she must have dreamt it, but the words were still imprinted on her mind ... 'be careful my darling.'

Katie sat up, half expecting to see her mum in the room. Did she really say those words or was she imagining it? For a few minutes she felt agitated about her ensuing date, compared to the feeling of elation earlier. But she soon calmed down when she looked at the roses on the bedside cabinet and she forgot all about those words of warning as she started to sort out a dress to wear.

Listening to Madame Butterfly a few minutes later, which was one of her favourite operas, made her feel good. There was a knock. It must be Bev, she thought, and quickly put on her wrap before she opened the door. It was another bunch of red roses which she took from the young Indian boy, who was still smiling as she thanked him. He hovered, so she dashed to the kitchen and took five dirhams from her purse and handed them to him; he nodded and grinned again as she shut the door.

The following morning Katie woke up about eight thirty which was quite late for her. Sitting on her balcony breathing in the morning air and smelling the sweet scent from the flowers below was heavenly. Marvelling at the blue sky and soaking up the sun's rays her whole being felt vibrant and alive. She thought about Nabil and

67

wondered what the future held for them. He had stood at the front door of her apartment at exactly nine o'clock the evening before, looking immaculate and extremely stylish. She liked a man who knew how to dress, and he certainly fitted that description. Class is written all over him she thought. But she believed class was something you were born with, regardless of whether you were rich or poor.

The Mercedes was parked downstairs and as she climbed in, she stepped into a different world. Katie happened to mention how charming Dubai looked in the evening, so he suggested a short tour first and his chauffeur obliged. Relaxing in each other's company felt natural and the warmth that emanated from him enveloped her like a cocoon making her feel cosy and secure.

Abdullah, Nabil's chauffeur, drove them around town and while she was enjoying the sights, she knew his eyes were on her. Mosques were particularly attractive buildings and at night they were lit up which gave them a golden glow; the flood of light enhanced the highly decorative façades, and the palm trees were silhouetted against these beautiful buildings.

In Dubai, the clock tower was a landmark to most local people. In the daytime it didn't have much character but at night it was transformed. Bursting from the middle was an enormous fountain with a golden glow around it. Emiratis seem to like illuminating everything. Palm trees everywhere were swamped with little white lights, and it reminded her of Oxford Street in the festive season.

The front doorbell rang, and she got up to open the door knowing it was her dear friend and neighbour.

"Morning Katie."

"Hello Bev. That was good timing the coffee's on."

"I've bought some fresh croissants for our breakfast," she said, waving the bag in front of Katie's eyes.

"Thanks. I haven't been up long. I'm just going to laze around today."

"I can tell you had a good time last night."

"Wonderful, but let's have something to eat first before we get into a deep conversation. Do you want strawberry jam on your croissants?"

"Yes please."

"You take the coffee out on the balcony while I do these. I wasn't hungry earlier, but I think I could manage one now."

Ten minutes later they were eating croissants oozing with strawberry jam and drinking their coffee. When they'd finished, Bev was bursting to know all about Katie's date with Nabil.

"Let's go inside, it's getting too hot out here."

They sank onto the sofa, the air conditioning cooling them down in an instant.

"Well?" Bev was unable to contain herself any longer. "Where did you eat?"

"The Penthouse French Restaurant in the Intercontinental Hotel."

"Umm, very nice too."

"A few people recognised Nabil, and we received some funny looks. Our table was waiting for us, but he asked for it to be screened off. Waiters were out of earshot but as soon as he looked up one would rush over. I got the impression I could have asked for anything, and they would have fetched it for me. Honestly, Bev, I felt like royalty."

"What was the food like?"

"I thought you'd want to know that." Katie laughed. "I've had French cuisine before but nothing so delicious. It was magnifique!" she said in her best French accent.

69

"And what was he like?"

She sighed with a dreamy look on her face. "What do you want to know first?"

"Was he boring, lively, irresistible? Did he undress you with his eyes?"

"You're so nosy Beverley Salter."

"Yes, I know, so come on tell."

"He was charming, considerate, lively, attentive and yes irresistible."

"Oh, come on, he must have some bad points."

"Not really, except you might say he's very sure of himself but not in an arrogant way. He's just a confident person, but then I feel confident about him too."

"What on earth do you mean?"

"I think I'm falling in love with him."

"What?"

"I think I'm in love with Nabil Khalifa. I've never felt like this about anyone before."

"But you've only been out with him once and you're usually so level-headed."

"I know, but it just feels right."

"So, he's rich, charming, and handsome but how can you be in love after one date? You don't know anything about him? He could have women all over the place. Anyway, you can't possibly be thinking about marrying a local man, it never works. You wouldn't be able to go to work; you'd have to change your whole way of life and your religion, and you'd have to live with his entire family."

"Oh, don't exaggerate."

"Katie I'm not exaggerating. I've been out here for three years, and I've seen it happen."

"I didn't say anything about marriage. I said I think I'm in love with him and I feel as if I've known him forever."

"You know what happens to young western females out here. Most of them are kept women living in huge luxury villas with servants, wearing Armani clothes and dripping with jewellery; they can have anything they want except freedom."

"Do you honestly think I would be a kept-woman Bev?"

"Well, no … of course not! But they rarely marry westerners and how do you know he isn't married. Mr Baker might have got it wrong."

"Nabil isn't married. His father died suddenly of a heart attack three years ago which was a great shock as he was only fifty-two. Yes, he does live with his mother and his younger sister Shazia. Yasmin, his married sister, lives in Abu Dhabi and he runs the family import business with his Uncle Mohammed."

"But how do you know it's all true?"

"I have such a warm feeling when I'm with him. I'm sure he wouldn't lie to me," she said emphatically. "We seem to have many of the same interests. He loves the arts as much as I do, especially the Opera, which he attended regularly when in England at University and on his frequent visits to London. He also admitted being a stargazer. He told me when he's at his Chicago Beach villa he loves to swim then sit on the terrace looking at the night sky while listening to the waves."

"Well, I am surprised at that. He doesn't sound like the usual type of Emirati man but why isn't he married?"

"Because he's never been drawn to any of the local women. Apparently, this angered his father when he was alive, and his uncle is furious with him." In her heart she knew he was going to be a part of her future.

"If he turns you on that much, why don't you jump into bed with him? You may find it's not love at all."

71

"Oh, he turns me on all right it was difficult to keep away from him last night. But it's more than that I know it is. Anyway, I don't want to jump into bed with him. I want a proper relationship."

"You are old-fashioned Katie."

"I suppose it was the way I was brought up."

"Yes, and you're too trusting."

"My mum used to say that."

"Well, if your mum used to say it, it must be true. I don't want to see you get hurt."

"I may have been a little over protected by my dad when I was young, but mum always encouraged me to follow my instincts. She especially wanted me to be my own person. Mum was a strong woman, and I am too. Besides, what about you and Greg? You haven't known him long either."

"That's different!"

"Why? Because he's not an Arab?"

"Katie don't take me the wrong way. I just don't want to see you upset."

"I won't be!"

"Did he talk about himself all night, or did he want to know anything about you?"

"Yes of course he wanted to know about me. He was genuinely interested in my life and showed great concern when I told him what happened to my parents. He said he now understands why he'd noticed such sadness in my eyes the first time we met at Dubai Airport. Anyway, do you want another coffee?" she asked, deliberately changing the subject, and getting up from the sofa.

"Yes please."

Bev knew she was annoyed but she hadn't meant to offend her. Nabil could be a genuine, honest man but he was still an Emirati, and she knew there would be trouble ahead for them.

The doorbell rang again, and Bev jumped up. I'll get it. It's probably Greg, we're going for a swim."

"Okay, I'll pour him a coffee," called Katie from the kitchen.

Bev showed Greg in, and he perched self-consciously on the edge of the armchair.

Katie came in with the tray of coffees. "Hello Greg," she said as she passed him a cup and saucer.

"Hi Katie, thanks."

"Bev hasn't told me how her meal went last night. Did you enjoy it?"

"It was brilliant," he replied with a look of pride in his eyes.

"She's a terrific cook."

"Yes, she is," answered Greg, who was not a great conversationalist.

"He certainly didn't leave much on his plate," Bev laughed.

"Are we going for a swim?"

"You bet!"

"Well, you've changed your tune. I can never get you in the pool."

"Didn't I have a swim with you the day before yesterday?"

"Yes, but I had to drag her in there, Greg. You must have something special to get her in the pool without a fight, I can tell you."

Greg looked embarrassed, so Bev thought they had better make a move.

"Are you coming down?" she asked as they walked out into the hallway.

"I might do later, but I'm waiting for a telephone call."

Bev gave her a funny look but didn't say anything.

Katie was so relieved to be on her own again. All she wanted to do was laze around after having two late nights. Now she was sitting quietly on her own she could think of Nabil. Seeing his happy smiling face and feeling his strong arms around her once more. At the door of her apartment, he had kissed her passionately, and it had set her soul on fire. His kiss was like nothing she'd ever encountered before, but she was determined not to let him in.

The telephone made her jump as she'd been absorbed in thought. It was a few seconds before she recovered and picked up the receiver.

"Katie."

"Hello Nabil."

"How are you feeling?"

"Tired, but good. Thank you for a wonderful evening."

"You don't need to thank me, but you can make me a happy man by agreeing to do it again."

"I'd love to."

"I will telephone you tomorrow to arrange something. Today I have work that won't wait but I wanted to hear your voice again."

"Nabil, you say the sweetest things," she yawned. "Sorry, I'm not used to dining out two nights running."

"You will soon get used to it. I'm going to take you to every restaurant in the Emirates where you can have anything your heart desires. My only wish is to spoil you and put the sparkle back in your eyes."

"Umm … unaccustomed as I am to being spoilt, I will say yes to all of that."

"I don't believe you. I'm sure there are many men who would want to spoil a beautiful woman like you."

Katie laughed. She really didn't realise just how attractive she was.

"I'll speak to you tomorrow, goodnight angel."

She couldn't focus on anything for the rest of the day as she lazed around listening to her music, wandering between the sitting room and the kitchen where she kept a pot of coffee on the go all day. Once or twice, she thought of going down to the pool but changed her mind. Several times she picked up the paper back she had been absorbed in for the last week, but she couldn't concentrate on it now. Giving up, she threw it on the coffee table and dozed off, but when she woke up, she thought of Nabil. He had called her angel. No man had ever called her that before. She admired the red roses round the room smiling to herself. Was she acting like a lovesick teenager? It was so unlike her to fall madly in love so quickly.

"What is wrong with me?" she said aloud. "I value my independence and I want to travel before I settle down … but … he is a lovely man."

Thank God it was the weekend because Katie would have to snap out of it when she went back to work on Sunday. A nice cool shower is just what I need, she thought as she looked at her watch and realised it was nine o'clock already. It was certainly becoming more humid now the winter was over, and she was not looking forward to the summer when temperatures would soar. No wonder most people go to Europe in July and August. Ellen was always inviting her to stay, and she certainly didn't have to worry about the expense. It would be a pleasant surprise for her aunt who had lived on her own since her divorce two years ago. She owed Ellen a phone call, but she decided she wasn't going to mention Nabil to her just yet.

The telephone rang as she was stepping into the shower, and she wondered if it was Nabil again; she quickly put a towel round herself and rushed to answer it.

"Hello."

"Hi Katie, it's Bev. I'm just checking you're okay as we haven't seen you."

"I'm fine. I've had a relaxing day doing absolutely nothing."

"I'm sorry about this morning. I hope you didn't think I was having a go at you."

"You don't have to apologize Bev. Did you have a good day with Greg?"

"Yep, brilliant. We didn't do much, just lounged around the pool and had a laugh with the rest of the gang. By the way a few of us are going to the beach tomorrow. Greg, Reece, June, and Don are going to do some wind surfing. I might even have a go myself. Do you want to come with us?"

She didn't want to seem unsociable. "Yes, all right. I was just about to take a shower, so I'll see you tomorrow

"Yes, I'm having an early night too. I'm going to curl up with a good book. See you in the morning."

Chapter Seven

The next six weeks of Katie's life seemed surreal and at times she felt she was living in two different worlds. Nabil surrounded her with luxury and thoroughly spoilt her, while at work she found it hard to concentrate. Staring into people's mouths and treating her patients' periodontal disease did not seem quite the same these days. But for the most part, she enjoyed her job. She always felt the satisfaction of having qualified and done something with her life and it made her feel independent.

Receiving bouquets of flowers from him was a common occurrence but three weeks ago he had given her a beautiful pearl necklace with pearl earrings to match. Sitting in the car on the edge of the desert, with only the glare of the headlights piercing through the pitch darkness, was an unusual but romantic setting. It was the first time she had ever seen him drive his own car and it was good to be on their own for a change.

"Oh Nabil, they're beautiful ... I don't know what to say?"

"You don't have to say anything, just a kiss will do."

It was a long, lingering kiss which left them both feeling dissatisfied.

"Katie, I want you so much," he whispered in her ear.

"I want you too."

"Do you think you could have a week off soon?"

"I don't see why not. I haven't had any time off since I started my job last November. Why?"

"Would you come away with me angel?"

"I'd love to. When?"

"As soon as you can get away," he said putting his arms around her and holding her tight.

The silence was wonderful but eerie as she rested her head against his shoulders; she wanted to stay there wrapped in his arms away from everyone. It sent shivers down her spine when she felt his lips gently brushing against the top of her head then his lips found hers and they both felt an uncontrolled passion. Suddenly she pulled away from him and screamed. He turned round to see a camel peering in through the side window.

"It's only a camel!"

"But it gave me such a fright."

Nabil thought it was funny and couldn't stop laughing until he saw another one approaching the car.

"I think we'd better leave. They're not always friendly creatures," he remarked as he started the ignition.

"Now you tell me." Katie looked anxious.

"It will be fine. If I drive slowly, they'll wander off," he said, trying not to laugh again.

"I'm glad you find it so funny, darling."

"I'm sorry, but you should have seen your face," he said as he slowly turned the car round. "Anyway, it was just as well we didn't stay any longer. I didn't want our first time together to be in the back of a Mercedes."

"Well at least it would have been in style," Katie chuckled. She was feeling more relaxed now the camels were out of sight.

"But not as much style as you deserve, angel."

Smiling to herself as she reminisced, she put the last of her things into her holdall, which had not been out since the day she had arrived in Dubai.

Only three weeks had passed since Nabil had asked her to go away with him. Mr Baker had not minded her taking some leave, as she only had a couple of patients booked and Bev had postponed their appointments.

There was a gentle knock at the door.

"You're fifteen minutes early," she remarked as she pulled it open.

"I am impatient to have you all to myself," he replied, as he gently pushed her into the bedroom took her into his arms then kissed her full on the lips.

"I'm all packed and ready," she said, as he relaxed his arms."

"Let's go then."

Katie went to pick up her holdall.

"You don't need to do that Abdullah is waiting in the hallway." She shrugged her shoulders and picked up her handbag. It was going to take her a long time to get used to being waited on.

They were sitting in the back of the car while Abdullah put her luggage in the boot.

"You haven't told me where we're going yet."

"Fujairah," he answered taking her hand in his. "It will only take about three hours through the Haggar mountains, then we will have a whole week together just the two of us."

"I can't think of anything better."

They arrived late in the afternoon and the scenery was magnificent as she gazed at the marble mountains rising up from the desert. It was breath-taking, especially with the sun glistening on the crystal waters of the Gulf of Oman. They entered the grounds of the Hilton International which was encompassed by beautifully designed gardens and such a contrast to the mountain scenery outside.

Katie adored their enormous suite, and they soon settled in. Luggage had been brought up, clothes put away and dinner ordered. They were going to eat on the

79

terrace overlooking the ocean, away from prying eyes. Nabil was bound to see someone he knew in the hotel and this they wanted to avoid as much as possible. His family were already asking questions after hearing about Katie, and they were naturally concerned. Mohammed approached him about his close relationship with an English girl and they argued when he insisted Nabil end it.

Mohammed expected his nephew to have been married a long time ago and to one of his own. Nabil, who had been educated in England like a lot of young Emiratis, had different ideals. Naturally, he was proud to be a Muslim and still agreed with most of the customs but not entirely. After refusing to give her up his uncle stormed out of the house red in the face and furious that his brother's son had ignored his demands.

Nabil had been expecting trouble and that was why he wanted a week away with Katie before he took her to meet his family. He had decided to face them and take her to meet his mamma and sisters and hopefully his uncle, although there didn't seem to be much chance of that. Preparing Katie for such an encounter was only fair.

Alone at last, there was a superbly prepared meal laid out before them which was much appreciated but they ate very little. Darkness had fallen suddenly as it always does in the Middle East and they both stood with their arms around each other looking at the vast ocean that lay in front of them. Nabil turned the lights off so Katie could see the star encrusted sky of an Arabian night; she was captivated.

A few minutes later he lifted her into his arms carried her into the bedroom and lay her gently on the bed. This was the moment they had been waiting for. Weeks of trying to avoid what was about to happen welled up inside them. Soon he lay down beside her and she could feel his breath close to her face. His hand moved slowly up her trembling thighs as he kissed her gently on the neck and breast. Katie shuddered with sheer joy. Their lips met urgently and putting her arms around his neck she ran her fingers through his thick, dark hair. Nabil moved his lips gently over her entire body and she thought she would explode as every nerve end tingled with his touch. The contours of their bodies blended as if they were one as they pressed themselves together in anticipation. She moaned softly as he entered her, and they clung together as if wanting to savour this precious moment. Their lovemaking came to a crescendo as they moved in perfect harmony; like figure skaters gliding in unison upon the surface of the ice.

It had been a night of passion and the fire that had raged inside her had at last been quenched. She looked down at him lovingly as he slept, his bronzed skin standing out against the white silk sheets. Smoothing back a lock of his hair made him stir and he reached out for her as he felt the touch of her hand; she snuggled into him and laid her head on his chest. They slept soundly unaware of the flood of morning sunlight coming in through the window.

Being happy and relaxed in each other's company meant they spent most of the week in their suite and on the terrace, talking, laughing, eating, drinking wine, and making love.

Nabil had also taken Katie to see the scenery in Fujairah. She liked to know the history of the places she visited, and he enjoyed showing her. Before she left England, she had bought herself a new Polaroid camera, which were all the rage, and she tried it out on Ellen and Sue the night before she left. It took brilliant instant photographs and some of her shots were quite artistic,

81

especially the ones she had taken in Fujairah. She laid them out on the coffee table, and they poured over them.

"These are excellent, but did you have to take so many photos of me?"

"Yes, and the best ones are when you're not aware I'm taking them. I prefer the element of surprise because it stops people from posing."

"Are you saying I'm a poser?"

"Well, if the cap fits, as we say in London."

They both laughed and he pulled her back against the sofa where she snuggled into him. These quiet moments were precious and sometimes there was no need to speak but Nabil wanted to talk to her, and this was the perfect time.

Katie was just nodding off.

"Are you awake, angel? I need to talk to you."

She opened her eyes and looked up at him.

"You sound serious. Is something wrong?"

"No, but I've been thinking it would be good if you were to meet my family."

She sat upright but didn't say anything.

"People are talking despite the fact that we've tried to keep our relationship secret," he took her hands in his. "My family know, and I want them to meet you then we'll no longer have to keep it quiet."

"But do they know I'm English?"

"I'm sure they do now because my uncle is bound to have told them."

"By the sound of your voice I take it he did not approve."

"You could say that, but I told him in no uncertain terms that I won't give you up. He is not my father or my keeper!"

"What about the rest of your family?"

Nabil could see the worried look on Katie's face and he took her into his arms. He wanted to protect her from everything, but he knew in his heart he wouldn't be able to.

"I'm not saying it's going to be easy, but I love you and I know you love me. I can put up with whatever happens with you by my side. But ... if you think it's going to be too much to cope with ... then I will have to let you get on with your life without me."

"But I can't imagine my life without you," she said, appalled at the idea.

They sat silently for a few minutes each with their own thoughts. The background music had finished and there wasn't a sound. It was Nabil who broke the silence.

"I never seem to do what is expected of a young Emirati man and when my father was alive, he couldn't understand. He would get exasperated because I refused to marry the local girls who were paraded in front of me. Well, not literally but you know what I'm saying."

Katie kept quiet because she wanted to know more about the man she loved; the man who wanted to break with family tradition for her and risk their wrath.

"Many men here have foreign lovers or mistresses if they're married. These young women are kept in luxurious homes surrounded by servants. They have the best jewellery, the most expensive clothes, and anything they could wish for, but they don't have respect; they are used. I'm sure you've heard this goes on."

"Yes."

"Mohammed is one of these men and it sickens me the way he treats women. He has such a lovely wife who has no choice but to put up with his appalling behaviour. She must be a good Muslim wife and keep quiet."

"I remember you saying they don't have children."

"That's right. My aunt couldn't have children, though it isn't often spoken about. Mohammed blames her for not giving him a son and he can be extremely nasty towards her."

"I know he's your uncle, darling, but he doesn't sound like a particularly nice character."

"He isn't and I've often wondered how two brothers could be so different. My father was very traditional, but he treated mamma and my sisters with respect. When he got angry with me because I refused to marry, we always made up a few days later. I was fortunate because the night before he died, he told me how proud he was. He said I had proved myself more than worthy of running the family business with Mohammed."

"That's a lovely memory to have, darling."

"Yes, it is! We could have so easily fallen out over my unmarried status before he had his heart attack … it doesn't bear thinking about. You know it's not easy being educated in England, mixing with the Brits, and enjoying the same freedoms they have whilst living there; then coming back to the Emirates steeped in tradition and old-fashioned ideals. On your return you are expected to 'toe the line' as you say in England."

"But you must have had relationships. I can't imagine a hot bloodied man like you being celibate for long."

Nabil laughed. "Of course, I've had women in my life, angel, but until now there hasn't been anyone special."

The following day he took her back to Fujairah. It was these moments when they were completely on their own that Katie loved the most and the wadis fascinated her. They were dried-up riverbeds that had been gouged out of the mountains by the flash floods. There were trees and plants growing in them and in one she had seen a family obviously making a home for themselves with a goat grazing nearby. They didn't seem bothered by Katie and Nabil looking down on them.

They visited the old fort and he surprised her when he opened a small box which held a diamond ring; it had the largest cluster of diamonds she had ever seen. It was their last day and he wanted it to be a truly special occasion. The old fort had an atmosphere which neither of them could fail to notice. There was a magic in the air that carried them back in time as they embraced amongst the ancient walls. The whole week seemed like a dream to Katie who was swept along by the sheer luxury which Nabil showered upon her. Taking the ring from its box he placed it on the third finger of her left hand. Her hand was shaking, and she looked questioningly at him.

"Angel, will you marry me?"

She was stunned into silence, although she was sure it would come to this, she was not expecting it to be so soon.

"Will you marry me?" he repeated, taking her hands in his.

She felt somebody close, and she turned her head but of course there was nobody there though she could smell her mum's perfume.

"Katie what's wrong?"

"Sorry, I thought I heard someone behind me."

"Don't you want to marry me?"

Nabil took her into his arms. He had seen the sadness come back into her eyes and he knew she was thinking about her parents.

"I want to kiss the sadness away. I want to help you forget the past. If you marry me, you will never have another worry for the rest of your life."

"Oh Nabil, I can never forget the past, but you've already helped me move on. I love you so much but …"

"No buts, just yes or no."

She had found a man with whom she felt secure, happy, and alive but she was also aware of the danger of two cultures colliding. He held her so tight she thought he was going to squeeze the breath out of her body. How could she resist him? Living without him in her life was not something she wanted to consider.

"Yes," she whispered in his ear.

Relieved she had spoken the word he was longing to hear he relaxed and letting go of her he raised his arms in supplication. "Thank you, Allah!" His words reverberating around the old fort. "You will never regret it," he cried, now holding her at arms-length so he could look at her beautiful smiling face.

Katie noticed his eyes were sparkling even more than usual and she knew she had made the right decision. He kissed her passionately then slowly pushed her thin dress straps aside; she sighed as he continued to run his lips lightly along her bare shoulder.

They arrived back at the hotel quite late which caused Abdullah some anxiety. He smiled with relief when he saw the two of them walking through the foyer. Having been employed by Nabil's father forty years ago meant they were on first name terms, and he was now considered an old family friend. Abdullah was the proud father of four grown up daughters, who were all married, but this young man was like the son he never had. He admired him for sticking to his values.

Nabil went over to him.

"Do not worry so, Abdullah. You won't have to send out a search party after all."

He smiled because he was happy to see them. "Would you like some dinner sent up?"

"No, we've decided a few snacks will do, but you can have a bottle of champagne sent up as we have something to celebrate," he remarked, looking at Katie who was smiling broadly. The gleam in her eyes which had been missing for so long was now back and he thought she looked radiant. "Oh, and could you have the car ready for eight o'clock in the morning please," he called after him as they walked to the lift.

"Yes of course, Nabil!"

Abdullah had not failed to notice the enormous cluster of diamonds on Katie's finger. He was a little afraid for them, wondering what his uncle was going to say about it. His dislike for Mohammed was intense, especially after he had questioned him about Katie. Driving Nabil to many a secret rendezvous was not something he was about to share with this spiteful man; if he wanted information, he wasn't going to have to get it elsewhere. But things were not so secret anymore and he sensed there was trouble ahead.

Chapter Eight

Once more, they were being driven through the Haggar Mountains on their way back to Dubai. Katie wondered what her friends at the complex would have to say; she was hoping to sneak in the back way, so as not to be seen. Nabil had asked her to meet his family soon and of course she had said yes, but now they were on their way home she was not so sure.

Nabil took her hand and squeezed it gently, feeling a rush of warmth and affection as he always did when she was close. Sensing what she was thinking, he wanted to take her in his arms and reassure her. He was wondering if he was doing the right thing, expecting her to meet with his mamma, sisters, brother-in-law and of course Latifa, his papa's mamma.

Marriage had not been uppermost in his mind until they met. From the moment he first saw her at the airport he had thought of nobody else, often wondering where she was and what she was doing. No other woman had ever affected him this way before.

It was Abdullah who broke the silence by announcing they were nearly home.

"Do you want me to come up with you?"

"No, you'd better not. It's going to take me a couple of days to settle down as it is and if you come up, I won't want you to leave. I'm going to miss you, my darling. When I should be giving all my attention to Mrs Pollard's bleeding gums, I will probably be thinking about you."

"Angel, I'm not sure I like being thought about when you're sorting out someone's bleeding gums."

Katie chuckled.

"You know you can move into the villa at Chicago Beach then you wouldn't have to worry about another thing, least of all Mrs Pollard's bleeding gums."

"I know but I don't want to live there without you, and I certainly don't want to be thought of as a kept woman. I'd rather stay here until we're married."

"As you wish."

"Don't be upset, Nabil," she said as they drew up outside the complex.

"I'm not upset. My only wish is to make you happy."

"I am happy. Happier than I have been in a very long time," and she kissed him lovingly then leapt out of the car as Abdullah was taking her holdall out of the boot. Nabil watched her as she disappeared up the back stairway to her apartment.

"Katie!" cried Bev, who was about to enter her front door, when she spied her friend out of the corner of her eye; followed by Abdullah at the end of the landing.

"Hello Bev, how's things?" They hugged but Bev let go and gave a little cough as she looked passed her friend. Katie had forgotten about the chauffeur. It was going to take her a while to get used to being followed.

"Sorry Abdullah, I'll let you in." She opened the door to her apartment, and he put her holdall in the hallway.

"Is there anything else I can do, Miss Morgan?"

"Yes, you can stop calling me Miss Morgan, Katie will do, and no, there's nothing else thank you very much."

He smiled at her while bowing slightly. He liked her a lot, but she had much to learn, and it wasn't going to be easy, he thought, as he walked back out onto the landing. Bev followed her in and was her usual bubbly self. "Is there anything else I can do Miss Morgan?" she

89

mimicked, and they both laughed at her terrible Arabic accent.

"Oh, we are going up in the world aren't we," Bev said not unkindly. "From an ordinary girl in West Wickham to the girlfriend of a wealthy Emirati in the Middle East. Wow!" Bev stopped in her tracks as she noticed the enormous diamond cluster on Katie's left hand. "Oh my God it's absolutely gorgeous!" she stared in amazement. "I don't know what to say."

"Congratulations, maybe?" suggested Katie amused by the expression on her face. "I know it's not the custom here to wear engagement rings, but I can wear it as costume jewellery when we go out.

"That's some costume jewellery."

Katie laughed.

"It's absolutely stunning … but … I thought you would have taken more time to think about it … after all ..."

"After all, what?" Katie interrupted. She had been expecting some opposition from Bev.

"Well, you haven't known him that long. Couldn't you have gone out with him for a few more months before having to decide?"

"I know what I'm doing." She was suddenly feeling weary and a little disappointed.

Bev noticed the change in the atmosphere and not wanting to spoil Katie's happiness, she said quickly, "I am happy for you."

"Really?"

"Yes, if that's what you want then I'm all for it, just don't forget to invite me to the wedding."

"Of course, you're invited, but you probably won't have to wear a hat." They laughed.

Bev got up. "You do look tired. I'll make us some coffee. Too many sleepless nights no doubt." She chuckled when she saw the mischievous expression on her friend's face and her eyes said it all.

Katie leant her head back against the sofa and she could see his smiling eyes in front of her once more which reminded her of something her mother used to say ... 'Eyes are the windows to the soul.' Her mum had always come out with things like that, and her dad had said to Katie many times ... 'You should listen to your mother ... she knows best.' A sixth sense, he called it, because she always said the right thing at the right time. In the business if she felt something was wrong, or if she had a hunch, her dad would go along with it knowing there was no point in arguing; her hunches were invariably accurate. It's a pity, Katie thought, she had not had any hunches about going to Cornwall on that fatal Friday afternoon or they might still be alive today. Tears trickled down her cheeks and there was a lump in her throat when Bev walked in with the coffee.

"Now what's all this about then? I thought you were supposed to be happy." Bev put the tray on the coffee table as Katie reached for a tissue.

"I was thinking of mum and dad. I wish they were here I miss them so much ... sometimes I feel them around, especially mum."

Bev kept quiet.

"I haven't told anybody apart from Ellen, but I feel her presence in the room. I turn round and expect to see her and when she's not there, I'm disappointed; then the feeling of calm comes over me like a warm blanket enveloping my whole being."

"Umm," Bev looked a bit perplexed.

"I knew it would sound odd, that's why I've never told you before, but I know she is here in the apartment with me."

"Doesn't it worry you?"

91

"Of course not, why should it? My mum wouldn't do anything to harm me."

"I guess not."

"I hear mum's voice in my head as though she is trying to talk to me."

"Oh, it gives me the creeps. Drink your coffee then you can tell me all about the trip. How did Nabil propose to you?" She asked, changing the subject.

Katie was transported back to Fujairah soaking up the atmosphere once more in the ruins of the old fort.

"Well?"

"Sorry, I was miles away."

"I could see that."

Katie smiled and Bev was glad to see her looking happy. All that talk about her mum being in the apartment had unnerved her.

"It was wonderful. I don't think I've ever really enjoyed sex until now and there's such a difference between making love and pure lust. Now I know what it means to be in paradise."

"Sounds like you two hit it off. Was it really that good?"

"Yes, it was. Nabil is such a gentleman. He is caring and gentle and he made me feel like I was the most important person in the world. It was as though we became one."

"Wow, most English guys just want to get your knickers off and finish as quick as they can before the football comes on the television."

"Oh, Bev you're incorrigible."

They both sat there giggling when the telephone started to ring. Before Katie could answer it, Bev got up to go.

"I'll see you later," she mouthed as Katie picked up the receiver.

"Hello angel. I love you."

"I love you too."

"I wanted see how you are after our week away."

"You're so thoughtful. You're not like any other man I've ever known. Not that I've know that many of course."

"And from now on I don't want you to think of any other man. I am going to give you everything your heart desires."

"But I only want you."

"You have me, Katie." He failed to mention the fact that she would also have to live with his mamma and sister; he naturally thought she would expect this.

"I'm going to miss you so much while you're away, my darling."

"I'll miss you too, but I will only be gone for five days, and it is an important business trip."

"I know, and quite honestly, I must try and concentrate on my job. So much has happened so quickly. I mustn't forget I have patients to attend to."

"You won't have to worry about them for much longer. Anyway, I must go. See you soon angel."

"Have a good trip, bye darling."

Katie went out into the hall to retrieve her holdall and unpack but she felt a little uneasy as she sorted through her things. 'You will not have to worry about that for much longer,' he had said, meaning her job. She hadn't thought about giving up work just yet, but it sounded as though Nabil had already decided. I'd better talk to him when he comes back from his business trip, she thought. Living such an affluent life means he's obviously used to having his own way. He probably doesn't notice it but when he lifts his hand people come running, especially in restaurants.

Feeling a presence close by as she always did when she was concerned about something was comforting. She smiled to herself as she put her holdall away. Poor Bev had looked so worried when she was telling her about her mum being in the room. Maybe she shouldn't have spoken about it, but it was too late now. Sensing and sometimes seeing spirit people around had been quite normal to her when she was a young girl. Her gran had died when she was twelve years old. How she missed her. She remembered how she used to thrust her smiling face into hers. Bouncing her on her knee when she was small, singing funny songs and reading to her were fond memories. Katie found it hard to accept she'd gone away so quickly. Every night she cried herself to sleep, but one night she sensed someone leaning over her. Opening her eyes and expecting to see her mum or dad she was most surprised and happy to see her gran, who then kissed her on the cheek and gently wiped her tears away as she drifted off to sleep. Katie was so excited in the morning when she remembered what had happened and she rushed downstairs to tell her parents. They were in the kitchen, and she can still remember their faces as they stared at her. Her dad thought she could have imagined it, but her mum had given her a hug and told her that her gran was surely watching over her.

Katie slipped into bed. She really needed a siesta, but she couldn't sleep. She put the radio on, but she couldn't concentrate on that either. All she could do was think of Nabil. The last week with him had been wonderful and she kept re-living every precious moment. Most of the time they had eaten on their terrace, but one day Nabil had surprised her by taking her on a safari in the desert; the picnic which followed was delicious. Arabic food was nothing like anything she'd eaten before. She enjoyed most of it especially the lamb, rice and raisins with its aromatic spices followed by fresh dates and Arabic coffee. But it was the night sky and sitting under the stars which was most memorable. You read about Arabian nights, but you cannot appreciate them until you're in the desert with no light pollution. Trillions of stars above you, like a painted canvas, is quite unbelievable.

Remembering the feeling of his warm body next to hers gave her a secure feeling. He was strong, positive, and very much in charge of his life, but he was also kind, gentle and romantic. Everything she had ever wanted in a man, and she came alive when she was with him; she knew he felt the same way and she loved him with all her heart.

It was becoming increasingly difficult to focus on her job. Nobody had any cause for complaint, but she found herself daydreaming when she was supposed to be writing up patient's notes. The hot weather didn't help. You had to go from the airconditioned hospital to an airconditioned car then to an airconditioned home; walking was out of the question because of the humidity.

She wasn't sure if she would ever get used to the summer heat in Dubai, and sometimes she found the aircon too cold, but she did appreciate it. Nabil had been pressing her to give up her job and leave the country with him for a few weeks holiday before the temperatures rise even more. It was tempting, but she wished he weren't so persistent. Coming to Dubai had meant a whole new way of life and she wasn't sure about making more changes so soon. It worried her sometimes at the thought of marrying and giving up her independence and she wished she could have both.

Mohammed was against the ensuing marriage and while Nabil was away, he turned up at Katie's apartment, much to her surprise and annoyance. She felt she had to let him in but regretted it when he tried to persuade her not to marry his nephew. He told her he wanted him to settle down with his own kind. He had the audacity to offer her money to forget Nabil and leave Dubai for good. She was stunned by this verbal attack and offer of cash and deeply hurt that his uncle was so sure she would take the money and run.

Obviously, he thought all she was interested in was Nabil's riches. Little did he know she had her own money; it wasn't a vast fortune but enough for her to live a comfortable life. He had asked her not to mention their conversation to his nephew. He gave her a telephone number to contact him in two days with her answer despite having already told him the answer was no. She was relieved when he left abruptly. The hate she had seen in his eyes had shaken her and she was convinced there was no good in him whatsoever; this was hard for her to admit.

Obviously, the reason Mohammed had chosen to call when he did was because his nephew was away. Nabil would often have to make new contacts abroad as they were importers of everything you could imagine; whatever the customer wanted they tried their utmost to obtain.

Katie would not have been able to hide her feelings from him had he seen her after Mohammed's visit. Bev was out with Greg too, so she was completely on her own. Feeling shaken, she sat on the balcony staring in disbelief for about twenty minutes, then she began to stir herself. True, she was frightened and hurt but now she was feeling anger towards that despicable man. She decided she would tell Nabil when he returned from his trip, but then changed her mind. The last thing she wanted was trouble and there surely would be if she told him what his uncle had said to her. She wondered if it would be better all round if she did return to England …

but ... how could she leave him? Never had she felt this way about any other man in her life and she loved him dearly. How dare his uncle intimidate her!

I will go to England with him she thought. A holiday will do us both good, but she was not prepared to give up her job just yet. Nabil wanted to take her away for two months, but he would have to be satisfied with four weeks. She could use her annual leave which was already booked. Not wanting him to sense there was anything wrong, she decided she would distract him by talking about their ensuing holiday in England as soon as he arrived home.

Katie knew she would have to phone Mohammed and give him an answer which she had already tried to do. One thing was certain, she couldn't give up her man and she didn't want to leave her friends either; they had helped her through such a tough time when she had first arrived in the Middle East.

Mohammed must have given her a direct line because he answered the telephone straightaway. Her heart began to thump. Finding it difficult to speak because her mouth was dry, she nearly put the phone down but instead she took a sip of water and stayed on the line. "It's Katie Morgan."

"Ahh, Miss Morgan, I was wondering when you would call. Have you decided to accept my generous offer?" He asked in a smug voice. She hesitated and Mohammed smiled to himself at the other end of the phone; he was confident she would take the money and leave the Emirates.

Chanel No. 5 wafted under Katie's nose. She knew her mum was close, and she found the strength to stand up to him. "I've already told you, I'm not interested, so the answer is no!"

"Miss Morgan, I think ...

Katie put the receiver down. She couldn't speak to that man any longer. Her heart was racing, and she was terrified he would turn up again. Reaching for the fridge door she grabbed a bottle of chilled white wine. Why was life so difficult? You could almost guarantee when things were going well, something would happen, and life would come crashing down around you. Maybe coming to Dubai was a mistake; perhaps she should have stayed in England ... so many thoughts made her head spin.

Working in Guy's Hospital had been secure, and she was happy there with no intention of leaving until ... Katie choked back the tears ... so much sadness. She was feeling thoroughly miserable while pondering on what she had done to deserve such disaster.

Pouring herself another glass she thought about her wonderful childhood; she'd been lucky to have such lovely parents. They'd had a good lifestyle but above all she'd had love and affection which she missed so much; how she longed to sit and talk to her mum and dad once again.

It wasn't like Katie to be so negative, but the last year had been a tragic one. However, she had the wedding to look forward to and she smiled to herself. Mohammed would probably give up now she had stood her ground. 'You have to stand up to a bully,' she remembered her father saying as she poured herself, yet another glass of wine. Stretching out on the sofa she decided she might as well drink the whole bottle.

Her head was swimming, and she began to feel peculiar as she tried to stand up; she fell back onto the sofa. "Oh, if Nabil could see me now," she said aloud. Suddenly she started to panic. What if Mohammed came round to her apartment again? She should have kept a clear head ... and she felt ill. Standing up again she steadied herself and walked slowly into the kitchen to pour herself a pint glass of water, but she turned the drinking tap on full and it sprayed all over her face, arms, and chest. "That's all I need," she cried while grabbing a clean tea towel to wipe herself down. She managed to drink most of the cool clear liquid, then made her way slowly back to the sofa. A few minutes later she had fallen into a deep sleep.

Waking early in the morning she was surprised to find herself in the living room and she felt terrible. There was a pain in her neck where she had slept awkwardly, and she had a terrible headache. Jumping up suddenly made her feel sick but she desperately needed the bathroom. Splashing cold water on her face made her feel a little better. Was she late for work? she thought, but then realised it was the weekend. On the coffee table was the empty wine bottle and her empty glass was lying on its side on the floor. She remembered the telephone call to Mohammed and was thankful Nabil was coming home today.

Looking at her watch, she was relieved to see she had plenty of time to have a shower and sort herself out. Making her way slowly to her bedside cabinet she knew the first thing she had to do was take some pain killers, drink plenty of water and hope for the best.

Abdullah picked her up on his way to Dubai Airport. She was looking more like herself and by the time they were in the arrivals, she felt much better than she had earlier.

Katie was searching the many faces for Nabil, trying to push all thoughts of Mohammed to the back of her mind. When she saw him all she wanted to do was run towards him, jump up, wrap her legs around his waist, put her arms round his neck and kiss him passionately on the lips, but she knew she could not; it wasn't acceptable behaviour in the Emirates. She smiled to herself wondering what the police would say and decided she would surely be arrested on the spot.

In the back of the car, it was a different matter though. She kissed him then held his hand tight.

"Is anything wrong, angel?"

"No, nothing," she answered quickly. "I've missed you darling, that's all!"

"Well, I hope you miss me this much every time I go away." Nabil was not keen to go back to her apartment in case it caused unnecessary gossip for her, but she had been insistent. He thought she seemed different, but he couldn't explain his uneasiness.

They discussed the wedding and decided November was a good month as it would be much cooler for Katie. But for now, all he wanted to do was get away from Dubai; he was pleased when she agreed to a trip to England. Four weeks was not what he had intended, but she wasn't prepared to give up her job yet. His uncle was still causing waves about the wedding so he would take Katie away from any unpleasantness; little did he know it was too late for that. Nabil's brother-in-law, Rashid, was taking on more responsibility in the business and Nabil and Mohammed had a good team around them.

Sleeping for most of the afternoon after making love wasn't surprising as they'd both had late nights and unbeknown to Nabil, Katie was still suffering from a hangover. Waking up and looking down at her while she lay still with her arms across his chest, he admired her beautiful face and her glorious raven-coloured hair draped over him as she slept peacefully. He didn't want to disturb her. At the airport he thought she looked tired and there was a trace of anxiety on her face which soon changed to a delightfully captivating smile when she saw him; he dozed off feeling contented.

Chapter Nine

England was a welcome reprieve from the hot weather and the constant need for air conditioning in Dubai. It was raining when they arrived at Gatwick Airport and the weather forecast was not very promising for the next few days, but typically English. A chauffeur driven limousine picked them up and drove them to London's Mayfair district, to Grosvenor Square to be precise. Nabil hadn't told Katie much about his luxury three-bedroom apartment because he wanted to surprise her.

Lavish was the word she used when he showed her round, and she absolutely loved the beautiful open plan living and dining room with a prayer room leading off from it. Huge windows looked out onto a large terrace overlooking the square and the kitchen was divine. At the back, the two spare ensuite double bedrooms were spacious and stylish. There was a garden view from the main bedroom, with an ensuite bathroom at one end and a dressing room at the other. Katie remarked on how superbly decorated the apartment was. Nabil told her that between himself and the interior designer, they had chosen a mixture of Arabic and English artifacts and décor.

It amused him when she was impressed by something, and it made him even more determined to make her happy. He wanted to help her forget the tragedy in her life and protect her as much as he could. Although, he knew she wasn't looking forward to giving up her career he hoped when they were married, she would settle down.

Spending time on their own for the first three days enabled them to unwind. Making love, sleeping until mid-morning, and having breakfast together was sheer joy. Going for walks was something Nabil was normally averse to because he was used to being driven everywhere. Katie, however, wanted to walk so she could admire this beautiful part of London and after a while, he found himself enjoying it too. On their first early evening stroll they walked past Claridge's Hotel and Katie stopped as she looked at the famous entrance with a wistful look on her face.

"It is beautiful, isn't it?"

"Yes, it is," replied Katie as memories came flooding back and she found it difficult to choke back the tears.

"Are you okay, angel?"

"Yes darling … I'm all right," she said as she wiped her eyes. "We came here for afternoon tea, and it was absolutely lovely."

"You mean with your mamma and papa?"

"Yes, and Ellen and her husband Pete. It was mum and dad's twenty-fifth wedding anniversary. It was something my mum had wanted to do for a long time, so I booked it as one of their presents."

"I'm sorry it makes you sad. I should have told you where my apartment was then you would have known Claridge's was nearby."

"It's okay you weren't to know but … can we book afternoon tea one day while we're here?"

"Of course, but won't it be upsetting for you?"

"It won't be easy, but it will be good to remember that wonderful afternoon. Besides with Claridge's on your doorstep who can resist afternoon tea."

He was relieved to see her smiling.

"It's certainly a contrast to the Burj Al Arab but I'm sure afternoon tea is just as good here," he said as they walked on.

"Well, that goes without saying, after all, we British did invent the custom," she said playfully, and Nabil laughed.

By the time they got back to Grosvenor Square the sun was out and it was a lovely warm evening. Gary the concierge was a friendly chap and had worked there for many years. He knew Nabil well as his father had owned an apartment in the same building.

Katie showered and changed into her favourite orange kaftan which she had bought in an Indian shop in Dubai. Nabil changed out of his dark suit, his usual apparel when he was abroad, into a white dish dash. Katie was used to seeing him in traditional clothes, and she loved the pure whiteness of it; she thought he was handsome whatever he wore.

Before they changed, he had ordered a light supper from the local deli because they had eaten a late lunch and weren't too hungry. It was delivered and even laid out for them on the terrace. Katie was amazed at the service, but it was standard for Nabil. She had offered to cook when they first arrived because the kitchen was exquisite, but he insisted it was her holiday and there was no need for her to do anything; even their breakfast came from the local deli, though she did say she would cook a full English breakfast before they returned to Dubai.

The maid service was excellent too. Nabil always expected the best and that's what he got. He became impatient when things weren't done properly, and this sometimes annoyed her. She made sure she spoke to the maids and servants with the utmost respect. Being waited on was his way of life and she decided to relax and enjoy the experience.

Their first week flew by. They'd been to art galleries, wonderful restaurants, and they even went to see La Boheme at The Royal Opera House in Convent Garden. La Boheme was one of Katie's favourite operas and she was thrilled when Nabil told her he had booked tickets. Sitting in a box all to themselves made her feel like royalty and it was something she could get used to.

Covent Garden and the surrounding area had looked sad in the seventies after the original flower market had moved to Nine Elms; now twelve years later it was thriving once again. It was a colourful part of London and somewhere Katie had met friends for lunch before her move to the Emirates.

Her aunt came to London and wasn't at all surprised when she was picked up at Victoria station by a chauffeur driven limousine. She decided to sit back and enjoy the short ride to Grosvenor Square. At least Katie had told her where Nabil's apartment was situated and she couldn't wait to see her lovely niece, spend time with her and get to know the man she was to marry.

Ellen had already told Katie she was only visiting for the day, as she didn't want to intrude on their holiday, but said she would visit again before they flew home. Their engagement had happened so quick, and she felt it was important for the two of them to have as much time as possible on their own, away from work and his family. By what Katie had told her on the telephone they were experiencing growing pressure, especially from Nabil's uncle.

She understood why a Muslim family in the Middle East would voice objections over an ensuing marriage to an English girl; it was a clash of two cultures. But if they loved each other enough it could work. A mixed marriage often brought feelings to the surface, and they weren't always good ones. You would think in 1986 that things would have changed for the better. As for Mohammed, she had the distinct feeling her niece was holding something back when it came to his opposition; she hoped she was wrong, and that they would be able to surmount any difficulties his animosity caused.

Katie and Nabil couldn't lie in bed this morning, but it was a chilly day and the pair of them just wanted to curl up together. When hearing the alarm, she stirred herself. Looking forward to seeing Ellen and introducing her to her favourite man was uppermost in her mind. She pulled the duvet off the bed, forcing Nabil to get up too. After getting ready as quick as she could she went to put the coffee on and placed croissants on the breakfast bar. Ellen was arriving around 9.30, and the plan was to eat a light breakfast then go shopping and have some quality time together.

Nabil had chosen a dark blue Armani suit. Business meetings and lunch with his associates had been arranged so that Katie could have time with Ellen. Thinking about her aunt she didn't hear him coming into the kitchen; he hugged her from behind and planted a kiss on her neck.

"I wish we could go back to bed angel," and he ran his tongue along her bare shoulders.

"Oh my God," she moaned, "please stop darling. You know how much I love you kissing my neck and shoulders." She turned round to face him and gently pushed him away. "Ellen should be here any minute and you have business to attend to."

"I'd rather attend to you."

They were both laughing when the intercom buzzed.

Gary the concierge had been expecting Mr Khalifa's guest and had given her a warm welcome while the chauffeur took hold of her bag. Protesting at first, but then realising he was only doing his job, she let him carry it for her. It held some books that Katie had asked for, so it was quite heavy. She smiled to herself when she stepped into the lift with deep blue carpeting on the floor and the walls.

Ellen was so pleased to be introduced to Nabil and she could see why her niece was so smitten with him. They ate breakfast together, then he had to leave for his meetings. He asked Katie if she minded using black cabs for their shopping spree and she assured him they would be fine. Walking to Oxford Street wasn't a problem anyway as it wasn't far from Grosvenor Square.

Shopping together was great fun especially the one and a half hours they spent in Selfridges. They then walked up and down Oxford Street popping in and out of shops and ending up at the arcade at Marble Arch.

"Shall we stop somewhere for lunch soon darling? There's nothing like a bit of retail therapy but we must eat before I pass out from lack of sustenance."

"Yes, good idea Ellen. We could go to your favourite, Liberty's, have lunch, then continue shopping in store."

"Sounds like a good plan to me but I don't think I can walk any longer, my feet are aching like mad. It's okay for you youngsters."

"We'll get a cab, as I've done enough walking too."

Katie held out her left hand, but the first two taxis were occupied. However, it wasn't long before an empty one stopped at the kerbside. They piled in with their bags and were glad to rest their feet though the short journey didn't take long even in the busy Saturday afternoon traffic.

Having paid the driver, they stepped out onto the pavement looking up at the enormous and ornate shop front.

"Liberty's is such an elegant building."

"It is darling. Your mum loved it."

"I remember when I was young, and you were both going on one of your 'shopping expeditions,' as dad called them. We stood at the front door waving you off. When you were out of sight, he would turn to me and say, 'Right Katie what mischief can we get up to today then?'

Ellen didn't get the chance to reply because a disgruntled shopper pushed passed, nearly knocking them over.

"We'd better get off the pavement before we get mowed down," and they laughed while hurrying into the store.

Making their way to the second-floor café wasn't easy because everyone had the same idea. They had to wait for two seats to become available but fortunately the lunchtime rush was soon over; it wasn't that long before they were sitting down.

"I'm famished, but we'd better not eat too much if we're having dinner in the Hilton tonight. I don't want to spoil my appetite when Nabil has kindly booked a table."

"That's true and I'm really looking forward to it, especially as you'll be able to get to know him a bit better."

"I can see why you've fallen in love with him. He is charming and very handsome and so is your ring. I noticed it glinting in the sunshine when you were hailing a taxi. Maybe you should have left it at home as you were going to."

"Normally I only wear it when we go out for the evening, but yes, I'd better take it off now," Katie replied as she took out the little box from her handbag and replaced the ring safely."

"Is it strange not being able to wear your engagement ring all the time darling?"

"Not really, if I'm honest, it does rather draw attention to itself, and I have to get used to the different customs."

"Yes of course."

They studied the menu, and both decided on smoked salmon because it was light.

"I can't believe how good Nabil's English is. Excellent in fact! Mind you it's often the case with non-English speaking people who spend a good deal of time in England. They usually end up with a better command of the English language than the natives."

"Well, you should know, Ellen, you're the English teacher."

"Have you learned any Arabic yet, darling? Or should I say Emirati?"

"It's not an easy language to learn and Nabil is not a good teacher."

"That's a no then!" They were both laughing when the waiter came to take their order.

Ellen wanted to hear as much about Nabil as possible and what they had been doing in London for the last week. Katie was only too willing to talk about him and their holiday. Secretly her aunt was concerned for her, but the last thing she wanted to do was cause upset by being negative, after all she was not her mother.

"I know you're worried about our engagement," Katie said after they'd finished eating, "but we really love each other."

"Darling, I would be lying if I said I wasn't concerned but it's only because I care about you. It's not going to be easy, not with the culture difference."

"I know and it does frighten me sometimes, but I can't give him up not for anyone."

"I can see that." Ellen patted her hand. "I just want you to be happy. Now come on let's continue shopping."

"I know exactly what you want to look at."

108

"Liberty Prints!" They said in unison as they picked up their bags.

Later that evening the three of them had finished dinner and were enjoying coffee and liqueurs. Ellen thought the opulence of the Hilton was something else and she thanked Nabil for a wonderful evening. Normally, she was not easily impressed, but she had to admit the food was exquisite and the service outstanding; she could tell he was used to and indeed expected such service which caused him to be demanding at times.

Trying to find the opportunity to have a quiet word with Nabil to voice her concerns hadn't been easy. Oh, how she wished her sister were still alive. Shirley was wise and would always choose the right words. Mind you, she thought, these two young people were so much in love that she doubted whether they would listen to anybody.

Nabil was a confident man. A little too confident perhaps, but she thought that was a lot to do with his rich background. However, she could see how much he loved Katie. One of her concerns was that her niece enjoyed independence and a good career, and she wasn't sure if she was ready to settle into married life yet; especially in a land that had its own traditions.

Katie went to the lady's room which gave her the opening to speak to Nabil, but it was he who spoke first.

"Ellen, I have the distinct feeling you want to talk to me. You don't have to worry about Katie. I wouldn't hurt her for the world."

"I'm sure you wouldn't want to intentionally, Nabil, but you're older and more ready to settle down than she is."

"But ..."

"No, let me finish before she comes back. I know you love her anyone with any intelligence can see that, but you cannot possess her. You can't expect her to change to your way of life completely. She's not going to find it easy being your wife in a foreign country."

"I promise I will protect her from as much as I can."

Katie was on her way back. Ellen leant across to Nabil and laid a hand on his arm. "I really hope you do."

"I can see you two are getting along," she quipped, as she reached her chair which was being pulled out for her by the waiter.

"Yes, angel, we are." Despite his assurance, she sensed a slight atmosphere.

It wasn't long before they were back in Mayfair standing outside the apartment block in Grosvenor Square. The chauffeur was waiting to drive Ellen home to Edenbridge which had already been arranged by Nabil earlier in the day. It pleased Katie because neither of them wanted her aunt travelling on a train late at night, especially with Selfridges and Liberty's bags on show.

"I'm going to miss you," she said, and gave Katie a big hug. "Good luck with the wedding plans both of you."

"Do come Ellen, you're the only family I have."

"I'll do my utmost to make the necessary arrangements at school. Don't worry darling I'll sort it out. I'll be there!"

"Let me know as soon as you can."

"I will Katie, but I'll see you soon anyway."

"Yes, and next time you must stay for the weekend."

Ellen turned to Nabil. "I'm so glad we had the chance to meet and thanks again for a wonderful evening."

"You're most welcome. It was a pleasure to meet you too and I hope we see much more of you in the future."

He liked Ellen and he knew how important they were to each other.

Soon she was sitting in the back of the limousine. It had been a lovely day, shopping, and lunch with Katie then dinner at the Hilton; she was feeling tired, but happy. Enjoying the luxury of the limo she watched the familiar streets of London go by and it wasn't long before they were on the outskirts.

She knew it was going to be difficult to have time off in the middle of term, but she had to be at their wedding. She knew how important it was to Katie. Yes, she did have reservations, but she wanted to be there more than anything in the world. I pray it works out for them she thought to herself. Loving him is all very well but marrying someone of a different culture can create all sorts of problems, the customs, the religion, the language barrier with his family. Ellen sighed. He is handsome, though, and charismatic and there's more depth to him than I thought there might be.

I can't blame Katie for falling head-over-heals in love with him. Maybe I'm worrying for nothing. Am I just a little bit jealous of all that romance? I'm forty-two years old, I have a great career as the head of the English department in a good grammar school and I have a beautiful home, but my personal life is a mess. Would I not love a little romance? Wouldn't I like to have luxury showered on me? Instead, I have an ex-husband who phones me to tell me how broke he is and how he regrets cheating on me and a boyfriend who does not even know when I'm in the same room; he has his eyes glued to the television most of the time. Steve has been a good friend, but I certainly wouldn't marry him. How lovely it would be to meet someone who noticed me for a change who wanted to wine and dine me and have interesting conversations. Someone like Nabil Khalifa? She smiled to herself. Let Katie enjoy her romance and the luxury, she deserves every minute of it after all she's been through. Loving each other the way they do will hopefully be enough to help them cope with any difficulties that a mixed marriage creates. I need to stop worrying. Katie must live her life the way she wants to and with my blessing.

Back at the apartment Katie and Nabil were getting into bed but the atmosphere was tense.

"What was said between you and Ellen?"

"Nothing you need worry about angel."

"Don't be patronising I want to know what was said."

"Sorry!" He took her hand in his as they lay side by side. "It was nothing much, really."

"But you were obviously talking about me, and I don't want to be treated like a child."

"No one is treating you like a child. Your aunt is concerned about you that is all."

"I know she is."

"It's only natural."

"But I don't want to be talked about. You could have included me in the conversation when I returned to the table, instead, it went quiet. Do you know how horrible that feels?"

She turned over with her back to him, something she had never done before, but she wanted to calm herself. About ten minutes had passed when he leant across and kissed her neck, then his arm went round her. In her head she could hear her mother's words … 'Don't go to bed on an argument!' Feeling his strong body next to hers helped her relax. She didn't feel irritable anymore and Nabil knew he was forgiven. It had been a long day and they both fell asleep.

Chapter Ten

The wedding had been an extraordinary occasion and had left an indelible impression on Katie's memory. Wearing a long red and gold wedding dress had been the right choice. A less traditional dress would have been acceptable, but they decided they wanted to please his mamma and grandma Latifa. She loved the glamourous style anyway, especially when she was draped in jewellery.

Nabil had given her an exquisite watch, two days before the wedding, and it was her favourite piece. Thinking about all the different customs in the forthcoming ceremony and hoping she would get it all right had made her nervous and she nearly dropped it.

She shrieked as she managed to stop it falling to the floor. "Phew, that was close!"

"Let me put it on you, angel, then it will be safe," he said as he took her hand and placed the watch on her slim wrist. "Perfect!"

"It's the most beautiful thing I've ever seen." She couldn't take her eyes off it. Diamonds encircled the small dial, transforming it into an elegant piece of craftsmanship. Katie appreciated good things, having been brought up with and surrounded by antiques; she had learnt much about craftsmanship in the Emirates too. 'The Old Quarter,' where the souks, artists and craftsmen were situated, was her favourite part of Dubai and she was happy to see it being historically restored. On their days off she would go with friends, and they loved crossing the Creek in the water taxis followed by their favourite Middle Eastern drink, Limonana; lime juice, mint leaves and sirop which was melted sugar. Not particularly good for your teeth, but delicious just the same.

Nabil had taken her on a shopping spree a week before the wedding, but she wanted to go to the souks as well as the expensive shops. In the gold souk there was a dazzling array of eighteen and twenty-two carat gold chains, bracelets, bangles, rings, and pendants. Bracelets studded with stones and headpieces and necklaces were gem encrusted. What beauty! Katie was amazed that there was so little crime in this part of the world.

Managing to get a week off work, Ellen arrived three days before the wedding so they could spend some time together. She also loved the 'Old Quarter.' Katie took her on a boat ride to see the famous pink flamingos at the end of what was a natural creek. It was a beautiful sight away from the bustling city and the ongoing wedding preparations.

Sue, had planned to fly to Dubai for the wedding and stay in the same hotel as Ellen, but she had cancelled quite early on. Her excuse was that she couldn't get away from work, but Katie sensed that wasn't the main reason. Sue had changed so much since she'd started living with her partner and they were drifting apart. Rob was extremely controlling, and she suspected he had stopped her from coming to Dubai for her special day. She had so wanted Sue to be there for her and she couldn't help feeling let down.

Ellen had been a bit concerned about her niece having to convert to Islam but to Katie it wasn't a problem, though she found it a bit of a struggle learning the Koran. Nabil always preferred to go to his prayer room and pray in private, and she now accepted it as part of her life. As far as she was concerned there was only one God whatever faith you followed. Spirituality was a personal thing, and she embraced all religions. Wearing abayas was something she would have to get used to but at least she could wear clothes of her choice when at home, in the garden and of course when they went to England.

On the morning of their wedding day, Nabil's sisters, Shazia, and Yasmin, painted her hands and feet with henna. Katie and Ellen watched in awe as the delicate patterns started to form. It seemed to take forever to do her make-up and arrange her dress, and jewellery. Ribbons and flowers were woven through her long, raven black hair and they all loved the effect when they put on the see-through head dress; even Fatima, soon to become her mother-in-law, looked pleased when they had all finished fussing over her.

"Thank you so much," she said as she turned to Nabil's sisters.

Ellen took her by the hands and stared at her. "You look amazing my darling and I'm so proud of you."

"I wish mum and dad were here," said Katie, with tears in her eyes.

"I wish so too, more than anything in the world."

"I know they're close."

"Now, don't let the tears flow or you will mess up your makeup after Shazia and Yasmin took so much time over it. Besides, you have a handsome man waiting for you."

"I do," she replied, with a beaming smile on her face. She felt extremely nervous but excited at the same time.

The wedding went on for hours and the ceremonies performed were surreal. Customary dress worn by the family and most of the guests made it colourful, and traditional music was played throughout the day. Katie, who was the focus of attention had no idea how beautiful she was and there were many gasps amongst the guests when she first appeared.

Nabil, who was stunned into silence when he first laid eyes on her, felt as though his heart would burst with pride. It was obvious just how much they loved each other. Some of the younger guests were secretly happy that he had avoided an arranged marriage despite the pressure that had been piled on him. His best friend Hakeem, who he had grown up with and went to university with, was never far away. He was thrilled for them and made sure the day went without a hitch.

The family looked happy too on what was meant to be a joyous occasion. All except one man. Ellen noticed him as soon as the wedding got under way, and she asked Nabil's sister Shazia who he was. Uncle Mohammed came the reply. All through the ceremony he looked stony faced, but when his nephew came close, he would smile. He did not seem enamoured with his new niece by marriage. Ellen feared Katie had made an enemy and it filled her with dread.

Spending their honeymoon in Fujairah had been Katie's idea. Nabil wanted to take her to America, but she preferred to go back to Oman where he had proposed to her; it had such romantic memories. On the beautiful wide, empty beaches they laid together sometimes in the moonlight. White sands stretching out to the Indian Ocean and a constant temperature of eighty degrees made it pleasant indeed.

She smiled to herself as she remembered the time Nabil led her into a small cave. It felt cold compared to the hot air outside, but she soon warmed up when he started to kiss her all over. Katie had been worried because it was early evening and she thought someone might hear them, but he reassured her. The sense of danger only added to their passionate lovemaking and by the time Nabil had caressed every inch of her body she didn't have a care in the world.

They looked so happy on their honeymoon she thought as she looked at the photos in the album on her dressing table. Nearly eight months had passed since then, and she was used to living in luxury and being spoilt by a doting husband. She continued looking at the photographs and gazed in wonder at the scenery of Fujairah especially the palm groves. This must be some of the country's most beautiful stretch of coastline, she thought. Remembering the mountains as they embraced the shore, enclosing many fine sandy bays. She tried to compare it in her mind to anything she had seen in England. The only place she could think of was the many coves of Cornwall where she had spent a lot of her childhood.

Nabil had taken her to see a few of the forts and watchtowers and at Bidiya she saw the most exquisite little old mosque. Closing her eyes and imagining herself back in the past was not hard in a country steeped with history. He had laughed and called her the biggest romantic he had ever met, and she was. It was not just the romanticism though, she had the ability to sense the mystery of a place, the people and customs from times gone by. Katie thought it was natural to be able to do this. There had been many spiritual happenings from her past that she didn't relate to her husband, but she did tell him that she often sensed her mum around; he didn't mock her, but he didn't pursue the matter either, so she left it at that.

She put the ornate photo album back on the dressing table, all the while thinking how unhappy she was living in the town house with his mamma and sister. Shazia was a sweet eighteen year old, extremely pretty with big brown eyes, long dark hair and a smile that seemed to

117

spread across her whole face; she looked just like Nabil, but his mamma was dominating. It was fine when Katie and Shazia were on their own but as soon as Fatima appeared, the difference in the atmosphere was palpable. Shazia would speak English to her sister-in-law which was a relief because as much as Katie tried, she could only manage a few Arabic words and phrases. Her mother-in-law knew this so she would speak Emirati most of the time, hardly ever speaking English unless Nabil was at home.

Fatima was crafty because she behaved reasonably well towards her son's wife when he was there, but when he was out, she was indifferent towards her. Katie, who was becoming more depressed, longed for their summer vacation. She desperately wanted to visit England to see Ellen and meet up with friends. She couldn't put up with Fatima for much longer.

Miserable and fed up with complaining about her mother-in-law, she suspected Nabil was fed up with her complaining. A few times he did confront his mamma, but she always denied she behaved anything but decent towards Katie. It was deeply frustrating hearing them have words and not being able to understand most of what they were saying.

Katie was bored when Nabil was at work, even though she had taken up painting again, loved reading her books and could swim in the pool. For the first three months she had enjoyed all these things but after a while she missed having a purpose; she also missed her friends in Dubai.

Having anyone round to the house was a nightmare because of Fatima's attitude and she could not even go for a simple walk on her own. Nabil preferred that she went everywhere by car and invariably she had Fatima tagging along with her. Trying to be friends with her wasn't easy and on the rare occasion her mother-in-law showed signs of softening towards her, she would soon put her guard up again. Katie was desperately unhappy.

Nabil was sitting in his office, but he couldn't concentrate on his work. Instead, he swung his chair round so he could look at the beautiful view of Dubai Creek from his window while thinking about his wife. In the last couple of months, he had started to realise just how difficult it was for her to adjust to the changes in her life and he was looking forward to their two months away. He knew she wanted to see her aunt and her friends. Secretly he was relieved that his mamma and sister were not coming with them. It had been arranged that Mohammed and his wife Aamira would go with them to visit friends in Italy.

Nabil knew the atmosphere at home was becoming unbearable and he thought a long break would help put things right. Since his papa's sudden death three years ago, his mamma had changed beyond all recognition; he didn't know the person she had become. In his heart he knew she was behaving badly towards Katie whether she denied it or not and he felt torn between the two. One thing they must do when they returned from London was to start making more use of the beach villa so they could have time alone; he knew his wife felt more relaxed there and she loved to swim in the sea. Watching the sun setting over the ocean from the terrace was something they both enjoyed.

Later that day, Katie was in the garden and was feeling utterly desolate. Even the sheer beauty of it could not cheer her up as she sat on the low wall round the water fountain; she always sat here when she was agitated because the sound of cascading water calmed her.

Fatima was being her usual spiteful self. Katie only wanted to do some cooking, but she would not even let her do that. She didn't like anyone in her kitchen and of course they had a cook. Nabil was never there to witness this sort of behaviour. She absentmindedly ran her fingers through the cool water and began to cry when she heard somebody close by; she wiped her eyes quickly with the back of her hand before realising it was Shazia.

"Mamma doesn't mean to be cruel to you, but she can't seem to help herself."

Katie didn't look at up but continued to dip her fingers into the water.

"She loves Nabil very much, but she wanted him to marry into a local family and she can't forgive him for refusing. The only way she can punish him is by being nasty to you."

"But that doesn't make sense."

"Nothing makes sense with mamma anymore. Since papa died, she has been a changed woman. She's bitter because he was only fifty-two and she misses him terribly."

"I understand that, but she can't be bitter for the rest of her life. She needs to move on, or she'll never be happy."

"Well, I can't see her changing for anyone, least of all you, Katie. Sorry, I didn't mean to sound harsh."

"It's alright."

"What I mean is, she seems to enjoy playing games with your feelings. I think it's bad how she behaves differently when my brother is here. I know she's jealous because you're so happy when you're together and it brings back memories for her. Anyway, in a few days you'll fly to England. I hope you two enjoy yourselves, I really do," Shazia said before turning to leave as her mamma was calling her from the house.

Katie continued to play with the water, listening to the fountain pouring the liquid back into the pond. A continuous cycle, she thought, and she watched and listened. Complete silence apart from the fountain was something she normally craved, but today she felt so alone; it was as though she was in a trance. Sensing someone close made her look round but there was nobody; just the fragrance of her mother's favourite perfume which lingered for a while and gave her some comfort. "Mum," she whispered, "I know you're here with me. I love you."

She sat there for a long time, tears streaming down her cheeks, and she didn't even bother to wipe the drips from under her chin. She was in this miserable state for a long time when she heard Nabil calling her; she stirred slightly. It must be late she thought but she didn't have the will or the energy to call back neither did she hear him approach.

"Angel, what is the matter?" he asked, as he sat down beside her on the wall.

Katie couldn't speak and she couldn't explain her feelings either, not even to her husband. Instead, she fell into his arms sobbing and clinging to him. Nabil was solid and true but nothing else seemed to be. His mamma didn't believe she belonged, but she felt she did belong in this sun drenched and mystical land. Katie felt she was a part of the Middle East, and it was a part of her. If only she could be free of her mother-in-law, then their marriage would stand more chance of surviving. What was she thinking … that their marriage was in danger? She was so confused she did not know what to think. Her sobs subsided but she still clung to her troubled husband then inertia crept over her once more.

I don't know how to cope with their social and religious snobbery, she thought to herself. It's like a glass wall, invisible until you overstep the mark.

Chapter Eleven

Flying over Dubai Creek away from the district of Jumeirah, the stifling way of life she had been living since she married Nabil, and the unreasonable behaviour of Fatima was a relief.

"Are you feeling all right, angel?"

"Yes, I'm fine, stop worrying," she said, as she squeezed his hand and looked down at the wonderful view of the creek and Dubai. It was hard to believe it had grown out of the desert in the past twenty years. Highways, airports, ports, roadways, flowers, plants, trees, beautiful emerald-green grass, with underground watering systems and the gardens had all sprung up in the last two decades. Katie enjoyed history and she thought it only fair to find out more about the country she was living in. The country where she had found both happiness and misery.

What am I going to do? How can I tell Nabil of my true feelings without hurting him? How can I tell him that I don't want to go back to the town house and continue living with his mamma? She laid her head on Nabil's shoulder. She always felt safe and secure when she was with her husband, but sooner or later she was going to have to confront him about their future together in Dubai. The town house was not theirs. They hadn't chosen the furniture or the décor and nearly everything in the house belonged to his parents. Like most young women she wanted a home of her own and she knew if they continued living in his parent's house, it would become her prison.

Katie dozed. She'd been feeling extremely tired lately and all she wanted to do was sleep. The doctor had told her it was depression, but she had never been the sort to be depressed and it shocked her to hear the doctor say this. True she'd been in a state after her parents died, but that was understandable. Deciding to pull herself together when she got home from seeing the doctor was not easy either. As soon as she entered the house, she could feel the oppressive atmosphere closing in on her and she went to their bedroom. She was spending too much time in their room lately waiting for Nabil to come home, albeit an extremely large and luxurious room with a living area at one end, and a bathroom at the other. Feeling lost and alone was not how she wished to feel, and it wasn't how she used to be; the old Katie was in there somewhere trying to get out.

Three weeks before she had visited Bev and it was so good to be out on her own even though she was chauffeur driven. Abdullah had always been kind to her, and she knew he understood the predicament she faced every day. Fatima was in bed with a bad cold, so Nabil had encouraged her to visit her friends. It was lovely seeing Bev again, but she had been concerned because Katie looked drawn and tired. It marred her visit because it wasn't what she wanted to hear. Nabil had also commented recently, and it had been his idea that she made an appointment to see the doctor.

Looking down at his wife resting her head on his shoulder he felt sad that she wasn't the woman he had married; he still adored her and was looking forward to their break in England. He would have to fly to Europe on business once or twice, but he was determined to spend as much time with Katie as possible. He wanted them to be free and easy as they had been on their honeymoon. Nothing had mattered to them then, but now everything was a problem.

Nabil planned to talk to his mamma on the telephone before they went back to Dubai; he was not going to put up with her behaviour towards Katie any longer. Shazia had spoken to him just before they left for the airport. She told him how their mamma treated his kind, caring wife when he wasn't around. Suddenly feeling tired himself he also dozed.

In England they had a marvellous time, dining out and visiting the theatre, but more importantly staying home at Grosvenor Square and relaxing in each other's company. Ellen came to London for the opera 'Othello' at the end of their first week and had stopped over which pleased both Katie and Nabil. Even Sue, who had been staying at her mum and dad's house in West Wickham, came up for the day. It was too hot to go shopping so they went to Hyde Park and had a picnic, just like old times, while Nabil stayed home to do some work.

Her best friend wasn't the warm, bubbly, audacious person she had grown up with. Every time Katie tried to talk about her relationship with Rob, she just changed the subject. It was hurtful, especially as she had opened-up to Sue about some of her problems in Dubai; after all these years there seemed no way of bridging the chasm that had formed between them.

Katie loved the apartment and even though they didn't use it as often as they would like, it still felt warm and inviting. Nabil asked her if she wanted to change anything, and she had insisted it was perfect the way it was. Being away from her mother-in-law and having her husband all to herself was bliss. She felt less tired and soon she was more like her old self.

At the beginning of their third week, Nabil had planned a three-day business trip to France. Ellen was coming up for the day and they were going to have a leisurely walk and a relaxing late lunch on the terrace. It had a low privet hedge growing along the wall and many plant pots with such an array of colour, so there was plenty of privacy.

Katie was also looking forward to meeting up with her friends from Guys Hospital the following day. It was going to be a reunion in Convent Garden where they would have lunch and watch the street entertainment. How she had missed interaction with others in the first few months of their marriage.

Nabil left in the early hours, but telephoned her from Calais, before his drive to Paris, as he said he would.

"Hello, angel. Did you go back to sleep after I left?"

"No darling, I couldn't, so I had a soak in the bath with music and candles on."

"You must be tired."

"Not really, we did go to bed early."

"That's true."

"Ellen will be here in about three hours," she said excitedly.

"And tomorrow you're meeting your hospital friends. You're going to be busy."

"Yes, and I'm really looking forward to seeing them all, but on Monday I'm just going to relax and wait for you to come home, and make mad, passionate love to me."

"I certainly look forward to that but ..." he hesitated.

"But what?"

"I was wondering ... now you're feeling much better, I think we need to talk about mamma's behaviour towards you and what to do about it. I'm sorry Katie, I hadn't realised just how bad the situation had become. You did try to tell me."

"But I didn't want to cause trouble between you, and she always behaves well towards me when you're at home."

"Shazia told me the same thing just before we left for the airport."

"Bless her, she's such a lovely young lady but why didn't you tell me about your conversation with her?"

"You've been so low, and I've been worried about you … about us. I didn't want to spoil the wonderful time we've been having together since arriving in London. I could see the difference in you after just a few days."

"It's been hard these last months … very hard," Katie said, reliving the feeling of oppression in the town house. "I was going to bring the subject up as well when you got home from Paris. It seems we've both been putting it off."

"But never again. My dad's mamma said to me once after I had fallen out with papa … 'It's better to talk than create a wall so big it can never be knocked down.'"

"Latifa is a wise woman, and we ought to make more time to go and visit her."

"Yes, we must, despite the fact that she lives with Mohammed."

Katie felt flustered at the mere mention of his uncle's name, but Nabil didn't notice because he had to hang up.

"I must go, angel. Enjoy yourself and say hello to Ellen. I love you."

"Love you too."

Feeling much more hopeful about their future knowing they would at last sit down and talk to each other about their concerns was a relief. Maybe she should tell him about his uncle's threats, even though he hadn't repeated them … she would have to think about that. "Anyway, we have the rest of our holiday to look forward to," she said aloud. She was determined to enjoy her freedom before they returned to the Emirates.

Would he also understand that she had to find something to occupy her mind besides painting, reading, swimming, and watching films? Nabil wanted to give her everything, but he didn't realise what she needed most was her own space and a sense of purpose. "Oh God, what if nothing changes? I can't stand being stuck in the house with Fatima any longer."

She went into the kitchen to put some coffee on, and Mohammed came into her mind. At least he has kept away from me, she thought, as she reached for the cups and saucers, but I don't trust him. As soon as she started thinking about him, she felt a black cloud forming. Trying to push it out of her mind wasn't easy but at least she knew he was staying in Italy or so she thought.

Katie went back into the bedroom for something when the telephone rang. Reaching for the receiver she put it to her ear thinking she would hear a friendly voice.

"Good morning, Miss Morgan!"

Her heart missed a beat, the palms of her hands began to sweat, and she couldn't answer the cold, callous voice at the other end of the phone.

"Miss Morgan are you not pleased to hear from me?" Mohammed was in a telephone box in Grosvenor Square.

"It's Khalifa not Morgan," she replied. "What do you want? Nabil isn't here." She regretted saying this as soon as the words came out of her mouth.

"I know, my nephew is away on business. I made sure of that."

"What do you mean?" Katie was scared and she didn't like the menacing tone in his voice.

"I have a proposition to put to you. I will give you more money than I offered you before if you stay in England and let Nabil go back to Dubai on his own."

"But we're married!"

"Women are your fields. Go into your fields, when and how you will," he cruelly quoted the Koran. "My dear Miss Morgan," he continued to goad her," Nabil can have more than one wife if he so wishes."

"Why do you hate me?"

"Leave now while you still have the chance. I have left an envelope with the receptionist, and it contains a cheque for twenty thousand pounds. This is the last offer I will make and it's there waiting for you."

"But I don't want your money just leave me alone!" she shouted down the telephone.

"If you don't pack and leave within the hour, I will send a friend of mine up to make sure you go."

"I won't let him in!"

"But I have a set of keys," he replied, triumphantly. "Oh, and you should know Miss Morgan, that he is a large unpleasant man who is partial to pretty, young women. I'm sure you will enjoy him, but he is liable to be extremely rough and he has no manners," he laughed. It was an eerie laugh that put the fear of God into Katie. She threw the telephone receiver down as though it had burnt her fingers, breaking the glass on her favourite wedding photo, which dropped onto the carpet. Running out of the door she did not know what she was doing or where she was going, but she had to get away, that much was certain.

Ellen arrived about three hours later, and Gary greeted her warmly. Not having seen Katie run out of the building, he assumed she was home. Maria, the receptionist, was busy dealing with a resident, so Ellen went straight to the lift. A few minutes later she found their front door ajar, and she went cold. Wondering why the door was open, she walked in calling out, but there was no answer. Entering the living room, she looked round and continued to call Katie's name; when there was still no reply, she checked every room including Nabil's prayer room leaving their bedroom till last. She was disappointed not to find her there either. At first, she didn't see anything untoward but then she noticed the telephone was hanging and a photograph was lying on the deep pile carpet. It was Katie's favourite wedding photo, but the glass was broken. It must have been thrown or fallen onto something for it to break because the carpet is so soft. Maybe Nabil didn't go to Paris after all. They could have argued this morning, but where were they now? Ellen replaced the receiver, and the telephone immediately began to ring, she picked it up hoping it would be Katie with an explanation.

"Hello, angel."

"Nabil, it's Ellen."

"Ellen, how are you?"

"Eh … I'm not sure."

"What do you mean? Is Katie there?" He could sense something was wrong by the tone of her voice.

"No, I was hoping you would know where she is."

"What are you talking about? Last time I spoke to Katie she had just got out of the bath and was looking forward to seeing you. It's strange but I had a very strong urge to phone her again before going into my meeting."

"Oh God!" She started to fear the worst.

"Where would she have gone?"

"Nabil listen to me," her voice sounded more urgent now. "I came up in the lift and found the front door open and …"

"And what?" Nabil was beginning to panic now.

129

"Your wedding photo, the one by the bed, I found it smashed on the floor and the phone was hanging off the receiver."

"But why would she do that? It's her favourite photograph."

"I'm not saying she did it on purpose ... I don't know what to think. Also, she hasn't taken her handbag or purse. Nabil you need to come back as soon as you can, please?"

"Ellen what if ..." he sounded panic stricken and she realised she had to stay calm for them both.

"Try not to panic, just drive back now."

"I will!"

Ellen heard the telephone click at the other end. Sitting down she prepared to wait for Nabil. What else could she do? She didn't know where to start looking for Katie and she couldn't leave the apartment in case she returned. She could walk through the door at any moment, but somehow, she didn't think so. Something was wrong, but what? Why had she been in so much of a hurry to leave without her handbag and purse ... and the smashed photograph didn't make sense at all. Deciding she must do something, she phoned the reception to speak to the concierge, but Gary hadn't seen her leave the building. He told Ellen he would ask Maria if she'd seen Mrs Khalifa and get back to her.

Katie ran out of their apartment and into the lift. When it reached the ground floor, she almost fell out and collided with a stocky, middle-aged gentleman who tried to steady her. She moved quickly away, hurrying past the reception area and through the main doors looking dishevelled. At the desk, the young receptionist just caught sight of her as she rushed past, and had called her name, but she had already disappeared. Gary wasn't on the door or in the lobby when she hurried out of the building.

She kept walking as fast as she could, terrified that Mohammed and one of his henchmen would come looking for her. Ending up in a busy street she melted into the crowd, a mixture of happy tourists, busy shoppers, and workers on their way to the office. Katie carried on walking; remembering Mohammed's cruel threats sent her into a blind panic. She started to run knocking into people as the feeling of utter confusion engulfed her. Thoughts ran wild through her head ... her parents ... the crash ... Nabil ... his mamma ... Mohammed ... his evil laughter ... the hatred ... nothing made sense and she ran headlong into the road. The driver of the black cab did not stand a chance, he slammed on his breaks, and the taxi screeched to a halt. Katie screamed as it smashed into her slender body tossing her like a discarded mannequin into the air, then darkness enveloped her. She didn't see the ensuing confusion around her. Neither did she see the stunned and horrified faces looking down on her crumpled body lying on the tarmac, blood pouring from her head and making a sticky pool beneath her. There was a young policeman frantically trying to control the chaos while he radioed for assistance. An ambulance soon arrived, sirens blaring.

Mohammed was sitting in his car with his driver who was an unsavoury character. He was waiting for Katie to leave the building with her luggage; instead, he saw her rush out of the apartment block in a panic, with no bags at all. Assuming she hadn't picked up the envelope with the money in either made him extremely angry. His plan had not worked. Sitting in the back of the car and thinking about what to do next he decided he must get the envelope back as soon as possible. Furiously, he

131

shouted at his henchman to go and get it so they could get away. The concierge knew Mohammed, and he did not want to be seen or implicated.

Katie wasn't aware of anything until she came round in the hospital and immediately felt an excruciating pain in her head. A friendly doctor was reassuring her and calling instructions at the same time, but she began to slip away.

"We're losing her!" The doctor called to his team.

The pain subsided and Katie found herself floating above her body. No more agony, just the feeling of peace and tranquillity, then she was halfway to the ceiling looking down on the nurses and doctors trying to revive her; she wanted to tell them not to bother because she was fine. One of the young nurses looked upset and the doctor who had spoken to her earlier was desperately trying to get her back. Quite a commotion followed but she did not care … she felt free. Above her now was a bright light, and the ceiling disappeared. It was so inviting as she floated towards a shaft of white light that sloped upwards. It embraced her and she felt happy and calm, vibrant and alive all at the same time; it was an energy she could not describe. Sensing somebody in the light was trying to reach out to her filled her with joy but she could only see the outline of people. Her mum and dad were there smiling and waving but she couldn't reach them, then she noticed a good-looking man wearing a western style suit with an Arab headdress. He smiled at her, and he looked like Nabil's father, Ibrahim. Nabil ... I can't leave him … he'll be desperately unhappy without me. As soon as she had this thought she started slipping backwards. Slowly at first, then faster and faster until she was back in her body, and she felt the intolerable pain once again.

"We've done it, she's breathing," cried the doctor. Tension eased and everyone looked pleased with themselves. The young nurse she'd seen getting upset was holding her hand.

"You'll be all right now. We'll take care of you," she said quietly.

Katie began to cry with the pain, but she also cried tears of happiness because she'd seen her parents and had experienced the remarkable feeling of floating and serenity. It was difficult to comprehend because it was nothing like she'd ever felt before. Nabil's father was such a handsome man and he had smiled at her. It was all so crystal clear, like watching a film, but it hurt her head to think about it and she wondered why she had come back to this unbearable pain? Why had she not stayed in the light? But she knew why? A few seconds later she drifted off into unconsciousness as the doctor removed the syringe from her arm.

"Nabil, I thought you'd never get here," Ellen cried as he came through the front door. She'd been walking up and down wearing out the same piece of carpet with a glass of brandy in her hand which she hadn't touched.

"I drove as fast as I could without getting pulled over. Is she back?"

"No, I think we ought to call the police."

The telephone rang and Nabil got to it first.

"Hello."

"Sir, it's Gary. There are two police officers here to see you. Shall I bring them up?"

Nabil felt paralyzed.

"Mr. Khalifa?"

"Yes please."

He sat staring at the telephone. Beads of sweat appearing on his forehead. Ellen took the phone from him and placed the brandy in his hand.

"Drink this, you look like you need it. Who was on the phone?"

"Gary … the police are on their way up."

Ellen's hands flew to her face. "Oh God!"

A few minutes seemed like hours when there was a sharp knock at the door. A policeman and a policewoman followed Gary into the apartment.

"Mr. Khalifa?"

"Yes," he replied as he got up from his seat. "What has happened? Is it my wife?"

"I'm afraid there's been an accident sir," and as he said it, he could see the look of fear in Nabil's eyes. "It's alright … your wife is alive."

"Alive?"

Ellen caught him by the arm to steady him.

"Mr Khalifa, we have a car waiting to take you straight to St Thomas' hospital."

They followed the two police officers out of the building. It was certainly different travelling in a police car rather than a chauffeur driven limousine, but Nabil did not notice; it all seemed like a bad dream.

They arrived at the hospital twenty minutes later. Katie was in the Intensive Care Unit with bandages on her head. Her face was unrecognizable. It was bruised and battered, and her eyes were swollen and closed. Nabil nearly collapsed when he saw her, and Ellen steadied him for the second time that evening. The police had explained that the only thing Mrs Khalifa had on her was a card in her skirt pocket. It had the phone number of the concierge. Gary had given it to her in case she ever needed it.

The vigil began and the wait to see if she was going to live; her fight for life as she knew it. Nabil sat numbly beside her for a few hours. Ellen was worried sick, but she tried to stay calm and did her best to reassure him. She plied him with coffee from the canteen and bought him sandwiches to keep up his strength. He would only take a bite then push them away and she couldn't eat much either.

Katie hadn't acknowledged him yet or stirred at all. Staring at all the tubes and machinery around her he tried to visualise her beautiful sky-blue eyes; her smile which encapsulated you and her long, dark silky hair which he loved to see cascading down her back. Silent tears rolled down his cheeks as he imagined holding her close.

"Angel, please live ... please come back to me," he whispered.

Ellen found herself praying. Something she wouldn't normally do, but these were desperate times. Nurses were close by, and one moved nearer to check her vital signs. Ellen stepped out of the way so they could get on with their job and she told Nabil she would be outside; he nodded, barely registering what she was saying. A few minutes later his wife moved slightly, and he jumped out of his chair to get closer to her. A nurse had seen it too and had immediately called for a doctor, but Katie opened her eyes before the doctor arrived. Nabil was by her side, tears clouding his tired and sore eyes; she was trying to speak so he put his face to hers being careful not to touch her injuries.

"I love you," she whispered.

"Katie, oh Katie ... my angel," his voice cracked because his throat was dry, and he could hardly speak.

"Don't cry my darling," she slowly and painfully lifted her arm and wiped a tear from his cheek, then drifted off to sleep once more; for the next twenty-four hours she was in and out of consciousness.

Not needing the respirator anymore meant she was taken out of the Intensive Care Unit and put into a private room; at least she was on the slow road to recovery. Nabil mentioned a private hospital, but he was advised that moving her would not be a good idea, at this stage; her condition was in a delicate state.

Ellen went home to Edenbridge, and Nabil returned to his apartment to tidy himself up. Looking into the mirror he could see dark circles under his eyes. His hair was untidy, and he couldn't remember when he had last combed it. He needed a long, hot shower to wash away the fear and anguish of the worst two days of his life. Even when his papa died of a sudden heart attack, he hadn't felt this agonizing pain inside him. Nabil had loved his papa. They hadn't always agreed with each other, but he had been a striking man at fifty-two; handsome with a broad smile which made you forget your differences. His energy knew no bounds and he had a wonderful charisma.

Nabil looked around the apartment. It felt empty and strange without her and as he walked into the bedroom, something nagged at the back of his mind. Something about this whole business did not seem right. Why had she left in such a hurry? He bent down to pick up the photograph and he could see Katie smiling back at him, they had both been so carefree when the picture had been taken on their wedding day. Lying on the bed repeatedly reliving the last two days her words kept going through his head … 'Don't cry my darling.' "How can I not cry when I see her lying there battered and bruised?" he groaned to himself.

What had made her leave in such a hurry without telling anyone? Where was she going? All these thoughts ran through his tired but questioning mind. The police said people witnessed Katie running out into the road as though she was running away from someone or something; they said they would investigate further. Investigate! Investigate what? Have I been so blind not to notice what has been happening? What or who could have frightened her so much that it made her run in front of a taxi. He vowed he would find out. Lying on the bed clutching the photograph to his chest, he drifted into a fitful sleep; the worry and trauma of the last two days had exhausted him.

Four hours later he heard the telephone ringing in the distance. He couldn't wake himself but when he realised where he was, he reached for the phone. Before he had a chance to say anything he heard the doctor's distinctive Scottish accent.

"Mr. Khalifa it's Doctor MacDonald." Nabil could tell from his tone there was something wrong.

"What is it doctor, is my wife worse?"

"No, but I need to talk to you when you return to the hospital."

"I would rather you talk to me now if there is something I need to know."

"Very well," he paused, "I'm afraid your wife has lapsed into a coma." Nabil fell into a shocked silence. "Mr Khalifa?"

"Yes, I'm here."

"I'm sorry to give you such bad news, but it may only be for a few days. We just don't know at this stage. I'll tell you more when you're here."

"Yes … yes of course. I'll be there soon. I must tidy myself up. Thank you for phoning Doctor MacDonald."

Nabil replaced the receiver and the next forty minutes were a complete blur as he showered and changed. He was driven to St Thomas' but did not remember anything about the journey. When he arrived, he went straight to her room. Seeing her sleeping like a baby was traumatic and he wondered if she would ever come back. For the first time in his life, he felt lost and alone, like a child without his mother. Being rich meant he could have almost anything he wished for, but right now all he wanted was his wife. He wanted to hold her in his arms, smell the familiar scent of her body. Putting his head in his hands he didn't hear the doctor arrive.

"Mr Khalifa."

Nabil looked up to see Doctor MacDonald, an eminent neurologist, who pulled up a chair beside him. He was a friendly chap with a kind and compassionate bedside manner.

"I must talk to you, while you're on your own. It's a delicate matter. Did you know your wife was pregnant?"

Nabil looked at the doctor in utter astonishment. "Pregnant? But … why wouldn't she have told me?"

"That I cannot answer, but it's a miracle she didn't lose the baby."

"Pregnant." Nabil repeated looking bemused.

"It is possible your wife didn't know herself. Had she been unwell at all which could have caused her to be irregular?" enquired the doctor.

"My wife has been depressed for some time, and extremely tired. I was going to insist on her having a thorough check up while we were in England."

"Well, by what you've said she probably didn't know she was expecting a baby, so don't go worrying yourself on that score."

Nabil sat looking bewildered.

"There is no reason for any complications. From the scan we can see that your wife's brain has not been damaged as much as we previously thought but she has sustained a severe head injury; pressure is being placed on the brain because of bleeding and there could be blood clots or a build-up of fluid. We don't know much at this stage, but we are monitoring her very closely you can be assured of that. We're hoping it won't be necessary to move her back to ICU. Effectively Mr. Khalifa, your wife is unconscious, but we can't be sure how long she will stay in this condition."

"How will the baby survive?"

"It will grow normally, and your wife's pregnancy will be monitored by a colleague of mine who is an excellent obstetrician."

Nabil looked tired and it was all too much to take in.

"We will do everything we can to keep your wife safe and comfortable and she will be fed with nasal and gastric tubes; the nursing staff are well trained and will see to all her needs."

"Thank you … thank you for all that you're doing," he said quietly.

Getting up from his chair the doctor put his hand on Nabil's shoulder and squeezed it slightly to give him what little comfort he could. Walking out of the room he wondered if they would be able to keep mother and baby alive.

Chapter Twelve

"When are you coming home?" demanded Mohammed.

"Not yet! I can't leave Katie."

"But we have a business to run."

"Is that all you can think of at a time like this. My wife is in a coma, and she is carrying our child," he answered, raising his voice in anger at his uncle's lack of concern.

"Very well, but life has to go on."

"Thank you, uncle. I will remember that when I'm sitting in the hospital," and he slammed down the receiver, wondering why he hated Katie so much.

Mohammed had been extremely eager for his nephew to return to Dubai from the time the accident had happened, and Nabil was beginning to wonder why.

Maria on reception had informed the police that she saw Mrs Khalifa rush past while she was dealing with another resident; she also told them she called out to her because an envelope had been left at the desk by a man she hadn't seen before. Nabil was puzzled by this mysterious envelope which had been collected by the same man as soon as Katie had disappeared. Feeling uneasy about the whole business, made him think more than ever that his uncle had something to do with his wife's rapid departure from their apartment.

Katie had been in a coma for seven months. It was now the end of March, and never before had Nabil spent so much time in London in the winter. Having to purchase warmer clothes was a must, but that was the least of his worries.

Everyone had been marvellous. Friends from Guy's Hospital had been in to visit her on many occasions. Ellen came up from Edenbridge as often as she could, and a couple of times Sue had joined her when she could get away from her partner Rob. Bev had flown over from Dubai and was devastated to see her lovely friend lying so still. This pleased the doctors who said the more visitors the better as long as they all spoke to her and not about her; advising them to talk of past, happy memories, about the things she liked to do and especially about the baby.

Ellen talked to her for hours about her childhood and she was certain she had seen the flicker of a smile on her niece's face a few times. But she didn't tell Nabil because she didn't want to raise his hopes; she wasn't sure how much more he could take. One good thing had come out of this terrible situation, she thought, Nabil seemed much less impatient with the maids in his apartment or the waiters in the exclusive restaurants he was used to dining in. He still expected the best, but he was humbler and that wasn't a bad thing.

Nabil often listened to Ellen and was fascinated to hear more about Katie's childhood. It made him feel closer to her even though she was so far away. He talked to her about how they'd met in Dubai Airport, their first trip to Oman, their wedding and honeymoon; they had been so happy and radiant. When he spoke about their future together as a family, he found it difficult not to break down, especially when promising her that everything was going to be different when they returned home.

Doctor MacDonald had suggested they bring something in they could play her favourite music on, and they had been doing this for a few months. Katie had a passion for opera especially Puccini's Madame Butterfly and the love duet. They played some of her classical discs, Antonio Vivaldi's violin concerto, La Tempesta di Mare which had a soothing effect on Nabil's shattered nerves; plus, Delibe's exquisite Flower Duet which he'd heard her listen to many times. Katie also liked jazz, blues, and soul, which they played endlessly, and of course traditional middle eastern had become part of her life as well. She had been brought up to appreciate all genres and she was often heard to say that 'music was the food of the soul.'

Nabil felt desperately lonely without, Katie, even though his mamma stayed with him in the apartment most of the time. Friends often phoned and Ellen insisted he go out for a meal a few times just to get him away from the hospital environment.

Hakeem, his best friend, met him for dinner when he was in London, and he phoned him as much as he could to give him the support he needed. Nabil had always been loyal to his friend especially since he had shared his secret; he hadn't been surprised to learn that Hakeem was gay. It was imperative they continued to keep it to themselves because he was married to a local woman in Dubai. It was a miracle they had created two beautiful daughters. However, he was finding it increasingly difficult to have a normal relationship with his wife. In fact, it was soul destroying having to lead a double life. He knew if it ever became common knowledge, he would be imprisoned, and he may never be allowed to see his daughters again; he was desperately unhappy.

Swearing allegiance to each other when they were seventeen years old was something they would never forget. They had taken a jeep into the desert and driven like maniacs for a couple of hours until they got bored. Watching the night sky was something they both liked doing especially when they turned the headlights off. The intensity of the stars gave them enough light to be able to see in the blackness of the night. Hakeem made a small cut on the palm of his hand with his penknife then passed it to Nabil. He hesitated at first, then proceeded to do the same. They joined their hands together, so their blood mingled; they were true blood brothers.

Continuously worrying about what would happen if Katie did not come out of her coma in time to have their baby was understandable. Doctors reassured him that his wife would have a caesarean section and that all the time she was alive, their baby was alive too.

Nabil prayed to Allah that she would wake up and have a natural birth; he couldn't think of anything worse than Katie not seeing or being able to hold their baby in her arms. Feeling his eyes well-up he wondered how many times he had cried in the last few months. Most men in his culture were frightened of showing their emotions, for fear of appearing weak. But spending so much time abroad and, especially in England, meant he had distanced himself from the more traditional way of life in Dubai; this riled his uncle plus his mamma didn't always understand.

Staying at Grosvenor Square made him feel close to Katie though he had flown home to Dubai a few times in the last seven months. It was difficult to concentrate but at least the business took his mind off his problems though he couldn't bear to be away from her for too long. What would he do if she didn't wake up? Yet, he knew in his heart they would be together again, but he didn't know when.

Having so much time to contemplate and think about his wife's anxieties made him face up to the flaws in their marriage. Realising now that showering her with expensive jewellery, taking her to the best restaurants

143

and the most exclusive shops was not important. Always the best beauticians and hair stylists visited the house in Dubai. He gave her everything and yet she had been miserable.

Before the accident he said he wanted to take her shopping to Harrods, and he remembered Katie's words so clearly. 'Darling, I don't want to go shopping in Harrods. I really don't need anything. Money alone, doesn't buy happiness.' It was hard for him to understand at the time because he thought money brought you all these things. How wrong he had been! Yes, he was rich, but money would not bring his wife back to him. Paying for the best doctors in the land would not help.

Lying there motionless, like a beautiful porcelain doll, she looked delicate and fragile. Our baby is growing inside her, but she is completely unaware of it, or so he thought. "One day soon I will wake up from this terrible nightmare and find you lying next to me angel. I would give anything if I could only have you back. Yah a beeba, I love you," he said aloud as he held her hand in his. Resting his weary head in the crook of his other arm he nodded off.

Nabil didn't know how long he'd been asleep when he felt a hand on his shoulder. It was his mamma who took him in her arms. Something she had not done for a long time. One good thing that had come out of this terrible situation was that his family had visited Katie a few times. Shazia was attending university in London, so Fatima had decided to stay with Nabil for the foreseeable future. Surprisingly, she had even asked him to find her a good teacher. She wanted to learn to speak better English so she could talk to her daughter-in-law in the hospital. He had jokingly said that his mamma was becoming a modern woman at the age of fifty-two. This made her laugh, something she had not done much of since Ibrahim had died.

Yasmin, his sister, and her husband Rashid had visited three times. But he was needed in Dubai, while Nabil was spending so much time in London, so they stayed in touch with him by phone. His uncle was the only one who had not been in to see Katie even though he came to London for business and pleasure on quite a few occasions. Today he brought Fatima to the hospital, but he did not come in with her, preferring to go back to his apartment in Knightsbridge.

Fatima had no animosity towards Katie anymore because she realised more than ever just how much her beloved son adored his wife. She also knew there would be no normality until her daughter-in-law and the baby were home. It was heart breaking to see him looking so miserable, and she'd made up her mind when Katie returned to Dubai that everything would be different.

How she wished she could tell her now, but her English was not good enough yet. "Alam dalala, peace be with you," she whispered. She wanted to make up for all the hurt she had caused. Feeling jealous when seeing Katie and Nabil happy together was irrational and she realised that now. It was all part of her grieving for Ibrahim, but she had decided she could not spend all her waking hours thinking of him. Concentrating on those who were alive, and that included Katie, was the important thing.

Nabil had been so relieved to know she was looking forward to his wife coming home and it was one less hurdle for them to face together. Standing behind his mamma, who was now sitting next to Katie, he looked lovingly at his wife lying so still, her face like alabaster against the white pillow. He then walked quickly from the room wanting to catch Mohammed before he went out for the evening.

"Nabil, just in time, I'm meeting friends for dinner. You must dine with us," he said, as he patted him on the back.

"No thank you."

"Oh, come on you need a good night out!"

"Unlike you Uncle, I love my wife," Nabil snapped.

"What has that got to do with anything?"

"You treat my aunt abominably. You have a kept woman here as well as back home and you have many dubious friends, who I don't want to be associated with. My father used to despair of you and now I know why."

"How dare you speak to me like that. What is wrong with you Nabil?"

"What is wrong uncle is that I've had plenty of time to sit and think and for all I know you could be the cause of my wife lying in a hospital bed."

"Now you listen to me …"

"No, you listen to me. You have always hated Katie and you did everything you could to stop us marrying. Since we have been married you haven't uttered a civil word to her."

"For the love of Allah, I have only done what I thought was right. You should have married your own kind, not some English piece," shouted Mohammed.

"My wife is a lady and has more kindness and compassion in her than you will ever have," Nabil shouted back.

"You could have kept her in a villa and still married a local girl, but no not you, you had to marry your English woman," he sneered.

Nabil ignored this remark as he didn't feel like playing his uncle's mind games.

Mohammed poured him a drink which he refused by an impatient wave of his hand.

"I want to know where you were on the day of the accident. You probably lied to the police, and I wouldn't

146

be surprised if you bribed a few people as well. You were supposed to be in Italy, but mamma said you were gone for a few days around the same time as the accident; you also made sure I was out of the way. It wasn't necessary for me to go to France. What made Katie run out of the building and who was the man who left an envelope then took it back again? Was he an employee of yours? Because we all know what sort of person works for you; and now he has conveniently disappeared!"

"I did not see or speak to her." Mohammed was becoming red in the face and was losing his composure.

"Why don't I believe you?"

"You are like a son to me, let us not argue," he begged putting his hands on his nephew's shoulders, but Nabil knocked them off.

"If you don't tell me the truth, I will go to the police myself and tell them of my suspicions."

"Come Nephew we are family and families stick together. I only did it for you."

"Did what?"

"Nothing ..." he hesitated.

"What did you do?" Nabil was standing right in front of him now.

"I offered her twenty thousand pounds to stay in England and let you return to Dubai on you own. It was more than the last time and she still refused."

"It was more than the last time? You mean you've offered her money before? He couldn't believe what he was hearing because even he didn't think his uncle would stoop this low.

"Yes, before you were married. I suppose it wasn't enough for a gold-digging English girl."

Nabil felt a heat rising through his trembling body. All the anguish and worry of the last seven months was coming to the surface and he wanted to strangle his uncle as he took him by the collar. It took an enormous amount of self-control and energy not to.

"Let me tell you something, Katie, does not need your money or mine; she has her own. My wife loves me and that is why she refused your offers. No wonder she was agitated whenever you were around. What sort of threats did you make to her, the sort of vile threats you always make to people who get in your way?"

Mohammed was speechless and alarmed, as his nephew's grip grew tighter on his collar.

"You are despicable, and you will not come near my wife ever again. As far as the business is concerned, I will only see you when it is totally and utterly necessary." He threw his uncle onto the sofa, stormed out and went back to his apartment to calm down. He had come dangerously close to harming Mohammed. Pouring himself a brandy to steady his nerves he thought of Katie. My poor angel why have I been so blind to what was going on? "I will make it up to you … I promise I will make it up to you," he vowed to himself.

Katie was paralyzed to the physical world around her but there was the occasional flicker of emotion on her beautiful features. This was so fleeting it usually went unnoticed by the nurses or the family. She was not living in the hospital room she was living in an unseen world; a kind of utopia she didn't want to leave because it was where she felt safe.

The pain and tragedy that had befallen such a young, sensitive woman had taken its toll. Her parent's fatal car crash and her marriage, which instead of bringing her happiness, had brought her to the brink of a nervous breakdown. Mohammed's wicked threats and the cunning way in which he hid it all from Nabil. The accident and the unbearable pain in her head and the dull but continuous ache in her heart, all this had made her withdraw from the material world.

When she was young, she used to retreat to the summerhouse at the bottom of the garden with her books, drawing pad and pens. Not hiding from anything tangible, but as much as she loved people, she also craved peace and tranquillity. Having her own space was important and it was something she did not have much of while living with Fatima and Shazia. Now she existed in an ethereal and peaceful place, but she didn't know what was reality, and what was illusion? In the present, she was happy, contented and her spirit was free. There were no shackles, there was no hurt, no pain and yet deep down she knew she had left something precious behind.

Drifting between the two worlds had become normal but hovering on the threshold of the physical world was happening more often. It was at one of these moments that she heard her aunt talking about her childhood. Wonderful memories … happy times … a carefree life … which she had now recaptured. She was with her parents once again and yet she knew she did not belong in the same existence as them. Katie wanted to reach out to Ellen and tell her that everything was alright, that she was fine. But she couldn't move her limbs which were as heavy as lead; instead, she would give up and drift back once again to her diaphanous world where she did not have to exert any physical energy. It was at this moment when her aunt saw a flicker of recognition on her niece's face. Ellen knew she was there somewhere in the distance listening to her. "It can only be a matter of time before you come back to us my darling … please God," she whispered.

Sitting and holding her lifeless hand while talking about their future together, as he had done many times before, was draining. Occasionally Nabil felt a surge of energy as if she were reaching out to him. Katie experienced this outpouring at the same time, and she knew there was something special between them but didn't remember much until he began to talk. She was on the brink of the threshold of her physical life once more. His voice sounded urgent and sad, she also realised he was exhausted. Katie wished he could be with her, then he could rest and be at peace in this place of sheer beauty.

When he talked about their baby, he sounded anxious and at this point she wanted to stroke his face and tell him his son was okay. She wanted to let him know their son was growing well but she could not find the strength. She talked to their baby knowing this beautiful soul was not yet a part of the physical world but was a part of her. One day soon she knew he would have to leave the security and comfort of her womb. But she did not want him to feel pain and unhappiness only joy and love. Yes, he would cry and protest at being thrust suddenly into the earthly existence, but Katie felt deep within it was meant to be. In her heart she knew she would have to go back with him to continue to love and nurture him, to somehow protect him from the harshness of life. Could she? Could she protect him from life which to a certain extent was already mapped out for him?

Increasingly Katie was gliding back and forth between the two worlds, and she was aware that the pull between her and Nabil was becoming more powerful. He often talked to her about his childhood and about his papa, he would tell her how she would have liked and respected him and how he wished they'd met. "But my darling, we have met," she would say in her head in her more lucid moments wishing she could tell him his papa was not dead, that he lived on somewhere else, and still cared about them all. Katie wanted him to know his papa was

150

there, helping to guide him and he was going to be proudly watching over his new grandson. Observing his wife for any signs of life and thinking about the terrible argument he'd had with his uncle a week ago left Nabil emotionally drained. Fatima was concerned about him and knowing that he'd argued with Mohammed worried her even more; her son did not want to talk about it and his uncle had left England suddenly. Too tired to even talk to Katie today he just wanted to sit and send his silent thoughts to her in the hope that she would somehow hear them. With all the suffering and mental anguish had come a new understanding and the love he had for her was now unconditional. Not the stifling overprotective love he had shown her in the past; he had learned a lot in the last seven months. Nabil thought he knew himself better now and he understood Katie much more than he had before. They would start afresh. A new baby … a new life. Inshallah, Allah's will!

Later in Grosvenor Square when he had gone home to shower and change the argument with Mohammed was going round and round in his head. He was so angry he couldn't rest so he booked a flight to Dubai. He informed Douglas he would be gone for a few days, and he was pleased that Nabil was having a break from the hospital, albeit a short one.

Mohammed had not been doing much work for a long time. There was an increasing demand month after month for all types of merchandise, especially from the many foreigners who lived and worked in the United Arab Emirates. They obviously preferred home comforts and some of the food they were used to in their own countries. They imported anything from the best Russian Caviar, to requests for crates of British baked beans which were not easy to import even in 1988.

151

Nabil spun his enormous leather chair round so he could look out of the window. He could see men in dhows going about their daily business on the creek. It was a hive of activity, the lifeblood of Dubai, the place he loved. Wishing his uncle loved it as much as he did, he sighed. He was hearing terrible things about him. He was drinking, gambling, and keeping some of the worst company imaginable. Nabil knew Mohammed was in Dubai so he phoned and asked if he could come to his office, even though he didn't trust his feelings towards him. It was a cowardly man who would threaten a young lady in the way that he had. He didn't know the full extent of the threats, but he knew only too well what his uncle was capable of.

There was a commotion outside his office which grew louder, and he could hear Mohammed shouting. About to open the door to see what was happening his uncle suddenly burst in followed closely by the security guard.

"I'm sorry Sir I tried to stop him making so much noise."

"It's all right John, you can go now. I will deal with my uncle."

"Yes, Sir. I won't be far away if you need me."

"So, you can deal with me can you nephew?" he growled sarcastically. "I thought you didn't want to see me again. Well, let me remind you I am your business partner and as such I demand respect." Mohammed who had obviously been drinking stumbled his way across the room. He sat in Nabil's leather chair which was once more facing his large mahogany desk.

Nabil was disgusted by what he saw. His uncle's eyes were blood shot and he looked unkempt. He rested his hands on his desk leant forward and looked straight into his cold eyes. "You don't deserve respect and it's a wonder you haven't been arrested."

"That's a fine way to speak to your papa's brother."

"You leave papa out of this. You're not half the man he was." Nabil was relieved his desk was between them; he didn't want to do something he might regret. He could feel the veins in his forehead throbbing, and he clenched his teeth so hard his jaw ached; his palms were sweating as he tried desperately to control his temper.

Mohammed sensing this, moved out of his chair, and began to make his way to the door. "Oh no you don't, uncle, we need to talk about my wife!"

"You must forget about her now. Get on with your life and marry a local girl. At least then you won't have a half breed son as an heir."

Nabil couldn't suppress his anger any longer. He leapt across the room in a matter of seconds and punched Mohammed knocking him to the floor. It was impossible to ignore his uncle's insults and he pulled him up by his clothes and threw him against the wall, taking him completely by surprise.

"What did you do to cause Katie to run out of the building? Why was she so terrified? Why? Tell me!" he shouted.

"It was n … nothing," he stammered.

"What did you do to frighten her?" By this time, he had his uncle by the throat, and he was so close he could smell the stench of drink on his breath.

"I threatened her."

"How did you threaten my wife? How?"

"I told her if she didn't take the money and go, I would send a rough friend of mine up to the apartment for some pleasure."

Nabil could not believe what was coming from his uncle's disgusting mouth. Hearing the commotion, the security guard came in the door just as his boss was about to tighten his grip around his uncle's throat.

153

"Sir, stop!"

Mohammed gasped for breath as Nabil let go and he fell to his knees holding his chest then he slumped forward to the floor in obvious pain.

"Your uncle's having a heart attack, phone for an ambulance," John called, as he knelt to see what he could do.

Nabil stared at his uncle.

"Call an ambulance Sir!"

Walking to his desk in a daze he reached for the telephone and dialled the emergency services.

Twenty minutes later when his uncle was carried away on a stretcher, he felt no compassion towards him whatsoever. He called his Aunt Aamira, to tell her that Mohammed had been taken to the hospital with a suspected heart attack and that he'd arranged for Rashid to take her there. No way could he tell his aunt what had happened in his office. She knew her husband was a wicked man because she had suffered enough in their marriage, but he didn't want to upset her even more. His main concern was the need to fly back to London to be with his wife.

Nabil slept throughout the flight after a couple of sleepless nights. He couldn't wait to get back to the hospital to see if there was any change in Katie's condition, but he went to their apartment first. He needed to shower, change, and spend some time in his prayer room. That's all he seemed to do when he was there, shower, change, pray and sleep, if it was possible. It wasn't much of a life, and Fatima was concerned about him.

Ellen phoned him to say she'd been with Katie for two of the days while he was away and there had been no change. Some of her friends had been in too and it pleased him to know she'd had company.

He arrived at the hospital later that morning and had been by his wife's side most of the day apart from Fatima's two-hour visit. The chauffeur brought her, but friends had picked her up and were taking her out to dinner. She had bought some food in for Nabil because she knew he wouldn't want to go out for a meal after being away from Katie for a few days.

Puccini's La Boheme was playing in the background, Nabil was not really listening to it, but Katie was. Familiar sounds floated to her ears. It was coming to a climax ... Mimi was dying. The music was soft and gentle, then it came to a dramatic crescendo as her lover cried out in anguish. Mimi ... Mimi! Haunting music played on, and Katie heard Mimi's lover's heart-rending sobs, then Mimi's last few words were serenely sung out as she passed from this world to the next. Something stirred inside Katie ... she did not want to die as Mimi had done. She would live! Nabil's soul was reaching out to hers and they became one; she could physically feel the torment he was going through. Katie gently tightened her grip on his hand, and he felt it.

"Nurse! Nurse!" he called urgently.

"Yes Mr. Khalifa, what is it?"

"Nurse, call a doctor ... call a doctor please ... my wife squeezed my hand ... she squeezed my hand."

Anne left the room excitedly. She had been nursing Katie for a few months and the whole medical team were willing her to wake up. In fact, the whole hospital knew of her condition, and it was often the topic of conversation.

Doctor MacDonald entered the room a few moments later with Nurse Anne close at his heels. Nabil looked up when Douglas came rushing in. They were on first name terms now as they had got to know each other over the last few months; it was the main reason he hadn't moved her to a private hospital. He trusted this man and the staff were so attentive and caring. It had opened his eyes and made him realise that money wouldn't buy any better treatment than she was getting.

"Nabil what exactly happened?" he asked.

"She squeezed my hand!"

"Now, I don't want you to get your hopes up too much, but it is a good sign," he remarked, as he bent down to examine Katie.

"Did anything else happen?"

"No." Nabil looked puzzled.

"What were you or the nurse doing at the time?"

"I had just come in doctor. I was going to do Mrs Khalifa's mouth care," answered Anne.

"Thank you," and he turned to Nabil. "Were you talking to her about anything in particular?"

"I wasn't talking to her, at least not out loud, but the music was playing."

"What was the music?"

"La Boheme. Why Douglas?"

"I'm trying to ascertain what may have stirred her enough to squeeze your hand, could it have been the opera?"

"It is one of her favourites and it was her mother's favourite as well when she was alive. We went to see it at The Royal Opera House last year. She was mesmerised, especially by the scene at the end where the character – I can't remember her name is dying; even I had tears in my eyes."

"Was that the part that was playing when she squeezed your hand?

"Yes, I believe so."

"Then I suggest you play it again and again."

"Douglas does this mean she could wake up soon?" Nabil sounded so hopeful, but he looked totally worn out.

"It is a good sign, but I cannot say more than that. You must get some rest."

"I can't rest, not now."

"Look, Anne was about to do Katie's mouth care and tidy her up, so let her get on with it. Go home, I'm sure your mamma would like to see you," he said as they walked to the door.

"Yes, you're right Douglas."

"Remember what I said before, when Katie does return to full consciousness, she may be vague and have loss of memory, her voice could be slurred, and she is going to be weak. We don't know for certain what the long-term effects will be because every case is different."

"But you also said there is a good chance of her returning to normal," insisted Nabil.

"Yes, in many cases this does happen and of course she will have the baby and you to help her; she has everything to live for," answered Douglas as his pager sounded. "Look I must go now. Get some rest or you will be no good to anyone," and he rushed off to the nearest telephone.

Nabil walked into the corridor with the intention of going home for a couple of hours, but he felt very restless and really didn't know what to do with himself. Something stopped him in his tracks. There was a tremendous feeling of elation within him, and he knew he had to return to Katie; he started back towards her room. This feeling permeated his whole being and the moment he entered the door she opened her eyes for the first time in months.

Chapter Thirteen

Word travelled fast after Katie woke up and the atmosphere amongst the hospital staff was charged. Three weeks later, on the twenty-first of April 1988 Katie gave birth to a healthy baby boy. She had a caesarean section because she was still feeling the effects of the coma. Some members of staff had taken bets on whether it would be a boy or girl and it did wonders for morale. Gifts and cards came flooding in and Katie and Nabil felt like celebrities. Tafiq Ibrahim Alan Khalifa showed them all what a fine pair of lungs he had as he came into the world right in the middle of Ramadan. It was a good omen. The new parents would normally be fasting especially if they were in the Emirates. But after all that had happened and in consideration for Katie's health, even a strict Muslim wouldn't be expected to stick to it.

For the first two weeks she couldn't do much for Tafiq because she was still fragile, but now he was three weeks old she was managing to look after him well. It had been difficult for her to move around at first because she had to learn to walk again with the help of the physiotherapist, but she was full of determination. The doctors were amazed at her rapid recovery. Nabil found himself continuously looking at his son and his wife thinking the whole thing must have been a terrible nightmare. Every time Katie went to sleep, he was frightened she wouldn't wake up again. Douglas reassured him many times and gradually he was losing his fear.

Doctors advised they be left alone to get to know each other again now that Katie's health was improving, so after his mamma's visit they had time to themselves.

Feeling vague at times and with slightly slurred speech was frustrating but the speech therapist was pleased with her progress. Health professionals could not believe how much and how quickly she had improved. It was as though she had a tremendous inner force driving her. But the doctors were still concerned about her mental condition because she didn't remember everything that had happened to her. She had switched off, particularly to the memory of the accident which had brought her to the hospital in the first place. It was strongly advised she go to a rehabilitation centre in Hertfordshire for a few weeks. Nabil and Katie both agreed this was a good idea. He would do anything to have his wife back to full health and her memory restored to normal.

She was packing her personal belongings as she prepared for the journey to Hertfordshire in the morning. Nabil had an important business meeting, but he was coming back to visit her and Tafiq later in the evening. Still feeling strange at times, it was difficult to believe she had been in a coma for seven months. It was a little unnerving that she remembered more about when she was asleep than about what had happened prior to the accident. It upset Nabil when she didn't recollect things about their life together, but he tried not to show it. Her memory was coming back slowly, and he was encouraging when she did remember. What Katie did not tell her husband, or the doctors, was the terrible feeling of dread within her and not knowing what it was that frightened her so. They suspected as much because she only remembered the good things; growing up in

England; her job in the Emirates; her friends; her engagement to Nabil and their wedding. But she didn't talk about going back to their home in Dubai. She could not face the future, instead she wanted to stay in the security of her present surroundings or that of the rehabilitation centre. Returning to Dubai was not something she felt safe about doing. Nabil was so patient with her even though she knew he was aching to have her home. She didn't feel capable, not yet, even though she wanted the three of them to be a happy normal family.

Looking down at Tafiq sleeping peacefully, she marvelled at his mop of dark hair and his olive skin which stood out against the white sheet; she loved him so much. Being in a coma for so long and pregnant at the same time, had strengthened her bond with her baby as she had been so aware of him growing inside her. Nabil was fascinated when she told him that she had known all along he was a boy and that she used to talk to him. Katie also told him she saw her parents many times when she was drifting in and out of consciousness. He wasn't sure if she had seen them or whether she had been dreaming but she became passionate about it, especially when she re-counted her near death experience.

Douglas told him that he had listened to many patients talk about their near-death experiences over the years. Most doctors dismissed these events and put it down to some sort of chemical reaction in the brain. Douglas however, felt different about these happenings, because the patient often described what they had seen when looking down from above. Nabil was only convinced when she told him about his papa describing his looks and character. But most of all she knew things that had happened between father and son that even he had forgotten about.

"My darling, your papa told me he is close to you at the times you need him most and he also said he would be watching over his new grandson. Don't you see Nabil, only the physical body dies, not the spirit," she had told him. She wasn't sure if he believed her until he admitted there had been times over the past few months when he had felt his papa around.

Looking at her watch she was surprised it was nine o'clock. Maybe Nabil wouldn't make it tonight, she thought to herself, but she would see him in the morning when they would be driven to Hertfordshire. One of the nurses had been in to do her observations and check if she needed anything, and now she was feeling tired. She climbed into bed deciding to have an early night.

Katie was already asleep when Nabil came quietly into the room twenty minutes later. Bending down over the cot he kissed his son then looking at his wife sleeping peacefully he thought about how much he wanted to take them home. But he knew he would have to be patient because she'd been through so much.

"Goodnight angel," he whispered, as he kissed her on the forehead then left the room. Katie stirred and opened her eyes. Nabil had not had a chance to shut the door when nurse Martin, stopped to speak to him.

"Mr. Khalifa there was a phone call earlier from Mohammed Khalifa. He was trying to find you because of an urgent business matter. I told him you hadn't arrived back, but that we were expecting you this evening. I asked if he wanted to speak to Mrs Khalifa, but he said no."

Nabil was furious that his uncle had phoned the hospital, but he tried to stay calm.

"Under no circumstances must you ever allow Mohammed Khalifa to speak to my wife, do you understand?"

161

"Eh yes, Mr Khalifa, I'm sorry."

"It's okay it's not your fault. Goodnight." He walked off towards the lift wondering why his uncle had telephoned the hospital. His mamma had said he was at home resting after his heart operation.

Katie froze as soon as she heard the name Mohammed. It was like a knife piercing her heart, but she didn't know why? Trying to call out Nabil's name she found she couldn't speak, and her body felt like lead. Her palms were sweating, her heart was beating fast, and she lay there for a long time in a panic. She kept hearing Nabil and Martin's conversation in her head.

She could not go back to sleep, instead she tossed and turned until she finally dozed off, only to wake suddenly and sit bolt upright. She had started to remember … the telephone call … Mohammed's cruel voice … his vile threats … the fear of his henchman coming after her. Reliving every moment was like watching a video. She could see herself throwing the phone down; knocking their wedding photo to the floor; rushing from their apartment; getting into the lift; bumping into the gentleman as she dashed out of the lift and into the street. Recalling the fear, she'd felt as she ran headlong into the road was terrifying. She hadn't seen the black cab. The next thing she was aware of was the pain and the voices of the crash team in the hospital, then … that floating feeling. Looking down on her own body as they tried to revive her, and that beautiful shaft of light filled with peace and tranquillity. Why did she come back? Hearing Tafiq stirring in his cot roused her and she leant over him with an immense feeling of love. "My son … I came back for you and your papa," she said lovingly picking him up and cradling him to her chest her tears flowing.

Nabil had not yet told Katie how his mamma's feelings had changed towards her. How she was sorry for all the upset, and he had not yet told her everything was going to be different when they returned to the Emirates; he didn't want to dwell on the bad things because she had obviously switched off to them. The doctors told Nabil that something would happen to trigger these memories and it would be frightening for her. They told him it would be much better if he was there at the time which is why he hardly ever left Katie's side. Now she was remembering on her own and the conversation between nurse Martin and Nabil had been the trigger.

She sat on the side of the bed holding Tafiq while rocking backwards and forwards and wondering what to do next. Not knowing that Nabil knew the truth about Mohammed, all she could think of was his cruelty. She felt total panic at the mere thought of him and what he might do in the future. Not thinking rationally, she just wanted to get away from Nabil's family and all the misery they had caused her, the past the present and the future blending together in her mind; she was thoroughly confused.

Hearing someone talking outside her door she hoped and prayed they would not come into her room, she just wanted to be alone to decide what to do next. Tafiq started to whimper, and she knew that if she were to escape from the hospital, she would have to do it as quietly as possible.

"I must get away," she said to herself, "I must get away."

Katie and Tafiq had disappeared from the hospital, and everyone had been puzzled and alarmed as to how mother and baby could disappear so easily without a trace. The medical team who had been caring for them were devastated, after all their hard work to nurse Katie back to health they felt they had failed her. There was such a hue and cry. Nobody had seen them leave the room, let alone the hospital and it seemed incredible this could happen at all. A night nurse had raised the alarm when she came in to check on Katie and found her bed and Tafiq's cot empty; their clothes were missing and some of his soft toys.

Nabil sat in the armchair in the corner of the room stunned at the turn of events. He looked in disbelief at Katie's empty bed and his son's empty cot. Holding the large soft brown teddy bear he had bought in Harrods the day Tafiq was born just made him feel worse. Soft toys were all round the room and the many baby cards and letters sent from family, friends, and well-wishers. Everyone had been so kind. Now these were all that were left, and his family had disappeared.

Douglas MacDonald entered the room. "Nabil the police want to speak to you. I've told them you're obviously upset. Do you feel up to it?" he asked with concern.

"Yes, it's okay I will speak to them. I'll do anything that might bring Katie and Tafiq back to me. Why Douglas? Why? She was doing so well. Recovering from the coma and coping with Tafiq, her memory was beginning to return. How could she do this to me?"

"I cannot answer that. I don't know what's going through her mind. She was looking forward to going to Hertfordshire when I spoke to her yesterday, and she even joked about how she was going to miss me administering to her. There was no sign of stress whatsoever. I really don't know why Nabil?" Douglas answered him feeling utterly helpless.

"I should have cancelled the business meeting yesterday. It's all my fault!"

"Don't blame yourself. You have done everything possible, and you couldn't be with her twenty-four hours a day. Come on now, the police are waiting, and it won't do you any good sitting here." Douglas felt close to this young man, who he now thought of like a son. They'd been through such a lot together in the last few months. Nabil gently laid the teddy bear on the bed and walked out of the room with Douglas, feeling more confused than he had ever felt in his entire life.

Katie sat outside the Shipwrights Public House looking across the small harbour at Padstow. There were many tourists milling around. A few of them were leaning over the harbour railings devouring their Cornish dairy ice creams. Others were sitting on the harbour wall savouring their home-made Cornish pasties and there were certainly plenty of local bakers to buy them from.

Many visitors were admiring the view across the harbour from the North Quay. Looking to her right she could see the many different roofs of the cottages as they sloped up the hill. To her left, she could look across the harbour and out to sea. Katie had always loved water … rivers, ponds, lakes, but especially the ocean. One of the most enthralling sights to her was a full moon glistening onto a calm indigo ocean. It was at times like these when she felt at one with everything.

"Excuse me, love," a tall thin grey haired man was speaking to her, but she had been so deep in thought she hadn't heard him.

"Sorry, I didn't hear what you said."

"I just wondered if I could take this chair next to you. I didn't know if you were waiting for someone?"

"No, I'm not. You can have this one too as I'm going now," and she got up and walked over to the harbour railings.

"Thank you," he said, thinking there was something sad about this young woman, then he turned back to his family who were waiting patiently.

Katie breathed in the fresh sea air. There was a slight breeze, but it was a hot day for the middle of May. In the distance she admired the view of the rolling hills and she marvelled at the patchwork quilt of colours blending into each other. Appreciating beauty around her was something she had always been able to do. She could never understand people charging around from place to place without ever taking time to observe the wonders of nature and the allure of the countryside.

Children were shrieking with delight, as she looked down onto the harbour steps. Eagerly clutching their plastic fishing nets trying to catch small crabs, sprats, or anything else they could fish out of the water; they were obviously enjoying themselves. It was strange to think that Tafiq would be playing like this one day.

It was three weeks since Katie had arrived in Padstow, and she loved the harbour town. For the first two weeks she had hardly ventured out, she just wanted to take care of Tafiq and settle in taking great care not to be noticed. She was sure there must be media coverage about them, and she was relieved that Dorothy, the lady she was renting a room from, did not buy newspapers; she was hoping to be seen as just another tourist.

It was difficult to remember how she had arrived in Padstow, she'd been so desperate to get away from the hospital, and it all seemed a bit blurred. She did recollect withdrawing a lot of money from her account over a two-day period, because she didn't want to draw any out when she arrived in Cornwall. Neither did she want to risk using public transport again, so she went to a small car dealer and bought a second-hand car. A blue Peugeot, which was a bit small, but she felt it would be less conspicuous. Giving the dealer an extra three hundred pounds if he promised not to tell a soul, not even the police, had worked. He promised and said he really didn't want to get involved that he was just trying to make an honest living and not an easy one at that.

She mingled with the tourists when she first arrived and looked for a café or coffee shop. Tafiq had fallen asleep against her chest in his papoose. This had been invaluable to her while she had a rucksack on her back and two bags to carry. Collapsing onto a chair in a café on the North Quay she ordered a cappuccino. She knew Tafiq would be waking up for his feed soon and she only had one more bottle made up, so she had to find somewhere to stay and quick. After drinking her cappuccino and resting for a while she decided to walk through the back streets. Feeling exhausted and apprehensive, but with something driving her on, she knew she needed time to herself.

Katie had not taken in much of her new surroundings because her mind was on automatic pilot but as she walked past a newspaper shop, she stopped suddenly; she had a strong urge to look on the notice board. Maybe there would be a room to let, she thought. She scanned the postcards in the window, bicycles for sale, a chest of drawers, a double bed and two cars, a lady offering an ironing service and a man looking for odd jobs, but nothing to let. Katie walked on disappointed but stopped a few feet from the shop knowing she had to go back and have another look. Oh, what is the point she thought, so she took another couple of steps, but something stopped her again. This time she walked back to the newsagents. She looked at the window with the notice board in and a tall elderly gentleman in shirtsleeves was pinning a postcard on the board. ROOM TO LET, use of bathroom and kitchen, clean and bright, ladies only, please enquire within.

Katie could not believe her luck and was so glad she had retraced her steps; she went into the shop. A few minutes later the gentleman in shirtsleeves, who she took to be the owner of the shop, telephoned a Mrs Jenkins. He told her there was a young lady enquiring after her room and he emphasised that this young lady had a baby. This unnerved her. It would just be my luck she thought if Mrs Jenkins didn't like children.

Fifteen minutes later she was sitting in Honeysuckle Cottage which was at the end of Parnell Court near to the little shop. Tafiq had woken up and she was holding him over her shoulder and tapping him on his back. Mrs Jenkins was in the kitchen making a pot of tea. It gave Katie a chance to look round the sitting room. It was cosy in an 'oldy worldly' sort of way, which of course was in keeping with such a lovely old cottage. There was an open fireplace with a dark wood surround and on the mantelpiece were some Cape Di Monte figurines and a photograph of a happy couple. A stylish dark wood corner unit had some beautiful ornaments on the shelves. An old-fashioned upright piano was on the other side of the fireplace and there were two small cream damask sofas; they went nicely with the pale pink carpet. Antiques and a few Indian artifacts caught her eye too. The wallpaper was pale green above the dado rail and a print of greens and creams below the rail and the oak beams gave the whole place such character. There was a lovely atmosphere and Katie felt very much at home.

"I must admit, my dear, I was not really expecting anyone with a baby, but I thought I would still like to meet you," Mrs Jenkins said as she walked in from the kitchen with a tray of tea and homemade fruitcake. She placed it on the coffee table and starting to pour. "Milk? Sugar?"

"Milk, but no sugar, thank you Mrs Jenkins. Would you mind if I heated up the baby's bottle?"

"No, of course not, my dear, go through to the kitchen, the kettle has just boiled and there's a jug on the side. He's a handsome little chap, what's his name?"

Katie hesitated, "Daniel," she answered as she walked into the charming antique pine kitchen with a table and chairs along one wall. The sink was in front of the window which overlooked a small but pretty garden; the window was open, and she could smell the scent of honeysuckle and roses.

"And your name?"

"Katie … Katie Mitchell," she called out.

"Well, you can call me Dorothy."

Katie poured the water into the jug and put Tafiq's last made-up bottle into it. Please let us stay here, please, please, she prayed to herself. I hope Mrs Jenkins likes babies. Daniel, what made me say his name was Daniel. I hate lying to her, she seems like such a pleasant lady.

"Are you okay? Did you find the jug?" Dorothy asked as Katie walked back into the sitting room.

"Yes, thank you, but I'll have to make up some more bottles soon. Do you think we can stay? Daniel is a good baby and I'm sure he won't disturb you too much."

"Well, I think we could give it a try," Dorothy smiled.

The children with fishing nets were making a lot of noise while proudly showing their mum and dad what they had caught; this brought Katie out of her reverie, and she smiled at them. Walking around the harbour, she looked at the variety of boats and wondered how the owners of these vessels came to choose their names. 'Boston Lady,'

'Speedjib,' 'Padstow Queen,' 'Lady Diana' to name but a few.

Divers were out today. Every now and again the locals would dive for anchors and if they were successful, they would sell them to the local ship chandlers. There was always plenty going on down at the harbour, but she slowly walked towards the shops. It was a break to get away on her own and Dorothy loved to look after the baby. Somehow, she had switched off to Nabil and the Emirates and she knew she was living a double life. Now she was Katie Mitchell, and her son's name was Daniel.

The little narrow streets were becoming familiar to her. Secretly she loved it when tourists started to go home or back to their caravans or guest houses, and it became peaceful once more.

The cottages were so colourful, with an abundance of flowers and well cared for hanging baskets. Walking past the florist on her left and the many little bay windowed shops, she looked at their wares. Jewellery, trinkets, clothes and of course the bakers with the proverbial Cornish pasties in the window. She breathed in the aroma, then stopped at the leather shop to look at the handbags. Katie hadn't bought herself anything for a long time, and she certainly had plenty of money. What she did not want to do was take the risk of visiting the bank again, so she was only using cash; at some point this was going to run out. Walking passed the butcher's shop she crossed the street to the alleyway and Parnell Court.

Honeysuckle Cottage was at the top and as you looked up towards it the plants and flowers and hanging baskets were prolific; it gave such a splash of colour to the outside of the buildings. Her favourite was the bow fronted antique shop at the bottom. The middle-aged couple who owned it had moved from London to start the business. She often browsed and admired the antiques and today she looked in the window to see if there was anything new that had been added. It brought back memories of her parents, sometimes painful and sometimes happy ones. She could still see their antique shop as if it were yesterday.

Last week had been the third anniversary of their deaths and she wished she could go and lay some flowers on their stone, but it was out of the question. Katie couldn't even tell Dorothy why she had been feeling so miserable. She stayed in her room for most of the day looking at a small photo of her mum and dad that she kept in her purse. Feeling them close to her had helped. It was as though they were trying to tell her it didn't matter that she couldn't visit the cemetery; only their ashes were there … not their spirits.

Strolling back to the coffee shop, which was still open, she walked in and sat down near the window. She was staring out of it, when she realised, the waitress was speaking to her.

Shirley was a friendly woman from Newcastle. Divorced at the age of thirty-eight she had come down to Cornwall with her ten-year-old daughter. She was staying with friends who had found her this part-time summer job while she worked out what to do with the rest of her life.

"Hiya Katie."

"Hi Shirley. How are you?"

"Oh, don't ask, it's been a helluva day! I think the whole of Cornwall must have been in here since lunch time pet."

Katie laughed, "Don't exaggerate."

"Well, it certainly feels like it to me. Anyway, what can I do for you? Would you like a piece of your favourite carrot cake?"

"No thank you, not this late in the afternoon. Dorothy is sure to have supper on and I like to do her meals justice. I'll have a cappuccino please. I just wanted to enjoy the peace and quiet before I go back to Daniel."

"He is a little smasher, pet."

"Yes, he is, but it's still good to have a break from him once in a while."

"You're not wrong there, every mum needs a break."

"How's Lilly?"

"She's loving it here, especially as my friends have a daughter the same age. I'll be loath to take her away, but I need to find a permanent job if we're going to stay in Cornwall."

"Yes of course."

"Now I'd better get your cappuccino."

Katie sat and drunk it in silence. Shirley was busy clearing the tables and tidying up. Getting up to leave fifteen minutes later she called out, "Bye Shirley."

"Ta-ra Katie. Give the bairn a kiss for me pet."

"Will do, and good luck with the job hunting."

"Thank you!"

Chapter Fourteen

Katie could hear voices as she opened the front door to the Cottage. Whoever was speaking had obviously not heard her turn the key in the lock. She stopped dead in her tracks as she heard Dorothy's sister Margaret talking about her in the kitchen.

"You mark my words Dorothy there's something mysterious about Katie. Oh, she's nice enough but she's hiding something. You must realise that?"

"Look Margaret she pays the rent, she is a wonderful lodger and Daniel is a little gem. I don't care what sort of life she led before she came to Padstow, that is her business. Why do you let it worry you so much, she hasn't done you any harm has she?"

"No."

"Well then leave well alone my dear. Now I must go up and check on Daniel." Dorothy turned and walked through the lounge. She looked up in surprise at seeing Katie by the front door.

"Sorry Dorothy, did I make you jump? I've only just come in. I'll go and check on Daniel you go back to your sister." Katie ran up the stairs as Margaret appeared in the doorway of the kitchen.

"Oops! Do you think she heard me talking about her?"

"I don't know Margaret, but I sincerely hope not. I'd hate to upset the poor girl."

"Here you go again. You don't know anything about her," Margaret said in a whisper this time.

"No not much, but I do like her. I know she needs peace in her life at the moment and that's what I'm trying to give her."

"Yes, but peace from what?"

"I don't know but she does look sad at times. I'm sure she will tell me in her own time my dear."

"Well, I'd better be off. I can see I'm getting nowhere talking to you."

"No, quite!" Dorothy answered curtly.

Katie came downstairs just as Margaret was sheepishly sliding out of the front door. "Isn't she stopping for supper?"

"No not tonight my dear, she has the grandchildren visiting." Dorothy answered as she closed the door.

After eating a substantial meal Katie washed up the dinner things then went upstairs. Before she laid on her bed, she stood in front of the window looking out into the semi darkness of the garden and the beautiful countryside beyond; she was deep in thought until she heard Tafiq murmuring in his sleep.

Her room was extremely comfortable. There was a single bed with the cot next to it and the quilt cover and curtains were silvery grey. The walls a pale pink, with a pretty border to match. In the corner there was a single wardrobe and next to it a chest of drawers both in antique pine. A tall bookcase made her feel very much at home. Many classic books were on the shelves, in fact all the books she had grown to love over the years. Jane Ayre, Middlemarch, Pride and Prejudice, Wuthering Heights, Lorna Doone, Great Expectations and many more. Katie felt a bit like one of the characters in these books, as if everything around her was an illusion; living in two different worlds did not suit her nature at all.

Tafiq stirred again as she sat on her bed. She rested her hands on her chin and looked at him adoringly.

Remembering the conversation between Dorothy and Margaret worried her and she did not understand why her sister was so concerned; she had done nothing to upset her. Was it so hard to believe she was a single parent trying to start a new life in Cornwall? She was beginning to think she really was Katie Mitchell and that Tafiq was Daniel.

Lying back on the bed she stared up at the ceiling. She was enjoying her stay in Cornwall, but she knew she should be somewhere else. Whenever she found herself thinking of the Emirates, she would push all thoughts of Nabil to the back of her mind. Tonight however, she was finding it extremely difficult not to think about her husband.

Katie tried to switch off to her life in Dubai. There was still the terrible fear and dread when she thought of her married life there, so she would suppress her feelings as much as she could. But his spirit was with her, she was certain of that. She could smell his body scent and she felt as though he was lying next to her, he must be thinking about me at this very moment, she thought to herself.

Nabil was lying on their bed. The bed they had shared together. Staring up at the ceiling he felt utterly desolate because he missed Katie and longed to hold her and Tafiq in his arms. His thinking had become totally unbalanced lately. One minute he was longing for his wife the next he was angry with her. When he was thinking rationally, he knew she must have been confused and still suffering from her head injury. But then he would feel anger because of what she was putting him through; she had taken their son away from him. Depleted of energy and ill-tempered with everybody, he was beginning to understand why his mamma had been

175

so angry and bitter after losing his papa. Although he felt very strongly that Katie and Tafiq were alive, it was never-the-less still a terrible loss, and he had a continuous ache in his heart. He wanted to blame everyone, the staff at the hospital, the police for not finding her, but most of all he blamed Mohammed for his despicable behaviour towards her. Nabil had still not got to the bottom of the whole affair. He knew he would not, until Katie was in a fit state to tell him herself. If she came back to him that was. "In the name of Allah, I cannot contemplate a life without my wife and son," he said aloud.

Knowing he would bump into Mohammed at some point he hoped it would not be for a long while; the way he felt about him there was bound to be bloodshed. How could you have two brothers so different in character? The disparity between Mohammed and Ibrahim was all too obvious. Why couldn't his uncle have died instead of his papa … he couldn't believe he was having such a terrible thought.

Douglas MacDonald had stayed in contact with Nabil ever since Katie had gone missing. Reassuring him whenever he could and telling him his anger was natural under the circumstances. But that he must remember Katie may not have been in a fit mental state when she disappeared. Something could have triggered off a bad memory or memories and she had panicked. He also tried to reassure Nabil that Katie would take great care of Tafiq and sooner or later when she was feeling clearer in her mind, she would turn up. "I hope you're right Douglas … I do hope you're right because I can't take much more," he said to himself.

Sitting on the side of the bed he suddenly found the apartment too quiet. His mamma and sister Shazia were in Abu Dhabi visiting Yasmin and Rashid. "I must do something. I can't sit here all day waiting for the telephone to ring."

He found himself thinking of his wife once more and he decided when they were all back together again the whole house would be redecorated from top to bottom. Katie had never felt it was their home and now he wanted to make it up to her. They would buy new furniture, fixtures and fittings, a new beginning without his mamma and sister. Although Fatima had softened towards Katie, she still thought it would be best if they went and lived in Abu Dhabi with Yasmin and Rashid especially as Yasmin was expecting their first baby after such a long wait. Nabil was relieved to hear this and did not try to dissuade her. They needed a fresh start and he wanted to make it as easy as possible for his wife and son to come home.

Trying to think of positive things to stop him feeling restless, the beach villa came into his mind; it held such fond memories. Those were happy days, and all he wanted to do was think of his angel as she had been then and blot out the last nine months of heartache. Remembering when they strolled along the water's edge on Chicago Beach in bare feet made him smile. He had never done such a thing with any other women. But he had never felt totally at ease with anyone else. Nature was something they both loved, not that he had much time to appreciate it, and they felt free from the rest of the family when they were there. Smiling to himself as he pictured them running and laughing along the empty beach when Katie had looked radiant made him love her even more. He remembered scooping her up in his arms on several occasions and carrying her back to the villa where they had made love.

Reminiscing made him feel better for a short while, but afterwards he was still agitated, so he phoned his friend

177

Hakeem to see if he was in England. Thankfully, he was in his Bayswater apartment. He answered the phone straightaway because he was about to call Nabil to let him know he was in London. Katie would have called that synchronicity he thought. But he wasn't to know that as soon as he left his apartment, to go and meet Hakeem, there would be a phone call from the detective in charge of the case; they had found a lead at last. They had discovered that a small car dealer in Exeter had sold his wife a blue Peugeot. At least now they knew she was somewhere in that area.

Katie went downstairs to sit with Dorothy who was in the lounge knitting something for Daniel. Listening to a play on radio four she looked up from her knitting when she heard her on the stairs.

"You don't mind if I join you do you Dorothy?"

"No, of course not, my dear. Would you like a sherry?"

"No, thank you," she answered as she sat on the other sofa and reached for a magazine. "You carry on listening to your play, I don't want to disturb you."

Dorothy listened to the last fifteen minutes and Katie browsed through the Woman's Weekly. Not her choice of magazine, but she was not reading it anyway. Wandering into the kitchen to get herself a glass of water, she sighed heavily.

"You're very restless tonight, Katie." Dorothy commented when her play had finished.

"Yes, sorry," she felt close to tears and was feeling utterly miserable.

"You don't have to apologise. Is anything the matter my dear? Did Margaret upset you this afternoon?" She suspected Katie had overheard her sister's remarks. "You mustn't take any notice, as I told her it's lovely having you here and Daniel really is a sweetie."

"It's good of you to say so, Dorothy and I'm glad you've had hardly any sleepless nights since we've been here."

"Now don't you go worrying yourself on that score. It's lovely having a baby in the house and he is so good. I could never have children you know."

"Oh, I am sorry."

"That's all right, my dear, I soon got over the initial disappointment. We lived in India for quite a few years, so I kept myself busy. It was a good life and there were always plenty of other people's children around," she said as she got up from the sofa and reached for the photograph on the mantelpiece. "George died ten years ago from a sudden heart attack; he never had a day's illness in his life."

"That must have been a terrible shock!"

"Devastating ... but I know one thing for certain, it was the best way for him to go, he would never have coped with being ill, or God forbid, bedridden. As much as I miss him, I wouldn't have wanted him to have had a long, drawn-out illness. It would have been a terrible end to the life of such a lovely man."

"I'd like to hear more about your life in India," Katie remarked as she looked at the photograph of Dorothy and George.

"Okay my dear, if you're sure," she said as she sat down once more and took a sip of her sherry. "We went to India in 1936. George was an officer in the Royal Army Medical Corps, as it was called then. We'd only been married for a few months, but of course in those days you always followed your husband. I knew before we were married George was likely to be posted to India. I had never been out there, but my grandparents had lived there for most of their adult life, and I used to love listening to their wonderful stories of the colourful

179

processions. I remember my grandfather describing the elephants, how magnificently dressed they were and how well the mahouts trained and looked after them; that's the Indian boys. He loved to talk about the way of life that he had known, so I felt as though I knew the country already. It's such a shame there was so much unrest in those days, but then I think there'll always be turmoil in India. Being such a vast country and with so many religions in one land often leads to feuding and fighting."

"Did you like living in India?"

"Most of the time I did. We were thoroughly spoilt, and we lived in luxury compared to many of the Indians. We had servants, but if they hadn't worked for us, they would have been poverty stricken. At least we treated them fairly and I often gave things to my maid, Chitra, who was such a sweet soul. I wonder what happened to her?" Dorothy mused and was lost in thought for a few moments, but she soon came back to the present when they heard Daniel crying upstairs.

"I think he's picking up my restlessness," said Katie and she ran upstairs to see to him.

"I'll make us some cocoa."

It was becoming a nightly ritual. Katie did not always fancy cocoa, but she knew it pleased Dorothy when she joined her for a cosy chat, as she put it.

"Is Daniel alright my dear?" she asked as she came back into the room carrying two steaming mugs.

"Yes, he went back to sleep when I gave him his dummy."

"Would you like anything to eat?"

"Oh no thank you, not after eating your wonderful steak and mushroom pie."

Dorothy laughed. "George always loved my cooking, not that I did much when we were in India of course. It would most certainly have caused trouble in the kitchen if I'd tried to take cooks job away from him and he used to make the most amazing dishes."

"What was your favourite part of India?"

"Oh, most definitely Rhaniket. Mind you it was a while before we could enjoy it. George contracted Diphtheria from a little girl in Lucknow, who had been rushed into hospital. It was such a bad case, and she was going purple because she couldn't breathe. George, with the help of a nurse, had to perform an emergency tracheotomy. Not having time to put on a mask meant as soon as he made the incision the force of the mucous was like a torrent and he got some of it in his face."

"Yuk, how awful!"

"Yes, it was rather, but at least he saved the child's life, even though he became extremely ill. I think the entire staff of the hospital must have visited George and they were wonderful. Then, we were sent to Rhaniket so he could convalesce. It was a cool hill station about two days journey from Lucknow, by train and car. Do you know my dear after leaving the train the journey was another fifty miles or more and along narrow roads; we were climbing up and round all the way. You've no idea how frightening it was at times, but I would not have missed it for the world. We would look over the sides and see the winding roads hundreds of feet below us. Roads on which we had already travelled."

"Sounds exciting!"

"It was and after a while it became more beautiful, with woodlands, plants and rare flowers along the roadside and the grey faced monkeys. I used to love watching them, they were so inquisitive. They followed us for quite a time, jumping from tree to tree." Dorothy's mind wandered for a few moments remembering those wonderful events in India long ago. "Well … after an exceptionally long and dusty journey we arrived. It was a smallish town with the usual native surroundings and the constant chatter and bargaining was going on in the bazaar.

The garrison compound was made up of people like George who had only arrived for the summer season away from the fierce heat down on the plains. It had a small hospital, but it was in such lovely surroundings with the most fantastic views. We could see the snow-capped mountain peaks of the Himalayas in the distance, hundreds of miles away. In between were deep valleys, rolling hills and woodlands." Once again, she had a dreamy, faraway expression on her face, as she was being transported back to the distant past.

"At first George was tired and didn't really have much energy, but as he became stronger and looked more like his old self, we went horse riding in the hills. It was beautiful scenery, and the sunsets were magnificent. We were quite upset when we had to leave. The only thing I had missed in Lucknow was our piano. Rhaniket always held such fond memories for us," she gave a heavy sigh.

"It's a shame I don't play the piano much now, but my fingers aren't as nimble as they used to be. I hope I haven't bored you my dear?"

"Bored? You must be joking! I want to catch the next plane to India." This made Dorothy laugh.

Katie was secretly wishing she was back in the Middle East. She would love to tell Dorothy about the sunsets in the desert and the wonderful night skies adorned with stars; like a panoply delicately woven as she had written in one of her poems.

"I think I can hear Daniel, my dear."

Katie brought him down a few minutes later and gave him his last bottle for the night. How lucky she was to have such a contented baby who was already in a routine.

"He is handsome. Where does his father come from?"

Katie hesitated, because she didn't want to lie to this warm-hearted lady anymore.

Dorothy saw the distress on Katie's face. "Oh, I'm so sorry, my dear, I didn't mean to upset you. I shouldn't pry."

"It's alright ... Daniel's father is Arabic ... well, Emirati," she answered with tears rolling down her cheeks. "I miss him so much."

"Here, let me take Daniel upstairs now he's asleep. I'll be back in a minute then we can talk if you want to that is."

Katie let the tears flow, suddenly realizing she could not live a double life a moment longer. She was not Katie Mitchell, and her son was not Daniel. Dorothy came back downstairs and sat next to her on the sofa.

"This is all because of what my sister said isn't it?"

Katie nodded through her tears.

"You don't have to tell me anything if you don't want to. It's really none of my business."

"His name is not Daniel, it's Tafiq. Tafiq Ibrahim Alan Khalifa."

"Well, there's a fine name."

"I'm only glad you don't read the newspapers but I'm sure your sister will soon put two and two together. What am I going to do? I don't want to go back, not yet, but I love Nabil and I long to see him."

Dorothy held Katie close while she sobbed. Having to suppress her feelings in the last three weeks, the fear of Mohammed, the awful memories of the accident and the thought of having to live in the town house with Fatima, plus suffering from the after-effects of the coma was just too much. She cried until the tears finally subsided, and she gently pulled herself away.

"I'm so sorry, Dorothy."

"Sorry for what? Crying? It's better out than in my dear. If you hold on to it, you will only make yourself ill and then who will look after that darling baby of yours? Come on dry your eyes," and she reached for the tissues from under the coffee table. "Do you want to tell me all about it?"

Now that Katie's memory had come back, she could tell Dorothy everything. By the time they heard the grandmother clock on the landing strike ten, she felt completely drained. Dorothy could not believe a twenty-five-year-old could have gone through so much since her parents had died three years ago; she felt this young woman's pain when she saw the look of despair on her troubled face.

"I don't know what to do, Dorothy."

"Well, if your husband loves you as much as you say he does then he will have to sort out your living arrangements and without his mother."

"I vaguely remember Fatima talking to me when I was in a coma. Her English had improved, and she was saying how much she wanted me and the bee, that's baby, to come home. She said that everything would be different, but I didn't hear anymore because I drifted off."

"I don't suppose you know whether to believe her after what she put you through."

"That's right … I don't know how sincere she is … and then there's Mohammed."

"He sounds like a nasty piece of work. The first thing you must do when you see your husband is to tell him the truth about his uncle. You can't keep it to yourself any longer."

"No, I can't!"

"If you don't tell Nabil all about it you won't be able to mend your broken marriage, then you'll be letting Mohammed win."

Katie was exhausted and couldn't think about it anymore.

"Now, you take yourself up to bed. You need a good night's sleep, and we'll discuss it again tomorrow."

"I don't know if I'll be able to sleep."

"You will. I'm going to bring you up a hot toddy. George used to swear by them, he said they were medicinal. Medicinal my foot!"

Katie laughed.

"That's better!" Dorothy remarked. "Now, up the stairs with you, you look fit to drop my dear."

Katie got herself undressed and into bed. She leant over to kiss Tafiq then she fell back onto the pillow. Dorothy came in with the hot toddy five minutes later.

"There get that down you," and she waited while Katie drank it all.

"Thank you, I didn't think I would like it," she said as she gave the empty glass back.

"Like it or not it will help you sleep. Goodnight and God bless you my dear. Remember tomorrow is the first day of the rest of your life.

Chapter Fifteen

Detective Inspector Marshall phoned for the third time that evening. Nabil heard it ring as he walked through the door of his apartment. Picking up the receiver in a hurry he nearly dropped it.

"Mr Khalifa?"

"Yes."

"DI Marshall here. I phoned earlier but you were out."

"Any news of my wife and son?"

"Yes, we have a lead. Mrs Khalifa bought a small blue Peugeot from a car dealer in Exeter. She paid him an extra three hundred pounds not to say a word to anyone, but when he was questioned by my officers he got scared. After a bit of pressure, he reneged on his promise. At least we know now your wife is in the West Country."

"That makes sense!"

"Why?"

"She might be on her way to Cornwall. Her parents loved it there. Katie often talks about their holidays in that part of the country."

"We need to speak to her parents then. It might …"

"No, you can't Inspector. They died in a car crash three years ago when they were driving to Cornwall."

"Oh … sorry to hear that. But it would help if we knew where they spent their holidays. It's a big county."

"Her best friend, Sue, used to go on holiday with them, but I don't know how to contact her. My wife keeps her address book in her bag in case she needs to phone somebody while she's out. But I can tell you Inspector they stayed in many towns and villages."

"We will follow the lead we have and concentrate on the Cornwall area then. It won't be easy for your wife to hide away much longer."

"You make her sound like a criminal instead of a patient from St Thomas' Hospital."

"Sorry! Bad choice of words. We will be in touch if we have any more news."

"Thank you."

This latest development helped Nabil feel more positive. Hoping it would only be a matter of time before Katie and Tafiq were found, he went into his prayer room for some solace. For reasons he did not understand, he felt closer to his papa when he was in there. He missed him so much, but if Katie was right, he was watching over them all.

The following day he tried to focus on business phone calls. Rashid was coping well, and they had a large competent team working for their company; it was a weight off his mind. Mohammed was still at home recovering from his heart surgery, so at least he wasn't causing any trouble. He felt sorry for his Aunt Aamira though, who must be desperately trying to cope with his mood swings. At least when he was well, he kept out of her way.

Nabil missed going to Sheik Mohammed's daily Majlis though he and Rashid couldn't always get there. It was so important to keep good relations with the Sheik and the government. Most businessmen attended these councils, and it was a tradition that went back centuries. You could raise serious matters with Sheiks, elders, merchants, and legal experts. He liked to know what was going on in his homeland but for now he had to make do with the newspaper; it was a bit out of date by the time it arrived from the Middle East.

The following day there was another lead. Katie had stopped at a cafe to feed the baby, so the police knew for certain she was in Cornwall. Nabil wanted to go there and search himself, but the police advised him not to.

"Please Mr Khalifa, leave it to us. At least if you stay in your apartment, we'll know where to contact you when we find your wife and son."

"Yes, alright." Having little energy left to argue, he resigned himself to staying put in Grosvenor Square while the police continued their search. Detective Inspector Marshall was right of course, and he was grateful for all they were doing. It was because Katie had recently come out of a coma and may have had some sort of mental setback at the time of her disappearance, that they were searching at all. Feeling exhausted, he sat on the large soft sofa and was fast asleep in a matter of seconds.

Katie slept soundly for a few hours. Chanel No. 5 had wafted under her nose as she settled down for the night, but she was even too tired to acknowledge her dear mum. Soon after drinking the hot toddy Dorothy had prepared for her, she was fast asleep.

It was difficult trying to rouse herself at five thirty in the morning when she heard Tafiq waking up for his feed. Opening her eyes wasn't easy either because they were swollen from all the crying the night before and her head ached. Feeling as though she could sleep for a week she reluctantly climbed out of bed.

Holding Tafiq over her shoulder she went downstairs to heat up his bottle and he nestled into her neck. She felt such love for her son. He smelled delicious and was so soft and warm as she kissed him on top of his head. What a comfort he was too her, but did she have the right to keep him away from his papa, she thought ruefully.

After breakfast, Dorothy had insisted Katie go back to bed for a while, if only to rest her eyes. Tafiq needed some fresh air, so she took him out in the small pram they had acquired. After putting a cold flannel on her eyes to try and take the puffiness away Katie dozed off; thankfully, her headache had subsided.

Later in the day Dorothy suggested she go to see a medium friend of hers, who lived in a village a few miles away.

"A spiritual medium?"

"Yes, my dear, why not?"

"I have nothing against mediums, I just hadn't thought about going to see one."

"I wouldn't have suggested it if I didn't think you believed, Katie. But you always seem to know when your mother's around and I was captivated when you told me about your near-death experience, and what followed it. To think that while you lay in a coma shut out from the physical world your mind and spirit were elsewhere. I find it fascinating!

"It's an experience I won't forget for the rest of my life," Katie said with a faraway look on her face that lasted a few seconds, then she brought herself back to the present. "Tell me a bit more about Hannah."

"Well, she's a good and trusted friend and I know she'll be able to help you. She paints too, and extremely well I might add. Her home is called Hillside Cottage and its beautiful though why it's called a cottage I will never know; to me it's a large house, but what do I know about these things? Her husband was a lovely gentleman who was left the property by his parents. Sadly, he died five years ago, and their son and daughter live in London."

"She sounds like an interesting lady, and I'd love to see Hillside Cottage."

"Would you like me to phone her my dear? You will get proof that your loved ones live on, not that you need it, but you could certainly do with some guidance."

"That's true!" She agreed, and Dorothy rang to make an appointment.

Hannah felt very strongly she needed to see this young lady as soon as possible and she had just had a cancellation for that afternoon. As she put the phone down, she smiled; synchronicity at its best, she thought.

Katie was feeling nervous when they arrived at Hillside Cottage just before three o'clock, but Dorothy reassured her. Hannah opened the front door with a beaming smile on her face and gave them a such a warm welcome; she insisted on showing Katie round while Dorothy watched Tafiq.

It was built into the side of a hill, but it was much bigger than it looked from the outside. They were shown into the large lounge where there were two huge midnight blue sofas, with lots of different coloured cushions scattered on them. An amazing Indian rug was in the middle of the parquet flooring and paintings seemed to cover every inch of wall. Through an archway there was a dining room with large French windows and a fabulous view of the garden. There was a door which led into a large and typical country kitchen with pots and pans hanging from the ceiling, bunches of sweet-smelling herbs dangling from hooks, two shelves full of cookery books and a black range. In the conservatory there was a large wooden table with matching chairs and plants in abundance; the door opened onto the garden and the wonderful smell of honeysuckle and Jasmin permeated everything. It was like something out of a magazine, an unusual shape with every plant and shrub

190

imaginable; a natural garden with a kaleidoscope of colour and obviously well-loved and cared for.

A friendly, calming atmosphere awaited everyone who entered this beautiful home, thought Katie, as Hannah showed her upstairs. There were three bedrooms and two bathrooms and a spiral staircase leading up to the most delightful art studio with plenty of windows overlooking the garden. It ran the width of the cottage and had obviously been an attic at one point. Hannah was an artist as well as a spiritual medium and she had some beautiful paintings on show. What an interesting woman, Katie thought as they made their way back downstairs.

After they checked on Dorothy and the baby, Hannah took her through to the conservatory once more because this was where she did her readings. Besides beautiful plants there were Buddhas and crystals everywhere, plus a water feature in the corner; the soothing sound of running water was bliss. Katie thought Hannah looked about sixty-five with a caring face that made you feel comfortable in her presence. Wearing colourful Bohemian clothes suited her. She also had a wonderful energy which filled the whole room. Not knowing what to expect from her reading because it was her first visit to a medium, Katie was feeling excited as well as apprehensive.

An hour and fifteen minutes later they walked into the lounge, just as Dorothy was putting Tafiq's bottle down. Katie took him and held him in the crook of her arm.

"My, he is a good looker," said Hannah."

"Thank you."

"Would you two like some tea and cake? It won't take me a moment to put the kettle on."

"It's up to you, my dear," Dorothy asked Katie, thinking she still looked tired.

"No, I'd rather go if you don't mind. I have a lot to think about. Thank you so much Hannah, especially for the spiritual healing, I feel more relaxed than I have done for a while."

"Remember what I said, your husband needs you and you are meant to be together. It was clear in your reading that obstacles are being swept away so you can be together. You will have a good life, but it will always be eventful. Follow your inner-feelings, Katie, and you will know what to do." Hannah gave her a big hug; she felt as if she'd known this young lady all her life.

"Thank you."

"I'll see you soon, Dorothy," said Hannah as they walked to the front door.

"Very soon I hope, my dear."

Waving until the small car was out of sight, she sighed to herself as she walked back into the cottage. Some people have so much to cope with, she thought.

Hannah had recorded the reading on a tape so during the evening they both listened to it. Sitting transfixed, Dorothy thought it was exceptional. It surely proved the hereafter, and it was so accurate going by what Katie had told her the previous night.

"Thank you for suggesting it, Dorothy, she really is good."

"I told you she was, she's quite well known around these parts you know."

"I can understand why. It's certainly given me much to think about and I feel calmer now compared to last night."

"That's excellent. You're going to need to be calm when making a decision."

"Indeed!" replied Katie wistfully.

"You're welcome to stay here as long as you like, but as Hannah said your husband misses you both and is beside himself with worry."

"Poor Nabil, I've put him through so much."

"You have my dear, but through no fault of your own."

"My husband may not see it that way. I took his son away from him and it was a cruel thing to do."

"But you weren't in your right mind, which is not at all surprising."

"I just remember lying frozen in my bed, after overhearing Nabil talking to the nurse. My memory was hazy, but I had a horrible feeling of foreboding at the mere mention of Mohammed's name. I was confused, but my overriding thought was that I had to get away," Katie looked agitated.

"Now, now, don't go getting yourself upset. You must remember my dear Nabil doesn't know that you overheard his conversation with the nurse. When you tell him and the doctors what really happened, they will understand."

"You're so wise and I'm so lucky to have found you."

"It's nothing to do with luck, my dear. It was your mother who guided you to the shop window and to me, and you know it."

"Yes, you're right of course … my parents continue to watch over me."

"And Katie, it sounds like Nabil's wicked uncle is very ill, so there's nothing to stop you going home."

"Yes, Hannah was quite clear about that, but she also said he's full of bitterness and there is a black cloud around him. I feel quite sorry for him at times." Dorothy patted her hand then got up from the sofa.

"Right, I'm going to make us some cocoa."

Katie sat back against the soft cushions. It had been a strange day, but it was only nine-thirty, and she felt a sudden surge of energy. Tafiq was down for the night, and she thought a walk to the harbour would do her good.

"Dorothy, do you mind if I skip cocoa?" she asked walking into the kitchen.

"No of course not. Do you want something stronger?"

"Oh no ... it's just that ..." Katie hesitated.

"What is it, my dear?"

"I really feel the need to go down to the harbour. I have a lot of thinking to do, but Tafiq might wake up and I don't want you to think I'm taking you for granted."

"Oh, go on with you, it will do you good."

"But what if you want to go to bed?"

"Look when you get to my age you don't need so much sleep. When I go to bed early, I always read for an hour or two anyway, so off you go."

Ten minutes later, Katie reached the harbour. Walking past the Shipwrights Arms she decided to sit on a bench in front of the railings. It was a beautiful warm June evening. Kicking her sandals off and drawing her knees up under her chin she wrapped her arms around them and gazed across the ocean.

It was interesting listening to a group of people outside the pub, their chatter was lively and there was plenty of laughter. Your whole world could be in tiny pieces and yet life goes on around you she thought.

Looking out to sea, she noticed how beautiful it was at this time of night. It was twilight, the lights had just been switched on and were glistening on the water. A strong breeze had started to blow, and she could hear the sea splashing against the harbour wall below. Dusk had always been her favourite part of the day in England.

Katie was astonished by the things Hannah had said to her in her reading and she hoped she was right about the many positive changes. It was easy to trust her, and she felt she was sincere. She also knew for certain that

Dorothy had not told her anything about her life prior to her reading. Sitting quietly, she found herself sending out thoughts for guidance not knowing whether she was asking God or her mum and dad; it didn't seem to matter either way.

It became quieter when the noisy crowd left the pub. Time seemed to stand still as she breathed in the sea air and let her mind drift. Katie stayed in this meditative state for some time when a thought suddenly came into her head … Douglas MacDonald … I must get in touch with Douglas. Feeling more optimistic she, intuitively knew this was the right thing to do. Energy seemed to have returned to her in abundance since Hannah had given her healing. Now she felt the same driving force she'd experienced when she had woken from her coma; an energy she found hard to explain. Doctors and nurses had been amazed that she walked so soon after being bed ridden for seven months, especially Douglas who cared so much about her well-being.

Aching for Nabil she knew she couldn't live without him, and her mind wandered back to Jumeirah, but not to the town house they shared with Fatima. Instead, she was in their villa at Chicago Beach, which was part of the Chicago Beach Village. It wasn't the luxury she missed but the tranquillity when they were completely on their own. It had not been often enough, thought Katie.

From the kitchen window of the villa, you could see the desert which seemed to give off an air of mystery. There were camels and goats wandering in amongst the palm trees and she loved to watch them. Their bedroom terrace looked across the ocean and they enjoyed sitting there after dinner; especially when there was a full moon shining on the water making silver paths. On nights like these worries seemed to pale into insignificance. Such precious moments, but little did they know at the time just how precious they really were.

Looking at her watch she realised forty minutes had past, since she first sat on the bench, and yet it only seemed like a few minutes. Dorothy's wise words came into her mind as she made her way back to Honeysuckle Cottage … 'Tomorrow is the first day of the rest of your life.'

Katie was resolved to give Douglas a call, she did not know why exactly but she knew it was important to speak with him. After all, he was a dear friend and had saved her life. She told Dorothy what she had decided to do.

"I think that's a splendid idea. You two young people could do with an intermediary."

The following morning when Tafiq was in his cot and Dorothy had popped to the shops she decided it was as good a time as any to make her phone call; she was nervous when she dialled the number."

"Doctor MacDonald's residence."

"Douglas," said a quiet voice at the other end of the telephone.

"Yes?"

"It's me!"

"Katie is that you? Where are you? No … don't answer that if you don't want to." Douglas knew he had to be careful not to frighten her off. "How are you feeling?"

"Good … I'm feeling good."

"And how is Tafiq?"

"He's doing well, and he's such a contented baby."

"You were lucky to catch me, I was about to leave to meet someone for lunch." He did not tell her the person he was meeting was her husband.

"Oh, I'm sorry."

"No, please don't worry," he replied, wanting to keep her on the phone for as long as possible.

"Douglas, I need to see you."

"As your neurologist or your friend?"

"Both! I want to meet up with you before I see Nabil. I'm trying to get my mind straight ... I've remembered a lot of things ... and I want to do what's best for all of us, do you think he will understand?"

"I'm sure he will when I explain it to him, and he'll be so happy you've contacted somebody. But I need to know where you are Katie?"

"I'm in Padstow in Cornwall. Can you get away from the hospital? I know how busy you are and how essential your work is."

"As luck should have it, I'm on leave for the next week with nothing special planned, so I can come down tomorrow."

"That's fantastic, thank you so much Douglas," Katie was relieved, and she gave him Dorothy's address.

"There is one thing that must be done before I drive down to Cornwall though, the police need to be informed. Nabil will have to do that, and I must find a guest house to stay in."

"Yes of course, the police need to be told. I was dreading it in case they turned up on Dorothy's doorstep after she's been so good to me." She explained to him that she was renting a room in Dorothy's cottage. "We can sort out a B&B for you Douglas. It's still only June so there will be plenty of vacancies. I'll see you tomorrow then."

"I look forward to seeing you both and being introduced to Dorothy too."

"Bye Douglas ... and thank you." Putting the receiver down, she felt as though a burden had been lifted off her shoulders; she had obviously done the right thing. It was no coincidence he'd been home when she phoned, and it was certainly no coincidence he was about to start a week's leave. The hand of fate was reaching out to her, and she knew she was being guided.

Douglas stood there for a while staring at the telephone listening to the purr of the dialling tone; he replaced the receiver then hurried out of his apartment because he was running late. It was such a stroke of luck he'd been home when Katie rang, or was it luck? Stepping out onto the pavement he hailed a taxi and twenty minutes later he arrived at the restaurant in Carlton Towers Hotel. The head waiter showed him to the table where Nabil was sitting. Not knowing how he was going to contain himself he tried to look calm.

"Douglas!" Nabil stood up and they shook hands. He waited for his friend to get comfortable before he sat down again. Douglas always admired his impeccable manners.

"I apologise for being late."

"My dear friend, there is much to worry about in this life and being late for lunch is not one of them."

"No, of course not," he replied, thinking about the telephone conversation he'd just had with Katie.

After ordering their lunch it was obvious Nabil needed to talk.

"Douglas when I was in Dubai, Mohammed had a massive heart attack in my office, and I think it was my fault. He's just come out of hospital after having heart surgery."

"What makes you say it was your fault?"

Nabil told him what happened three weeks ago from the time his uncle barged into his office in Dubai until his collapse. Although he despised him for what he had done to Katie, he was feeling guilty about the argument and the way he had gripped his collar so tightly. Feeling sick to the stomach when Mohammed told him how he had threatened his wife if she didn't take the money and leave, had been the last straw.

"So, you had a terrible argument. If I had been in your position, I'm sure I would have reacted the same way after his dreadful revelations. And to call your son a half-breed was utterly contemptable. Look Nabil, your father had a heart attack and Mohammed's heart condition meant he was like a walking time bomb. It could have happened at any time, whether you had a fight or not."

"I know what you're saying Douglas, and I certainly didn't feel any emotion for a few days, but now I keep seeing him on his knees, gasping for breath."

"Just be glad he didn't die!"

"But sometimes I do wish he had died instead of my papa. My thoughts are all over the place."

"It's been nearly nine months since Katie's accident, and you've been through an unimaginable amount of stress. It's put a strain on you and finding out your uncle is responsible for your wife ending up in a coma is hard to take. It's not surprising your thoughts are muddled."

Nabil looked dejected.

"Do you want the police to know what your uncle has done?"

"No. In our culture we tend to deal with family troubles ourselves and mamma wouldn't like it because it would bring shame on us. Plus, if it got out it could have an adverse effect on the business. I don't want to risk that after my papa built it up to where it is today."

"Then somehow you must try and let go of what your uncle has done, and Katie will have to try as well. Don't forget she doesn't know you've found out about it and when she does, you'll be able to face the future together. Try and focus on your wife and son coming home safely."

"And when will that be, next week? Next month?" He sounded bitter.

"It could be sooner than you think," replied Douglas feeling guilty because he had not yet told him about the telephone call.

"Every night I dream they are home safe, and we're starting a new life together. I pray to Allah for their safe return."

Douglas placed his hand on Nabil's arm trying to give him what little comfort he could. He took his hand away when the waiter came up with their meal. But seeing the tears in his eyes he could stand it no longer and decided to tell him about the phone call. "I have some good news for you."

Nabil looked up. He was not hungry and was just moving the food around on his plate, feeling thoroughly miserable and pessimistic.

"News? What news?" He looked puzzled.

"To my surprise, Katie phoned me just before I left to meet you, that's why I was late."

"My wife phoned, and you didn't think to tell me until now," he cried, dropping his knife and fork onto his plate. It made a clattering noise and caused people to look over to their table.

"Please calm down and listen to what I have to say." Douglas repeated the conversation word for word that he'd had with Katie. Understandably Nabil was beside himself and he wanted to go with him to meet her, but Douglas insisted he could not.

"I cannot go against her wishes, surely you must see that my friend." It took all his strength and reasoning to pacify him.

"Let me meet her first," he insisted. "Katie trusts me and wants to see me as a friend and her doctor, and I need to see for myself how she is health wise."

"Yes of course you do." Nabil had calmed down and agreed that Douglas must go on his own. "I will speak to Detective Inspector Marshall. I just hope they haven't found her already because they're in Cornwall as we speak."

Driving over the Tamar Bridge the following morning felt right. Knowing that Nabil had informed the police yesterday afternoon, meant there was no risk of them turning up before he did, and he was grateful for that. They were only doing their job, but it could have set Katie back if they'd knocked on Dorothy's front door looking for her. This break may have helped her sort herself out, or she may still be confused, but he would soon find out.

Leaving Nabil behind was tough, but he knew he had to, he could not let his wife down. He wanted to do what was right for these two young people; he found himself praying even though he hadn't been inside a Catholic church for many years. It was a delicate situation, but he cared about them, and the baby of course. Until he knew Katie's state of mind, he had to tread carefully, though he was not unduly worried about Tafiq. She would love and care for him. Having the baby had probably kept her going throughout her present ordeal. He had given her the reason she needed to recover from the terrible effects of the coma, and yet it was more than that; she had an inner strength which helped her through, and it had been blindingly obvious to the medical team.

Nearing Padstow, he was trying to admire the scenery, but he had too much on his mind and he had to stop and look at his map.

201

Chapter Sixteen

Douglas arrived at Honeysuckle Cottage about eleven thirty and he thought it looked charming. He enjoyed the scent from the honeysuckle growing over the front of the cottage while he waited for Dorothy to open the front door.

"Doctor MacDonald?"

"Yes, Mrs Jenkins, pleased to meet you," he replied holding his hand out to shake hers.

"Oh please, call me Dorothy." She showed this eminent doctor into the lounge.

"Then you must call me Douglas."

Katie was sitting on one of the sofas holding Tafiq over her shoulder and it was heartening to see them both. Obviously, she was nervous, but she soon felt at ease in his company. He couldn't help showing his relief at seeing this brave young woman who had been in his care for nearly nine months. He admired Tafiq and noticed how well he looked.

Dorothy had arranged a double room in an award-winning guest house. It was only a few minutes away and was run by her friends, so he could check in later. She suggested the two of them go out for lunch on such a beautiful day, and they both agreed it was a good idea. Tafiq had just had his bottle and Katie had been about to put him down when Douglas arrived.

They walked to a popular cafe on the North Quay and ordered a ploughman's lunch. Neither of them had eaten breakfast, so they were hungry. He was extremely pleased to see her, but he let her chatter away realising she was trying to avoid asking about Nabil. He asked her about Tafiq and about Padstow and said Dorothy sounded like an interesting lady; she'd obviously been extremely good to them both. At least now he could see, as far as possible without an examination, that her health had improved vastly. She had been looking after herself well since fleeing the hospital while frightened and no doubt confused.

Douglas sincerely hoped their meeting would help to re-unite these two young people who had suffered enough. He had grown extremely close to them. His own wife had left him a few years ago because she could not stand the pressure of being a doctor's wife. They never had children of their own because she didn't want a family and she didn't have an ounce of maternal instinct. She preferred her cats. But this ill-fated Khalifa family had come into his life and now he felt he was a part of theirs.

"Douglas?"

"Yes Katie?"

"You won't laugh at me if I tell you something."

"I promise not to laugh, but what is it you want to tell me?"

"Do you believe in mediums and psychics and such like?"

"Pardon?"

"You heard me, Doctor MacDonald!" she quipped.

He smiled, pleased that she was relaxed enough to make a jibe.

"I haven't really thought about it, but one thing's for sure there has to be a lot out there we don't know about."

"Out there … meaning the universe?"

203

"Yes, I suppose it does, but most doctors won't entertain the idea. If they can't see it with their physical eyes, they dismiss it out of hand."

"But you don't?"

"Not entirely. I've always tried to keep an open mind on most subjects. There's enough intolerance in this world of ours. Mind you I'd still have to be convinced. Why are you asking me?"

"I went to see a spiritual medium recently," answered Katie, and she went on to relate what happened when she had her reading and healing with Hannah.

Douglas did not say much at first, he didn't want to interrupt her, but he was quite taken aback. Particularly when Katie said she'd never met Hannah before, and that Dorothy had most definitely not told her anything about her or her family. "And everything she said about your parents was true?"

"Yes, even things I had forgotten about. Oh, I've always known they were around, especially my mum, but it was still confirmation for me and proof that life carries on."

"Well, I don't know about that?"

"It felt right to see Hannah. I needed guidance. I've been leading a double life pretending to be Katie Mitchell and my son was called Daniel. I felt terrible lying to Dorothy, but I had to escape from everything. Do you understand?" Douglas nodded. "I adore Nabil and ..." a sob rose in her throat as she struggled to fight back the tears.

"Come on, let's go for a walk I've never been to Padstow so you can show me the harbour." After paying the bill he gently took her elbow and guided her out of the cafe and across to the harbour railings where they stopped for a while. He wanted to admire the view and he thought it would give Katie time to compose herself.

Katie thought Douglas had a wonderful attitude towards his patients, but it was more than that. She could talk to him and trust him because she knew he cared about her, Nabil and Tafiq. He was a lovely man and she thought it was sad he had never re-married. But she was thrilled to find out that while she was in hospital all those months, he had taken her aunt out to dinner a few times.

"Hannah mentioned you, you know."

"Did she? How did you know it was me?"

"Because she said I had a true friend, who was well-known in the medical profession. Although she didn't give me your name and position, she did say your initials were DM and that you would help to get us back together."

"Interesting! You do know the police have been on your trail, Katie."

"Yes, I guessed as much."

"I'm just glad you reached out to me before they found you."

"I hope I don't get you into trouble Douglas, especially a man of your standing."

"Nobody at the hospital knows I'm here. Besides, I am allowed time off you know. I'm not arrogant enough to think I can carry on working without a change of scene now and again. If I work until I drop, I'll be no good to my patients. All I'm concerned about is the three of you. Nabil is distraught, and he misses you both so much."

"I've really hurt him, haven't I? Can we walk out of town Douglas? There are too many people around here."

"Of course, I can't remember the last time I went for a walk," he laughed, trying to ease Katie's tension.

"Maybe you should have more time out."

"That's what my wife used to say, but I had to learn the hard way."

"What was she like?"

"Miranda? Well, she looked immaculate every day and she certainly knew how to spend all my hard-earned money, not that I minded. We weren't suited, and she didn't have a maternal bone in her body. Her two Persian cats were her babies. Surprisingly, I missed them after she left."

"Is that why you didn't have a family?"

"Yes. She told me a few weeks after we married that she didn't want children; she said she would make a terrible mother. There was never any thought about my feelings on the matter." Douglas changed the subject. "Then there were her ridiculous dinner parties which she always wanted me to attend and when I couldn't because of work, she would sulk for days afterwards."

"Why were the dinner parties ridiculous?"

"Her so-called friends were constantly trying to outdo each other, the wives that is. It was a game of one-upmanship. In the end the food became more and more elaborate, and our dining room looked like it had been transported from the Ritz. Oh, and most of the guests were like cardboard cut outs."

They both laughed at the thought of cardboard cut outs sitting round an elegant dining table and it was a few moments before they composed themselves.

"Oh, Douglas you are funny."

"It's so good to hear you laughing."

Walking passed the Aquatic Centre they headed out of town. They were both quiet for a while and it was Douglas who broke the silence.

"Katie what was it that made you run away? Was it something you remembered?"

"Yes."

"Can you talk about it?"

"I can now, as long as I am nowhere near him."

"Who?"

"Nabil's uncle," she said, looking troubled.

"Katie." Putting his hands on her shoulders he gently swung her round to face him. "You don't have to worry anymore, Nabil knows everything. Why you ran out of the apartment, about the threats and the money he tried to bribe you with."

"He knows?"

"Yes."

Katie leant against Douglas. He put his arms around her to give her what little comfort he could. "Mohammed is incapacitated. He had a massive heart attack and nearly died. He's only been home from the hospital for a short while and he's still weak."

"Incapacitated. Is he really that bad?"

"Yes, and I don't think he will be threatening you again," Douglas said trying to reassure her. "He must have had heart problems for a few years, and he led a degenerate life which wouldn't have helped either. Come, we'd better start walking back you look worn out."

"I'm all right!"

"Let me be the judge of that," he replied trying to look serious. "I am your doctor after all."

"Yes doctor!" Katie saluted.

"Are you always as cheeky as that to your doctor young lady?"

"Only when he's also a dear friend."

"I'm just glad to be of help," said Douglas in his usual humble way.

"Glad to be of help? she repeated. "You saved my life and my baby's life a few months ago and now you have rescued me again. I don't know how to thank you, Douglas."

"As I said, I'm just glad to be of help."

"Oh, you're incorrigible."

They walked in silence as they made their way back towards town. Katie was trying to digest the news about Mohammed. She felt such relief because at least now Nabil knew the truth.

His uncle couldn't harm her anymore, but it was going to take her a little while to get used to the idea. It was nothing more than he deserved, she thought to herself, quite stunned at the strength of ill-feeling she felt towards him. However, she knew this would pass, as she had a great capacity to forgive, but forgetting was another thing entirely.

"You're very thoughtful," Douglas commented.

"I feel a bit guilty."

"What about?"

"Because I'm glad Mohammed had a heart attack. I don't like thinking this way."

"I'm not surprised you do though. As I told Nabil his behaviour towards you was despicable. I know it's not easy, but try and let go of the past, and think of yourself now. You, Tafiq and that adoring husband of yours."

"How did he find out about Mohammed?"

"I'll let Nabil tell you that."

They had reached Honeysuckle Cottage and Douglas turned to her with a look of concern on his face.

"Do you want me to give Nabil your address? I can't keep him away from you any longer."

"Yes," she said quietly, "yes, you can."

"Oh, and I nearly forgot," he fumbled in his inside pocket. "I have a letter for you from your friend Beverley, she sent it to the St Thomas' when you were due to go to Hertfordshire and I've kept it for you ever since. I hope it cheers you up."

"Thank you. I'm sure any letter from my friend Bev will cheer me up." Katie looked sad. "I've neglected all my friends, haven't I?"

"If they are real friends, they'll understand that you've been through a dreadful ordeal. Now you'd better get back to that handsome son of yours and I need to check in to my guest house. Dorothy has kindly offered to show me where it is and introduce me to her friends. I must admit I'm looking forward to a holiday, especially as your aunt has agreed to join me."

"Oh Douglas, that is wonderful news!"

He smiled broadly.

"I can't wait to see Ellen. I know she must have been worried sick."

"There's no denying that. She just wants to see you well and happy."

Later, when they had to gone to the guest house Katie took Bev's letter upstairs. She ripped open the pink envelope and took out the pink writing paper. Stretching across the bed she laid it out before her. Feeling excited when she saw Bev's handwriting; she had not realised how much she'd missed all the news.

Dearest Katie,

I hope this letter finds you feeling strong. If it doesn't reach you before you leave St Thomas,' I've asked Doctor MacDonald to send it to the rehabilitation centre.

I haven't been able to visit you since you woke up from your long sleep (that's how I think of it), but I did visit you twice over the last few months. You may not have been aware of me in the room with you, but I was willing you to wake up as all your visitors were. I can't begin to tell you how relieved I am. It was heart breaking seeing you just lying there and now you're on your way to Hertfordshire. My thoughts are with you dear friend.

Greg and I will be able to visit you soon and I have such a lot of news. We are to be married in October. I've been bursting to tell you face to face, but a letter will have to do. It's just going to be a small ceremony in Greenwich registry office, but I'd like you to be one of the witnesses, if you're well enough that is. We're going to live in London. He is already happily ensconced in a one-bedroom flat in Greenwich. It's a bit expensive but everything is going well, and we've managed to save quite a bit from our years in Dubai. He's working in Guys Hospital Radiology Department and I'm leaving the UAE next week to start a Hygienist course at Guys Dental School, where I expect I'll meet some of your old friends.

I'm sure you remember me telling you about my brother, Michael, who has his own dental practice in Blackheath. Well, he thinks by the time I've finished my course, he'll be ready to expand and take on another Hygienist. Everything is falling into place.

I've heard lovely things about your darling son, and he sounds gorgeous. Nabil has so many plans for you all. I know I was a bit concerned about you marrying him, but he has certainly proved how much he loves and cares about you. He can't wait to have you home so you can tell him how you want the town house refurbished. I think he wants you to feel it is your home now that Fatima and Shazia are going to live in Abu-Dhabi, with Nabil's sister and brother-in-law. Shazia will be in England most of the time at university and she is enjoying it.

Hasn't Fatima changed? I was amazed at the welcome I received when I called round to see how you were doing and she's really looking forward to having you back in Dubai with her gorgeous grandson. How about Katie?

Well dear friend I do miss you. I'll be in England next week and I'll visit you in Hertfordshire so we can have a natter like old times. Nabil reckons it will do you the world of good. He's learned a lot in the last few months, and he does adore you Katie but of course you deserve the best.

Love you lots,
Bev xxx.

Katie sat up in amazement. Fatima and Shazia are moving to Abu Dhabi … Fatima can't wait to have me home … the town house will be ours and … it will be refurbished. She had a strong feeling of déjà vu as a memory came back to her and she recollected hearing her mother-in-law talking to her when she was in her coma. Some of these memories were vague and hadn't really registered; even when they came back into her mind, she couldn't always trust them to be true. Oh, Nabil I have put you through so much and you're trying so hard to make a new life for us. Tears fell onto Bev's letter, and she quickly put it to one side and grabbed a tissue.

Nabil paced up and down the apartment in Mayfair. He should have telephoned by now. Why didn't I insist on going with him? I can't stand this waiting. No, Douglas was right, he reasoned with himself. I must be patient. Only a few more hours and I maybe in Cornwall myself.

I will never let you out of my sight again angel …What am I saying? For the love of Allah wasn't it my short-sightedness and expecting her to live an insular life that triggered her depression in the first place? I was so blinded by my love for her. But I'm sure we would have

211

worked it out in the end until my uncle made things worse. Nabil's thoughts were all over the place again.

Sitting down he sipped the brandy he had poured absentmindedly. He hardly ever drank, but the brown liquid warmed him as it slid down easily. He stopped himself reaching for the bottle again because he wanted to keep a clear head. Water, that's what I'll drink, he said to himself, and he poured a glass, his hand shaking slightly.

Looking round the apartment, he realised everything reminded him of Katie, even the water he was drinking. Smiling to himself, as he remembered how he used to make fun of her because of the amount of water she drank. It must have been at least two litres a day he smiled. 'It's good for your skin,' she would say, and he would certainly agree with that. She has the most beautiful skin and the complexion of a typical 'English rose' as Ellen would say. Yes, my English rose, he mused.

Feeling like a caged animal and not knowing what to do with himself he paced up and down for a few minutes then walked into their bedroom. He lay on their bed and closed his eyes, but they were not closed for long; he turned to their wedding photo. It was in its new silver frame, and he reached for it and held it to his chest. Memories of that appalling day were still clear in his mind. The untidy bedroom and this photo smashed on the floor, proof of a hasty departure. It was on this telephone that Mohammed had threatened Katie. Would he really have carried out those evil threats? It did not bear thinking about. Suddenly, he began to feel warm and calm, and he knew his papa was there with him. He fell into a deep sleep.

Hearing the telephone ringing he tried to wake himself up. He'd only been asleep for an hour, but he found it difficult to stir himself.

"Nabil, are you okay?"

"Yes Douglas, I was asleep. I thought I'd never hear from you."

"I've only just left Katie. I didn't want to rush things and from a medical point of view I wanted to see for myself how she was coping."

"Yes of course. How is she? How is Tafiq? Does she want me to come to Cornwall?"

"Let me answer one question at a time." And he went on to tell him of his meeting with Katie, about Tafiq and how well Dorothy had been looking after them in her quaint little cottage in Padstow.

Nabil listened intently. He wanted to hear what his wife had been doing in the last three and a half weeks since they had gone missing. It was the not knowing that had been agony. At least now he knew they weren't that far away, and they were safe.

"Inshallah."

"Yes, it's Allah's will, they are safe, my friend."

"Does she want to come home, Douglas?"

"That young lady loves and misses you very much, but you must discuss these things together."

Nabil wanted to go to Cornwall immediately.

"Be patient just a few hours longer. Katie wanted to talk, but she also needs to digest the fact that your uncle is too ill to intimidate her anymore. You could see the relief on her face when I told her that you know about Mohammed's terrible threats and bribery. She feels guilty because she's glad he had a heart attack and is weak."

"Guilty after what he did?"

"Yes, but it's a natural reaction to someone so sensitive. I hope in the future that you two, talk to each other about anything that might be worrying you. It saves considerable heartache."

"Yes, you're right Douglas and I'm sure we both realise that now."

"I'm convinced she is over the worst because she now remembers the bad things that have happened to her in the last three years. As you know she had been blocking these out since emerging from her coma. It will enable her to come to terms with the past and look forward to the future. Cornwall has been her rehabilitation it seems."

"I do hope her future is with me."

"Nabil, I am a neurologist not a psychologist, but I do work closely with my colleagues in a case like Katie's. You must talk to each other, but more importantly you need to let her talk like she has never talked before. Let her tell you her feelings now that she remembers everything prior to the accident."

"I will Douglas, I will."

"It's not going to be easy, but I know you'll get through it."

"What would we have done without you as a doctor and a friend? I do not know how to thank you."

"Oh, I'm sure you would have figured it out, eventually."

"You are much too modest Douglas, and I cannot thank you enough."

"You still have a long way to go Nabil, just get yourself down here tomorrow because your wife and son will be waiting for you. And I suggest you take up Dorothy's friend's offer and stay in Hillside Cottage for a week. They showed me round and it's a beautiful place with a stunning and secluded garden."

"But … I thought I would be bringing them straight back to Grosvenor Square?"

"Think about it Nabil. The last time she was there she was so terrified she ran out of the building. You must give her time."

"Yes of course I wasn't thinking. If she wants to spend a week in Hillside Cottage, then that's what we'll do. You'd better give me the address." Reaching for Katie's note pad and pen from her bedside table he began to write the details carefully.

"Now try and get some sleep if you can."

"I will try and thank you again, goodnight, Douglas."

"Goodnight, Nabil."

Katie was not able to sleep. In fact, at two o'clock in the morning she found herself writing a poem, something she had not done for a while. Her father used to love her poems and he would show his colleagues at work, like the proud father he was. She smiled at the thought of him boring them all silly. She had quite a collection but had never done anything with them. As she picked up the pen she was in a philosophical mood, and she wrote ...

We are souls as we form in our mother's womb.
We are souls from whence we came.
Our spirit was ignited by two people's love,
as the kindling of a flame.

Experiences permeate our souls,
from the time of our creation,
bringing forth unhappiness, unease, fears,
Joy, peace, and realization.

When we understand ourselves and are whole,
answers will be revealed.

215

Our existence will become more meaningful,
and our lives will be fulfilled.

She felt her father close as she was writing. Certainly, she'd had more than enough unhappiness in her short life, but did she now have peace? Clearly, she felt much more at peace than she had done a few days ago and infinitely more than before her accident. She knew she was facing up to everything that had happened, and she felt more positive about life in general. But what about my life with Nabil, she thought? There are plenty of changes for the better going on around us. Mohammed can't hurt me, and we can have the town house to ourselves now that Fatima and Shazia have moved out. But Katie still felt uneasy about what she would do all day once she was back in Dubai; she knew there was no way she could lead a sedentary life again. Nabil would have to let her do something with her days, but what? She didn't want to go back to working in the hospital and it certainly wouldn't fit in with her new affluent lifestyle or the culture into which she had married. With all the events that had taken place in the last three years she knew she had to move on, and she realised the job she had once loved, did not enthuse her anymore.

Feeling happy knowing her husband would be arriving tomorrow did nothing to help her sleep. She was so looking forward to seeing him though not completely sure what to expect. Hannah had kindly said the three of them could stay at Hillside Cottage for a week while she stayed with Dorothy; to enable them have time on their own. Douglas said he would tell Nabil when he phoned him so he could pack some clothes. There were some beautiful people in this world and Hannah was one of them. Confident that her husband would agree, she finally drifted off to sleep.

Chapter Seventeen

Nabil had not been able to sleep much either and he wished he had a telephone number for the cottage. Directory enquiries had told him it was x directory, which you would expect with an elderly lady living on her own. After watching Michael Douglas in the 'Wall Street' film using one of the new cell phones, he had bought one for himself. It won't be much use in the car tomorrow if I don't have a phone number to contact Katie on though he mused.

Trying to imagine Dorothy's home was easy because his wife had shown him many photographs of Cornwall and the pretty cottages they had stayed in when she was a child. Quaint and so different to what he was used to. Hillside Cottage sounded interesting too and he thought Dorothy's friend was extremely generous to lend it to them. Nabil could afford the best hotels, but this was what Katie wanted and that was more important than luxury. However, he would compensate Hannah for allowing them to stay, it was only fair.

It seemed strange they had only spoken through Douglas, but not to each other. Katie said she preferred to wait to see him in person. Speaking to each other on the telephone would seem strange and impersonal. She was probably right about that, but it wasn't easy.

Now he was being driven towards the West Country. Sitting back and trying to make himself comfortable was difficult because he could feel the tension in the back of his neck. Sometimes Katie would massage his neck and shoulders for him when he came in after a hard day; often it would end up a full body massage, he smiled to himself as he pictured it. But trying to visualise her journey to Cornwall nearly four weeks ago wasn't so easy; it was even harder to fathom what had been going through her mind. How he wished she had told him from the beginning about his uncle's threats. Why did she hide it from him? Well, he would find out soon enough and he knew he would have to let her tell him everything in her own time.

Leaving the business in the hands of Rashid, was a relief. It meant he could concentrate on a reconciliation with Katie and Tafiq. They would have to make him a partner soon after all the work he had done in Nabil's absence and Mohammed's neglect.

Douglas had only just left Hillside Cottage. It was almost midday, and he didn't want to be in the way when Nabil arrived. Staying on for a few more days in his comfortable guest house was something to look forward to. It made a change from his usual demanding life, and he wanted to be close to Nabil and Katie in case they needed him. He was still concerned for her health, and she hadn't been officially discharged from the hospital.

Ellen would be arriving tonight, and he hoped she wouldn't catch the Friday evening rush on the motorway. She had to be back at the school on Tuesday, but they would have the whole weekend together. Meeting Ellen at the hospital after Katie's accident seemed a lifetime ago, but now they were extremely close. He had been nervous the first time they went out together because he was out of practice, but he need not have worried as they were relaxed in each other's company. They laughed a lot which he found refreshing after his disastrous marriage. There was ten years difference in their ages, but it didn't seem to matter in the grand scheme of things, and it certainly didn't bother Ellen.

Neither of them wanted to encroach on the time Nabil and Katie would have together but naturally she wanted to see for herself that her niece was well; she couldn't wait to cuddle her great nephew.

Nabil could not believe his eyes when he arrived at Hillside Cottage and saw his beautiful wife waiting for him. She had seen the car, picked up Tafiq and rushed to the front door. He fought back the tears as he stood and looked at Katie and his son in front of this charming Cornish cottage. They were a family again, at least he hoped they were, he had learned not to take anything for granted. It was a hard lesson and one he was never likely to forget. Here on the doorstep was his angel and his adorable son who he had not had the chance to get to know yet.

It was a wonderful reunion and Tafiq seemed to sense the excitement as he gurgled with contentment for the rest of the day, except when he needed feeding or a nappy change. Nabil was fascinated by him and even learned to give him his bottle. It was bliss to be together away from the outside world. They didn't need to venture out as they had all the food they needed. Dorothy had made sure of that.

Katie gave Nabil a proper tour of Hillside Cottage and he was amazed at how large it was especially when she showed him the art studio at the top of the house. He thought he was going to feel claustrophobic staying in a cottage, but this was no ordinary cottage and he loved it. Katie thought it had a soul of its own.

When their gorgeous son had settled down for the evening, they were happy and content to lay in each other's arms. Nabil just wanted to feel her close. They had a whole week to talk and neither of them wanted to break the silence until Katie started to cry tears of happiness. He held her close for what seemed a long time and he found it hard to hold back the tears himself. They made love for the first time since before Katie's accident. Nabil was gentle and it was beautiful to become one again.

The following morning Katie packed a picnic and put the basket under the pram. They walked for what seemed like miles to Nabil, but it wasn't that far. He enjoyed the English countryside but the picnic they ate sitting in a peaceful meadow full of buttercups and daisies was something new to him; it was certainly different to being in the desert. He remembered Katie telling him about their family picnics and he didn't want to spoil her fun. When they had finished eating and Tafiq was asleep she sat making a daisy chain and hung it round his neck.

"My lord and master accept this token of my friendship," she quipped.

He gently took her hands in his. "I will never be your lord and master angel. That I know for sure, neither do I want to be."

"But you've been through hell waiting for your family to return to you and I think that deserves a lot more than a daisy chain."

For a few moments he could not speak but she could see the sorrow on his face. It was then she realised just how much he'd been affected by their disappearance. She lay against his chest. They could hear the sounds of nature around them; the buzzing of the bees as they collected their pollen from the meadow flowers; the familiar sound of grasshoppers in the long grasses swaying in the breeze; the melodic song of a blackbird in a nearby tree and unfortunately the occasional car on the road two hundred yards away.

Tafiq slept soundly which gave them a chance to talk. Katie knew they must never keep secrets from each other again however painful the truth. She told him she had not been honest with herself from the time they had married and moved in with his mamma and sister in the town house. Instead of standing her ground she had allowed a bad situation to become intolerable. She attempted to explain to Nabil that she had been trying to spare his feelings and that even when she had mentioned his mamma's behaviour, she didn't think he believed her. This made him feel ashamed. She told him about the first time Mohammed had threatened her and how she had hidden it from him when she met him at the airport. Nabil listened intently, to everything she had to say. She reminded him of the day he found her sitting by the fountain in the garden and how wretched she had been as the feeling of helplessness washed over her.

"I know angel. I was horrified when I found you in such a state and it was then I decided I would have to do something. I thought a long holiday in England would do the trick, but of course I didn't know Mohammed was planning such a heinous attack on you. I wish he had died and gone to hell!"

"Please don't wish hell on him, whatever he's done. I must admit I was relieved to hear he'd had a heart attack and was confined to home, but I felt bad after having such thoughts."

"Altruistic as always Katie. That's a part of your personality I have always admired, your capacity to forgive people so readily. It will be a long time before I can feel charitable towards him. I can't believe I didn't realise something bad was happening right under my nose. By then he was already becoming a liability to the business with his drinking and womanising. Thinking back, I had noticed you were nervous whenever he was around. I should have realised there was something wrong."

"It was my fault for not telling you in the first place." She looked up into his tense face. "What made Mohammed that way and why was he so different to your papa?"

"I asked papa that once and he said that my uncle became a religious fanatic when he was about thirty-five years old and realised, they couldn't have children. He was jealous of my parents because they had me. He met a hard-line Islamic cleric and became great friends with him. It was about this time that he started treating my aunt appallingly for not giving him a son and heir. I'm not blaming the Cleric's fanaticism. My uncle must have had an evil streak all along regardless, but it certainly brought the worse out in him."

"Surely religion is supposed to promote kindness, tolerance, and compassion. All the things your uncle didn't show any signs of."

"In other words, he was a hypocrite. That's the trouble with extremists, they can't live up to their own ideals. Islam is a peaceful religion, but you wouldn't think so the way my uncle interprets it."

"Your poor Aunt Aamira is having to put up with him all the time now he's at home but hopefully he hasn't got the strength to bully her anymore."

"Don't worry I hired a full-time live-in nurse, so she doesn't need to have much contact with him. She's too gracious to talk about her terrible marriage to the family, especially in front of Latifa; however badly he has behaved he is still her son."

"We must invite your aunt and grandmother to the town house more often. The mood in their house can't be good. Your uncle might be frail, but he can still cause a bad atmosphere."

"Yes, we must do that. Latifa can't wait to see her great grandson. In fact, she said on the phone I had to hurry up and bring you both home before she gets too old to enjoy him. She likes you, Katie."

"I like her as well … very much, and I love her stories about Dubai when it was just a small fishing village. It fascinates me."

"It fascinates me too considering that it's now a successful business hub between east and west. What a difference twenty years can make. Papa used to like hearing his mamma reminiscing, but Mohammed hated admitting he came from a small fishing village," Nabil sighed. "It seems my uncle has always had 'a chip on his shoulder' as you say in England."

"Well, we can move on now."

"You seem different angel … more philosophical. After all that has occurred, I didn't expect to find you so calm."

"I've had nearly four weeks to come to terms with all that's happened over the last three years. I did a lot of thinking in my room and Dorothy left me alone, when she sensed I was in a reflective mood. A few times she looked after Tafiq while I walked down to the harbour. You know how much I love the ocean. I'm so lucky he's a contented baby otherwise I wouldn't have been able to leave him with her."

Nabil was listening attentively.

"Learning to accept is the best therapy and when I went to see Hannah, she confirmed this for me. I also realised I couldn't live a double life and I knew deep down I couldn't live apart from you or keep your son from you. Please forgive me for taking him away."

"There's no need for forgiveness after what you've had to endure, angel. I had no idea you had overheard my conversation with the nurse outside your room when he

223

told me Mohammed had phoned the hospital. When I looked in on you and Tafiq you were both fast asleep. If only I had shut the door behind me then you wouldn't have had such a fright."

"The worst thing was I didn't know why I froze at the mere mention of his name until my memory started to return. But what's done is done and we can't change it. In a strange way it may have done us a favour."

"How can you say that?"

"I don't say it lightly but my time in Cornwall has helped me put a different perspective on things."

"Douglas thinks staying with Dorothy in such a loving and caring environment may have been all the rehabilitation you needed."

"He said something similar to me and I hope he's right because I don't want to go to Hertfordshire now."

"I would like to take Hannah and Dorothy out to lunch before we leave. I have much to thank them for."

"I'm sure they would love that. Are we going to Grosvenor Square from Cornwall?"

"Only if you can cope with going back."

"If it had been two weeks ago, I would have said no, but now I feel strong enough to face my emotions. I know it will be tough remembering what happened last time I was there and your uncle's ice-cold voice at the other end of the phone. But … he can no longer threaten me, and I do so love your apartment, my darling."

"It's not my apartment, it's ours."

Tafiq started crying because he needed a nappy change, so Katie laid his mat on the grass. He enjoyed the freedom when she took his soiled nappy off, and she let him kick his legs happily for a few minutes while they watched him with pride.

The next morning Tafiq was a bit restless, so they decided they would take full advantage of Hannah's beautiful home. By lunch time he was more settled, and they enjoyed eating in the garden while he lay in his pram happy in his little world. They made use of the turquoise painted wrought iron furniture which blended in with the stunning colours around them, from the many shrubs, plants, and trees. Classical music was playing from the dining room and they both felt the energy of the house and garden doing its magic on them.

It was Sunday and Nabil had booked a table in an elegant restaurant for four so Douglas and Ellen could join them in the evening. Naturally, she was anxious to see her niece and great nephew before she drove back to Edenbridge. She wanted to see for herself that they were okay, despite Douglas reassuring her several times. The last nine months had been an ordeal for them all.

After Katie and Nabil had finished their lunch, she wanted to talk some more. "I didn't know how it was going to be possible for us to live together again darling, with all the aggravation from your family. Then I read a letter from Bev that Douglas passed on to me, telling me how things have changed for the better in Dubai. She also wrote that your mamma and Shazia had moved to Abu Dhabi."

"I wasn't able to tell you when you woke from your coma because the psychiatrist said you had shut all the bad things out. He said I had to be patient a little longer before bringing the subject up. Were you aware of my mamma talking to you a few weeks before you came back to us? She had English lessons while she was staying with me so she could tell you of the changes being made on your behalf."

"I do appreciate your mamma taking English lessons and I must admit it's not what I would have expected but as for recollecting," Katie hesitated. "I vaguely remember ... some things entered my mind while others did not," she said feeling impatient with herself.

Nabil became emotional at the mere thought her lying in the hospital bed. "Do you want to come back to Dubai angel?" he asked tentatively. He was feeling insecure and not so sure of himself anymore. Is it enough that Mohammed is in poor health, he thought to himself, and my mamma and sister have moved out?

"Darling there is nothing I want more, but there are other things to consider."

"But you do want to come home?"

"Yes, I do, but there's something you need to understand."

"Tell me!"

"I need more freedom and I want my independence back."

Nabil started to speak but she put her fingers over his lips. She sighed heavily. She didn't want to hurt him, but they had promised to be honest with each other. "I want a life outside the home. I need to be able to use my brain. I can't come back to Dubai and lead a sedentary life. I just can't do that anymore. You know how depressed I was stuck in the town house day in day out with hardly any intelligent conversation. When you came home from work sometimes you were too tired to listen to my moans and who could blame you. If I had something else in my life we would have so much more to talk about and I would not feel so useless. We come from different cultures, but surely love can conquer all."

"What is it you want to do?"

"I could start my own antiques business, she said excitedly."

"I know you want more freedom Katie, but isn't that a little ambitious after all that you've been through?"

"It's precisely because of what I've been through that I want to start my own business. I want to be fulfilled as a wife and a mother but also as a person in my own right. When I had the near-death experience, it gave me a fresh perspective on life. If we don't follow our true feelings then our very existence becomes pointless, and we wander aimlessly not really knowing why we are here."

"You have done a lot of thinking."

She smiled at him. "Yes, I have, and I know I can do it. I still have all my parents contacts, plus, I can make new ones in the Middle East."

"I don't doubt it for one minute, but it won't be easy for you as a businesswoman in Dubai."

"I realise that, and it makes it all the more challenging."

Nabil sighed. He knew he could lose her forever if he insisted on her giving up this idea. It was a male dominated society in the Emirates, but he had always thought the culture and beliefs were too strict on women. Knowing he would be frowned upon by some of the locals for allowing his wife such liberty seemed a small price to pay for her happiness.

"You've gone very quiet."

"Well, you've given me much to think about."

"It will work. I know it will. You can sponsor me, and I will do the rest."

"Just like that!"

"No, not just like that! I know it will be hard work and I won't leave Tafiq unless it is necessary, but we will have a nanny too," she sighed when she saw the expression on his face. "My darling it's only an idea at the moment, but it's something I really want to do."

"Then you must do it!"

"You mean it?"

"Yes, but I'd rather you didn't work in the shop yourself. We can break with convention to a certain extent, but it may be going a bit too far for my wife to be seen on the shop floor."

"Of course, I do understand that and the last thing I want to do is antagonise the locals. I will have enough to do setting the whole thing up and going to the auctions. Thank you for having faith in me." She flung her arms around his neck. Tafiq began to gurgle in the pram, and they looked at each other and laughed.

"I do love you, you crazy woman."

They enjoyed their time in Padstow and it was just what they needed but they were also chauffeur driven to different parts of Cornwall. Katie wanted to show her husband some of the beautiful places where she had stayed with her mum and dad. It had a positive effect on her when she revisited these charming towns, villages, beaches, and clifftops; it really was a time of healing and letting go. Nabil was pleased to learn a bit more about her life too, especially as she was looking so well and happy.

One of the highlights of the week was their meal with Douglas and Ellen. Not only was it an excellent restaurant where Katie enjoyed her favourite Lobster Thermidor, but her dear aunt announced their engagement.

"Wow, that's wonderful news," said Katie, who was a little shocked.

Nabil was extremely pleased, but he wasn't shocked because he had seen them together in the last few months. He shook hands with Douglas.

"Congratulations, my friend."

"Thank you."

"You look surprised, darling." Ellen said to Katie finding it amusing.

"I hope you're pleasantly surprised," asked Douglas looking concerned.

"I most definitely am, Doctor MacDonald! But don't forget, I've been on the planet Zogg for most of the last year and I haven't had a chance to catch up on the gossip."

They all laughed and were delighted that Katie was able to make a joke about one of the most traumatic times of her life.

Nabil wondered what Katie's reaction would be when they arrived back at Grosvenor Square. Much time had elapsed since she had set foot in the apartment. It was nearly July and about ten months from the time of her accident; Douglas said it was bound to feel strange. He longed to take his wife and son home to the Emirates, but he was advised not to rush her. A bit more time in London would help her to come to terms with all the changes, also Katie and Tafiq needed hospital check-ups.

Douglas and his colleagues, who had been caring for her since her accident, also worked at the London Bridge Hospital, so they had arranged for her appointments to be held at the clinics there. It was the same private hospital that Nabil had wanted to move her too, all those months ago.

The chauffeur stopped outside the apartment block and Katie hesitated when he opened the car door for her. Nabil came round and took Tafiq so she could get out. Gary, the concierge was so pleased to see them, but he had been warned not to mention the day of the accident. After it had happened, he told Mr Khalifa and the police how upset he was for not being on the door on the day Mrs Khalifa had rushed out of the building; he thought

229

he might have been able to defuse the situation. Nabil told him right from the beginning not to feel guilty and when he found out about Mohammed's part in what had occurred, he certainly wasn't going to share the information with the concierge.

They walked briskly past the reception area and straight into the lift because they didn't want to stop and talk to anyone. Katie was feeling apprehensive. As soon as they entered the apartment she felt as though she was reliving her sudden departure that had happened so long ago.

"Are you okay, angel?" Nabil asked, seeing the look on her face.

"Yes, it just feels surreal like watching a film on my mind's eye."

Tafiq started to cry, and Katie took him while Nabil found a made-up bottle in his baby bag; as it was heating up, she walked round the apartment with Tafiq over her shoulder. It was good to be back and having her son to take care of would certainly help her face her memories. She went into every room, apart from their bedroom. In one of the guest bedrooms his sister had left some of her stuff.

Nabil came up behind her. "You don't mind Shazia leaving some of her things here, do you?"

"Of course not! You told me she and your mamma stayed to support you when I was in hospital."

"Shazia only stayed for the odd weekend."

"How is she getting on at university?"

"She loves living on campus, but I haven't been able to keep an eye on her as much as I would have liked."

"I'm sure she'll be okay, darling."

"You forget I went to the same university, and I know what some of the students get up to. She's enjoying her freedom now but when she goes back to Dubai she'll be expected to marry. It was arranged when papa was alive."

Katie knew better than to comment on Shazia's arranged marriage as much as she disliked the custom. Mixed marriages could only work with compromise on both sides, and she wasn't about to alienate his family with outspoken thoughts on their traditions.

They were learning a lot about each other, especially since the first nine months of their marriage. Nabil had been far too over-protective, and it had nearly suffocated her. He dear dad used to indulge her in much the same way, but he stopped at being possessive, anyway, her mum would never have allowed it. It's uncanny, she thought, the way the law of attraction works. He husband adored her the same as her dad did and they both felt compelled to protect her, despite her need to be a free spirit. You often attract people into your life with similarities to your parents.

"Well, at least she has two more years in London, and you told me she's enjoying reading art history."

"Yes, she is but it's a shame she probably won't ever put what she's learning into practice."

"That's sad ... she's so intelligent."

"Intelligent and cheekier than ever since she's been at UCL."

They both laughed.

"She was so looking forward to seeing you and her nephew, but she didn't want to be in the way, so she flew home to Abu Dhabi."

"It's great news that Yasmin and Rashid are expecting their first baby."

"Yes, it is though it's been a long time coming. Needless to say, mamma is thrilled. She was beginning to think she wouldn't have any grandchildren until our son was born. To think that he ..." Nabil hesitated.

231

"That he what?"

"I was going to say … to think that he may not have survived when you had the accident." He couldn't help feeling emotional.

"He was meant to survive, my darling, and he is our beautiful baby."

"Talking of babies. Do you want me to find a nanny while we're in London?" Nabil asked, when Katie sat down to feed Tafiq.

"Definitely not! We eat out most of the time and the deli brings us delicious spreads when we want them, we have maids to do the laundry and the cleaning, so all I have to do is look after our son. Anyway, we'll be flying home to Dubai eventually."

"Are you sure?"

"I am."

"Have you been in our bedroom yet?" Nabil asked with a worried look on his face.

"No, but I will when I put Tafiq in his cot and I can't wait to see it."

"As I said to you in the car if there's anything you don't like I will send it back to Harrods and you can choose something else. I had to buy baby things ready for your return, but mamma and Shazia helped me."

"I'm sure your mamma enjoyed herself in the baby department."

"Yes, she did, and she can't wait to hold her grandson."

Tafiq fell asleep after he was sick on Katie's shoulder, so she had no choice but to go into their bedroom to change her top.

"Do you want me to come with you?"

"Yes, please."

Nabil had been advised to change things in their bedroom. He had put their wedding photo away, the one that had been smashed, and he'd changed the telephones to the newer cordless type; they were a different colour too. He was desperate to shield her from as much upset as possible. It certainly helped when she saw the baby things scattered around.

Do you like the cot?" It was a large stainless-steel cot, with an embroidery anglaise white canopy and bedding to match.

"I love it and I'm sure I would have chosen the same one myself," she replied, as she laid Tafiq down. He looked so small in such a large space, but he was fast asleep without a care in the world. "But do we really need so many things while he's still a tiny baby?" Katie smiled and shook her head as she looked round the room. "It's going to be quite a while before he needs a baby walker or a highchair you know."

Nabil put his arm around her shoulder and kissed the top of her head. "We can put them in one of the guest rooms and have it made into a nursery for when we're in London. I just wanted you to see everything and tomorrow we can choose a pram."

It certainly helped Katie to see their bedroom looking different than the last time she'd been there. She couldn't help noticing the new telephones and the missing photo.

"Where's out wedding photo darling?"

"I put it in the drawer next to your bed."

"I know what you're trying to do, and I do appreciate it, but that's my favourite photograph," she said, as she opened the drawer and took it out; she put it on top of her bedside cabinet where it belonged.

"That's better!"

"But I thought …"

"I know what you thought but I'm okay, honest. Now, I'd better change my top before I stink the place out. Oh, the joys of motherhood."

That night Katie found it difficult to sleep when memories of Mohammed's phone call came flooding back into her mind. Nabil cursed his uncle for what he had done to his wife, and he cuddled her until she finally closed her eyes.

Chapter Eighteen

Katie was happy to be back in Grosvenor Square. It had felt strange at first after being away for so long, but she soon felt safe and secure. She was now sleeping better at night. Reminding herself that Mohammed was no longer a threat, and that despite everything, her and Tafiq were alive helped her deal with her initial feelings.

Ten days after they'd been back in Mayfair Nabil mentioned that he had a business trip coming up, but it wouldn't be until after Katie's hospital check-up. She assured him she would be alright if he went away for three nights. He was anxious about leaving her and she was getting exasperated with his fussing. Since her accident, she had become more impatient.

She had a full check up at the London Bridge Hospital at the end of their second week and all was well. But she did mention to Douglas that she became irritable sometimes. It wasn't like her to be touchy with people, especially Nabil. She also had bad headaches occasionally, which was something she had never suffered from before. He explained that her serious head injury and subsequent coma could have altered her personality slightly and would more than likely be the cause of her headaches. He said they would monitor it and she was to tell him if the headaches got any worse. But overall, he was extremely pleased with her progress as her neurologist and as her soon to be uncle-in-law.

Ellen had told her over the phone that they had decided they didn't want to waste any time as they weren't getting any younger; a Christmas wedding was planned. She was looking forward to a family celebration and wished her mum and dad could be with them, but she knew they'd be there in spirit.

Katie received an unexpected telephone call from Sue a couple of days after her hospital check-up. She had left Rob and was living with her parents once again in West Wickham. She longed to catch up with Katie in person, so it was arranged that she would come and stay while Nabil was on his business trip. He had extended it to four nights away, now he knew that his wife would have company.

Tafiq was in his cot and Katie was on the terrace watching for Sue's arrival. She was elated that her best friend was coming to stay. A black cab pulled up outside the building, and she saw Gary helping Sue out with her holdall. As soon as she came through the front door, they hugged each other, rocking from side to side as they had done when they were teenagers. Ten minutes later they were sitting on the terrace drinking coffee.

"It's so posh here, Katie, and what a fabulous view of the square and the gardens you have."

"Yes, we sit out here as often as we can, weather permitting. It was one of the reasons Nabil bought it a few years ago. His papa had an apartment in this building for many years and since Ibrahim's death he's been renting it out. Now the lease is coming to an end he's going to let Shazia live in it while she's at uni."

"Lucky girl!"

"You could say that, but I'm sure she would prefer to be renting a house with some of her new student friends away from Grosvenor Square. She knows Nabil has asked Gary, the concierge, to keep an eye on her when he's in Dubai so she won't be having any wild parties."

They laughed.

"It's wonderful to see you, Sue. I'm so glad you phoned."

"Ellen told me you were back in Mayfair when I spoke to her. I had no idea you had been in Cornwall though. The last time I saw you, you were lying in your hospital bed, and it was awful. I talked to you about the things we used to do when we were growing up, but I had no idea whether you could hear me or not," she said with tears in her eyes.

"I've tried to explain to friends and family that sometimes I did hear your voices and apparently my eyes flickered when something registered with me."

"How scary for you."

"Not really, I was just resting, or sleeping as Nabil prefers to think of it. I'm sure it was much more frightening for all of you. I can only try and imagine what it was like when my husband was sitting by my bed day and night waiting to see if I was going to survive; and then to find out I was pregnant must have been such a shock."

"Yes, it must have been. I'm sorry I missed him today. What time did he leave?"

"About an hour before you arrived. He had a plane to catch. He wouldn't have gone at all if you weren't coming to stay. He was so worried about leaving me on my own and I was getting impatient with him."

"Cut him some slack Katie! Last time the poor man left you in the apartment to go on a business trip, you ended up in hospital and nearly died."

"Yes, you're right Sue, of course you are. He has coped with so much over the last year. Ellen did offer to come and stay but she's got the decorators in. Hopefully, they'll be finished tomorrow so you'll see her before you leave. She's going to be spending a lot of time with Douglas in his apartment in Marylebone."

"Her intended. How exciting to have a Christmas wedding to look forward to."

"Yes, it is, and I'm so pleased for them."

"Who would have thought the doctor who saved your life would end up becoming a member of your family."

"I know it's amazing! Anyway, I want to hear all your news. What happened between you and Rob?"

"I finally got away from him, but it wasn't easy. You must have guessed he was a control freak. I'm so sorry I wasn't at your wedding but if I had flown to Dubai, he would have made my life a misery."

"Sue, it became obvious he was dominating you after just a few months of you moving in with him, but I couldn't say much on the phone. I knew he was there listening because you sounded as though you were on your guard all the time. You were like a different person."

"Well, the old Sue is back now!"

"And thank God for that but tell me more."

"As you know, he's an architect, which means he works at home most of the time, and you're right, he always seemed to be hovering. When I was on the phone, which wasn't often, he insisted on knowing who I was talking to."

"You mean he spied on you?"

"Yes, I suppose so if you put it like that. Thankfully, I got a nursing job soon after I moved in, or I swear I would have gone mad."

"But why did you move in with him so quickly?"

"You know how loving he was towards me, and he was charming."

"He was a bit over the top if you ask me, Sue. I thought he'd been to charm school the first time you introduced him to me."

Sue laughed. "Plus, I couldn't wait to get away from mum, she seems to get worse as she gets older."

"That's true!"

"After four or five months he started to show his true colours, and it came as quite a shock. I'm telling you the short version, in case Tafiq wakes up."

"It's okay, he's not due a feed yet."

"Rob watched my every move when I was at home. I couldn't do anything without him, and he didn't like me making friends either. In the end I gave up trying to arrange a night out with some of the staff from the hospital. It just wasn't worth the aggravation."

"Did he hit you?"

"He used to bend my arm back sometimes or even pull my hair when he thought I wasn't listening to him."

"Oh my God Sue, that's dreadful. I bet you're glad you didn't start a family."

"I kept taking the pill and he didn't want babies either, so at least we agreed on that. I still don't want children … well, never say never I suppose. One thing I do know, it will be a bloody long time before I'm interested in men again."

"I can't say I blame you."

"The mental abuse is even worse. He would belittle me so much it even started affecting my mood when I was at work. When somebody puts you down day in day out, you're in danger of believing the nasty things they say about you; it's like 'brain washing.' He was angry with me all the time in the end, and I couldn't do anything right. Everything was my fault even though it clearly wasn't, but there was no arguing with him. I realised he was a narcissist, and you can't reason with one of those.

It wasn't long before the sister on the ward noticed a big change in me. One day she called me into her office, and I thought I had done something wrong; she could be a bit of a tartar. I had lost all my self-confidence by then. It turns out she had recognised the signs because she'd been through something similar herself when she was younger. We couldn't talk for long, as it was a busy ward, but she gave me a book to read called, 'The Power of Positive Thought.' She wrote her address and phone number on a piece of paper and put it inside the front cover, in case I ever needed it."

"How kind of her."

"Yes, it was! I saw a different side to her that day. It was a while before I started reading the book but once I began, I couldn't put it down. I had to make sure Rob was busy in his office. He would not have approved and would have torn it up if he'd read the title. The author, I can't remember his name, helped me to realise there is always a way out of a bad situation; it gave me hope."

"And you were given the book at the time when you needed it most."

"It seems so, yes. It empowered me to start believing in myself again and things came to a head soon after that. About four weeks ago, we had a huge row. I really let rip because I wasn't prepared to put up with it anymore. He pushed me to the limit when he raised his hand to hit me. I quickly grabbed a large frying pan and threatened to use it on him if he came any nearer. He stormed out of the house, but not before ordering me to make sure his dinner was on the table when he got back from his meeting. As soon as he left, I rang home and thankfully my dad answered the phone. I was sobbing and it took me a while to make him understand what was wrong. He told me to pack my things and go and stay in a guest house. I was to phone him with the address, and he would leave for Manchester first thing in the morning."

"So, you got away before Rob came home?"

"Yes, I knew he'd be gone for about three hours, so I packed my clothes and personal belongings in my large suitcase and pinched one of his. I looked in the yellow pages for a small hotel or guest house and found a vacancy straightaway then I called a taxi. I can't tell you how elated I felt as soon as I shut his front door double locked it and pushed my set of keys through his letterbox. I was lucky because the taxi driver was a friendly guy who could see I was distraught. He helped me with my cases and asked if I was all right. I was worried in case Rob came back early and caught me, but thankfully he didn't. The driver took me to the guest house which was in a different part of Manchester."

"You must have felt so alone in your room."

"I did at first but then I had such an overwhelming feeling of relief I cried tears of happiness. I opened my case and was surprised to see the book Sister Marianne had given me on the top of my clothes; it must have slipped out of the back pocket, but I don't know how. I had used the piece of paper with her address and phone number on as a bookmark. Fortunately, I had a week's leave booked, but I needed to tell her I wouldn't be going back to the hospital. The last thing I wanted was Rob storming onto the ward, so I phoned the landline and left him a message to say I no longer worked there and that I had left him."

"Was the sister okay about it?"

"She was marvellous and said she would explain everything to the hospital management. Having been through it herself she knew how important it was for me to put as many miles between me and Rob as possible.

She asked me to keep in touch and said she was sorry to lose such a good and capable nurse."

"Sue, I'm so sorry."

"Don't be … I'm not! It's the best thing I could have done; I feel free to be me again." She flung her arms wide with such gusto it made them giggle.

"Have you heard from him since you left?"

"Yes, he phoned home and my dad answered. Rob said he was coming to take me back to Manchester, but dad told him if he came anywhere near our house, he would call the police. We haven't heard from him since. Dad has never found it easy to show me love and affection, as you know, but he was certainly there for me when I needed him."

Tafiq started crying just as she finished speaking.

"That was good timing."

"Ooh, I can't wait to see him," Sue said, as she followed Katie into their bedroom. "Wow this is something else! It's like a hotel suite."

Katie laughed as she lifted Tafiq out of his cot. He quietened down when she held him close, so she passed him to her eager friend.

"He's absolutely gorgeous," she said as she held him in the crook of her arm and gazed at him in wonderment, "He's such a handsome boy which, is not surprising since he has such good-looking parents."

Katie went to put Tafiq's bottle on then showed Sue round the rest of the apartment.

"What's this door Katie? Is it a cupboard?"

"No, that's Nabil's prayer room. I can show you if you want."

"Do you mind if I just have a little peek? I've never seen a prayer room before."

"Okay," she said as she opened the door.

"Wow, I wasn't expecting such a big room and it's so ornate and beautiful."

Tafiq was becoming fractious, so Sue went to unpack her things while Katie gave him his bottle.

"I can't get over what a luxurious place this is," she remarked, as she came back onto the terrace fifteen minutes later.

"I love it, even though it was here that I had the dreaded phone call from Mohammed."

"Do you want to talk about it?"

"No thanks, Sue. It's not easy to forget but I'm learning to let go now I know he can't hurt me anymore. He hasn't recovered well from his heart attack or his operation."

"It's no more than he deserves, the bastard!"

The next four days were just like old times, except now Katie had her adorable son with them. His baby sling was perfect when they went shopping, but his Silver Cross pram was better when they had picnics in the London parks; the picnic basket fitted nicely underneath the large pram, and the local deli packed a great lunch.

Nabil phoned every day to make sure Katie and Tafiq were okay, even though he knew she had company. She tried hard not to get impatient with him, because as Sue had reminded her, the last time her husband had gone away terrible things happened. He had to find a way to let go of the past the same as Katie was doing and work helped him.

Sue was fascinated to hear all about her near-death experience after the accident, especially when she said she had seen her mum and dad. She was upset when Katie told her about the first nine months of their marriage and how traumatic it had been. They hadn't been in contact with each other much at that time with them both having their own problems to deal with.

243

"You poor thing, Katie. I had no idea it was that bad living with your mother-in-law, but it sounds like she's changed. I really hope so, for your sake."

"Fatima and Shazia have already moved out of the town house. They seem happy living with Yasmin and Rashid in Abu Dhabi, especially now Yasmin is expecting her first baby. So, we will have the town house all to ourselves and Nabil says I can change everything if I want to."

"He is certainly trying to make it up to you and it can't be easy for him ... I mean ... with their customs."

"I know what you mean, Sue, and we'll both have to make compromises. The main thing is we want our marriage to work, and we love each other very much."

"And now you have this gorgeous little baby too," Sue said as she watched Tafiq gurgling on his changing mat.

It was so good to talk and laugh together like they used to and even better when Ellen joined them while Douglas was at work. The three of them had such wonderful, shared memories of her parents. Sue and Ellen were extremely interested in her plans to open an antique shop in Dubai too.

"I'm so happy to have my crazy friend back again, Sue," remarked Katie on their last day together. They had just eaten a delicious lunch. "But what are you going to do about a job?"

"Ah ... I wanted to talk to you about that. One of the few good things about Rob is that he's an exceptional architect and earns pots of money. He would rarely discuss such things with me, but I was able to save from my salary while I was there. I hardly ever went out, so I didn't have much to spend it on anyway."

"It's unusual for you to save, Sue."

"I know but something in the back of my mind told me it was the right thing to do. I can't explain it, but you understand about feelings and such things. Anyway, it's given me time to think about my future without having to worry about money for a few months."

"You're not going to give up nursing, are you?"

"No, I'm not, but I've decided I want to work abroad. Dad's okay, but as you know, I can't live under the same roof as my mum, even though I'm grateful they're letting me stay. I've thought about it a lot and I'd like to work in Dubai."

"Really, but that's marvellous!"

"I got in touch with a nurse friend of mine from Farnborough Hospital. Her sister works in Dubai and loves it. She made enquiries for me and says I stand a good chance because they are recruiting at the moment. I've sent my application form and CV, so now I must wait and see."

"Well, if you want something bad enough, it will fall into place."

"Your mum used to say something similar, bless her."

"She did," replied Katie, thoughtfully.

"So, what do you think?"

"I'm excited of course … but one word of warning." Sue was puzzled when she saw the serious look on Katie's face. "You won't be able to swan around Dubai in your punk outfits on your days off. It might be 1988, but that doesn't matter in the Emirates. You would most certainly scare the locals and probably get yourself arrested." They burst into fits of giggles.

"Oh Sue, not only do I have my best friend back but she's coming to live and work in Dubai."

"I haven't been offered a job yet."

Just as she said this, they both smelled the beautiful scent of Chanel No. 5. Katie knew without a doubt that Sue would be starting a new life in the sun.

Chapter Nineteen

The antiques shop had been in its embryonic stage in Katie's mind when they flew home to Dubai from London, but she decided to put it on hold for a while. They had certainly had a rough ride in the last year and the need to settle down in the town house with their son was imperative.

Abdullah met them at Dubai Airport, and he was so happy to see them all together. He made Katie feel very welcome and said she had been missed, then he admired the new addition to the family. Seeing Abdullah after all this time gave her a warm feeling of familiarity, and she was genuinely glad to be home.

All the family were waiting at the town house and the cook, with the help of extra staff, had laid on some of her delicious food. Rashid and Yasmin looked extremely happy; in fact, Yasmin was blooming and had quite a baby bump. They couldn't wait for November. Luckily for them their arranged marriage had worked out well. Shazia seemed so grown-up and had a beaming smile on her face when she greeted Katie. Her future husband, Haidar, was there too but he seemed shy and quiet compared to Shazia who had a new-found confidence. She still had the same cheeky laugh and sweet ways that had endeared her to Katie when they had first met. Fatima greeted her warmly and absolutely drooled over her first grandchild. She was delighted to show off her English and Katie was impressed, which pleased her mother-in-law. Aunt Aamira looked awkward, which wasn't surprising after what her husband had done. She had only found out the full extent of his misdemeanours after she questioned Rashid. Katie made a mental note to talk to her as soon as she could to give her the reassurance she so obviously needed. Latifa, who liked to think of herself as the head of the family, was sitting and waiting impatiently to hold her great grandson. She had a habit of looking sterner than she really was and today was no exception. Katie took Tafiq over to her and placed him in her outstretched arms. She said something in Emirati, "I've waited long enough!" When it was translated it made Katie laugh as she sat down next to her. Nabil was relieved to see how happy his wife was to be home, and he would do everything in his power to keep it that way.

It was a lovely family reunion, but they were both tired and relieved when they all went home. Katie had been touched by the show of affection especially from her mother-in-law. It was indeed a transformation from the Fatima she had known before her accident. The house was to be transformed from top to bottom, but a few of Ibrahim's things would be kept out of respect for him and because there was no good reason to change them.

Fatima had taken all her favourite possessions to Abu Dhabi. She had an extremely large ensuite bedroom and her own beautiful sitting room. Shazia was content with her large ensuite bedroom, which had an onyx desk and two luxurious sofas at one end; she was in London most of the time anyway. It wouldn't be long after finishing her degree that her marriage with Haidar would take place and they would be moving into their own home. The thought of it, was not something Shazia relished. She wasn't ready for marriage, but she had little choice in the matter as her papa had made all the necessary arrangements before he died.

Her intended came from a respected local family who had been friends with the Khalifa's for many years. Haidar's papa had made plenty of money with different businesses and his latest venture would be importing Ferraris to the Emirates. His son was to be made a partner when he married Shazia.

A nanny was engaged, and Katie had chosen well. Irma was a twenty-five-year-old from the Philippines and was used to babies because she came from a large family; she was a natural with Tafiq. Nabil seemed pleased with her too. He didn't usually get involved with staffing matters, apart from Abdullah, but he paid more attention to Irma because she would be looking after their son. Katie found it difficult to leave her baby with a nanny at first but as she became more involved with the refurbishing she started to let go of her uneasiness.

Nabil offered to fly over the interior designer who he had hired to transform his apartment in Grosvenor Square. But Katie was artistic and capable, and she was looking forward to choosing fabrics, furniture, and colours for their home. He gave her carte blanche but would employ decorators and anyone else when they were needed. The refurbishing wouldn't inconvenience them too much, and they could always stay in the beach villa if they needed to, which was no hardship.

The town house was capacious with high ceilings and plenty of windows, with extremely ornate ceilings and walls; completely different to houses in England. She chose, with Nabil's help, the more traditional Middle Eastern forms of art and some Persian rugs and silks. One of them was a beautiful Arabic woven silk wall hanging in red, yellow, and green with a yellow fringe. A design incorporating desert camps, Arabian buildings, figures and camels, Arabic lettering, and geometric designs. She also chose some European art and a few water colours of different landscapes in Britain; this had always been her favourite medium.

The water colours, especially of Cornwall, were hung in the hallway at the bottom of the magnificent winding staircase. Her favourite one was of Padstow Harbour which she had bought from Hannah after seeing it in her art studio at Hillside cottage. It always reminded her of Dorothy who had been so good to her and Tafiq. She was a prolific letter writer and said she would keep in touch with her adopted family. In fact, Katie had received a letter from her when they were staying in Mayfair. She had replied and sent a couple of polaroid photos of Tafiq so she could see the change in him already.

Mixing old and new was something Katie had learned from her parents, and she was becoming quite adept at combining Eastern and European artefacts as well; the end result was amazing. One of their most treasured paintings, by a local artist, was in their bedroom, hanging over the large dressing table opposite the four-poster bed they had chosen together. It was of flamingos flying majestically over Dubai creek. A sight they had both come to miss when they had been away for so long. On the odd occasion Nabil had flown to Dubai for business, while Katie was in hospital, he had found solace when watching the activity on the creek from the huge windows in his office.

Three months had passed since their home coming. They were settled and happy and enjoying normal married life. Katie was used to wearing abayas again and Nabil was glad to be back in traditional clothes for most of the time. She was loving being a young mum and they both noticed new things about Tafiq every day.

Katie enjoyed having a project that was both time consuming and fulfilling. Sadly, she had to miss Bev and

Greg's wedding which was in October. They'd only been home for six weeks and after a year of hospitals and trauma, they all agreed it was too soon to fly back to London. She had stayed the best of friends with Bev, and she kept a framed photograph of their wedding on her desk. Silver framed photos were one of her weaknesses, and she had them all over the place. It was lucky they had two large homes in Dubai. One of her favourites was of Latifa sitting and holding Tafiq with her and Nabil standing behind.

Katie knew Bev wanted one of the new Kenwood Mixers, so she had one sent to their Greenwich flat from John Lewis a couple of weeks before their wedding. Bev was thrilled with her amazing new toy and couldn't wait to try it out.

Another happy event was when Yasmin gave birth to a healthy baby boy at the end of November when Tafiq was seven months old. The family were thrilled to meet Yusef especially Fatima and Latifa and it was good that Yasmin and Katie could talk about babies together. Yasmin had everything she wanted, a good loving husband, a beautiful home and now they had started a family. She was happy being a wife and a mother and was easily contented by life's simple pleasures. Rashid was hard working and a good family man. He loved Yasmin very much and they wanted at least four children.

Katie knew marriage and motherhood would never be enough for her. She wouldn't say this in front of Nabil's family, apart from Shazia who completely understood. She had flown home when the university broke up for Christmas and she was pleased to meet her new nephew though she soon got bored with baby talk. Enjoying her freedom in England meant the last thing on her mind was marriage and babies, even though Haidar talked about nothing else. They got on well when he wasn't talking about getting married, but she found him dull compared to her student friends in London. His name meant Lion, but she thought he was more like a pussy cat, and she wished she could get out of her arranged marriage.

One evening when Nabil had gone out with Hakeem, Katie and Shazia sat in the garden listening to the rise and full of the water in the fountain.

"I remember the day you sat out here running your fingers through the water. I had never seen you look so miserable," remarked Shazia.

"It seems like a lifetime ago now even though it's only been two years."

"And what a painful two years it's been for you and my brother."

"You could say that." She smiled at her sister-in-law.

"I think you're marvellous after all that you've been through. It's a miracle you're still alive after what my uncle did."

"He didn't actually make me walk in front of the taxi."

"Well, he might as well have done, the nasty bastard."

"That's what my friend Sue calls him. Mind you, I've heard her say a lot worse." This made them chuckle.

"I never liked him you know. He hardly ever spoke to us girls when we were growing up. Nabil was his favourite and of course he always wanted a son but I'm glad he didn't have children. It's a shame for Aunt Aamira but can you imagine having a monster like him as a father."

"It doesn't bear thinking about, but he might have been different with his own kids."

"You're too nice that's your trouble, Katie. You always try and see the good in people. I wish I could. My uncle should have died and gone to hell!"

"Shaz, you sound like Nabil."

252

"Good!"

"I did feel anger towards Mohammed for a while, but I had to let it go. I didn't want anything to spoil my future with your brother which is what your uncle would have wanted. Anyway, he is living in a kind of hell, being at home most of the time with an elderly nurse watching over him."

They both giggled.

"My brother had the last laugh. He was determined not to hire a young pretty nurse for uncle, just in case he got any ideas, which he would have done without a doubt. He makes me cringe."

"Let's change the subject. How long are you staying?"

"Until I fly to London for Douglas and Ellen's wedding with you and Nabil," Shazia said with a beaming smile on her face.

"Oh, that's great news but what about Haidar? Won't he miss you?"

"Mamma said the same thing and it took me a whole day to persuade her to let me go. Anyway, I will have lots of studying to do straight after Christmas and she couldn't argue with that."

"You might as well enjoy yourself while you can."

"Oh, don't you worry, I'm having a great time at uni." Shazia winked.

Katie laughed. She looked at her sister-in-law knowingly remembering the fun she had when she was studying at Guys Hospital. Students must work hard if they want to succeed, so the need to play hard is understandable; it's a release.

Shazia fell silent suddenly, looking sad and vulnerable.

"Is something wrong?" Katie looked concerned.

"No ... yes ... I was just thinking." She had tears in her eyes which started trickling down her cheeks.

Katie guessed what the problem was.

"I don't want an arranged marriage … I don't want to marry anyone!"

"I wish I could help. I don't like seeing you unhappy."

"Mamma would be devastated if I went against papa's wishes. It would shame our family and we would never live it down. Don't take this the wrong way, Katie, but it's so unfair that Nabil was allowed to marry for love. I was only young when I used to hear him arguing with papa, but Yasmin says our brother refused his demands from the time he was eighteen."

"Yes, he told me before we were married. I didn't comment much then because it's part of your culture and who am I to criticise your religious beliefs? But a couple of months ago when I had one of my headaches and was feeling irritable, we had a terrible argument about your arranged marriage."

"Did you? I don't want you two falling out over me. I know my brother would help me if he could."

"Well, like I said I was feeling irritable, and it was me who brought the subject up."

"Thank you for trying, Katie. It means a lot."

Hakeem was particularly morose, even though he was in his favourite restaurant with his best friend and blood brother. Nabil tried everything to raise the vibrations to no avail. He talked about their childhood and teenage years when they had got up to some tricks, but nothing seemed to work. He was becoming extremely concerned about his friend.

"It's no good, Nabil, I can't shake off this terrible depression."

"What can I do to help you?"

"There is nothing anyone can do. My wife desperately wants more children, and I can't give them to her. I just can't bring myself to …"

"It's okay, you don't have to explain to me I understand."

"I don't think you fully understand my predicament because you're happily married. You've certainly had your share of troubles and I'm so pleased that everything has worked out for you and Katie. But … there's something I must tell you."

"I'm listening."

"A few months ago, when I was in London on business, I met a man and he … he became my lover."

Nabil didn't say a word.

"Your silence says it all, my friend. You disapprove."

"It's not disapproval Hakeem … it's concern. You know what can happen to you if this ever gets back to Dubai."

"Of course, I know. Prison or even death, though I think the latter is preferable."

"Please don't say that."

"Why? My wife and daughters will be better off without me."

"Leena and Mira don't want to grow up without a papa."

They had paid the bill and it was getting late, so they left the restaurant. Nabil didn't want to leave Hakeem in this state, but he assured him he was going straight home.

Katie could see something had upset her husband because he was unusually quiet and looked thoughtful. He leant over and kissed Tafiq lying peacefully in his cot; they hadn't moved him into the nursery yet. He climbed into bed without a word. Taking Katie in his arms, he held her knowing how lucky he was compared to Hakeem and Usha. Ignorance and prejudice towards gay people, was bad enough in England, but in the Islamic world it was unacceptable and against their religion. Hakeem was taking a great risk.

255

It was nearly Christmas in Europe, and they had an important wedding to go to, so the town house refurbishment was put on hold. There wasn't much more to be done, and it was good for them to have a break from it all. They flew to England in time to buy Christmas presents and the atmosphere in Mayfair was electric. They took their nanny with them, not just to help with Tafiq, but Katie wanted Irma to see London, especially at this magical time of year. It was the first time she'd been to England or anywhere other than the Emirates; she was excited to say the least and was extremely happy with her new employers.

Shazia, who had persuaded her mamma to let her fly to London with her brother and sister-in-law a week before the Christmas wedding, was her usual bubbly self. The following day Sue arrived and hit it off with Nabil's sister straightaway. Shazia asked her if she wanted to stay in her apartment because she had more empty bedrooms than her brother. Sue was happy with the arrangement and was simply glad to be free from her mother's indifference towards her.

Katie was to be matron of honour and had sent her exact measurements to Ellen a few weeks before. She tried on her dress as soon as she arrived in case it needed altering, but it fitted perfectly. Her aunt thought it would because her niece's figure always seemed to stay the same. Ellen's best friend, Doreen, from Edenbridge, was also matron of honour but she'd had her fitting two weeks before.

Four days before Christmas Katie, Ellen, Sue, and Shazia were looking forward to shopping in the West End despite the continuing IRA bombing threats. They weren't going to let that stop them visiting the big stores. It was manic, but they managed to buy what they wanted even though they were exhausted at the end of the day.

Irma stayed home with Tafiq because it would be far too busy for a baby; plus, she enjoyed taking him out in the pram so she could see more of Mayfair. Katie and Shazia had shown Irma the sights when they first arrived, and she had been thrilled with the Christmas lights in both Oxford and Regent Street.

Nabil was meeting up with business associates for a pre-Christmas lunch while the women were shopping; he liked to keep their English business partners happy, and he was pleased to be surrounded by men for a change. Secretly, he was glad that Sue was staying in Shazia's apartment because he found her a little overpowering. He wondered how she was going to find life in the Emirates when she started her new job at Dubai Hospital. Katie defended her best friend and said she would fit in fine. She was really looking forward to having Sue so close. A new year, a new job, and a new beginning! It reminded her of the day she had arrived in Dubai in 1985. The day that had changed the course of her life and it had certainly been an eventful three years since.

A few friends had come up to London to join them for Ellen's hen night. They had a marvellous time in the Ivy Grill, Covent Garden. Plenty of wine and champagne were flowing which is why it hadn't been arranged for the night before the wedding. The bride wanted to look and feel her best on her special day.

Sue and Katie had arranged a kissogram for Ellen, which had been a complete surprise. He was handsome and sexy dressed in a fireman's uniform with his jacket open, showing his wonderful pecs and rippling muscles. Holding his yellow helmet under one arm, he sat on Ellen's knee and put the other one around her shoulders. They all laughed at the look on her face when he invited her to run her hands over his chest, which she did of course. A few others in the restaurant enjoyed the spectacle as well and they cheered and clapped as he left fifteen minutes later. The girls were still giggling as they fell out of the restaurant and climbed into the waiting black cabs.

The following morning, when Douglas was at the hospital Ellen and Doreen relaxed after a night of drinking and fun. He hadn't planned a stag night because of work, but at St Thomas' the staff put on a party for him. Nurses, doctors, and ancillary staff all joined the celebrations, but some had to leave if they were on call or if there was an emergency. It was a typical lively hospital party with staff coming and going. Being the modest type who didn't like too much fuss, he found himself overwhelmed by the good wishes, presents and cards. They had both said they didn't want presents because they had all they needed in their respective homes. But they still received a few, plus money and vouchers.

Katie offered to help Ellen with any last-minute preparations, but everything was organised by Claridge's Hotel. The ceremony and the wedding breakfast were being held there and of course it had lovely memories for Ellen and Katie. Douglas went along with whatever his future wife desired; not because he didn't care, but because he wanted to make her happy. She was not as demanding as his first wife had been and she was so much more fun to be with; he didn't think he would marry again until Ellen came into his life. He was pleased she had asked Nabil to walk her down the aisle; she wanted to keep it in the family.

Douglas took him and his brother, Alex, who was the best man, to the tailor. Nabil had sent Ellen his measurements a few weeks ago and fortunately there was only a slight alteration needed much to the tailor's relief.

The wedding plans had all happened so quickly, but everything was working out perfectly.

On Christmas morning the atmosphere was building in the Claridge's wedding room they had chosen. They didn't want anything huge as they both had small families. Douglas' Elderly mother Agnes, brother Alex, his wife, Maureen and their two teenage boys came down from Scotland. Their mother, Agnes, was a lively eighty-two-year-old but sadly their father had died five years ago. It had been a blessed release as he'd suffered from bad health for several years. But they did have many friends, especially from the medical and teaching professions.

The wedding room looked stunning with its enormous ornate arched windows, elegant drapes, and stylish chairs for the guests. Beautiful floral displays matched Ellen's small pink and cream rose bouquet and huge church candles in glass jars were placed all around the room, setting the scene for a Christmas wedding. It certainly looked chic.

Katie was in the hotel with Ellen, and they were waiting for her friend Doreen, the hair stylist and beautician to arrive.

"While I have you all to myself darling, I want to tell you something. It's been so hectic since you arrived from Dubai, and I haven't had a chance. What with Christmas shopping, wedding rehearsals, fittings, and my hen night we've hardly had a minute on our own."

"What do you want to tell me, Ellen? You haven't changed your mind, have you?" She smiled at her aunt.

"Oh, very funny … no I most definitely have not. It's many years since I've been this happy."

"I can see that, and I'm thrilled for you both."

"I haven't even told Doreen yet … I wanted you to be the first to know … I'm pregnant!"

259

"What?" Oh my God I wasn't expecting to hear that. How wonderful!" Katie squealed with delight and hugged Ellen excitedly.

"It is and Douglas is so happy about it."

"Did you plan it?"

"I supposed we did when we decided I would stop taking the pill, but neither of us expected it to happen this quick. Mind you, the quicker the better, considering my age."

"You're not old, Ellen."

"Maybe not, but my biological body clock is ticking away. That's why we thought we'd try sooner rather than later. But it's not a shotgun wedding as I'm hardly showing." Ellen insisted, with a huge grin on her face.

They both giggled.

"Did you give in your notice at the school like you said you were going to?"

"I did and it felt like the right thing to do after all these years."

"I'm sure you'll be missed!"

"The staff were half expecting it because I've been spending so much time in London at the weekends and through the summer break. I'm sure the students have had fun discussing my love life too."

"They've probably been taking bets on whether you'd marry or not."

"Probably! I had such a lovely leaving party and besides wedding presents they gave me a first edition John Betjeman book of poems as a keepsake."

"Another book to add to your library."

"Funny you should say that Douglas has quite a library too, mostly medical books and journals. We were laughing the other day because if we ever bought a home together, we'd need one huge room to put them all in."

The thought of this made them chuckle.

"But won't you miss Edenbridge?"

"I'm sure I will darling, but we plan to spend as much time there as possible when Douglas can get away. He's starting to do more teaching and less practical work these days."

"Really?"

"He says that although him and Miranda were incompatible, he was married to his job throughout their twenty-year marriage, which didn't help; he doesn't want to make the same mistake again."

"He must really love you."

"I know, bless him, but he says he enjoys teaching and lecturing and helping the young doctors of the future. And I'm looking forward to doing some part-time private tutoring in London, plus I want to write that book that's been in my head for the last two or three years."

Before Katie had the chance to reply Doreen arrived followed by the hair stylist and the beautician; Sue and Shazia arrived a few minutes after that. Even though they weren't part of the ceremony Ellen wanted them to be pampered as well.

The wedding was held at midday. Douglas was feeling nervous while waiting for the bride to be. He had asked his brother Alex at least twice if he had the wedding ring as millions of other bridegrooms do at their weddings. Alex reassured him while patting his breast pocket and said the speeches were safe too. The music started playing and when he turned and saw Ellen he was filled with pride and couldn't stop smiling. He thought she looked stunning and exuded happiness with her arm linked in Nabil's, who took great delight in walking her down the aisle. She looked fabulous in a midi v neck cream silk dress with three-quarter length sleeves and a pill box hat. The full skirt swung as she walked, and her elegant high heeled sandals were gorgeous. Douglas had bought her an eighteen-carat gold heart shaped pendant with earrings to match, which completed her wedding outfit. Katie and Doreen walked behind in midi salmon pink dresses with leg of mutton sleeves carrying small posies to match Ellen's bouquet. They looked beautiful but neither of them could nor indeed wanted to upstage the bride. The men were extremely smart in their dark suits, cream waistcoats, and salmon pink cravats.

It had been a wonderful day. The wedding breakfast was excellent and the speeches that followed were both witty and appropriate. This was a relief to the men, especially Nabil, who had never been asked to make a speech at an English wedding before. Katie had helped him write it and he had practised on her too. She was delighted when he got through it without any hitches.

That evening, the newly married couple stayed in the honeymoon suite and were thoroughly cossetted as you would expect. It was a wedding present from his family, and they even had a personal butler. Douglas found this a bit ostentatious, but his wife loved it. Ellen thought they deserved to get pampered. The day after their wedding they had a delicious breakfast of smoked salmon and scrambled eggs served in their suite, followed by champagne and strawberries. But they were ready to leave at mid-day so they could get back to Marylebone. They wanted to spend time with his family before they returned to Scotland the following day and Douglas and Ellen went off on their honeymoon.

Nabil and Katie had booked a week at the Hilton International in Fujairah, Oman, as a wedding present. Ellen had heard them talk about it a few times and had expressed an interest in staying there. It was a shame it couldn't have been a surprise, but Douglas needed to take leave from the hospital and make sure he had cover. He worked so hard he deserved two weeks away, which included travelling time. Their last few days would be spent with Katie and Nabil in Dubai. Nabil's family were looking forward to seeing them both, especially Douglas, the doctor who had saved Katie and Tafiq; typically, he would say it was down to his whole team.

Chapter Twenty

Mohammed was thoroughly bored with his sedentary life and sick of the old dragon nursing him, but he didn't have the energy to argue with her. He had met his match but wouldn't admit it. Aamira had told him how pleased she was that Nabil had brought his wife and son back to Dubai. "The infidel and the half-breed!" he muttered to himself. She had also taken great pleasure in telling him that his nephew was allowing Katie to refurbish the town house and he was seething. "How dare she think she can change my brother's house to her own liking. She's an infiltrator!" His thinking was as distorted as ever, and he was deliberately forgetting that the house now belonged to his nephew. "I need to think of a way to get rid of her." He kept his voice low so his nurse couldn't hear. If she suspected he was hatching a plot, she would report back to Nabil, of that, he was certain. "I must find the strength to get out of this prison; it is full of spies." He even included his mamma, Latifa, in this.

By the beginning of April, the only rooms that hadn't been refurbished in the town house were the majlis. Nabil didn't want the men's one changed, and Katie love the ladies majlis with its elegant greys and pinks, so she just added a few personal touches. She was used to the low sofas and tables, and it was a beautiful place to welcome her visitors. There was an archway on the left of the large entrance hall which led to the men's majlis and an archway on the right leading to the ladies. She had been in there a few times in the past with Fatima and her friends, but most of them had spoken Emirati, so she had not enjoyed it at all. These days, however, she was finding the language a bit easier to grasp and she certainly understood more. Fatima had put in a lot of effort into learning English, so Katie felt it was only fair to return the compliment. Her teacher came to the town house twice a week because she wanted to learn to write Emirati, as well as speak it. Nabil was impressed.

Hospitality was a big thing in the Emirates and the history of the Majlis fascinated Katie. She was looking forward to inviting some of her girlfriends from Dubai Hospital, especially Sue who had settled in well and loved her new nursing job. It felt strange when she visited her at the complex and even more so when she found out she was living in Bev's old apartment.

Shazia was trying to talk her sister-in-law into having a certain type of women's only party where there would be the presentation of sex toys and lingerie. Yasmin had one, while Katie and Nabil were in England, after her sister had pleaded with her. Once the local women had relaxed and played a few party games, most of them ended up laughing and enjoying themselves. It was secretive, but harmless fun, though unlike England, there was no alcohol. Shazia said the informal and private setting of Katies majlis would be perfect. Obviously, she didn't mention any of this in front of her brother. What they did in the ladies majlis was of no concern to the men who held their own councils and gatherings. Shazia was going to organise it and Katie would only need to supply the food and hospitality.

Katie said yes because she wanted to see for herself what occurred at one of these parties. She had heard about them in England but with all the things that had happened to her and Sue they didn't get round to booking one. She loved her sister-in-law's mischievous ways, and she found it difficult to say no to her. Hosting the party would give her a chance to meet some more of the young local women, especially those with children.

She booked it for three days before the beginning of Ramadan while Nabil was away on business. Yasmin and Shazia brought a few local ladies with them. Two of whom hadn't seen Katie before, and they were curious to meet Nabil Khalifa's English wife. Most of the local families had accepted her now, but she wasn't naïve enough to think they all had. There was still a lot of intolerance and suspicion amongst the Emiratis but after all she'd been through, she wasn't going to let a few prejudices affect her. The Khalifa family were well respected which helped enormously.

Sue arrived with two of Katie's former colleagues from Dubai Hospital and it was lovely to see them. Some of her friends had moved on which was inevitable, so she was really happy to have her best friend in the Emirates. She welcomed and relaxed her guests just as her mum would have done, though her dinner parties were a slightly different affair. The party planner was ready and waiting with all her gear. Patter came easy to her, but it was a bit of a slow start, so she was grateful to Sue who was good at helping the ladies lose their inhibitions. The representative said she would make a good party planner herself and they all laughed.

Katie's first gathering in her majlis was a great success and she smiled to herself after they had all left; feeling satisfied as she looked round her domain. It was a far cry from the days when Fatima and some of her friends had made her feel like an outsider. How things had changed. She wasn't tired, so she went upstairs to the lounge, poured herself a glass of wine, then wandered out onto the terrace over-looking the swimming pool. It was lit up and looked extremely inviting. Sue had an early shift in the morning otherwise she would have stayed. The lights around the garden made it look even more beautiful with the many exotic plants and trees and amazing splashes of colour; the sound of the fountain was mesmerising. It was so quiet, and she sat soaking up the peace for a few minutes until she heard Tafiq crying. Although he was now sleeping in the nursey and Irma had a bedroom attached to it, she decided to go and help because she knew he was teething.

Tafiq's first birthday was in the middle of Ramadan. Katie and Nabil decided to have it mainly in the garden so the children could play in the pool. Food was laid out in the garden room, but the adults would not be eating until after the sun had set around seven-thirty. They had a few guests: Hakeem, his wife and two girls; Yasmin, Rashid, and baby Yusef who was nearly five months old; Abdullah brought his wife and two of his younger grandchildren and Katie had invited two local mums she'd got friendly with; they had two children each. Shazia was on a short Easter break from university and Haidar couldn't hide his pleasure at being in her company again. Aunt Aamira looked happy and relaxed while enjoying watching the little ones play and Irma was in her element.

Latifa and Fatima were looking forward to having more grandchildren when Shazia and Haidar married. Her mamma said this just as she walked past, and it didn't go unnoticed; she chose to ignore her mamma's comments.

Sue came of course, but it was a surprise to Katie when she turned up with Reece, though she was pleased to see him.

267

Ellen was sad she couldn't be there for her great nephew's first birthday. She was nearly seven months pregnant and as a mature mother to be she was advised not to fly. Katie missed her aunt and was looking forward to seeing the new baby when it arrived. She spoke to Ellen and Douglas regularly on the telephone and they sounded extremely happy. They couldn't hide the excitement in their voices when they talked about the preparations for their son or daughter. It was the best thing that could have happened to them.

Mohammed was sitting on his terrace feeling nothing but bitterness and rage towards his nephew's wife. He had too much time to think and his unbalanced thoughts were getting more obsessive by the day. In his warped mind she was the cause of his near fatal heart attack, and it was because of her he was leading an inactive life. He ignored the fact that his life had, until recently, existed of debauchery, gambling and drinking which would have had a lot to do with the deterioration of his health. His thoughts would have seemed illogical to anyone else, especially as he was the one who had threatened Katie which nearly led to her death.

Knowing all the family were at his nephew's house enjoying the half-breed's first birthday party made him even more angry. He knew his chauffeur had driven Aamira and Latifa to the party, leaving him with his nurse for company; not that he sought anyone's company, not even his mamma's. She sometimes came to see him in his rooms, but he preferred to be on his own. He detested his wife and hardly ever spoke to her these days. Latifa wondered what had happened to the decent young man he had once been. Since her son had become fanatical about his faith, instead of being understanding with his wife, who desperately wanted children, he became hostile and unreasonable.

Latifa felt he had brought shame on her and Aamira, but she only said this to him once because he had lost his temper. She was a tough old woman but even she was frightened by the strength of her son's anger and bitterness.

He was surrounded by luxury, but nothing could bring his health back, so he decided it was time to put his plan into action. Earlier he had added a sleeping draft to his nurse's drink. He walked into her room next to his bedroom where he found her slumped in her chair snoring like an old hag. He smiled to himself then walked back to his room, went over to his bureau, unlocked a secret compartment, and pulled out a handgun. He had already phoned for a taxi. The family had an account if they needed extra cars.

Making his way slowly downstairs, because he couldn't rush anywhere these days, was frustrating and made his black mood even darker. The staff had been given the night off, so the house was empty and there were no spies. The driver came to the door just as Mohammed opened it and he offered him help when he noticed he was breathless. But the man with a mission stubbornly refused and walked to the car unaided. He gave the driver the address of his nephew's house and they were there in no time.

One of the extra maids who had been hired for the day opened the door for Mohammed because the other members of staff were busy. She didn't know who the gentleman was, and he wouldn't give his name. He asked her where the family were, and she said she would take him through to the garden room; he said he preferred to make his own way, so the maid went back to the kitchen.

The Khalifa's, their friends and family were eating downstairs because some of the older children were still up and playing round the pool. Ramadan was a time for them all to eat together when the sun had gone down. Nobody heard or saw Mohammed hiding in the shadows of the archway with the handgun poised because they were all talking and laughing. Mercifully, Tafiq was upstairs in the nursery with Irma so he couldn't harm the child he hated with a vengeance.

He stood in the shadows watching the happy scene, which only made him more furious. How he loathed seeing his nephew's English wife being a hostess to most of the people he knew. It had taken all his strength to get here and despite the pain in his chest, he wasn't going to give up now.

Katie was sitting at the table and had just finished eating when her mum's perfume became suddenly overpowering. She could feel her so close as if she were trying to warn her about something. Nabil saw the look on his wife's face and wondered what was wrong. He was about to ask her when his uncle suddenly appeared holding a gun. "English infidel!" he shouted, then he fired a shot.

The next few seconds were like something out of a film set. Nabil flung himself in front of his wife, taking the brunt of the bullet. The force of him toppled her and the chair backwards onto the floor. Everyone was screaming, some ducking under the table, plates, cutlery, and food went flying and the children were crying. It was utter chaos. Hakeem went to disarm Nabil's uncle but as he grabbed the gun Mohammed collapsed holding his chest. Realising he had hit his nephew instead of Katie made him repentant but only Hakeem heard him whisper, "what have I done?" He died from a massive heart attack.

Katie lay stunned at first as her husband lay on top of her with blood pouring from a wound. "Somebody, call an ambulance!" she screamed, but Abdullah had already done it. Rashid lifted his brother-in-law from Katie and Abdullah picked her up from the floor, still on the chair. While this was happening, Sue checked Mohammed's pulse and proclaimed him dead though nobody seemed to notice, except his mamma. She then went to Nabil as Rashid laid him gently on the sofa putting her fingers to his neck as he was out cold; everyone waited anxiously with bated breath. She could sense the fear and panic all around her. "He's alive," she called out and although this was her best friend's husband, she put her professional hat on and went into emergency mode. She looked to see where the bullet had gone. "It's missed his heart." There was a collective sigh of relief. Fatima, who found some hidden strength, brought a first aid kit and Sue stemmed the flow of blood by applying pressure to Nabil's wound while they waited for the ambulance. She knew it looked worse than it was, and she tried to reassure them all.

Yasmin and the rest of the women were trying to calm the children down. Latifa was sitting crossed legged on the floor next to her dead son and was desperately praying for her grandson. She was pale and suddenly looked extremely frail. Shazia had her arms around her sister-in-law and for a few seconds Katie was in a daze; she pushed Shazia off and ran over to the sofa.

"Nabil." She knelt on the floor next to Sue just as he opened his eyes."

"Are you okay, my angel?"

"Yes, I am but you're not, darling."

"Don't worry, I think he shot me in the shoulder, at least that seems to be where the pain is coming from."

"Don't waste your energy talking Nabil you've lost a lot of blood," Sue told him just before he fell unconscious again.

Rashid was sickened, "I wish the ambulance would hurry up," but just as he said this, they heard the sirens coming down the road. Abdullah and Hakeem went out to meet the paramedics and took them through to the back of the house.

Sue told them where the bullet had gone, and they thanked her for stopping the bleeding. They took over after gently pulling Katie away from Nabil, who was still unconscious. It wasn't long before he was put in the ambulance with his wife by his side. Another ambulance arrived to take Mohammed away. Rashid said the family would follow them to the hospital. Aamira was worried about Latifa, but she insisted on going too.

Terrified staff, after getting over the initial shock, started to clean up the mess. There was blood everywhere but Abdullah, Hakeem, Haidar and Reece took over and told them to go home. The rest of the horror-struck guests left after Sue checked they were all okay. She was covered in blood so when Abdullah had finished clearing up, he drove Sue and Reece back to the complex. His wife and grandchildren had already gone home, and Irma was taking care of the babies while the family were at the hospital. Everyone was stunned by the whole affair and none of them would be doing much the next day.

It was one o'clock by the time Katie, Rashid, Yasmin, Fatima, Shazia and Latifa were allowed in to see Nabil. It had taken the surgeon a long time to retrieve the bullet because it was wedged in a bone. The family had been worried about Latifa, but she wanted to stay; she wouldn't rest until she saw her grandson alive.

He looked peaceful lying against the pillows with his shoulder strapped up, but he was oblivious to the world around him after having general anaesthetic. It was just as well under the circumstances. The family were pleased to see he was okay, but they weren't allowed to stay long; they were told to come back in the morning.

Abdullah was anxiously waiting outside the hospital when they at last appeared. Rashid told him Nabil was going to be all right and thanked him for all his help. He was a true friend to the Khalifa family, but when they got back to the house, they told him to go home to his wife; she must have been worried sick.

Rashid and Katie were still covered in blood so the first thing they did was shower and change but none of them could sleep so they met in the lounge afterwards. Suddenly Katie started shaking violently when the realisation of what had happened dawned on her.

"Mohammed … tr … tried to kill me."

None of them knew what to say. Fatima had been crying most of the time since her beloved son had been shot by her husband's brother, but she knew she had to stay strong for her family. Wiping her eyes, she went to her daughter-in-law, who looked like she was going to pass out. Rashid poured her a brandy but before he got to her, she crumpled to the floor. He carried her up to the bedroom and Fatima called the doctor. Rashid was doing his best to take care of everyone in the aftermath, but the night of terror had affected him greatly.

Shazia and Yasmin were comforting Latifa, who also looked ill, so when the doctor came, he examined them both. He said they were suffering from shock, but because of Mrs Khalifa's past medical history and the fact that her lips were going blue he was concerned. He told them, if she were still the same after he had examined Latifa, he would call an ambulance.

273

Shazia sat with her sister-in-law, who was the only person in the world who really understood her. She covered her hand with her own while keeping vigil knowing that Katie would hate to have to go back in hospital again.

Thankfully, she came round, her lips had returned to their normal colour, and she looked much better; everyone was relieved. The doctor examined her again and was satisfied but advised her to rest. He told them the best thing for Latifa was to be in her own home and bed. Aamira had tried to stay strong for her mother-in-law but was feeling shame, anger, and incredulity at her husband's actions; she was glad he was dead but did not voice her opinion.

In the morning when they had all finally had some sleep Abdulla came to drive them both home. He helped Aamira take Latifa to her bedroom because she looked weak and broken. None of them had given the nurse a thought and because the sleeping draft had been so powerful, she hadn't long been awake. Abdullah gave her a broad outline of what had transpired at the party. She was revolted and puzzled as to why she had slept while her patient was able to leave the house and carry out such a dreadful deed. Then it dawned on her that he must have put something in her drink and Abdullah agreed.

Her charge may have been dead, but she was kept on to nurse Latifa, who would surely be a far better patient. The strength had gone out of her, which was not surprising. She had lost her husband at the age of forty-six, then her son Ibrahim who died suddenly and now Mohammed. She didn't know how she felt about him. He had tried to murder her nephew's wife, the wife he adored and had been through so much with. Katie was the mother of her great grandson, yet he hated her enough to try and kill her. The more she thought about it, the more confused she became, so she slept trying to shut out the terrible truth.

Aamira was concerned for her mother-in-law, Katie and Nabil and the horrific situation they found themselves in. But she was relieved beyond all measure that her husband was dead. She was surprised at her strength of feeling but the atmosphere in the house was already much lighter. In fact, she felt free for the first time in many years. Free of his bullying and mental abuse, free to be herself; she had lived in fear for so long she hardly knew where to start in finding the real Aamira, but she was going to enjoy trying.

Katie was such a kind caring person and had spoken to her husband's aunt a few times about the things her Mohammed had done. Yet, her only concern was for others. She recalled Katie's wise words. 'Somewhere inside you, there's a wonderful, strong woman trying to get out of the protective shell you've put around yourself.' These words came back to her, and she knew it was time for the butterfly to emerge from the chrysalis.

The Dubai police visited the family the day after the attempted murder. Katie was in no fit state to answer questions and as they had all been witnesses, they answered their enquiries as best they could. They had been into the hospital early in the morning too but were told by the doctor that Mr Khalifa was not well enough to be questioned. It was clear Mohammed had died of a massive heart attack so there wasn't a case to answer. The police left and said they would be in touch.

Later in the morning Katie willed herself to get out of bed. She had one of her headaches and the doctor had told her to rest. How could she with her husband in hospital? Ellen and Douglas needed to know too, so she phoned them, and it was lucky they were both at home. To say they were stunned by the news was an understatement. Her aunt was beside herself with worry and wanted to fly to the Emirates, but it wasn't possible.

After the telephone call Ellen couldn't get her head round what Katie had told her. Mohammed had attempted to murder her niece and had wounded Nabil when he dived in front of her. Douglas had to calm her down which wasn't easy, but he didn't want her going into early labour. They were both shocked and he was glad he didn't have to go into work as he couldn't leave her in such a state.

Feeling bad about having to give them such terrible news knowing her aunt was seven months pregnant made Katie feel even worse. Her head was thumping, and she went into the bathroom for some pain killers. She laid back on the bed for half an hour to give the tablets time to work, but she certainly felt better than she had the night before. Yearning to see her son helped her to rouse herself again; a cuddle would do her the world of good.

A warm shower made her feel half human again and she dressed, then went into the nursery. Irma, Tafiq and Yusef weren't in there, so she went downstairs. Yasmin and Rashid were cooing over their son and Fatima was holding Tafiq, though he was straining to get down, so she let him crawl. Katie watched this scene of domestic bliss from the doorway and wished Nabil was there. She had tears in her eyes as she thought of him lying in a hospital bed and how he had saved her from possible death.

Fatima looked up. "Katie, are you feeling strong enough to be out of bed?"

"I am thanks, and at the moment all I want is a cuddle with my handsome boy." She leant down and picked him up and as soon as he saw his mamma his face lit up with the most gorgeous smile. It filled Katie with strength. "Where's Irma?"

"She's preparing lunch for Tafiq, and I've just fed Yusef," replied Yasmin. Shazia is in the pool. She's more upset than she likes to admit, and a swim will do her good."

"I phoned the hospital and Nabil had a fairly comfortable night," Rashid told her. "They said, he is feeling depressed after what happened which is hardly surprising; he's looking forward to seeing you but only when you're well enough."

"Did they say we can visit?"

"Yes, but we've decided you both need some time alone, so we won't stay long."

Katie was trying to push last night's events to the back of her mind unsuccessfully and she knew she needed to be with her husband.

Rashid told her how Hakeem, Abdullah, Reece and Haidar had cleaned up the garden room after the family had left for the hospital. "They couldn't do much with the sofa, which is still covered in blood, but I've arranged to have it taken away, so you don't have to see it. You can buy a new one … when you're up to it I mean."

"Yes … thanks," she replied absentmindedly. Rashid, Yasmin, and Fatima exchanged looks. "That was so good of them. I must remember to say thank you." She suddenly felt sick to the pit of her stomach and sat down abruptly, letting the struggling Tafiq crawl on the floor again just as Irma came in; she gathered him up in her arms.

They all looked concerned when they noticed how pale Katie had become.

"You must have something to eat."

"I'm not hungry, Mamma."

Fatima was touched when her daughter-in-law called her mamma, and it showed just how far their relationship had come. Her heart went out to her when she thought of what her brother-in-law had tried to do. How she wished her husband were still alive. Ibrahim would have been a calming influence on them all. "You need to eat, or you won't have the strength to go to the hospital."

Katie reluctantly agreed and Fatima went to see if cook had lunch ready. Praying for her family was something she had been doing continuously. She prayed they would all stay strong and be able to help her son and his wife get over this latest appalling episode in their lives. At least now Mohammed was gone but she prayed for his soul.

Later that day when her headache had subsided, Katie was able to go and see Nabil. It was so good to find herself alone with him and he was more alert than she had expected him to be, though he looked as tired as she was. Thankfully, the morphine was easing his pain.

"Come and sit on the bed next to me, angel, so I can put my good arm around you."

She smiled and didn't have to be asked twice.

"You look exhausted, so I don't want you staying too long. Mamma told me they had to call the doctor and you've been ordered to rest."

"I promise I will as soon as I get home. Poor Latifa she was in shock too and Abdullah took her and Aunt Aamira home this morning."

"She's lost her husband and both her sons. Is it any wonder she's in shock? And what must she think of Mohammed? It doesn't bear thinking about, the burden she must be shouldering. We should visit her as soon as we can."

Leaning against him never felt so good and he kissed the top of her head. They were struggling to fight back

278

their emotions as they thought of Mohammed standing in the doorway pointing a gun; they both ended up tearful. Nabil gave her a squeeze, recognising her fear, but so proud of the strong woman she was.

"I can't stop thinking about what might have happened if I hadn't seen my uncle … you could have been …"

"But you did see him, and it was such a brave thing that you did, darling."

"It's not brave, to save my wife from a bullet. I will always do my best to protect my family angel. I thank Allah that you're alive and we are finally rid of … I can't even bring myself to say his name. I'm glad he is dead!"

"I won't argue with that."

"It keeps replaying over and over in my mind. What if he hadn't have called out, 'English infidel,' before he fired his gun? I may not have seen him in time to save you."

"We can't think about what ifs. It is done and worrying about what might have happened isn't going to help us get over it any quicker," Katie said with conviction. But she knew it wasn't going to be easy for either of them to forget such horror.

"Tell me … what were you thinking just before it happened?"

"What do you mean?"

"You looked worried, and you turned round as if you were looking at somebody. I was about to ask you what was wrong when my uncle appeared."

"Oh, I'd forgotten. It was my mum. Her perfume was overpowering, and I sensed her close by. It definitely felt like she was trying to warn me about something."

"Well, if it was your mamma trying to warn you, I wish she had done it a bit sooner."

They both smiled weakly.

"We seem to spend most of our time in hospitals." Nabil sounded so miserable. Katie sat up to face him. She pushed a lock of his dark, thick hair away from his eyes. She gently took his handsome, sad face, in her hands and kissed him on the lips, then leant against him once again. She hated seeing him so downhearted.

"I love you so much, angel, and nothing or no one will ever come between us. I promise!"

Chapter Twenty-One

Having plenty of visitors when he was in hospital helped to raise Nabil's mood. Katie went in everyday taking Tafiq to see his papa as often as possible. Being a lively little boy meant he wanted to be on the floor all the time and he was trying to walk. This cheered Nabil up no end, but he often became fractious when he couldn't get his own way like any normal baby, so they decided it was best to leave him with Irma.

Sue managed a few short visits when she could get away from her busy ward, and he thanked her for her valuable help before the paramedics arrived; he had certainly seen a different side to Katie's best friend on that terrible night. He also asked her to pass on his thanks to Reece for helping the men clear up afterwards, which would have been no mean feat.

Ten days later and with his arm still in a sling, Katie went with Abdullah to pick him up. The family were all at the house to meet him, even Latifa, who was feeling a little better. Strong pain killers made him drowsy, and he needed to convalesce. The surgeon told him because the bullet had been difficult to remove it would still cause him pain for a while. Fortunately, it was his left arm so he thought he would still be able to use the phone and do some paperwork in his home office. All the family protested, especially Katie. Nabil had to agree to recuperate at the beach villa away from the business. It would also help them both to try and come to terms with what had happened.

He enjoyed nothing better than seeing his wife swimming in the ocean after the tourists had gone back to their hotels. Nabil also enjoyed watching Irma and Katie taking Tafiq to the edge of the sea; the waves gently lapping over his little toes and feet. At first, he wasn't too sure, then he started stamping his feet splashing himself and getting excited; he laughed aloud. There's nothing better than hearing a child's laughter and it is a great healer, Nabil thought to himself.

Swimming looked so inviting and he couldn't wait to get his sling off and be free of pain so he could join in too. The pain wasn't just in his arm and shoulder but in his mind. Bad dreams had plagued him since the shooting and Katie hadn't slept well either. He couldn't stop thinking about what might have happened to his wife, who never did anyone any harm. The memory played out in his mind all too often as he tried to come to grips with what his own uncle had tried to do.

Rashid was running the business again, but he kept Nabil informed and they discussed things together on the phone. He loved and respected his brother-in-law and was only too pleased to be able to help by keeping things running smoothly. Yasmin, Fatima, and baby Yusef came some days, but Shazia was back at university, though she rang often to see how they all were, especially her brother.

Hakeem brought his wife, Usha, and their daughters, Leena, and Mira, to the beach as they had a villa in Chicago Village as well. One hot, humid evening when the children were playing in the sea with Katie, Usha and Irma, Nabil and his best friend had a chance to talk privately.

"I have something to tell you," Hakeem said in a serious voice.

"You're not going to do anything stupid are you?" Nabil looked disturbed.

"No! Quite the opposite in fact."

"What's changed?"

"After the shooting, which I know you don't want to talk about, it confirmed to me how precious life is. I knew if I carried on with my affair in London and it got back to Dubai ... well ... you know what would happen ... so ... I've ended it." His throat muscles tightened, and his voice cracked with emotion. "I have to think about my wife and the girls."

Nabil put his hand on Hakeem's shoulder. "It's for the best my friend. But I thought you found it difficult to have sex with Usha?"

"It's not easy and of course it's not her fault but I am trying. She's very astute and I'm sure she knows my secret, but she is loyal too, and she often says Leena and Mira couldn't wish for a better papa."

"Well, that's true but what about your manfriend in London? Can you trust him not to talk?"

"Yes. He is also a Muslim, and his family would be mortified if they found out he was gay. There's no way he would tell anyone about our relationship."

"I'm pleased to hear it. I've been worried about you ever since you told me about him."

"And that's the last thing I want. You and Katie have had your fair share of worry and upset for as long as I can remember."

"You can say that again." They both went quiet for a few moments each reflecting on their own thoughts.

"It must be so distressing when you can't be yourself. I hope it works out for you. I really do."

"Thanks, that means a lot," said Hakeem. "Come on let's go and watch the children."

Occasionally, Irma would take Tafiq back to the town house for the night so they could be completely alone. He had started walking, much to the delight of his proud parents, but he was into everything; after having so many visitors it was good to have time to themselves.

On one such evening, when the sun was going down, and they were sitting on their terrace after dinner, the colours of the sunset were incredible. Flaming orange bleeding into ambers and reds right across the sky above the blue ocean. It was breath taking and Katie tried to catch it on her new camera that Nabil had bought her for her birthday. Her polaroid wasn't up to the task, but she had great affection for it and had put it safely away. She then picked up a pen and note pad for the first time in ages and started writing a poem.

A dragon sucks fire from the setting sun,
and breathes orange flames across the evening sky,
scorching the heavens in its wake.

"Show me."

"You can read it when it's finished. By the way a few of our friends suggested we have a beach party to celebrate the fact that you're alive and well. What do you think?"

"I don't feel like celebrating. I want to spend time with my family and friends but I'm not in the party mood. Do you mind, angel?"

"Of course not! And I agree with you about not being in the mood for a party. I just want you to get better before we fly to London after the baby is born. Poor Ellen could have done without such a shock, but Douglas is keeping her calm so hopefully she'll go full term."

"Yes, your poor aunt. I'm so glad she has a doctor in the house." Katie chuckled. "If she does have the baby

284

early, you'll have to go on your own. I really need to concentrate on the business before we take our summer break. It has grown so much. We have so many more employees since papa's day," he said wistfully. "I like to be a hands-on boss and so does Rashid."

"I know you do darling, and your papa is so proud of you."

"I'm sure he was with me when I woke up from the anaesthetic."

"I'm sure he was. I wonder what he thinks of his brother?"

"Surely my uncle is in hell and nowhere near papa?"

"I don't think there is such a place."

"What do you mean?"

"I'm sure hell is a state of mind and your uncle's mind must have been in some state. Until he sees the error of his ways, he will not be free from his own hideous thoughts."

Nabil had a look of disgust on his face. "His mind was a cesspit!" He didn't mind his wife voicing her opinions on religion and he found her way of thinking quite refreshing at times. Forcing Islamic beliefs on her wasn't his way; he knew she was happier being a free spirit. Yes, they did have a terrible row over Shazia's arranged marriage, but that was in private; she was always careful what she said in public. They both made compromises, and this is what made their marriage successful. "Well, whether hell is a place or not, I hope he is suffering." He started reliving the shooting once again and Katie could see the anguish on his face. She put her note pad down and went over to sit next to him, taking his hand in hers. They sat quietly for a few minutes listening to the waves.

"How are you feeling now you've cut down on the pain killers?" Katie asked trying to ease the tension."

285

He pulled back from his thoughts. "Much better … I can't believe it's only been three weeks."

"But you're still in pain, darling."

"Yes, but much less than it was, and it eases a bit more each day. It will do me good to be back in the office."

Katie knew what he meant. He wanted something to take his mind off what his uncle had done. She knew he was finding it difficult to come to terms with it. Neither of them would ever forget, especially as their son's birthday would always be a reminder. She had taken up yoga and meditation while Nabil was still in hospital, and it helped immensely. Her husband would throw himself into his work and enjoy his family when he came home at the end of the day and at weekends.

"Yes, darling I know it will."

Nabil and Katie had their usual summer break in Mayfair. They spent some quality time with the happy couple and their new daughter, Lauren Shirley MacDonald, who was born on the tenth of July; surprisingly two weeks overdue. Douglas was overjoyed to have a daughter, especially as he thought he would never have children. She was a very pretty baby with huge blue eyes and an unusual mop of blonde hair, but this could have been because she was two weeks late.

Holding her new cousin made Katie feel broody, which was to be expected now their son was a toddler. Tafiq was fascinated by this little being at first, but he tried to climb on mamma's lap when he thought she was getting too much attention. This made them all laugh.

Katie followed Ellen into their bedroom where she was about to change Lauren's nappy. The men were chatting in the lounge and Irma had taken Tafiq for his afternoon nap.

"She is such a gorgeous baby."

"Aren't all babies gorgeous?"

Katie pretended to be affronted. "Yes, but this is my new cousin." Her aunt laughed as she laid Lauren on her mat then unbuttoned her baby grow so she could remove her wet nappy.

"Now the men are in the other room we can talk mothers and babies. How are you feeling?"

"I'm tired most of the time, but it's only to be expected. I thought she would never come into the world. I was so heavy Douglas had to help me in and out of the bath. I felt like a bloated whale." Katie laughed. "It's no picnic having a baby is it … oh sorry, darling." She looked up from what she was doing. I forgot, you couldn't have Tafiq the normal way and I didn't mean to remind you of …"

"Mohammed? It's okay, I hope I've moved on enough to be able to cope when the subject is raised, especially when 'he who should not be named' is mentioned."

"Nabil still won't talk about his uncle then, since the shooting?"

"He did at first but … oh Ellen … the pain in his face every time he relived that dreadful night … it was awful to witness." She wiped a tear from her eye with the back of her hand. "He admits the only way he can cope with it now is by locking it away in a box and placing it in the back of his mind."

"Compartmentalizing."

"Yes. I really think it's the only way he can deal with the fact that his own uncle tried to kill me. He feels guilty because he mistakenly thought he was tucked away in his house with his nurse watching over him and I was safe at last."

"Poor Nabil. Thank God that man is dead. I knew when I first set eyes on him at your wedding, he spelt danger. But how are you coping?" Ellen asked, as she changed

Lauren's clothes. All she wanted was her niece to be happy.

"Nabil's family have all been incredibly supportive. Sue has been there for me too, but yoga and meditation has helped me enormously. Zac comes to the house or villa once a week to teach me new positions. We don't broadcast it as these practices are often frowned upon, but Nabil is okay with it. I love my sessions and it's now my morning ritual. I still swim but getting in the pool with Tafiq is more fun than counting lengths."

"Does meditation really help?"

"Yes, it does, it helps me to stay calm and relaxed which wasn't easy at first. It took a lot of effort and practise. Zac has taught me a few techniques, deep breathing, body awareness and we found a mantra that suited me. Continuously repeating the mantra and learning to match your breath to it helps to clear the mind. Like I said, it wasn't easy at first, because all I could think about was that man pointing his gun and Nabil throwing himself in front of me."

"I wouldn't expect anything less of Nabil … anyway it seems to be working. I never expected you to be so calm."

"I have my moments! Some days are harder than others."

"Your mum tried to get me to meditate when we were teenagers."

"Really? I never knew that."

"Shirley was always interested in that sort of thing, and she read a book about it. She thought it would help us cope with dad's drinking, but I was hopeless. I could never keep my thoughts under control." Ellen smiled at the memories. "She gave up in the end."

Katie laughed. "Mum often comes close when I'm meditating and it's a great comfort." They both went quiet each with their own thoughts about Shirley and Alan, until Lauren broke the silence with a gurgle.

"Here, take your cousin and have a cuddle before I put her in her cot."

"Ooh yes please!"

Nabil had a few business meetings in London and a couple of business trips in Europe planned while they were staying in Grosvenor Square. The first time he went away, Katie took the opportunity to visit Bev and Greg in their flat in Greenwich. They were expecting her but were surprised when a chauffeur driven car dropped her off; she found it much more relaxing these days than having to drive herself around busy London and find somewhere to park.

She loved the atmosphere and the history in Greenwich, especially the amazing Cutty Sark, which Tafiq was too young to appreciate. They enjoyed walking round the craft market with him in his baby Dior stroller which Nabil had bought when Katie was still in hospital. He only ever bought the best and it was certainly much better than the flimsy buggies that most parents had. But it didn't stop Tafiq trying to grab colourful items from the stalls. He protested when they were taken away from him and apologetically giving back to the stallholder, so Bev bought him a small handmade unicorn. It kept him amused while the others looked at various items.

Greg took them all out for lunch and Tafiq was surprisingly well behaved while sitting in a highchair. He was a good eater and the food placed in front of him kept him occupied for quite some time. Afterwards, they went for a long walk in Greenwich Park, and he enjoyed running around like a mad thing. He was fascinated by the squirrels but was a bit nervous when they came too close; throwing the nuts down for them then running back to mamma made them all laugh. Katie, Bev, and Greg took it in turns trying to keep up with him, so they decided to walk back down the hill towards the swing park.

Greg, who didn't seem so self-conscious these days, picked him up. "I'll take this young rascal to the swings so you two can have a proper catch up."

"Are you sure?" asked Katie.

"Yes, he is a little smasher and I need to get some practice in for when we start a family." He looked lovingly at Bev who smiled.

The two of them sat on the grass. When Greg was out of earshot Katie tuned to Bev with a grin on her face. "You're not …"

"No, I'm not. We want to wait until I'm qualified and have been working as a hygienist for at least a year before we start trying."

Bev was enjoying her training at Guys Hospital, and she had met some of Katie's former colleagues. Being the sociable kind meant she had made quite a few friends there and she felt she had found her niche. They wrote to each other occasionally and Bev thought that Katie and Nabil had finally found the true happiness and peace they deserved. Like everyone else she was shocked when she heard what had happened on Tafiq's first birthday.

"It's good to see you looking so happy and well, especially after what happened. Do you want to talk about it?"

Katie's smile faded. "Not really, Bev. I'm all talked out after spending time with Ellen and Douglas. I know you're concerned but honestly, I'm doing okay. Tell me more about your life and what you've been up to since we last wrote to each other."

Bev didn't have to be told twice and she chatted about their lovely neighbours and the wonderful dinner parties they had. How she loved her Kenwood mixer and about some of her creations which friends, family and neighbours enjoyed. She said her brother Michael's dental practise in Blackheath was doing well and she was looking forward to working with him at some point in the future. They now had two children and she loved seeing her niece and nephew.

Katie and Bev talked about their time in Dubai Hospital and how wonderful the life had been when they were carefree. Reminiscing about their trips to the souks, the water taxis on Dubai Creek and the beautiful flamingos brought back lovely memories for Bev. They were still in full flow when Greg brought Tafiq back from the swing park.

"I think he wants his mum cause he had a little grizzle." Greg was used to children as he came from a big family. Katie held out her arms to her son.

"But we had a great time didn't we little man." Tafiq smiled at him.

"He obviously likes you. Thanks so much. It was nice to have a little break. It's Irma's day off today so it's been full on." She put him in his pushchair. He was worn out with so much excitement and it wasn't long before he was asleep.

Three and a half months passed quickly, and it was soon the middle of November. The business kept Nabil occupied, which is just what he needed. They had some extremely important clients who expected the best. The attempted murder was hardly ever spoken about. He had well and truly locked it away in his mind and his bad dreams had stopped. No one mentioned it in front of Latifa either. She wasn't the same spirited woman she

291

had once been. Life, loss, and shame had worn her down and it made them all sad to see her fading away. However, Aamira was much happier and was enjoying new hobbies at home. Katie had suggested she re-connect with girlfriends who she had lost touch with over the years because of her controlling husband; she now enjoyed regular gatherings and had even started a craft group. She tried to cheer her mother-in-law up and on the odd occasion she saw a spark, especially when the family visited with the babies. The first time Nabil and Katie went to see Latifa after her own son tried to murder her grandson's wife was emotional; she touched them both on the cheek and looked into their eyes. No words were necessary.

Sue supported Katie as much as she could in the months following that frightful night and she visited her on her days off. They swam in the pool at the house and Sue often joined in with Katie's yoga sessions, having learned some herself when in England. She loved visiting Katie and Tafiq in the Beach villa, but often, it was when Nabil was at work, because she didn't want to outstay her welcome.

One day, Sue and Reece and a few of their colleagues from the Hospital planned a sundowner in one of the catamarans. They were there for anyone's use and Sue loved these trips. Nursing could be stressful at times, and it didn't take much for her to let her hair down. Katie had never liked boats, so she wasn't too bothered about not being included. It wouldn't be correct for her to join them, and her abaya certainly wasn't appropriate attire. It was one of the downsides of her marriage not that there were many.

"It's such a shame you can't come, but I know you're not keen on being on the ocean just in it."

Katie laughed. "That's true, I do love a swim."

292

Sue looked thoughtful. "Do you ever get fed up with the restrictions?"

"Not that much. I can fly to London and stay in Mayfair anytime I want to though I prefer to go with my husband. When we're there I can wear jeans and jumpers whenever I like. We have a great social life and I catch up with friends when Nabil is working. I have the best of both worlds and I thank my lucky stars every day. You know I don't have nearly as many restrictions as a lot of wives do in the Emirates."

"Yes, I know that but ...

"Sue, you know Nabil has made many compromises for me."

"As you have for him."

"Of course, it works both ways. He has continuously shown me how much he loves me especially when he threw himself in front of a bullet."

"I'm sorry Katie ... I didn't mean anything by it."

She was cross with Sue, but the feeling didn't last long. "It's okay, but I can read you like a book."

"What do you mean?"

"I think you're getting restless."

"Umm. I love working in Dubai Hospital, I have good friends, a good salary, a lovely apartment with a swimming pool, plenty of sun and free catamarans for sundowner trips." She smiled.

"But?"

"Don't you ever wish we could go to a pop concert and scream ourselves silly watching one of our favourite bands get drunk and wake up our Emirati neighbours?"

Katie laughed out loud. "And get arrested?"

"That's what I mean. We're not free to do what we want."

"But you have a great life here, Sue. Many would give their right arm for all those things you've just mentioned."

"I know … I'm so ungrateful. There's me complaining when you've been through so much. You are the bravest woman I've ever known, and I love you for it."

"Bless you, Sue."

"But it's true. Losing your lovely parents so tragically, leaving the country you knew, then being threatened by Mohammed. You survived a serious head injury, came out of a long coma relatively unscathed and then had a baby; as if that wasn't enough for any one person to deal with, you then got shot at."

"Yes, okay I get the picture."

"Well sometimes you need to know just how remarkable you really are woman because you're too damn modest!"

They laughed at the depth of feeling in Sue's voice, and it relieved the tension.

"But going back to concerts," said Katie.

"What concerts? There are none out here."

"Look if it helps, we can book tickets for one in England. George Michael will be playing in London from April. You can use some of your leave and stay with me in Grosvenor Square. Irma can look after Tafiq. You can be as outrageous as you like, and it will be just like old times."

Sue looked like she was warming to the idea. "Maybe Shaz would like to come too if she can spare the time from her studies."

"I'm sure she'd love to. It won't be that long before she finishes uni altogether and then … marriage."

"Yes, an arranged marriage. It's not right."

Katie frowned. "Well, there is nothing we can do about it. And changing the subject, I've been meaning to ask you if anything is going on between you and Reece?"

"No, we're simply good friends, and I want to keep it that way. He knows about Rob and what I went through. I'm not ready for a relationship with anyone. And ... I'm working on myself, as you suggested. If I can learn to love me and be happy with who I am, then somebody will come along at the right time. The last thing I want to do is attract another control freak."

"Very wise."

"Oh my God I'm getting maudlin."

Katie was about to reply when Reece called out from below. The others were further down the beach standing by a catamaran with their snacks and beers ready to be loaded.

Sue's just coming Reece, sorry we got chatting," she called out to him.

"It's great to see you looking so well."

"And you! This life suits you. How is Mr Baker?"

"Still the same, but he's a great boss."

"Say hello to him for me."

"Will do!"

Sue had joined Reece and they both waved to Katie before walking off. Nabil arrived home a few minutes later and they were going to have a swim before dinner on the terrace. No, she didn't mind missing out on the sundowner because she would watch the sunset with her husband. The husband who could have died saving her life.

Chapter Twenty-Two

It is often said that Christmas is for children, and it certainly proved to be the fact in Mayfair. A wonderful time was had by all in their Grosvenor Square apartment. Douglas, Ellen and Lauren, Hakeem, Usha, and the girls spent most of the festivities with Nabil and Katie. Tafiq sensed the atmosphere building and at times became over excited; especially when the nine-foot Christmas tree was delivered.

Lauren, who was nearly six months old, was sitting up and trying to crawl which amused Tafiq. He was now a lively eighteen-month-old toddler and was enthralled by the tree lights and decorations. On several occasions he had tried to pull the lower branches. He was curious about the brightly coloured parcels underneath, however many times he was scolded. This made Leena and Mira giggle and they were disappointed when Irma took him for his afternoon nap.

Nabil and Katie wanted everything to be perfect, so it was decided that instead of eating in a restaurant or hotel with four children, they would eat at home. On Christmas Eve their favourite deli delivered an amazing spread but for Christmas Day, Nabil hired a chef who brought somebody to help and clear up after him; the food was exquisite. Assorted canapes were to die for; their favourites were Oysters with beef and horseradish jelly and the dates in gorgonzola wrapped in pancetta. Beetroot-cured salmon and salmon pate for starters were amazing too and the goose Christmas dinner was the best

Katie had ever tasted. They didn't have any room for desserts, but they promised the chef they would eat them later in the day. She thought her mum and dad would have loved it and it made her sad to think of them not being there to celebrate with family and friends. It had been Shirley's favourite time of the year.

Katie had to tell Irma to sit at the table with them because she was still shy. She was happiest when she was with children, and she adored Tafiq. They made sure she had plenty of chance to enjoy her food as well, so they took it in turns to see to him in his highchair. Lauren was able to sit in a highchair as well, but she was over tired, so after eating and playing with her food Ellen took her for a nap. It worked out well because her and Douglas were able to eat in peace.

They all decided it would be good to have a long walk on Boxing Day, so they took the children to Hyde Park. Feeding the ducks on the Serpentine would keep them amused and they all needed fresh air and exercise after eating so much. Katie had insisted that Irma have a break, so she walked around Mayfair and Oxford Street drinking in the atmosphere and watching people queuing for the sales. She always had plenty of news to write about in her letters to her family back home in the Philippines.

Hakeem and his family flew home the day after Boxing Day. He didn't want to risk bumping into his ex-lover when he was with his wife and daughters. Nor did he want anything to spoil the wonderful Christmas they'd had. It made him realise that ending his affair had been the right decision.

Douglas had invited Katie and Nabil to Scotland so they could experience their first Hogmanay and it was a New Year's Eve they would never forget. Douglas needed to spend time with his family, especially Agnes, his eighty-two-year-old mother, who was thrilled to see them all. They had a wonderful time attending torchlight parades in Edinburgh and celebrating with the villagers in Gullane, where his family lived.

It was Nabil's first time in Scotland. He loved the scenery and the culture, especially the ancient village which was now more like a small town. But sometimes he found it difficult to understand the Scottish accent which made Douglas and his family laugh. His brother, Alex, didn't drink as much scotch as the other men because he had a suspected ulcer. Nabil, who wasn't used to drinking much was persuaded to down the whiskey offered, so him and Douglas had thick heads on New Year's Day.

Alex, his wife Maureen, and the boys had gone back to their house just outside the village. Agnes enjoyed Hogmanay and the odd malt whiskey, but she needed more rest these days, so she hadn't emerged from her bedroom. Douglas and Nabil were woken up by the children who weren't concerned that it was only seven o'clock on New Year's Day.

Katie and Ellen managed to leave the children with Irma and the men. They had not drunk that much themselves, so they weren't going to pander to their husbands for overdoing it. They wanted to walk round the beautiful village before breakfast. It was a short drive from Edinburgh and was where Douglas and his family came from.

Ellen sighed as they left Agnes' house, "At last, I thought we'd never get away." She remarked as she tied her scarf tight to keep out the chill and pulled her woollen hat down over her short pixie cut. Katie had much more hair to keep her warm. They had wrapped themselves up against the freezing Mid-Lothian winter. The wind wasn't so biting as it had been when they'd first arrived, and they both wanted some fresh air.

"My poor husband. He's not used to drinking, especially in the company of hardened Scots."

They both laughed as Katie hooked her arm into her aunts and they walked towards the ancient church.

"It's been a wonderful Christmas and New Year. I'm glad you came to Scotland with us darling. Agnes was so looking forward to seeing us all again, especially the little ones. She had given up hope of more grandchildren, so she was delighted when we told her I was expecting; now she has a granddaughter as well as two lovely grandsons."

"They seem very well balanced and happy young men."

"They are and they've had a good start in life. Peter wants to be an engineer like his dad and Alexander wants to be a doctor like his uncle Douglas. Agnes is so proud of them all, but I know she misses us when we're in London."

"She is a character isn't she, bless her."

"She most certainly is. Apparently, their dad, Tavish, was the quiet one."

"Well, they say opposites attract."

They found themselves standing outside the ancient church.

"There's been a church here since the ninth century. Do you want to take a look inside?" Ellen knew how much Katie enjoyed history.

"Later probably, but at the moment I just want to walk and blow the cobwebs away. And have a chat."

"About anything in particular?"

"Yes, as a matter of fact."

"I'm all ears."

"A few weeks ago, at the end of November, I reminded Nabil of his promise to let me start my own antiques business. I waited a few months, so we could all move on from the effects of the shooting, before bringing the subject up. But I couldn't leave it any longer. I really need this."

Ellen's face broke into a huge smile. "I'm so glad you've talked to him about it darling. Living a life of luxury is all very well, but everyone needs a purpose in life, especially someone as intelligent and determined as you."

"I get my determination from dad."

"And your insight from you mum. Plus, you have all their business contacts, so what can go wrong? What did Nabil say when you reminded him?"

"He was reluctant at first but only because he's happy with our life as it is after all we've been through together."

"I can understand that. But he runs a large successful business, so he has a reason to get up in the morning. You didn't argue, did you?"

"Not really. We are quite good at talking things through these days. After I reasoned with him, we agreed I would start planning straightaway, which I did, but not to do anything practical until the new year."

"And now it is 1990."

"Yes, it is, and I've decided it's going to be my year!"

"Good for you darling. Your mum and dad will be so proud."

Katie looked sad. "I hope so, Ellen. I really hope so."

"You know so!" Now cheer up and remember this is going to be your year."

They walked on in silence.

Douglas poured Nabil a pint glass of cold water from the drinking tap and handed him a small banana from the fruit bowl. "We're having a late breakfast today. A good hearty Scots breakfast and Alex, Maureen and the boys will be joining us."

"Why the banana? I'm not hungry."

"You need to keep your blood sugar up after a night of drinking and water will help you hydrate."

"Yes doctor."

Douglas chuckled. "We should have drunk more water with our whiskey last night then we wouldn't have ended up with headaches. I must remember to practise what I preach in future."

Nabil's face broke into a smile. "You can't be perfect all the time." He felt better, after eating something and slowly drinking most of the water Douglas had given him.

"The children are with Irma in the nursery. Mother won't be down just yet and the girls have gone for a walk; let's go through to the lounge and make the most of the peace and quiet. I get the feeling you want to talk to me about something."

Nabil told his dear friend about the conversation he'd had with Katie about starting her own antiques business. How reluctant he was at first because he was happy with their life as it was. But he soon realised that the germ of an idea in her mind had already taken shape.

"You knew it would come to this. You can't expect her to lead a sedentary life."

"I know Douglas and I don't want to lose her."

"I've never seen two people so much in love. You are more likely to lose her if you don't allow her the freedom to realise her dreams. I don't mean you'd lose her physically, but she would become resentful and that can't be good for any marriage." Douglas left him to his thoughts while he rested his head against the back of the armchair.

Nabil was lost in thought. Katie's English upbringing and her wish for a certain amount of liberty within their marriage wasn't as difficult as he'd thought it was going to be. She had always been confident but since the tragic accident and her experiences whilst in the coma she'd had this phenomenal energy and zest for life. Everyone noticed it, and as soon as they entered the town house, they would soak up the positive atmosphere. His beloved wife endeared people wherever she went which of course would help in the early days of her business venture. He would not want her any other way. She had come back from the brink of death and had been shot at by his uncle. They were together against all odds, and he was not going to jeopardize his marriage, by being as strict as most Muslim men were with their wives.

"I know you're right, Douglas. I'm just nervous she'll end up doing too much and it will take her away from me. Does that sound selfish?"

"It does rather, but I can understand. The way of life you were born into is completely at odds with a wife who wants to start a business. But you chose to marry a westerner and Katie is an extraordinary young woman."

"She certainly is, and I will do anything to make her happy."

"Then stop fretting."

Agnes appeared at the door with Lauren in her arms and Irma followed behind with Tafiq. "Stop fretting about what?" She asked.

Neither of them had a chance to reply because Tafiq launched himself at his papa and made everyone laugh.

In the new year home life wasn't disrupted too much when Katie started to put her ideas into action. She spent

302

as much time with Tafiq as she could even though they had Irma. Nabil missed them when they flew to England so she could renew some of her parent's contacts and attend the auctions. He suggested to Rashid that they make space in their warehouse for the antiques she was going to import. It was a very secure building and meant it was one less thing for her to have to worry about.

What a busy year 1990 was going to be. Katie, Sue, and Shazia were looking forward to the George Michael concert and plans for Shazia and Haidar's marriage were already under way. It was to be a mid-November wedding, but the bride to be reminded them all that they would have a graduation to go to first. She was looking forward to collecting her degree. Katie suggested to her sister-in-law, in private, she could use her art history degree by helping her with Khalifa's Antiques.

"Really?"

"Yes, really, if Haidar doesn't mind you working part time as a consultant. And of course, I will pay you."

"Oh, Katie that would be wonderful. I've been feeling a bit despondent lately while writing my dissertation, wondering why I bother."

"You bother because you need to use your brains and, like me, you need a goal in life. But I don't want to cause any trouble between you and Haidar. He seems a reasonable young man and he adores you."

"He does and I've grown very fond of him. Haidar is 'putty in my hands' as you say in England. But I will have to be discreet because his papa wouldn't approve, and I certainly can't be seen working in the shop."

"If Haidar agrees and we promise to be discreet, I'll make sure you won't have to go to the shop. I know a lot about antiques but I'm no expert when it comes to art. If I see a painting at one of the auction houses which looks promising, I can phone you on my mobile, tell you who

303

the artist is and describe it to you. You can check the paintings out properly in the warehouse and catalogue them. I don't think anyone will be concerned about you going there and if they are we can say it's because you want to see the paintings."

Shazia had a big grin on her face. "You have it all worked out!"

"I do and I'd love to have you on board, Shaz. It's going to be a while before I'm ready to open Khalifa's Antiques. You can concentrate on your dissertation and your wedding for now."

Shazia was near to tears as she thanked Katie. She was so glad that Nabil had married this wonderful English woman who was now a dear friend.

It had not taken too long for Nabil to gain sponsorship for Khalifa's Antiques. This was necessary because although Katie was married to an Emirati, she was still a foreigner. But it did take a few months for a shop to become vacant in Dubai's Al Ghurair Shopping Centre. A modern and spacious shopping mall, which had two hundred and fifty shops and boasted nine restaurants.

She stood in the large empty unit which had beautiful marble tiles throughout finding it easy to imagine the whole place filled with antiques and customers. It was exciting. Nabil, who was used to his wife's hunches turning out right, had no doubt the shop was going to be a success. His concerns about the changing dynamics in their relationship had receded to the back of his mind.

Katie knew about antiques, but he was always there if she needed advice on other business matters, although he tried not to interfere too much. He sensed how important it was for her to do this on her own, so he gave her plenty of encouragement and support. It was soon common knowledge amongst the locals and some of the older men frowned upon this venture as was to be expected.

Buying a mixture of antiques from different countries but with the emphasis on Middle Eastern culture was key; she did not want to alienate anyone. Securing a collection of Victoriana pleased her because she hoped it would prove popular with the ex-pats if they wanted to buy something British for their Emirati friends. There were artifacts from India, Turkey, Egypt, and many other countries. It was quite a collection, but it was the Arabic collection that she was most proud of and some things she would be reluctant to part with. This Middle Eastern flavour gave the shop an ambience all of its own.

She had managed to buy three exquisite antique Hope Chests, or Dazza as they are known in the Emirates, made of wood, and decorated with ornate brass. Arab men give them to their brides. Female members of the groom's family prepare the Dazza. It includes jewellery, perfumes, a prayer mat, Quran, mehr (bridal gift) and a very extravagant trousseau including a garment embroidered in expensive lace and jewels. She had one or two Khanjar short knives in beautifully decorated sheaths; there were camel trappings woven from goat's hair and dyed in a variety of vibrant colours; miniature Arabic coffee pots; incense burners and pearling knives which were used by the local divers in the creek at one time.

On one of her trips to England she had interviewed Peter Harris for the position of manager at Khalifa's Antiques. He had been recommended by one of her dad's closest colleagues in the antiques business. Peter was thirty-five and divorced. He had lots of experience and he was looking for a challenge, especially in a new part of the world. He certainly knew all there was to know about antiques and he had experience in running a large concern in Kent. Katie was feeling extremely proud of herself because she would be ready to open Khalifa's Antiques in November, after the wedding of course.

Fatima was getting excited about the wedding, but Shazia was more excited about receiving her degree in London late in October. Fatima was sad that Ibrahim couldn't be there to see their daughter receive a first-class honours degree. He had wanted his girls to be educated as well as Nabil, although Yasmin chose not to go to university. She was already madly in love with Rashid at the age of sixteen and all she wanted was to get married and have children.

Haidar accompanied Fatima to the ceremony, and they were as proud as could be. It was a shame the rest of the family couldn't be there too, but they all met up afterwards and had an excellent meal in the Savoy Hotel. Shazia loved her graduation cake which was cream and drizzled with chocolate. It was decorated with a mortar board and degree on the top and said Congratulations Shazia BA Hons. Katie had more beautiful silver framed photographs to add to her collection.

The wedding followed in mid-November, and it was a beautiful day. Unlike most brides Shazia didn't want a big fuss, but she had little choice. Her family and Haidar's family were determined it was going to be a wonderful ceremony and celebration. Nabil took the place of the father of the bride. He was so proud of her and loved both his sisters very much. The bride and groom looked happy despite Shazia's· reservations. Secretly she was looking forward to working with Katie; in fact, she was eager to start, but she wanted Haidar to think the grin on her face was because they were pronounced man and wife. She knew she had to get used to having a husband and she had no doubt he would be a good one.

Haidar was made a partner in his papa's business on the eve of their wedding day. He was looking forward to the future especially as they were going to be the first to import Ferraris. Their showroom and service centre had been built and he was happy to oversee this side of their business. He had appreciated cars since an early age when his papa had taken him to Beaulieu, home to the national motor museum in England. His love of cars helped him to understand Shazia's love of art and the need to do something fulfilling.

A year had passed since she had started planning her new business and the grand opening of Khalifa's Antiques was held at the end of November 1990. The invasion of Kuwait by Iraq in August had caused an influx of Kuwaitis to the Emirates escaping the invasion. Hotels, which would normally have a twenty percent occupancy, suddenly became full. Katie wondered if they should postpone the opening due to the ultimatum by the UN and the impending war. But Nabil said they might as well take advantage of there being many more people staying in the Emirates. He reckoned that the Kuwaitis who could afford to stay in hotels must have some spare cash to spend on antiques.

What a wonderful day it proved to be. The family and their many friends were there especially those who had supported them throughout their troubled times, including Sue, Bev, and Greg. Ellen and Douglas came over and they stayed on for ten days as they needed a decent holiday. Irma was on hand to help with Lauren, who she loved. Even Dorothy at her great age was determined to make it and she did, staying for three weeks because she was so impressed by the lifestyle in The Emirates. She became partial to the sticky sweets and found it hard to resist the variety of pastries soaked in honey. Katie promised to send her some, every month, which she did until Dorothy suddenly passed away a year later.

Katie made her opening speech and thanked everyone for their help and support, especially Nabil. She told her guests to enjoy the food and champagne and admire the stock while it was still there. Standing in the middle of the shop floor watching her guests she looked around to survey her new premises; she had realised her dream. She knew her parents were there too because earlier at home when she was getting ready, she had smelt her mum's perfume and her dad's aftershave. They were trying to impress on her how immensely proud they were, and for once she didn't get choked.

The opening had been planned for months, even her elegant long sleeved abaya style dress suit embroidered with gold on the bodice and along the edges. A beautiful blue silk outfit, which enhanced her figure. It showed off her gold high heeled sandals exquisitely. Nabil couldn't take his eyes off her as she stood there looking sophisticated and pleased with herself.

He came up behind her putting his arms around her slim waist. "Angel, you've done it! You have opened your first antiques shop. How do you feel?"

Her face broke into a smile. "Wonderful," she sighed. "But what do you mean, my first antiques shop?" She turned round to see the cheeky grin on his handsome face. Laughing she went off to mingle with her guests. She noticed Peter, her manager, showing off some of the beautiful craftmanship in the Hope Chests; they were beautiful, she thought to herself, but she couldn't get sentimental about them as they were there to be sold.

Later that evening they arrived home and Katie yawned as they entered their bedroom.

"How tired are you?"

"Extremely tired, but I'm sure you can revive me." Before she had time to do anything Nabil was kissing her passionately on the lips.

"I've been wanting to make love to you all evening. You looked stunning in your new outfit," and he began undoing the back.

Katie laughed. "If I look so good in it my darling, why do you want to remove it?"

"You're about to find out, angel."

Chapter Twenty-Three

Nabil longed for a daughter, especially after Yasmin and Rashid had twin girls the following year. They were concerned when Katie wasn't able to fall pregnant so easily the second time. He came home one evening at his usual time and felt there was something in the air.

"What is different about you angel?" he asked, as he wrapped his arms around her, but Tafiq was pleased to see him too.

"Papa, yella, yella, come here!"

"Tafiq wait a minute, I have something to tell your papa."

"What's wrong?"

"Nothing, my darling husband," she replied looking cheerful. "It's just that … I'm pregnant."

His eyes met hers. "For the love of Allah, well done!"

"What do you mean, well done? It takes two you know."

He couldn't stop grinning. "I am so happy. Tafiq you're going to have a brother or sister." Nabil scooped him up and his arms entwined them both.

He was concerned about Katie's health, and she admitted she needed to slow down. She had not had much time for herself in a long while and she knew she needed space to relax. He suggested that her and Tafiq should go to England to see Ellen, so she could have a break. Nabil knew her aunt and Douglas would make sure she relaxed, and it would keep her away from work. He went to the airport to see them off.

They were sitting in Baskin Robins at Dubai Airport, Tafiq's favourite ice cream parlour, where he was tucking into an ice cream sundae.

"Do you remember when we first met in this airport?" asked Nabil.

"How could I ever forget. I bumped into you, and I was so embarrassed."

"I loved you from that moment, Katie."

"And I couldn't take my eyes off you. We were meant to meet which is why I nearly took your leg off with my trolley."

They laughed at the memory.

"Can two people love too much?" he asked as their eyes locked across the table. "Nothing in my life has meaning without you, angel. We must not let anything come between us."

"What has brought this on?" He didn't say because Tafiq had pink ice cream on his nose and round his mouth and made them laugh. Katie cleaned him up.

"I will miss you both, but I want you to rest, and I know you won't do that here."

"I promise I will. Anyway, I'm looking forward to spending some time with my gorgeous little cousin. We have lots of things planned while Douglas is away on a conference then when he comes back, he'll spend time with us all. Tafiq give papa a kiss."

"Yes, you must get going, you haven't got long before the gates close," he kissed Tafiq. While waving them off he thought again about how much he loved her. A few of the locals still frowned upon his life with his English wife. She had endeared herself to most people, but a couple of the local wives were jealous of her success as a businesswoman. They were envious because she had more freedom than they had; luckily, it was only the minority.

Peter was such a good manager at Khalifa's Antiques and was more than capable. She certainly had enough stock in the warehouse, and she had left Shazia checking out and cataloguing some new paintings which she was only too pleased to do.

Katie had a wonderful break with Ellen. They visited Hay-on-Wye for three days, a pretty but small market town on the edge of Wales, often referred to as 'the town of books.' It was somewhere she had always intended going, and they were both in their element. Fortunately, they took Irma to Hay with them so they could browse undisturbed. They spent the best part of two days hunting for the books of their choice, and they ended up with seventeen between them. Katie was thrilled when she found a beautiful old copy of 'The Vicar of Wakefield,' by Oliver Goldsmith; for years she had wanted to replace the scruffy copy she had. They both loved the musty, but familiar smell of old books.

They stayed in a beautiful and very large three-hundred-year-old house in a village near Hay-on-Wye and they soaked up the atmosphere. The owners were friendly and during their stay they got to know the lady of the house. Ray and Susan lived in one half and Susan ran bed and breakfast in the other half. Proudly showing them around, she was pleased that Katie and Ellen were so enamoured with the place. The furniture was exquisite, and every room was perfect for the guests, as Susan had thought of everything they could possibly need.

The lounge was enormous and ran the whole length of the house, so you could see the well-kept walled gardens at either end. There were statues and the original old flagstones, which was a lovely surprise. The dining room where they went for their breakfast, was charming with an interesting collection of porcelain teacups. There were oak beams and a beautiful old winding staircase going up to the bedrooms.

They spent quality time with Douglas when he wasn't working, and Katie thought he was a brilliant dad. He managed to get time off for the last few days of their visit, so they stayed in Edenbridge. Lauren, now a lively toddler, loved running round the garden with Tafiq. He helped her climb up the slide by pushing her bottom, which amused the adults. They had picnics in the surrounding countryside reminding Katie and Ellen of lazy days with Shirley and Alan.

Not able to keep away from Khalifa's Antiques entirely, she visited it once a week when she returned to Dubai. Everything was running smoothly, and when she wasn't there Peter kept her informed on the telephone. He coped well without her.

Katie had a fairly comfortable pregnancy. She hadn't carried Tafiq in the normal way because she'd been in a coma but at least she had been spared the heat. By the time she was eight months gone, she preferred staying in the air-conditioned town house. She was happy to relax and listen to her favourite music and operas, especially La Boheme. One day Nabil came home unexpectedly and stood in the doorway of the lounge with tears in his eyes. "How can you listen to that?"

She looked up in surprise. "Oh, you made me jump I wasn't expecting you."

"You know it brings back bad memories," he snapped, as he walked over to the stereo system and turned it off. I can still see you lying in the hospital bed."

"I'm sorry darling but I didn't know you were coming home early."

He turned round to face her. "No … it's okay … it's not your fault. I wanted to surprise you."

She stretched out her arms to him. "Come and give me a cuddle, if you can get your arms round me?" They sat on the large sofa for a long time enjoying the peace and quiet. Now there was no music playing they could hear the water fountain below. It had the desired effect and calm reigned once more.

Nabil noticed Katie's headaches had been more frequent and she'd been irritable lately or was it just that he was looking for something to stress about. He telephoned her from the office at least twice a day. It disturbed her period of relaxation when Tafiq was at nursery, but she knew how worried he had been when she was pregnant the first time. These recollections seem to come to the surface of his mind at times and were still raw. She knew she was lucky to have such a caring husband, but it bothered her that he had never let go of the painful memories.

He phoned his favourite doctor to voice his concerns. Although he was family now, he still regarded him as a good friend and confidant. Douglas reminded him that Katie had only had a check-up a few months ago and everything was good. He was more worried about Nabil and told him it would be beneficial if he could find a way to let go of the past. Holding on to the pain and hating his uncle for what he had done could be bad for his health.

Katie had told him the same thing. She tried to make him understand that forgiveness helps you find peace within and enables you to move forward. She even attempted to teach him meditation to no avail; he had too much nervous energy, so he gave up.

She had been trying to get into 'Samuel Pepys' Diary,' one of her favourite books that she hadn't read for a few years when the telephone rang. She knew it was Nabil.

"Yes, darling I am fine, just a little tired that's all. No, I don't have a headache today. I'm trying to read but I can't seem to concentrate on anything."

"Let me hire you a nurse."

"Darling, women have babies everyday all over the world and they don't have nurses to look after them."

"I don't care what other women do I only care about you."

"But I have telephones all over the house and there's always someone around, please try not to worry so much."

"How can I not worry about you after the last time. And you still have the effects of your head injury."

"But I had a check-up at the London Hospital not long ago and this is a normal pregnancy. I am well, besides, there's only a month to go now. You know I would feel uneasy if something wasn't right."

"That's true, angel."

Seven days later Katie went into labour three weeks early. She'd had a few twinges during the morning, but nothing major. Cook was trying to get her to eat something to keep her strength up, but all she wanted was a chocolate milkshake; she'd been craving these for in the last few months. There had been no chance of any cravings when she was carrying Tafiq. Maybe that wasn't such a bad thing, she smiled to herself.

Irma wanted to call Nabil at his office. "No, not yet Irma I'm fine. I just have a bit of back ache that's all, but you could take Tafiq to the beach when you pick him up from nursery. I've got a feeling this baby is going to be born sometime today."

Fatima arrived just before Irma left to collect Tafiq. She was going to be staying for a couple of days. She looked concerned when Katie told her she had a bad backache. "I think I will call Nabil."

"But I haven't had any contractions yet, though, I do feel a bit peculiar."

"Katie, when I gave birth to Yasmin and Shazia, I didn't have normal contractions either, but a bad back ache; they both came much quicker than Nabil had done."

"Okay mamma, you'd better phone him."

He arrived home twenty minutes later. "Are you okay angel? Do you want me to call an ambulance?" he asked as soon as he saw her trying to get comfortable on one of the sofas.

"No, we don't need an ambulance."

"Okay, Abdullah is downstairs, but will you be okay to walk down to the car? Are you in much pain? The baby is not due for another three weeks."

"Nabil stop panicking! It won't help Katie," cried his mamma.

But he couldn't help himself. "Why do you have an ice pack next to you? Do you have one of your headaches?"

"Son, let's just get her downstairs."

Abdullah drove them to the hospital, and it didn't take long but Katie's back was killing her by the time they arrived. Nabil had been rubbing it for her, but she got irritable with him because it didn't help. He ran inside to warn the staff, and a porter she recognised came out with a wheelchair.

It all happened so quick. She barely got through the door of the maternity room before the baby started coming. The staff worked fast getting everything ready and it wasn't long before Latifa, Fatima, Shirley Khalifa was born. It was the 20th, May 1992 and Tafiq was four years old.

Nabil was beside himself with joy and like all papa's, he thought she was the most beautiful baby he had ever seen. He was besotted and Katie was concerned that she

316

would be thoroughly spoilt. It reminded her how her dad had over-indulged his daughter, however, it hadn't done her any harm. She smiled at the memories.

"Well done, my angel," Nabil said as he sat down next to her on the bed. She was cradling Latifa, and he was looking down with admiring eyes. "It was much quicker and easier than I expected it to be."

Katie pretended to be offended. "Easier for who? You or me?" He laughed out loud.

Tafiq was fascinated by the new addition to the family when his papa took him into the hospital to visit his little sister. He found it difficult to pronounce Latifa, so he started calling her Lati; after that it stuck. This was Fatima's fifth grandchild and Shazia, who had now been married for about eighteen months, was expecting too. Not able to take her eyes off little Latifa she longed for her baby to be born which was quite a turnaround for her.

Chapter Twenty-four

The next few years were relatively uneventful for Katie and Nabil. They enjoyed the comparative peace that had followed so much trauma. They both travelled to Europe for business, and they had holidays in Singapore, Hong Kong, Bali, New York, and Italy. Lati was a normal, lively, but stubborn six-year-old as her mamma had been at that age. Her ten-year-old brother, who had a lovely disposition, adored her. He had the looks and aplomb of his papa and the kind, caring nature of his mamma; everyone loved him. Lati followed Tafiq everywhere, but when she had one of her tantrums, he would roll his eyes and walk calmly away. This often had the desired effect and would quieten her down; it certainly amused the family.

Fatima, who always telephoned before she visited these days, could not see enough of Tafiq. He reminded her of Nabil when he was a child and he seemed to bring out the best in her. Spoiling her grandchildren was one of her favourite pastimes, but she often wished Ibrahim could have seen them all. Sometimes she felt lonely although she would never admit this to anyone in the family. Katie guessed so she would invite her to stay so she could be near the children.

Recently Katie had started to feel uneasy, but she wasn't sure why. Nabil had always been a hardworking man and he thrived on it, especially when he was trying to shut out the past. She began to worry when he looked more tired than usual, and she tried to get him to slow down. Feeling edgy and trying to push the feeling to the back her mind she found she could not, so she spoke to Douglas on the telephone. He suggested that Nabil have a thorough check up as soon as possible. He might be only forty-three years old, but they had to bear in mind the family history he told her.

It wasn't easy persuading him to make an appointment with the clinic. But when she told him how uneasy she felt, he decided to do something, although he insisted, he was only tired. Making him promise not to go into the office again until he had seen the doctor meant they could stay at Chicago Beach and relax. It was heaven and Katie felt less concerned as they enjoyed lunch on the terrace. Making love just the once in their bedroom overlooking the ocean was enough. They wanted to lay in each other's arms and talk about what the future might have in store for them.

"I think my adorable daughter will have to marry a Sheik or someone equally impressive."

"But what if she falls madly in love with someone ordinary?"

"My Latifa will not do that, she will be the most beautiful and striking young lady for miles around and will attract only the best."

"Oh, Nabil you are funny."

"I'm being serious, angel."

Katie laughed. "Yes, I know darling that's what worries me."

"Why should it worry you because I want the best for our children?"

"Don't you think I want the best for them? Of course, I do but we can't live their lives for them."

"No, I know we can't, but you must indulge me a little."

"What about Tafiq, what have you in store for him?" she asked, as she propped her head on her elbow so she could see the expression on his face.

"Oh, I think he will be the president of a giant international business."

"But he might want to do something completely different, and he is sensitive."

"Yes, but I am sure we can toughen him up."

She playfully punched him in the shoulder. "Don't you dare toughen him up and make him into some sort of macho man. Tafiq would never be happy that way."

He smiled when he saw her looking so serious. "I didn't mean it."

They talked about her possible new venture in the Emirates. He thought it was a great idea to expand with the reputation she had gained in Al Ghurair.

Later that day he did not seem his usual self and Katie began to feel agitated again especially as she sensed her mum close by. Putting on something light they went out onto the terrace. The children were staying with Fatima for a few days, as it was holiday time.

That evening there was a full moon and it seemed to light up the whole of the ocean. The stars were clear and bright, and it was peaceful apart from the occasional reveller they could hear in the distance. They both loved the villa, and it was the only place where he ever truly relaxed.

Standing on the terrace looking at the wonderful view and soaking up the atmosphere, he put his strong arms around her and squeezed her tight. "Angel, I love you so much!" His voice sounded strange, and she felt a knot in the pit of her stomach. "You must promise me that whatever happens, you will always be strong, for yourself and the children."

"What is it? What's wrong, my darling?"

"Maybe I'm feeling a little apprehensive before my check up."

"No, it's more than that, what is it?"

"I'm just feeling tired again, that's all."

"Why don't you sit down, and I'll go and make some coffee."

He wanted her to stay with him, but he kept quiet because the last thing he wanted to do was frighten her. If he didn't feel better soon, he would ask Katie to call an ambulance. As she left him on the terrace, he saw a shadowy figure he recognised as his papa. He was standing close by and so much love was emanating from him.

Katie went to make the coffee. They had given the maid the night off so they could be alone. Abdullah was visiting family a few streets away and would come back if they needed him.

Walking into the bedroom a few minutes later with the silver coffee set on the tray she knew something dreadful had happened before she reached the terrace. Nabil was slumped forward in the chair and the tray went crashing to the tiles. She tried to rouse him but couldn't, so she laid him on the floor. Remembering what to do from her training at Guy's was one thing but this was her husband! Calling the emergency services, she told them the front door was open. Katie couldn't believe this was happening; she had to get him back begging him not to leave her as she did emergency resuscitation. It seemed like hours before the medical team arrived, but it was only a few minutes. The paramedics took over immediately and she sank back on her heels pleading with them to save him.

Katie watched as they did everything they could. They got a pulse and rushed him to the hospital. It was the second time Katie had been in an ambulance with her husband. She felt numb but when they arrived, she managed to follow the trolley into the emergency department. One of the nurses took her to a seat while the crash team worked on Nabil. Tears were falling now, because she knew in her heart, they could not save him. She hoped and prayed she was wrong.

"Mrs Khalifa, can I call somebody for you?" said an elderly nurse who must have witnessed this scene countless times.

"Yes, I must call mamma, oh my God what am I going to say?"

"Do you want me to help you?" she said kindly.

"No, no it's all right, I … I'll do it. Could you show me where the telephone is please?"

The nurse took her to the reception area where Katie called Fatima and she heard her anguished cry at the other end of the phone. She said something about history repeating itself. The nurse led her back to her seat where she sat looking dazed. She waited for some news any news of her beloved husband. It was not long before a doctor appeared. She got up as soon as she saw him coming towards her.

"I am so sorry, Mrs Khalifa we could not save your husband. I'm afraid he died a few minutes ago."

"No!" Katie's hands flew to her face in disbelief, and she fell back onto the chair.

"Would you like to see him?" he asked sympathetically.

She nodded and he gently led her through the double doors to the room where he lay.

"We will leave you on your own for a while, the nurse is at the far end of the room if you need her. We did everything we could," the doctor stated apologetically. She nodded at him again; she didn't have the strength or the inclination to reply.

Katie sat staring at her husband holding his hand. "My darling, I can't live without you. Why did you have to leave me?" she cried. She put her hand to his cheek, and it still felt warm. "I can't bear it." Feeling all the energy seep from her she laid her head on his lifeless body. A few minutes later she felt a hand on her shoulder. It was Fatima and they fell into each other's arms, sobbing uncontrollably. The rest of the family was outside except for the children who were being cared for at home.

The doctor came back in. "Do you want the rest of the family to come in now? We will be moving your husband soon Mrs Khalifa?" She looked at the doctor with her tear-streaked face. His heart wrenched. He hated losing a patient and he could never get used to having to tell the relatives that their loved one had died. She nodded to him and turned back to Nabil.

"We have to say our goodbyes now, mamma." And in turn they held his hand and kissed him. Fatima still sobbing kissed him on the forehead and Katie kissed him on the lips, those beautiful lips she had kissed a thousand times now felt cold to the touch. "Goodbye my darling, I will always love you."

Katie was totally grief stricken. Ellen flew over straightaway with Lauren and stayed for a few weeks. She had written the words of the Romantic poet, Alfred Lord Tennyson in a card, 'Tis better to have loved and lost than to have never loved at all.' Katie kept it close to her and read it when her grief became unbearable.

Douglas came for the funeral of the young man who had been like a son to him. It saddened him greatly that Nabil had been taken away from them at such a young age. He wanted to be there for Katie, but he could only stay for six days; he had to get back to his patients but promised he would return as soon as possible.

Sue couldn't be there for her best friend because she was in Kent nursing her mother. She had cancer and didn't have long to live. Sue was so upset and even her mum, who didn't show much emotion, was affected by the tragic news. She spoke to Katie as much as she could on the phone, and they often ended up crying together.

Peter ran Khalifa's Antiques and Rashid was running the family business once again, though he found it difficult to focus. Fatima and Katie tried to be there for each other and the only thing that helped them recover from the shock were the children. Yasmin and Shazia were equally heart-broken at losing their big brother and Rashid and Haidar were devastated. Hakeem already missed his blood brother and was distraught to say the least.

Latifa couldn't take it when her beloved grandson left this world. She retreated into herself even more and only showed a slight interest in life when the children came to see her. Fatima was absolutely crushed after Nabil's death. Tafiq seemed to be the only one who could make her feel that life was worth living, even though he missed his papa terribly. He had such winning ways and was older than his years suggested. Lati was too young to really know what was going on, but she knew her papa had gone to heaven.

Irma was marvellous as usual, although she had been as shocked as everyone else. All Katie could do was think of Nabil. She cried at the mere thought of him unless the children were around then she tried desperately to check her tears. The feeling of emptiness engulfed her. There was a great void in her life. One thing was sure though, Nabil would always live in her heart whatever the future held.

It was the children who kept her going and she could still hear Nabil's words in her head. 'You must promise me that whatever happens, you will always be strong, for yourself and the children.'

How she missed him. She stood on the terrace where he had suffered a fatal heart attack two years ago to the day. There were times when she felt she could not go on without her soulmate, but she knew he was close, driving her on.

In fact, she had been compelled to start the process of opening a new business in Abu Dhabi six months after Nabil passed away. It took all the strength she could muster, and it was ready to open on the first anniversary of his death. As much as Katie was hurting inside, she took this to be a good omen. She knew she couldn't have done it without the support of her family and Irma. It was what Nabil had wanted for her it and it certainly kept her busy.

Spending the holidays in Grosvenor Square helped her to stay in touch with her English friends. And of course, it was great to spend time with Ellen, Douglas, and Lauren. She loved the apartment because it was here, they had spent their first summer together doing the things they loved doing.

Thirteen years had passed since they had first met and despite all the terrible things that happened at the beginning of their marriage, they had the most wonderful relationship. Tears trickled down her cheeks as she stood on the terrace overlooking the ocean. Suddenly she could smell his favourite after-shave even though she had thrown all his bottles away a long time ago. The aroma grew stronger, and she felt a slight breeze on her face but there was no breeze, it was hot and still. There was a hazy outline a few inches from her in the form of a figure and she felt a warm hand touching her cheek. "Oh, Nabil my darling I know it's you!" She felt his familiar strong arms around her; he held her close for a few wonderful minutes then he was gone. "Don't go, my darling, don't go!" she cried, but the smell of his after-shave subsided, and she knew she was on her own once more.

Tears were flowing freely now, but not just tears of sadness; she cried tears of happiness too. Nabil had been there with her of that she was certain. She had felt his arms around her, and she could still feel the warmth where he had touched her cheek. It was the one and only time she'd had such a strong feeling of his presence, though she sensed he was never far away. It had been an incredible experience and one that left her with such hope for the future. She now knew for certain that one day they would be together again.

Printed in Great Britain
by Amazon